RYDER
MACKLIN
COREY

SEALs of Honor, Books 14–16

Dale Mayer

Books in This Series:

Mason: SEALs of Honor, Book 1

Hawk: SEALs of Honor, Book 2

Dane: SEALs of Honor, Book 3

Swede: SEALs of Honor, Book 4

Shadow: SEALs of Honor, Book 5

Cooper: SEALs of Honor, Book 6

Markus: SEALs of Honor, Book 7

Evan: SEALs of Honor, Book 8

Mason's Wish: SEALs of Honor, Book 9

Chase: SEALs of Honor, Book 10

Brett: SEALs of Honor, Book 11

Devlin: SEALs of Honor, Book 12

Easton: SEALs of Honor, Book 13

Ryder: SEALs of Honor, Book 14

Macklin: SEALs of Honor, Book 15

Corey: SEALs of Honor, Book 16

Warrick: SEALs of Honor, Book 17

Tanner: SEALs of Honor, Book 18

Jackson: SEALs of Honor, Book 19

Kanen: SEALs of Honor, Book 20

Nelson: SEALs of Honor, Book 21

Taylor: SEALs of Honor, Book 22

Colton: SEALs of Honor, Book 23

Troy: SEALs of Honor, Book 24

Axel: SEALs of Honor, Book 25

Baylor: SEALs of Honor, Book 26

Hudson: SEALs of Honor, Book 27

About This Boxed Set

Ryder

Having lost the one good thing in his life, Ryder wants only to forget, to help others and defend his country. After a mission goes south and his SEAL brother is hurt, Ryder checks on him in Medical and finds the one that got away working there. In no time at all, the same damn feelings he used to have for Caitlyn are back as if they'd never gone away. She's not his anymore, but maybe friendship is enough…

That's the *last* thing Caitlyn wants with Ryder. She isn't here by chance. Realizing she screwed up their relationship big-time, she'll do anything to get him back in her life, even if it means working overseas on the off-chance of seeing him sometimes.

When the outpost is attacked, medical supplies go missing and Caitlyn is grabbed, all bets for a fairy-tale ending are off. What's really important is all that matters now, and the two of them need to figure out what that is before they lose that very thing again—this time permanently.

Macklin

One damaging relationship in his life refuses to end when the woman insists it's not over between them for her. Marsha makes Macklin's life hell…until she turns up dead and the evidence points straight at him.

As the new detective on the Coronado Police force, Alex is determined to make a good impression on her superiors and colleagues. That goal is thwarted by Macklin, who's the chief suspect in her murder investigation—and someone she longs to know a whole lot better. Whether she wants to or not, she can't let herself foolishly forget that his last girlfriend now occupies an ice-cold bed at the morgue.

During his thorough interrogation at the precinct by the sexy-beyond-belief detective, Macklin finds himself furious...and intrigued. Seems, alive or dead, Marsha is determined to make his life miserable. Alex intends to find out the truth, and, as an elite warrior himself, he admires her grit and ethics in pursuit of the answers. Damn that she's the first woman in a long time he'd love to get to know better.

With no other option, Macklin has to help the detective solve the mystery—hopefully before Alex has no choice but to charge him with murder.

Corey

A voice from the past cries out for help and Corey finds himself reunited with the only woman who'd ever rocked his world straight off the axis. But twelve years is a long time apart. Both of them have moved on, but, tragically, Angela is no longer the lighthearted woman he once knew and loved.

Caught in a nasty divorce and custody battle, Angela will do anything to keep her son with her. After seven years of a rocky marriage, she's only just beginning to figure out what kind of a man her husband truly is.

Angela makes it clear to Corey she doesn't want or need his help. She's got her own insurance to secure her case. But Corey is determined to shield his old flame anyway because she doesn't seem to realize her "insurance" is more than likely to get her dead sooner rather than later. Given that Corey's up against a man with no intention of letting his son go, it's a race to see who ends up in a casket first.

RYDER

SEALs of Honor, Book 14

Dale Mayer

PROLOGUE

MARKUS'S BACKYARD BARBECUE was rocking, and the San Diego weather was perfect for outdoor entertaining. Markus was another SEAL and a member of Mason's unit. He and his partner were celebrating with all their friends the end of some serious renovations on their house.

Ryder Lewis settled back in his folding chair, beer in hand, and watched as Summer, Easton's ladylove—the newest to the group—completely won over the large gathering around her. Summer didn't seem fazed at all by the crowd. That she was busy taking photographs of couples didn't hurt.

The gathering's laughter was contagious. Even Ryder was smiling. Normally he was not an upbeat personality, but lately …

"Hey, you. Still nursing that same beer?" Corey sprawled in the folding chair next to his buddy. "Personally I might need something harder."

Ryder glanced at him. "Why's that?"

"A little too much lovey-dovey stuff here. I never expected to feel so lost by being alone."

"You brought a girlfriend," Ryder pointed out. "You aren't alone."

"A friend, yes. A girlfriend, no." Corey slid Ryder a sideways look. "No way would I come alone. You're braver than I am."

"Damn, I didn't think of that."

Corey chuckled. "You need to plan ahead. If you had the sisters I do, you'd come up with that camouflage in an instant."

"Ha, if I had that many sisters, I'd have left town." Ryder shook his head. "I also don't think I know a woman I could have called to step in and help me out in a situation like this."

"Sure you do. What about Caitlyn?"

Ryder's heart hiccupped. "Hell no."

"And why is that?"

Corey's curious tone said he didn't understand anything about Ryder's more recent history with Caitlyn.

"You took her to prom. You were there for her when she graduated from nursing school, gave her away at her wedding and got her drunk to celebrate her divorce. Dude, that's a major friendship. She'd have been delighted to show up here today."

Ryder shook his head, but he didn't say a word. He couldn't.

"Unless something's changed?" Corey asked, leaning forward. "As in, you had a fight?"

"No fight," he said, keeping his voice neutral. Corey was no fool.

"If no fight, then it's the opposite."

Silence was Ryder's only response.

"Ah, hell."

More silence followed.

Corey took a deep breath. "Don't tell me. When the two of you got drunk, you slept with her."

Ryder lifted his beer and poured the cool liquid down

his throat. Anything to shove the hot painful memories to the back. The hurt. The loss.

"And it didn't work out?" Corey pushed cautiously.

"Work out? She got up Monday morning and walked away. I haven't heard a word since, despite all my calls to her. It's been two years. I'd say that fits the definition of *it didn't work out.*"

Corey reached into the cooler at his side and pulled out a couple more beers. He handed one to Ryder. "Sorry, man. Here's to staying single." Corey was quiet for a long moment, then added, "Now I understand the change in your behavior. You went a little off for a time. I wasn't sure what the deal was, but you seemed to pull out of it so I put it aside."

The two men clinked cans, and a commotion at the corner of the house caught their attention. Another arrival. The party had already swelled to close to sixty people. What were a few more?

"Isn't that Mac and Quinn?"

"Looks like it." Ryder settled at the sight of more men he knew. A break in the crowd showed they'd arrived with dates. "Figures. I think I'm the only one who came alone."

"And you might want to prepare yourself. I could be wrong, but I think that's Caitlyn on Mac's arm."

Ryder's heart froze, then shattered. He shoved his beer can into Corey's hand. "Here. I'm done." He got up and walked down the opposite side of the house. He could handle a lot of things in life. But seeing the only woman he'd ever loved with another man—again—was not one of them.

CHAPTER 1

T HE SILENCE WAS deafening.

Ryder shifted his gaze across the deserted buildings on his left. The intel was good. That just made this Iraq mission all the worse. This bomb maker had gone to ground now, pinned inside the dilapidated structure in front of Ryder. He wanted to make sure the bomb maker didn't set booby traps to allow him to escape. The US military wanted him for questioning regarding the two bombs that blew up a stadium in Baghdad. Twenty-two people had died with another seventy-plus severely injured.

Devlin and Easton were on the far side of the building, tracking enemy movement. Corey watched Ryder's back. Another four-man team checked out other buildings. Ryder's headset crackled. "Beta team moving in."

Ryder swept forward, silent and deadly. Nothing in front or to the side. He dropped low and did a fast sweep inside from the doorway. No trip wires. Good.

In sync, Ryder and Corey went through all the ground-level rooms while Easton and Devlin maintained surveillance of the perimeter. Ryder and his partner found … nothing. Ever aware, Ryder kept moving. This was not the time to drop his guard. Too much at stake.

Gunfire sounded in the distance. *The other SEAL team.* Devlin's voice crackled in Ryder's headset. "Watch your back. Bullies coming up on the outside."

Instantly Ryder and Corey faded into the shadows. If somebody was coming, Ryder wanted to see them first. Anybody who knew the bomb maker was of interest to them. More wild gunfire sounded. Ryder exchanged a look with Corey. Ryder knew exactly what that meant. *The other SEAL team taking more fire.* But they couldn't help. Not just yet. He and Corey had done a full sweep of the downstairs, but they had the rest of the building to check.

"Sweep completed," Easton whispered in Ryder's headpiece. "I'm on the other side of the front entrance. We have company."

Silently Ryder signaled to Corey before slipping around the outside of the building, following the wall toward the front. He peered around the corner. One man stood guard, his back to the entryway. A second man crouched against the front door and placed something on the step. *A bomb.*

Ryder warned the others with the appropriate *click*s of his comm.

Of course it would be a bomb. As a weapon they were so damn unforgiving. Ryder had no way to calculate the devastation this one could bring, and he had no plans to find out. At the single tap on his comm, he lifted his semiautomatic rifle and waited.

From the far side he heard, "Step back away from the bomb. Hands in the air."

The crouched man spun, lifting a rifle.

A single shot clipped the air. Ryder sprang from his hiding spot, his weapon on the man still standing. The other man had collapsed on top of whatever he'd placed on the front step. From his position, Ryder could see the wires connecting to the doorknob. It was crude but effective. The questions of the moment were, did the bomber die with the trigger in his hand and was the bomb ready to go off?

Ryder returned his gaze to the other man. The guard inched backward as he stared at his fallen comrade.

"Everyone take cover," Ryder yelled into his comm before diving to the ground. Seconds later the bomb exploded, sending clay and body parts flying. Ryder rose immediately, his weapon once again on his prisoner who'd been thrown down by the blast.

With Ryder's alpha team now at the designated rendezvous spot, but earlier than expected, Devlin and Easton pushed forward to the far side of the town where the earlier gunfire came from. The beta unit hadn't checked in on the comm. Ryder had to assume they were in trouble, and he wasn't taking any chances. Shoving his weapon into his prisoner's neck while backing him against a wall, Ryder asked, "Where's the bomb maker?"

Black eyes flashed his way as the man stayed silent.

Ryder shrugged. "We'll get the answers one way or another."

He didn't for a moment believe the man who had died in the doorway was the bomb maker. Men like him had a dozen faithful helpers who'd die to protect him. So many young men had died for nothing.

Devlin reported in for him and his partner, Easton. "Alpha team still in search of beta team."

Ryder wanted to leave too but with another mission in mind. He studied the prisoner, wishing for an easy way to get him to talk. But men like this would take a bullet rather that give away their secrets.

Ryder glanced at Corey and said, "Keep him here. I'll be back in five."

Corey protested. But Ryder wanted to check the bomb maker's house. Now that they'd left the bomb maker's building, Ryder wanted to know who had showed up. The bomb blast would have alerted the rebels. Ryder raced back to where the remains of the dead man lay. Ryder kicked open the door, sending a hail of gunfire inside. Cries ripped through the house. He didn't go inside but slipped around to the back and sent a message to Easton and Devlin.

Gunfire shot out from the floor-to-ceiling windows. The men were disorganized. As far as Ryder could tell, only two gunmen were inside. Ryder took a quick look through a broken window, popped off a shot, and one gunman dropped. Now that was more like it. The second gunman stood in front of an older man who cowered behind him. This then was the bomb maker. As soon as Ryder had a shot, he took out the final gunman and stepped through the window, holding his weapon on the bomb maker. "Ahmed Amin?"

The man glared at him, hate in his gaze.

Ryder nodded. "I'll take that as a yes." He motioned the man to move toward the front door. The bomb maker shook his head and dropped to his knees.

This wasn't a kill mission as the bomb maker was wanted back at headquarters. Ryder quickly tied Ahmed's hands, stripped him of his weapons and forced him outside. Within minutes he had him in the rendezvous enclosure beside Corey and the other prisoner.

With both prisoners now secure, Ryder gave Corey a hard grin. "Time to go to the extraction point."

As they pulled back, Ryder's comm crackled, and Easton said, "One man down. Mac's been hit."

Ryder's heart sank. "Copy that."

Following directions, they picked their way to where the beta team was pinned in a corner. With Corey holding the bound and gagged prisoners to the ground, Ryder slipped forward. He took out two insurgents and managed to get into the beta team's hideout. Macklin was out, his left shoulder and chest bloody. "How bad?"

"He's unconscious, but I'm sure he can walk when he's awake again," said Keenan, one of Mac's unit.

Ryder slid a hand down and checked Mac's pulse, his heartbeat strong and steady. A lot of blood stained his chest, and … air bubbles surfaced. Shit. Definitely a compromised lung. Time for a field dressing of the roughest sort. They had to get everybody to fall back so they could arrange for an emergency medical evac.

Mac needed care. *Now.* Ryder slapped a piece of thin plastic over the hole in Mac's upper chest. The bubbles stopped, and Mac breathed easier. From his view of the position of the injury, Ryder figured the bullet just caught the tip of a lung. That was bad enough. Breathing would become damn near impossible soon. The blood-clotting field dressing was temporary at best.

With Mac's wound bandaged, the men lay out a quick plan of cover fire and an even faster retreat. They had two vehicles available. They'd need both to get back behind enemy lines. Mac was big; then again so was Ryder. And time was running out for his friend.

One of Mac's team said, "You okay to do this?"

Ryder shot him a frown and nodded. Why the question? Did everybody know Mac was with his best friend, Caitlyn? Or should Ryder say his ex-best friend? It didn't matter. They were still a team. They'd never let women come between them before. He wouldn't let one now. Although he had avoided Mac as much as possible and apparently that had been noticed. Some things hurt even after two years' time.

Carrying Mac, Ryder retraced his steps with the other men covering his retreat.

With Easton and Devlin pulling up the rear, they returned to the vehicles. There, Ryder lay Mac on the back seat. They were at least an hour outside the next town and, if driving, another several hours from a medical center. All they could do was make Mac as comfortable as possible and try to keep him alive while arranging for a helo. Ryder did not know if the enemy had given up or been taken out. They saw no one as they drove to town. That, in itself, was suspicious as hell. No way to hide the direction they traveled or where they'd come from with the sand and dust they stirred up. They could only hope the cloud of dust at least hid them as targets until they could get clear.

This place was so damn riddled with land mines that they'd be lucky to get out in one piece as it was. Still, mission accomplished thus far, but, until Mac was safe and the prisoners were handed over, Ryder wouldn't consider it a success.

Watching for enemy traffic coming in behind them, they raced toward the helicopter as arranged. Mac's breathing was labored; his color was gray, and the blood, although sluggish, still pumped slowly from the wound by the time they reached the bird.

"Go. Go."

Ryder picked Mac up and raced him to the helicopter. They strapped him down on a stretcher and watched as the chopper took off, heading in the opposite direction where the fighting had been.

"Ryder, let's go."

He raced back to the truck, and they continued on to the camp. There, the prisoners were transferred from their care to be transported to one of the main bases. This was just a temporary headquarters.

Four hours later Ryder stood in front of his commander with the others of his alpha team.

"What happened to Macklin?" the commander asked in a hard voice.

Ryder gave a brief account of what he knew, followed by each team member adding his details.

The commander nodded, listened to each person, writing a few notes at the same time.

As the others turned to leave when dismissed, the commander called out, "Ryder, a moment."

Ryder turned back. "Yes, sir."

"Is there a problem between you and Mac?" The commander leaned against his chair. "Normally I wouldn't bring it up, but there were murmurs a while ago. One of his men brought it up as well."

Ryder let one eyebrow rise slightly. That was the only reaction he'd let himself show. Inside though was a different story. "No, sir."

"As rumor has it, a woman is involved."

"No, sir. Caitlyn and I are longtime friends. We never were together," he lied glibly. *Other than that one magical weekend where we made love for three days straight after two decades of being just friends—the best of friends. Then I said I love you, and she bolted. Refused to speak with me afterward— for the last two years.*

The commander studied him intently.

"Caitlyn is dating Mac."

"Are you okay with that?"

Ryder nodded. "I am."

"Good. Make sure you are. I don't want anything to come between our team members."

Inside Ryder was angry at the inference he'd be less than professional over a female. Sure it was the woman he loved, but she wasn't his. Whether he liked it or not, he had no choice in the matter. "That won't happen, sir."

The commander nodded. "Dismissed."

Ryder spun on his heels and headed out.

Corey waited for him. "Did I hear that right?" Corey asked in a low voice.

Ryder gave a clipped nod. Corey shouldn't have heard anything, but, on a base like this, sounds carried.

"Jesus, I'm sorry, man."

Ryder gave a shrug. "Nothing I can do about it." The trouble was, he loved Caitlyn, but he'd lost her. Of course she'd found somebody else. He headed to the medical tent, hoping an update on Mac had been shared with the base. Macklin was a good man. If Caitlyn was happy with him, it didn't matter one bit how Ryder felt about it. She'd made her decision two years earlier, and Ryder had to live with it.

He stopped at the tent, cleared his throat. The medics turned and looked at him. A small blonde stood with her back to him. He frowned at the familiar profile, his heart slamming against his ribs. Why wasn't she at the main base hospital outside Baghdad with Mac? "Caitlyn?"

She turned.

He stared in confusion at her and then backed up one step toward where the helicopters sat. "What are you doing here?"

She shrugged. "I'm a military nurse, remember? I have

another few weeks in my tour."

"And Mac?" he asked hazily.

She frowned. "Mac's a good man."

He felt the shock of surprise go through him. "Of course he is. I just helped save his sorry ass. I came for an update."

A businesslike look came over her expression. "He'll make it. But he's got a tough few days ahead. Depending on the damage he could be off for months of physical therapy."

"Why aren't you with him?"

"Because I'm working."

"He's your partner. You would get leave to be at his side."

She gave Ryder a long hard look. "He's my *friend*. He'd expect me to do nothing less than stay here and look after the rest of you."

Unfortunately that was all too possible. Still Ryder felt bad. Macklin shouldn't be alone.

Everyone needed someone.

Even Ryder.

CAITLYN WATCHED AS the only man she'd ever loved exited the tent—obviously frustrated, with anger and concern on his face. She'd barely seen him since their infamous weekend—which had about torn her apart. She regretted only one thing in her life, and that was not setting things straight with Ryder earlier. And in all this time she hadn't found a way to put it right. "Ryder, Mac will be okay."

Ryder retreated as fast as he could.

She watched until he disappeared from sight. Even though little love was lost between the two men, they were teammates. They would still be concerned about each other.

She hated that she'd come between them. She hadn't intended to. Mac knew some of what had gone down between Ryder and her, and Mac had been there to help, hoping she'd patch things up. But she'd refused to answer Ryder's many initial attempts to contact her because she wasn't in a mental state to do so.

After he stopped calling, and she took over reaching out, she'd turn mute on the phone once Ryder answered and would hang up in exasperation. This went on for months. Followed by her *stalking Ryder* phase. Which hadn't led to any communication between the two of them either. When Ryder had seen her with Mac, that had been it. Ryder had walked away from her at the barbecue without giving her a chance to say a word to him. And that was the only reason she'd gone to the party—because Mac had told her that Ryder would be there.

Now she realized it hadn't been the best decision. Of course Ryder would've taken things out of context and would have believed she was with Mac. She'd seen the anger on his face—the hurt. Mac and Ryder had been good friends, until Ryder had seen her with Mac at the barbecue. Mac said things had changed after that. Not in a major way but, if Mac joined them while they were hanging out, Ryder would inevitably find an excuse to leave. Or, if they arrived at the gym at the same time, Ryder would head in the opposite direction. Subtle changes but obvious ones to Mac.

She knew Ryder's walls would be higher, bigger and stronger after the barbecue. Another event she had to make up for. She had to get him past all that history in order for him to understand that Mac was her friend, not her lover.

She stared down at her hands, wondering at the foolishness of her actions. She'd specifically asked to come overseas—hoping on the off chance Ryder would show up wherever she was posted. That she'd see him, talk to him.

Afterward, she realized she had to talk to Ryder face-to-face, so she'd stalked him for months. Mac had caught her midstalking and finally wrangled the truth from her. She'd felt like a fool. Mac had alternated between angry and horrified. She remembered his words clearly.

"Well, I'll be damned. As much as I'd love to know a woman cared enough to track me down, stalking is damn creepy," he said.

And that's when she'd stopped. Mac was right. She wanted to apologize to Ryder for being too scared early on to discuss what making love had done to their decades-long best-friends-only friendship. Hence the barbecue and her overseas assignments.

Yet, why hadn't she said something now? Why did she keep avoiding this? She stood outside the medic tent to detect the direction he'd gone.

She could've gone into the private medical sector and made a killing, but here she served her country, putting herself in danger every day. Mostly as a punishment.

And for a chance to see Ryder. As she turned, somebody stepped up and blocked her way. She glared up at Corey. "What's your problem?"

He thrust his face toward hers. "Leave Ryder alone. You've done enough harm already." On that note Corey spun on his heels and stormed off.

Inside she broke a little more. She hadn't wanted to hurt Ryder but knew she had. His declaration of love—after twenty platonic years as best friends—had been like a bomb of awareness going off inside that had confused and devastated her to the point she no longer knew what was real and what wasn't. Like an injured animal, she'd hidden away, trying to find a new normal in a world gone awry.

It was foolish to say she was just young and immature. Ryder had always been there on the sidelines, watching, friendly and supportive.

He'd been at her graduation, her wedding. He'd been her best friend, but she'd been sure he wasn't *the one*. If there was one thing she could count on, it was that he was her best friend. Forever. And he would never be the love of her life.

She found out the hard way how wrong she'd been.

That weekend she lost her longtime best friend … and her newest lover.

She didn't remember how they had ended up in bed that night and stayed there for the entire weekend. Might have been the wine, but neither of them drank much. Ever. Might have been her devastation mixed with joy over her divorce. She'd been a mess at the time, finding George's complaints about their marriage so off base. Was there anything more confusing than a major breakup? First there'd been George. Then no George. And through it all there had been Ryder. The mainstay of her life—until that weekend. The sex had been phenomenal, overwhelmingly hot, passionate, fun, caring. When she woke up after that marathon and saw his face, heard his whispered declaration, her *heart* wanted to rejoice, but her *mind* had rejected everything. Her feet had picked up and followed her mind.

Her heart and mind at war never led to anything good. Look at what happened with George.

It had taken her months to figure it out because she'd been so busy looking everywhere but inside. Finding out the truth had been shocking and delightful. Followed by her horror as she realized she'd let too much time go by. Ryder's hurt had gone too deep by now, and life had never been the same after that. Not for Ryder. Not for her either.

The next few months had been really rough. He had been sent on mission after mission, training after training. Too much distance between them. As if he'd volunteered for every opportunity possible, hoping to get killed. And now she sat in a world she wasn't terribly comfortable in, or wanted to be in, because this was Ryder's world and the only way she knew to be a part of his life. Her plan had worked. They were both here in Iraq now. And that was terrifying enough.

Yet, she didn't want to mess this up, her attempts to reconcile with Ryder.

Where was Mac when she needed him? He had proven to be a good friend. He understood her heart lay with Ryder, and Mac had threatened to take Ryder around back and beat the crap out of him until he was willing to listen to her. But she hadn't wanted that. She also didn't want Ryder to know she had cried all over Mac's shoulder. Many times.

If there was one thing Ryder had, it was pride. She'd taken it and shredded it unintentionally. But, when he put it back together again, it was stronger and thicker and harder than ever before. And she didn't want to tear it open. *Again.* She went back inside and checked her watch. Almost 1800 hours. She grabbed her jacket, put it on and headed for the mess tent. She had no patients at this moment, so it was a good time to eat.

Just then the area to the left of her blew up, and she was tossed to the ground. Coming to after momentarily being knocked out, she bounded to her feet and raced in the direction of the blast. The camp was heavily manned. There would be injuries.

As she ran, the smoke thickened. She was grabbed from behind, spun around and slammed up against a hard chest. She struggled to get free. "Let me go. Let me go. I have to help."

Arms squeezed her tight. "You'll go in a few minutes, not until the scene is secured."

Ryder. She fell limp against his body. Of course it was him. She glanced up, but he wasn't staring at her. His grim face was locked on the devastation behind her.

Moments later he let her go, and she raced into the chaos. She could see at least two dead so far, three more injured. It could've been much worse. As it was, she mourned the loss of those who died. She knew them both. They were good men and didn't deserve this. Not for the first time it came home to her just how close she'd been to dying. Another few feet to the side, and she'd have taken a direct hit.

THE NEXT FOUR hours passed in a haze. She patched, swabbed and disinfected, then readied patients for transport while the camp disassembled and moved behind the new frontline. The attack had taken them by surprise, and now there was organized chaos. Between the gunfire and the orders coming from every direction, she kept her head down and worked.

With the last of the patients attended to, she was rushed to the last helicopter. High above, she gazed down at the turmoil below, fervently saying a prayer for Ryder and the others. No way would he retreat from such an attack. The fighting had been brutal. She glanced down at her patient who studied her face. She smiled, reached out and covered his hand with hers. "You'll be all right, soldier."

He smiled too and closed his eyes.

At the main base, she supervised the transfers of her patients, went through a debriefing and then headed for the showers. Everything hurt from the blast, and her headache, instead of easing, had gotten worse.

She finished shampooing her hair for the second time, then turned off the water, finding blood mixed in. With a towel wrapped around her hair, she stepped from the shower and dried off. She sat down on the bench with a second towel wrapped about her body and reached up to the back of her neck. Her fingers came away with more blood. She stood up to check in the mirror but couldn't find the wound hidden in her hairline. A doctor would have to take a closer look.

She hadn't told anybody she had lost consciousness at the site. They'd been shorthanded for medics as it was. But the headache she'd ignored up until now started to pound. After getting dressed, she folded some paper towels and held them against where she guessed the wound was.

One of the doctors stood outside her tent, calling for her, his schedule in his hand. When she approached, he took one look and nodded toward the medical center. He walked beside her. "What happened to you?"

She gave a quick rundown as he led her into an examining room. Another nurse came. She clipped Caitlyn's hair at the nape of her neck, then gave her a local anaesthetic. Dr. Carter, according to his name tag, stitched up the cut. "Good timing. I needed to see what your schedule was to put you into the roster. But you're taking twenty-four hours to rest up, and we'll see how you are then. Do you have time off coming?"

"Not sure." She shrugged. "I've only got a few weeks left in my tour as it is. I think I do though."

Nothing like a concussion to ensure confusion. By the time she reached her quarters, her thoughts were scrambled as to whether she was due leave or not.

Feeling unsteady and woozy, she lay down, stretching out with a blanket over her shoulders. She hadn't even been aware of her injury until the blood flowed in the shower. But now that she knew … She had been given something for the pain but hadn't even touched it yet.

With all the confusion, she'd forgotten to ask for an update on Mac. And that made her feel like a crap. She'd gotten so busy with everything that had happened after his exit that she hadn't had a chance to even think about him.

She reached up and tentatively winced as her fingers came in contact with the stitches. If she could get a good night's sleep, she'd be fine in the morning.

Just as she was about to drop off to sleep, she heard footsteps at the entrance to her eight-bed tent. Still, she hadn't seen anybody else bunking here since she had arrived. A man called out, "Caitlyn?"

She froze. "Ryder?" Why was he here? She so wanted to see him but not when she was like this.

He stepped into the tent, his gaze searching the quarters before zooming toward her. A frown appeared. In several strides, he reached her bedside. "What the hell happened to you? And when?"

"I can't remember," she said. "Maybe flying debris from the blast clipped my head. I don't know."

"How bad?"

"Just a few stitches. And a mild concussion, so I'm off for the next day."

She dropped her gaze, wishing he'd sit down and pull her into his arms. Dangerous thoughts. She just didn't have the energy to keep her blocks up right now. She had to apologize but feared there was no going back to what they had. That she still loved this guy with the chasm between them made this all so impossible. That he was here, available to talk to, but she wasn't ... not when she was like this, made it worse again.

"Can I get you anything?"

She shook her head and then moaned as waves of blackness swam over her eyes. Gasping, she whispered, "No, I'll be fine. I just need to lie here. Hopefully when I wake up, it will be okay."

"Fine, you do that. I'll come back in a couple hours to check on you."

"You don't have to." She closed her eyes, sinking deeper into the bedding, hoping he'd leave. Pain still rolled through her like a rocking boat in a terrible storm. She kept waiting for calm weather.

Her stomach churned alarmingly. She sat upright, shuddering as what little was in her stomach flew up her throat and out her mouth. And into a bucket. She accepted the container from Ryder even as she wondered how he had known. The trouble was, her stomach wasn't done emptying. Three more heaves and she lay back, gasping in pain.

"Take it easy."

She didn't have a choice. Obviously her body wasn't letting her do anything *but* take it easy. The shivers started next. She pulled the blanket over her shoulders, wishing she could disappear. There was no reason to feel ashamed, but it was hard not to. She groaned. "Go away."

"Like hell," he said good-naturedly. "I get you don't want anything to do with me, but I'm not leaving you in this condition. Why aren't you in the clinic?"

"Not that bad."

"Right." He picked up her hand, wrapping her fingers around a bottle. "Here's some fresh water if you want to drink."

With his help she sat up enough that she could fill her mouth, rinse, then spit. He held the bucket. She repeated the motion several more times, then finished with a long drink of water. She collapsed back down again, holding out the empty bottle to him. "Take this and thanks."

"You're welcome. I'll bring you another one."

She didn't care what he did just so long as he left her alone. Thankfully she heard his footsteps fade away.

She drifted in and out, her stomach still queasy, her head still pounding. She didn't think it was anything serious, wasn't exactly sure why her stomach had decided to react since she had eaten very little. Now she could get no food down. If only the shivers would stop. She curled into a fetal position with the blankets almost over her head and waited for her body to warm up. She heard his exclamation before she recognized he'd actually returned.

"That's enough," he said. "I'm taking you back to the clinic."

"I'm fine," she said, her teeth chattering so badly it was hard to talk. "They have bigger problems to deal with. I just need to get warm."

Instantly, she was shifted gently to one side, and he lay down behind her and tucked her up close. With his arms wrapped around her, his legs pressed up against hers, it was like coming up against a heated blanket. Slowly, ever so slowly, she started to warm up.

Finally her teeth stopped chattering, and she whispered, "Thank you."

He dropped a gentle kiss on her head, bringing tears to her eyes. And he whispered, "No problem. Now go to sleep."

Too tired and sore, and still too cold to argue, she let her eyes drift closed and finally fell asleep.

RYDER HELD HER close. Her vomiting had really worried him.

He'd seen a lot of different reactions to head injuries,

and, from where he was, he counted only a few stitches, six or eight at the most, at the back of her head. She also might have more than a concussion. The doctor had clipped her hair around the torn skin at her nape and had pulled the edges together. It didn't look deep but was raw and ugly looking. He'd seen much worse. However, what he didn't know was if she'd sustained other injuries. No way would he sleep. Somebody needed to keep a watch on her overnight.

He glanced around the tent and saw two of the beds appeared to be claimed as duffel bags were underneath. The rest of the tent was empty. He didn't really have any right to be here, but it was either this or he took her to the clinic. If nothing else he should let them know what kind of reaction she had had.

Had they given her drugs? Maybe she'd reacted to those? Worried, he went over the possible scenarios, afraid something much more major was going on.

Another woman walked into the tent and froze at the sight of him. He held up a finger to his lips, checked on Caitlyn to make sure she was still sleeping and slowly sat up. He walked over to the woman and said, "She was injured today. She just emptied her stomach and couldn't get warm. She's asleep now."

The other woman was one of the supply chain clerks. She nodded. "I'm just here to collect my bag. Then I report to work."

He nodded. "I want to update the doctor on her condition. Can you stay long enough for me to return?"

She frowned, checked her watch and said, "Only if you're fast."

He was gone instantly. He found Dr. Carter, standing at the entrance to the med center, catching a breath of fresh air.

Ryder introduced himself and said, "You put stitches in Caitlyn's head today. I don't know if it's important or not, but she just had a violent upchuck session and couldn't get warm."

The doctor frowned and said, "Are you keeping an eye on her overnight, or do you want me to watch her here?" He turned and looked inside. "We're really short on space after the last attack."

"That's what Caitlyn said," Ryder said. "She refused when I mentioned it earlier."

"Keep an eye on her. If her symptoms persist or get any worse, bring her in. Likely she'll be fine come morning."

Ryder had to be content with that. He quickly retraced his steps to her tent. The supply chain clerk smiled with relief. "Thanks for being as fast as you were." And she bolted out the door.

At Caitlyn's side, he noted her deep relaxed breathing contrasted by her ashen-white cheeks and an almost bruised look under her eyes. He still had a bucket of nastiness to dispose of. Something he needed to do now. He hated to leave her alone, but the latrine was next door. He dumped the bucket, rinsed it out, dumped and rinsed it a few more times and then went back.

There was no change in Caitlyn's condition. She slept deeply. Good. That was the best thing for her. He took her water bottle and raced out to the mess tent for several new ones, and, since he hadn't had anything to eat, he grabbed a sandwich and some coffee.

Back at her tent, he sat at the end of her bed to keep watch.

His phone went off several minutes later. Corey asked, "Where the hell are you?"

"Caitlyn was injured. I'm at her bedside." He glanced down to make sure he hadn't awakened her, but she slept soundly.

"Are you sure that's a good idea?"

"I can't do anything less," he said simply.

After that came no answer. Then again what could Corey say? He knew Caitlyn wasn't Ryder's best friend anymore, yet Ryder could hardly leave her like this.

He was a better person than that. And, although he understood the need to protect his heart, he wasn't at all sure it was possible. She'd had a place deep inside for such a long time.

CHAPTER 3

C AITLYN OPENED HER eyes, grimacing at the taste in her mouth. For a moment she didn't understand where she was. She shifted to look around the tent, gasping at the pain in her neck. She closed her eyes for a long moment, and, when she could, she opened them. Ryder sat at the end of her bed, his eyes closed, his cell phone in his hand, looking as if he was thinking. She winced. Apparently she'd been a little more injured than she'd thought.

With uncanny vision he turned his head, opened his eyes and glanced at her. "How are you feeling?"

She gave him a small smile and just barely stopped herself from shrugging. "Better. As long as I don't move, I might survive this," she said only half-joking.

He nodded, but his gaze was intent on her face. "Whatever you do, when you're ready to move, make sure it's slow," he warned. "That blast hit you hard."

"A piece of debris caught me too. Plus, I just might have reacted to the stress of the situation and the heat. I hadn't had any lunch or breakfast," she said.

He glanced at her in surprise. "Your stomach was empty? You threw up several times."

"Mostly acid." She gave him a small nod. "I did have a muffin somewhere along the line, but I'd been up most of the night too."

He nodded in understanding. "It's tough when that happens."

Lying here, she smiled up at him, thankful they were talking as friends, not as combatants or as lovers on the rocks. "So true." Then she remembered. "You have any update on Mac?"

Instantly he withdrew. She felt the distance he put between them. Damn. She should have kept her mouth shut.

He shook his head. "No, not yet."

She frowned. "I guess that's not too surprising. It's been really busy here."

"I'm sure he'll get in touch with you as soon as he can," Ryder said quietly.

"I'm sure he will." Her tone was as formal as his. Wanting to say something to move them forward but not sure how, she said, "He's a good friend." And then she winced inwardly because the only other person she would have said was a really good friend was Ryder. And they'd been friends since they were kids—until they weren't anymore.

"Good for you." He stood up. "If you're feeling better …"

She rushed to reassure him. "I'm fine. Thanks for staying and looking after me. You make a great nursemaid." Her words were said warmly, but inside she cringed. This was a perfect opportunity to broach *the* subject, yet she didn't know how to start. How she hated this wishy-washy avoidance. He stood up, and she blurted out, "Mac is just a friend."

"Sorry?" He turned back to frown at her.

She groaned. "I wanted to let you know that Mac is *just* a friend."

He studied her for a long moment. "Like I was just a

friend?"

Her mind filled with images of the two of them. From the first moment they had kissed, they'd been consumed in a passionate fire she'd never experienced before or since. It had taken her by surprise, terrified her actually. She shuddered as heat swamped her.

When she regained her voice, she said, "No, not like we were good friends." She took a deep breath. Maybe it was because she was sick. Maybe it was knowing he'd stayed and looked after her all night. But she wanted to get this out. "I've missed you."

His gaze gentled. "I've missed you too," he admitted. "You were such a major part of my life for so long."

"Then why are we like this now?" she asked. "Even if there is nothing else, I'd like to know we're friends enough that you don't have to leave a party when I arrive."

His face closed down, and he resumed his walk toward the entrance. She could see his fists clenching and releasing.

"I never meant to upset you," she called out. "I'd hoped to see you, to talk to you, at the party."

He froze for a long moment, then continued to walk out the doorway. He paused, turned and said, "There is a limit to where friendship can go." And he disappeared.

What did that mean? She went over his answer, tearing it apart, looking for any innuendo that would give her a little bit of hope. Had she said enough? No, probably not. What did he mean? There was a limit to how friendly he could be? He wasn't prepared to go back to the way they were? Or had she jumped into a space where she wasn't welcome? Those at the party were all his friends. Was that the problem? Maybe he felt like she'd intruded. Trying to explain after so long a break between them was awkward.

And then there was Mac. He had been her shoulder to cry on. He'd been a stalwart friend at her side whenever there was an event she wanted to go to but didn't dare go alone. Mac was dealing with his own problems, his own heartbreak and hadn't wanted to get involved either. They'd been safe together. No pressure. No expectations. And she'd needed that then.

As she considered Ryder's quick retreat, she realized it didn't look like Ryder would let her back into his life any time soon. And that was heartbreaking.

She felt so damn weak; it was hard to focus on what else she could've said to him. Could say to him next time. She'd been looking for a way to delicately open up the subject of their passionate weekend. That weekend was when everything had changed. That's when everything had broken down between them. She knew it was her fault, and it wouldn't be easy to fix.

Today they'd spoken without animosity. Last night he'd looked after her. It was a start. She lay here regretting not having said so much more. How would she get that opening again?

But for now she had to go to the bathroom. She threw back the blanket and slowly propped herself up. The room swam, and she moaned. "Damn it." She should've asked for his help to get there. But the last thing she wanted was to show any more weakness. The military was bred on strength, and she had to tell the injured to ask for help when they needed it. Yet, she'd been the one to refuse help any chance she could get. She started to realize, when the chips were down, she was just like the others. Then, as everyone said, medical professionals made the worst patients.

She gained her footing and walked very slowly toward

the entrance. Once there, she held onto the doorway and took several deep breaths before walking in the direction of the bathrooms. Halfway there she realized she still wasn't as strong as she should be. She faltered. Instantly an arm came around her waist, and Ryder hooked her arm over his shoulder.

"Let's get you there and back again," he said quietly.

She let out her breath. "Sorry. I thought I was strong enough."

"I know the feeling. But sometimes our body doesn't let us get away with that stubborn stance." He helped her to the entrance to the latrine.

Afterward she washed her hands and face and went back out. The shakes were still there. She took a deep breath, saw him waiting for her and smiled. "This sucks," she said. "I was hoping to work today."

"Not happening. If you pass out on me, I'll take you to the clinic. I talked to the doctor last night about your condition as it is."

Outraged, she glared at him. "I told you that I just needed sleep."

"And you puked your guts out several times, collapsed and then couldn't get warm. Pardon me if I was worried."

She had to give it to him. As reasons went, they were pretty damn solid.

Back in her tent, he helped her to the bed where she sat down. "My stomach might be empty now, but it sure wishes it wasn't. Is there *any* chance I could make it to the mess tent and get something to eat?"

"You're not getting a chance to try. Tell me what you want, and I will get it for you."

She thought about it a moment. "How about a yogurt,

some fruit and a sandwich? Something that might stick, yet something not too heavy." As he walked through the door, she said, "And coffee."

He continued outside without acknowledging the last bit, so she could only hope he heard. She did love her coffee. She drifted off a couple times, waking just enough to see if he had returned. Soon Ryder walked in holding a tray. She slowly sat up, propped the pillows against the end of the bed, shifted until she sat cross-legged. He set the tray on the bed beside her.

"Glad you slept," he said. "I also went to the doctor and reported in on your condition again."

"I'm fine. I feel better but tired, and, then again, maybe that's hunger." Her stomach growled. She smiled and looked at the feast in front of her. "What's in the bags?"

"Sandwiches for later and a couple muffins. I don't want you heading to the mess tent on your own until tomorrow."

"I said I was better," she protested.

"That's what you said the last time and lulled me into believing it. That won't work again."

She gave him a look of outrage, but the smell of the food in front of her was more than she could resist. She picked up a small yogurt, pulled off the top and devoured it in a few bites. With that gone, she started in on the fruit salad. When she was halfway finished, she realized she needed to slow down. She settled back, picked up her coffee and took several sips. She glanced at the food and over at him. "Have you eaten? You want to share this with me?"

He shook his head. "No, I'm meeting some friends in a little bit."

"How's Corey?"

Ryder's lips quirked. "The same as ever."

"Good. I miss him too."

"I'll pass it on."

She took that to mean Corey wouldn't be coming to see her any time soon. At least other than to warn her to stay away from Ryder. She'd seen that SEAL brotherhood in action many times before. They stood up for each other; they felt the pain for each other, and they formed a line of defense to stop it from happening again. "What have you been doing for the last couple months?" she asked. "I've hardly heard anything about you."

She picked up half of the sandwich in front of her and took a bite. Eating much slower, she nibbled her way through it, thankful everything appeared to be settling in her stomach. She saw the bucket was beside her just in case. That was enough to bring a grimace to her face.

Ryder didn't appear to notice. "Busy," he said. "With the state of the world right now, I'm sure you can imagine."

"It's a scary place out there."

"It is, as you know, a scary place here too." He looked at her, his gaze intensifying by the minute.

She frowned at him. "Now what's the matter?"

"You shouldn't be here. It's dangerous."

She raised an eyebrow. "Then you shouldn't be here either."

"It's what I do."

But she knew he wasn't a sexist. It went much deeper. He still cared, just like she still cared. They couldn't be friends for twenty years and not have something between them still.

"I want you to stay safe too," she said in a low tone. She thought she saw a softening in his gaze.

Then he said, "I got an update on Mac."

She brightened. "How is he?"

RYDER FELT SOMETHING sink in his stomach as he watched her eyes light up and soften with a loving smile forming on her lips. She had said she and Mac were friends. Was that how she'd looked whenever Ryder's name was mentioned? He wished. No way were she and Mac just friends if she looked like that at the sound of his name.

Pulling back his jealousy and sense of helplessness, he said, "He'll be fine. He's recovering in one of the main base hospitals. They'll send him stateside as soon as he's well enough to travel."

She nodded her head. "That makes sense. He'll need physiotherapy for a few months, I'm sure."

"And you? Are you content to stay here when the reason you came overseas was to be with him?"

Surprise darkened her gaze, and the soft look left her face. "I did not come here to be closer to Mac," she said firmly. "I'm happy to serve, and I saw no point in staying home when I could be of more help here. Yes, Mac was here, but then so were you and Corey."

He gave her points for that. He glanced at his watch. His time was up. "Do you think you'll be okay alone now?"

"I'll be totally fine, thank you." She glanced toward the door and said, "It's late anyway. So if I can sleep through the night, I'll be much better in the morning."

"You promise to talk to the doctor first thing tomorrow?"

She chuckled. "I promise."

He smiled. "Good enough. In that case, I'll take my leave."

He turned to walk out, but she called out, "Why do you hate me so much?"

He froze, his stomach sinking. He couldn't do this. She had to know how he felt already. He turned and glanced at her. "I don't hate you. I've never hated you." Then he walked out.

Outside Corey, Devlin and Easton waited for him. He glanced at them and raised an eyebrow. He hoped they hadn't heard the conversation, but, knowing these guys, they would have gotten the gist of it anyway. "What's happening?"

"We're heading out in two hours to lead the fight against another militant army. The local group we left behind was attacked hard. They need reinforcements. They've got troops coming in from the northern part of the country, and we're taking troops from here until theirs arrive."

Ryder nodded. "Good." As they walked away, he muttered, "Glad she's here, not back on the frontline again."

"Ryder, apparently she volunteered for that position."

Ryder glanced at Corey. "Say what?"

Corey nodded. "I talked to the doctor earlier. Anytime there's a dangerous position, and they need a medic up in the front, she offers to go."

"Damn her. What has she got, a death wish?" He couldn't believe she continually put herself in harm's way like that. The girl he'd known all these years hadn't been as daring or as reckless, nor had she been that brave. What brought about that change?

"You may have to admit she's not the same as she used to be," Easton said quietly. "Women change. They grow up, go through strife and trouble and become somebody else. If you're lucky, they become somebody you admire all that much more."

Ryder didn't bother answering. "As long as she's here recovering and not in the middle of the fighting, I don't care."

"Did you say goodbye to her?" Corey asked.

"We'll be gone for days, so you might want to," said Easton from the other side of Corey.

Ryder tilted his head and considered that. "Maybe it's better if I don't go back."

It was Devlin who gave him the sagest advice. "Walk forward because it's right for you. But don't avoid going back and saying goodbye because you're scared."

Startled, Ryder looked at him. "I'm not scared." What a concept. He figured Devlin might've been joshing him. But when he took that serious, hard look straight on, he realized Devlin could see a whole lot deeper than Ryder wanted him to. He shrugged, repeating, "I'm not scared."

There was silence from all the others.

He protested. "Why would I be? It's not like she's in my life anymore."

"Then go tell her that you're leaving. We'll wait here."

The men literally stopped. He glared at them, shrugged and said, "Fine."

He walked back the short distance to her quarters and stepped inside. He saw her face light up before she recognized who it was, and she sank back.

Pain punched him in the gut. "Not quite who you were expecting?" he said, trying to mask the bitterness in his tone. "The guys seem to think I should tell you that I'm heading back out in a couple hours, but, from the look on your face, they need not have worried as you don't care."

"That's not fair," she protested. "I'm happy to see you.

But you didn't look like you wanted to see me. So of course I stopped smiling."

He snorted, not totally convinced.

She frowned. "How bad is it out there?" She swung her feet around and sat up.

"You're not returning to work, so it doesn't matter." Seeing the lost look on her face, he sighed.

"I still want to know."

"We're reinforcing the allies' numbers until their own men arrive. They took a major hit yesterday."

"We took a hit at camp. So I'm sure they were hit much harder." She touched her stitches. "Maybe I should go back out."

In two steps he was at her side. He grabbed her by her shoulders firmly but gently. "Like hell," he said, biting off his words. "Stay here and get better. Then go home."

She stood, thrust her chin up and glared at him. "Like hell," she repeated his wording. "I'm here to help. I'm not hiding away in my tent if my services are needed elsewhere."

The two of them, nose to nose, gazes hard against hard, glared at each other until finally she sagged. "But at the moment, I don't think I'd make it."

He let his hands fall away.

She collapsed back against her bed, pulling the covers against her shoulders. "You guys go take off. I don't need you anyway."

He frowned, not liking the hurt tone in her voice. "You've done well without me. I highly doubt you'll miss me now."

She snorted. "Like you know anything."

He'd already walked several steps away, but, at her words, he turned and looked at her. "Was there something I should know?"

"Would you believe me?"

"If you told me the truth, I would." He shoved his hands on his hips and glared at her. "I know you were in my bed. We had the best weekend we could possibly have wanted. I told you how I loved you. How I've always loved you. Yet you walked away, and you kept on walking. Obviously you didn't want any more of me or what I had to offer because you never once picked up the phone and called me." He upped the wattage of his glare. "How's that for the truth? Or do you have something to add?"

Devlin's voice called from outside. "Ryder, we're leaving now. Let's go."

CHAPTER 4

SEVERAL DAYS LATER, back on her feet and feeling more like her old self, Caitlyn heard about the increase in fighting on the frontline. She'd spent the entire week trying to get an update on both Mac and Ryder only to find out Mac was doing fine, but there was no word on Ryder. No one told her more than that. That was so typical. She turned to Dr. Carter and asked, "Do they have a medic still stationed at the outpost?"

He nodded. "Same as when you were there."

"Can I go back?"

He shot her a look and asked, "Why?"

She dropped her gaze and shrugged. She was busy restocking the cabinet supplies, something that always needed to be done. Their inventory changed fast as this was a busy clinic. "I like to be of help," she said simply.

"How much does it have to do with one of the men who might be there?"

She glared at him. "Nothing."

His face neutral, he didn't say anything further, but he didn't drop his gaze.

Her shoulders sagged. "Okay, so maybe a little. I'd like to make sure that, if anybody on the frontline needs assistance, I can help."

"I'll see. As far as I'm aware, nobody else is needed."

"Good enough." Caitlyn finished the restocking and glanced down at her watch. "I'll grab lunch."

It seemed as if she had to force herself to eat since being injured. She hadn't told anybody about that curious symptom, and she was dropping weight, which wasn't good. The minute any sign of weakness, fatigue or dizziness set in, she would be sent home, and that was not what she wanted. Not while Ryder was here.

She only had a few weeks left on her tour, and maybe, if she was lucky, it was enough time to fix things between her and Ryder.

She walked along the food line trying to find something that would appeal to her touchy stomach. She had food on her tray, but only because she needed to eat, not because it looked appealing. At the far end of the counters were packages of granola and yogurt, prewrapped muffins and sandwiches to go. She grabbed several and headed for the coffee. With a couple bottles of water, enough liquid to last her to dinner, she found a table off on the far end where she could be alone.

Again, since the injury, she was alone a lot. That was not something she'd expected. She'd always had friends, shared space with others well. But, at the moment, maybe she was sending out this big barrier to tell everyone to stay away. And how much of that was due to Ryder's unexpected return to her world?

However, it wasn't long before several other nurses walked in and saw her. Rose and Teresa came over to her table, Rose saying, "So tell us, Caitlyn, have you picked up a new partner yet?"

Caitlyn's eyebrows shot up. "What do you mean, a *new* partner? I didn't have an old partner."

"You and Macklin were pretty tight." Teresa chuckled. "We haven't seen much of you lately."

"Old friends," she said dismissively. "I've not been feeling great, that's all."

"How about Ryder? He looks like he's a hot number."

Caitlyn shook her head. "There's nothing between Ryder and me."

Teresa leaned forward with a big grin and asked, "Can I have him then?"

Caitlyn glared, then rolled her eyes.

Rose chuckled. "I'd watch what you say, Teresa. Caitlyn might take your head off. She's got Ryder and Mac wrapped around her little finger. Although Mac is crazy good looking," Rose admitted. "I wouldn't mind a go at him myself."

"Mac's a big boy. If he wants, he can go out with you one night and Teresa the next," Caitlyn said with a grin. "Neither of you want long-term relationships. Mac doesn't either."

Teresa studied her. "You're serious, right?"

Caitlyn nodded. "Mac and I are just friends."

"Of course you say that now because he's not here."

She laughed. "That could be my reasoning. But not likely."

The two women grinned, their eyes twinkling. They'd made friends soon after Caitlyn had arrived. All of them had a similar mind-set in that they were here to help out. But, unlike Caitlyn, these women were enjoying the singles' life. Something Caitlyn hadn't enjoyed in a long time.

When she finished eating, she saw Dr. Carter looking around for a space to eat. She lifted her hand in greeting. He walked over with his tray. As the two nurses excused themselves and joined somebody else, Dr. Carter sat down with a smile.

"Is it something I said?" he joked as he watched the two women leave.

She chuckled. "No, but you're married, so you're not exactly on their radar."

He rolled his eyes. "Those two are deadly."

Caitlyn had to admit they had a bit of a reputation they might not like to know they had. But they were happy, and who was she to spoil their fun?

The doctor looked at the tray in front of her. "That's a lot of food. Glad to see your appetite is back."

"It is a lot of food. I'd hoped to find something that tasted right." She shrugged. "Food just doesn't sit well since the explosion." She picked up a muffin, taking a little bite. "I'm doing better with small meals."

"That's good. Got word the outpost could use a nurse. A team of one doctor and one nurse—same as before—is coming in, but we're short one nurse to go back. It would be for four days. There's a permanent replacement coming at that point. Interested?"

She brightened. "Can I go?"

He nodded. "As long as you're back to full health."

She grinned. "Somehow this tray looks very appetizing now."

"It has been pretty quiet apparently. The rebels moved farther off into the distance. And the casualties have been minor."

"Even better." With a fork she dug into the plate of pasta and salad. "Leaving later today?"

"Tomorrow morning, early."

She grinned. "Thanks. I appreciate this."

"I've never seen anybody as hell-bent on getting to where

the action is."

"I feel like I'm doing something useful there," she protested.

"Let's hope you still feel that way when you get there." He grinned.

It was only for a few days. How bad could it be?

RYDER PULLED UP behind the rest of his team, dust settling heavy in the still air. "The place is quiet. It's too damn quiet."

Easton nodded. "I hear you there."

"It's been that way since we came back," Corey said. "I can't help but feel like they're getting ready for another attack."

"My thoughts exactly," Devlin said. "They are watching us. Planning ..."

Off in the distance he studied the rebel camp below. He wanted to go in and attack, take them all out to show how the game was played. But, as long as they were peaceful, Ryder and his team would be peaceful. This was a reconnaissance mission for the moment.

They had to keep an eye on the enemy at all times.

They slipped around the hills for a closer look. There was nothing to see. There were buildings but no people, no animals. In a low voice Ryder muttered, "Have they abandoned camp?"

"Do we have any intel on an alternate one?" Devlin asked.

"No, but it doesn't mean they don't have one."

As he studied the place, Ryder realized there was no smoke. There was nothing. "It's deserted," he announced.

"It looks deserted, but that doesn't mean it is." Devlin swept his heat signature reader to the left, checking the first four buildings. He shook his head and whispered, "No sign of anyone yet."

With Easton giving cover, Ryder and Devlin moved to the closest building. Ryder knew in his gut the place was empty. And, if it was empty, that was bad news. If the occupants had moved out, where the hell did they move to?

Corey slipped to his side. "A heavily traveled trail runs on the far side, going between the hills. A unit could circle back around, coming up on our flank."

Silently the men shifted to a better vantage point to study the trail. At least eighty men had been below. Ryder would like to think they'd withdrawn, but … They also hadn't made any attempt to hide their tracks. That in itself was unusual.

Since the bomb maker had been collected, the group had scattered, disorganized. Ryder knew his two teams had taken out several leaders. Somebody was obviously back at the helm, pulling the scattered soldiers together again. That would always be an issue. Not only was an eager rebel soldier always ready to step forward to fill an empty spot but even more rebel soldiers were eager to create an empty spot.

An hour later Ryder's team finally reached a fork in the trail. The men studied them, faces grim. "One leads back around."

"And one with a lot less people is heading north. Possibly to get reinforcements?"

"Or taking away their wounded."

Ryder's team needed to know, but they were short on men, so intel-gathering would have to wait. The priority was to stop another attack. That meant following the tracks of those circling back.

With Easton running communications to the outpost, the four men moved, keeping to the shadows of the trees. The rebels would have sentries on duty, but, in this half-light, it was hard to see everything. Another SEAL team from the outpost was en route.

Plus, the outpost was on alert. The countryside was hilly, sporting lots of hiding places, and the dark depths were deceptive. The dust was strong, making it difficult to keep the cloud down as they traveled on foot. When gunfire erupted about a mile out from their position, they picked up the pace. Unfortunately that made things difficult. The gunfire stopped. Swearing under his breath, Ryder approached the top of a hill cautiously. He peered over the edge to see a larger group than they anticipated milling below, holding guns on prisoners. One of the teams from the outpost had been taken. His eyes quickly scanned below, his mind sorting through options.

With perfect timing, their backup team arrived.

And the balance of power shifted. It took less than ten minutes to organize a plan, and less than half that to implement it. Ryder slipped down the hill and took out the first rebel. Like dominos falling, the other sentries were taken down the same way. That was all it took. Within minutes things changed hands. The guards were now prisoners themselves. Not wasting any time, Ryder's unit gathered all the prisoners and headed back to the camp.

As a day went, this was a much better outcome than they could've anticipated as they'd survived remarkably unscathed.

He stood outside the medical tent and waited until the numbers within reduced. Hearing a kerfuffle, he stepped in to watch one of the guards run into a prisoner, slamming him onto a chair. The man didn't speak English. One of the nurses was trying to ask him some questions. Ryder's gaze locked on the nurse, and he swore heavily. The guard turned to look at him. Ryder shook his head. "Jesus Christ, Caitlyn. What are you doing here?"

She shot him a hard look. "I'm doing my job."

And that was all she said for the next few hours as she and Dr. Robertson cleaned, swabbed, stitched and bandaged those in need. When done, she walked toward Ryder. He couldn't help note the fatigue in her slumped shoulders and in her gaze. Then he caught sight of her stitches. Damn. She shouldn't even be here.

"You should be with Mac," he said abruptly.

She thrust her jaw out at him. "What's your problem with Mac? You keep bringing him up as if he's my lover. I told you that he's not."

He glared at her, wanting desperately to believe it, but, at the same time, he wasn't sure. At least if Mac and Caitlyn *were* together, she'd be safe right now. "I don't want you here," he snapped. "It's dangerous."

"Got it. Just over a few weeks, I'll be home."

"Please stay safe in the meantime." He turned and strode from the tent.

"You could keep an eye on me," she whispered under her breath.

But he heard. He turned. "I will always try to do that. But I can't have my focus split. When I'm here, I have a job to do. I can't be worried about you too."

"I was joking," she said with a bright smile. "You don't need to worry about me. I'm fine."

He snorted and stormed off.

CHAPTER 5

C AITLYN SANK SLOWLY to the bench on the side where she could still see. The first day back here at the smaller outpost, at the edge of the action again, had been on the rough side. She had a mess to clean up here at the clinic. Plus, she needed to find water. Not just for her but for the patients too. She sent one of the men to grab a medical case and told him to bring food as well. She had four men she was keeping overnight. The doctor was currently talking to two of them.

Dr. Robertson walked back over and said, "Good thing we brought plenty of medical supplies with us."

"Yes," she added. "I thought it had been calm lately, but obviously I was wrong, given the lack of supplies."

"Some of the medical supplies were stolen," Dr. Robertson said. "It's happened a couple times. Some young boys were caught."

"That explains it."

It sucked, but she felt almost sympathetic to anybody who needed medicine. She wished to God there was a way to call a peace treaty. But it never seemed to make any difference what she wanted. The fighting continued regardless.

She was still confused after seeing Ryder. She didn't have the time or the energy to argue with him, but that didn't stop her from constantly turning to see if he was entering her clinic. The problem was, she expected to see him. Twenty years of friendship was hard to give up. Even though they had missed out on the last two years, he was here now. She needed to do what she could to get them back on their natural footing.

That she wanted so much more was another story.

One of the men returned with crates of water. She grabbed a bottle, opened it and took a long drink.

Dr. Robertson turned and said, "You haven't even had a chance to drop your things on a bed. Take an hour and get settled in. Come back for your shift at eight p.m."

With that order, Caitlyn grabbed another bottle of water and headed out to make sure she had a place to lay her head tonight.

After dropping her bags on the floor beside a bed, she carried on to the mess tent for food. The meals would be a lot simpler here, but it would still be plentiful. She walked inside, headed for the coffee first, and then some hot food. With a tray full and an appetite to go with it for once, she sat down.

Within seconds, four shadows surrounded her. She glanced up, startled to see Ryder and his unit. She smiled at Corey. She'd been good friends with all of Ryder's unit in the day. But life changed for her and also for her relationships to them. Still, she was delighted to see him.

He gave her a guarded look in exchange.

Ryder put down his tray, swore and headed back to the food. She presumed he'd forgotten something.

Taking the opportunity she said, "I missed you guys."

Corey sat down, but his gaze never left her.

"I never meant to hurt Ryder."

Corey lifted an eyebrow. "For somebody who didn't

mean to, you sure did."

She winced. "Yeah, well, I'm trying to fix it, but it's a little hard, given the circumstances." She glanced at Easton and Devlin. Both gave her half smiles, willing to be friendly, but she understood the code. She'd hurt one SEAL so she'd hurt them all. She upped the wattage of her smile. "And I hear you two have ladies."

Devlin grinned. "Absolutely."

Easton nodded.

Caitlyn said, "Rumor has it they're both remarkable."

Devlin chuckled. "Well, I'd agree with that. Mine is Bristol, a busy lady, inventing drones and all kinds of weaponry for the military."

"Wow, that's impressive." She turned to Easton. "Is your lady mechanically minded or computer minded?"

The three men chuckled.

"No. Summer is the exact opposite," Easton said with a shy grin. "She's creative. She's a photographer."

"That's nice too," Caitlyn said with a laugh. "Sounds like you men have found exactly what you need." She glanced at Corey. "And you?"

Corey snorted. "Hell no. After what happened to Ryder, no way."

Her stomach sank. "More than just me or just me?"

"Just you."

She stared at her tray full of food, and her appetite fled. "I guess I have a little bit more to make up for than I thought," she said quietly.

"Maybe," Devlin said, "you could start by explaining to him exactly what happened."

Keeping her gaze down, she nodded. That was the hardest part. Especially as it had taken her months to understand it herself. But Devlin was right. It was time.

Just then Ryder returned. He sat down across from her without a word, digging into his food. He had enough meat on his plate to feed four men. But then he'd always been a huge eater. He expended tons of energy, and he was heavily muscled, so she knew his system could handle it just fine. She was a little bit jealous of how much he could consume.

Silence fell at Ryder's arrival. He glanced up, shifting his gaze from one to the other. "Don't stop the interesting conversation because of me."

Heat flushed her cheeks. Caitlyn murmured, "We weren't talking about anything specific."

A snort came from Corey, but, outside of shooting him a glance, Ryder stayed quiet. For that she was glad. As much as she had wanted to see these men, she really wanted to heal her relationship with Ryder. She didn't want to explain unless she and Ryder had privacy. It was all about the right moment to make this happen. So far she hadn't seen it.

HE HADN'T WANTED to sit at the same table with her, but it seemed he was unable to stop himself. Like a moth to a flame he kept coming back to the light and got burned again and again. It made him angry, frustrated, and, at the same time, he couldn't stop himself from seeing how she was. "How's the injury?" he asked abruptly.

She glanced up from her plate of food and shrugged. "It's fine."

"You still have stitches."

She nodded. "They're coming out in another few days. Stitches themselves aren't enough to stop anybody from working, as you well know," she said with spirit.

He had to acknowledge that. They'd all been in situations where they had worked with minor injuries. But this wasn't the same. "In your case you could've waited in relative safety until the stitches were out."

"I could've." She picked up her coffee and took a long sip, closing her eyes, enjoying the moment. "I don't know if it's just that it's been a really long day, but this cup of coffee tastes wonderful."

Devlin nodded. "I think they brought in a shipment of the specialty coffees by accident."

"Lovely for us," she said with a smile. "Every once in a while, these accidents turn out for the best."

Easton chuckled. "More often than not we end up with dishwater. This isn't bad." He took a healthy sip, then stood. "Speaking of which, I could use a second."

She watched as he walked around the many tables to the coffee. "He looks happy," she commented.

Nobody at the table said a word.

She shrugged and finished her meal. She'd spent so much time wishing she could be with Ryder again, yet now that she was … She moved her tray off to the side and sat with both hands holding her coffee cup. She was really looking forward to getting some sleep tonight, but she had to be at the clinic at eight p.m., so sleep was a long way off.

Easton returned with a cup of coffee. In a low voice, he leaned down and said something to Ryder and Corey. The look on their faces changed, became hard. They bounded to their feet and took off.

"Is something going on?" Caitlyn asked.

"Talk of a potential attack. You need to go to your room and stay there."

She shook her head, standing up. "I'll head to the clinic." She glanced at her watch. "I'm almost on shift anyway." Without giving the men a chance to argue, she bolted.

Ryder watched her leave. He'd been ready to race out of the tent at Easton's words, only to stop and look back at Caitlyn. She shouldn't be alone.

While she went one way, Ryder took off the other. He'd swing around to check on her later. If she was on shift tonight, that was shitty news. But at least he'd know where to find her.

As he walked in to the meeting, the rest of his team lined up at his side. They all listened, realizing the attack looked to be an attempt to free the rebel prisoners held in the outpost's medic facility.

"How many are injured and being held in medical?" Ryder asked.

The commander glanced down at his notes and said, "Twelve."

Ryder gave a hard nod. "Okay, how many guards holding the men?"

The commander studied him for a long moment. "Six."

His frown was instinctive. A two-to-one ratio was not bad as long as everybody understood what was coming.

The commander looked at him. "You don't like those odds?"

Ryder gave a quick shake of his head. "No. I don't."

Devlin spoke up. "Do we know the status of the twelve injured? Are any of them their leader?"

One of the other men spoke up. "One leader is here. He took a bullet in the hip."

"Surgery?" Easton asked.

"Bullet went right through. The doctor stitched him up, but he shouldn't be moved."

Ryder considered the odds. "I'd like to be assigned to medical," he said calmly. "We need a strong presence."

"No," the commander said. "You and your team are to find out where the attack is coming from, how many rebels are involved. We need intel to understand what we have coming."

Ryder wanted to argue, but he knew there was no point. Besides, that was where his skills would be best used. He had to trust the others would keep Caitlyn safe.

Within minutes the men were geared up and already sliding through the night. They were expecting an attack from the north, so the enemy couldn't be too far out. With the comms on Silent, the four of them with another team of four on their flank raced through the darkened terrain.

Two miles out, he knew something was wrong. His comm confirmed as everyone came to the same conclusion. The attackers had either changed their approach, their timeframe or had somehow avoided them. Given the full moon and the lack of tracks, Ryder figured it was the first scenario.

The men split up and came back to the camp from east to west. Ryder didn't like this one bit. It was all too possible a large force was coming, but, if the enemy had chosen a couple silent and stealthy invaders, hoping to free the prisoners and then take over medical, that was something else. It made sense as they had a dozen men there, mostly mobile. Once free the rebels had an army already in place.

In virtual darkness, silence hung heavy on the grounds, and Ryder's gaze caught a movement to his right. He watched as one man separated from the hillside and slipped to the outpost, heading to medical. Ryder tapped his comm hard twice and pointed.

The others acknowledged what he'd seen, and Devlin sent a coded message to the outpost. One man was easy enough to take out. But how many others were out there? They waited another ten minutes. There was no sign of gunfire or disturbance of any kind. Which meant the intruder had been taken out.

Soon two more shadows separated from the trees in different directions, heading for different parts of the camp. From their profiles, it was easy to see they were heavily armed. As they reached the bottom of the hill in the distance, Ryder watched six more men separate from the far side.

His gaze turned feral.

Now he could do something. His team moved in.

CHAPTER 6

I T WAS HARD to still her nerves while she made sure all her patients were comfortable. The camp was on high alert, expecting the enemy to free their men held here. The guards had been doubled up inside the medical center. She had many injured rebels as patients. One man in particular had been sedated. A bullet had gone through just above his hipbone. It had missed everything major—stitches had been required, and he'd lost a lot of blood. He was holding his own, but would be transported in the morning.

She bustled around, checking everyone else. Dr. Robertson was here with her. She'd been delighted to see the extra guards in the center, but she'd hoped one of them would be Ryder. Instead, they were strangers.

Of the twelve injured rebels, most were ambulatory and under heavy guard. A couple of cracked bones, several bad burns, open wounds and, yeah, several bullet holes. Two of her own men slept in the back room, separated for ease of guarding. One had a dislocated shoulder, and the other had a bullet burn along his throat. It was nasty, and it would take some time to heal. He should be shipped to one of the main bases just out of Baghdad with a full hospital facility, but he'd argued pretty fiercely about staying here. She admired the sentiment, but, at some point, it was just foolishness.

Then Ryder's words echoed in her head. He was as concerned since she had done the same thing.

By the time she finished checking on her patients, a sense of awareness, a readiness came over the men guarding the prisoners. A small light was on in the center of the medical tent. One of the guards blew it out.

She sat down at the desk by the doctor, and the two of them looked at each other. There was a protocol to follow. If they were attacked, they had weapons of their own. She was a good shot, but she'd never been field tested. It certainly wasn't anything she wanted to try today either.

One guard flattened against a nearby cabinet. Then another moved to a better hiding spot along a wall. As she watched, everyone took a spot where their shadows weren't as easily seen from outside the tent. They blended in well. Medical was large enough to sleep a half dozen but could treat a lot more in a pinch. It also held offices and medical supplies. But it wasn't a permanent base, and, for the first time, she realized just how very little separated her from whoever was outside.

One of the guards motioned for her to go under the desk. She pulled out her own firearm, but he motioned a second time. She shrugged and sat cross-legged under the wooden structure. She wasn't going to argue. Her heart slammed against her ribs, and she breathed through her mouth silently as she waited.

Suddenly three men burst inside. Two were immediately attacked and dropped to the floor. The third man fired randomly. One of the men at her side took a shot, then dropped to a crouch. Caitlyn crossed her arms over her head. Dr. Robertson was behind her somewhere.

Why couldn't everybody just get along? Instead of these constant war-torn countries where a dictator was always being overthrown—terrorists trying to take over somebody else in the name of one religion or another. It seemed that, no matter how much the military did, there was just no improving this.

Gunfire ripped through the camp. Men shifted in and out of the center. Several others fell. She didn't understand who was who as chaos reigned. And then several more men burst in, guns firing, but they were quickly taken out.

She counted six rebel bodies on the floor now. Still four shadows outside. A guard straightened, lined up a head shot and popped one through the tent material. She clapped a hand over her mouth, wanting to cry out that he didn't even know if it was an enemy or a friend. But, when the rebel rush came the third time, it came from the front, the back and the sides. She realized that, while they'd all been watching the front, somebody had been opening the back wall, giving them access from a different angle.

Suddenly her hands were full. One guard collapsed beside her amid a flurry of gunfire. He bled from a graze across his throat. She clasped her hand over the wound to stop the bleeding. Then she saw a second bullet in his shoulder. His eyes were open, but he struggled to breathe. As he gasped for air, she whispered against his ear, "Stay quiet. Let me work on you."

He gave her a grateful look and tried to stay still as she grabbed bandages from the cabinet beside her. She quickly slapped one against his throat. It wasn't bad, but a few stitches would be needed to hold the tear together. Right now it was a case of holding pressure to his shoulder to stop the more major bleeding.

Gunfire rattled over her head to the side. Shouts and screams followed as though some were badly wounded.

Prisoners tried to fight back.

And then suddenly the men appeared to double and then triple in numbers. All she could do was keep her head down. She didn't know who the hell was who in the dark. A heavy hand landed on her shoulder, and Ryder's voice was in her ear. "Are you okay?"

Shuddering at the shock of his presence, she nodded. "I'm okay."

"Stay down," he ordered.

With her hands still pressed against the man's throat and shoulder, she tried to get an idea of what was happening. But as the gunfire stopped after one last bullet, she figured it was over. She just didn't know who had won.

It took a few minutes before the power came back on. She glanced around, saw Dr. Robertson working his way through the patients and ordered several men standing guard to pick up their fallen comrades and place them on available beds. Two came to help the man she'd been working on. Dr. Robertson soon came to assist.

Once able, she did a quick search to find several of the prisoners they had treated earlier were now dead, collapsed on the floor. Six of the men who attacked them were also dead. The leader with the bullet above his hip had taken a bullet in his forehead—almost execution style.

Bodies were everywhere. She ran her fingers through her hair and pulled her hand over her face. Under her breath she said, "Jesus." It was more prayer than profanity.

She'd seen a lot of dead, seen what people could do to each other. But still, she'd never get used to it. However, she had no time to think about that. People needed her. She did a quick triage through the downed men. One of the guards had taken a bullet through the stomach. He would be stabilized and air-lifted out now. She redirected the doctor to those who needed him most, then moved out as many of the able-bodied guards as she could, so she'd get the room back in order.

"Go, go and go. We need room to work here." She caught sight of Ryder. "Please remove the bodies."

Within minutes arms and legs were grabbed, and the bodies were taken away. Caitlyn didn't know what they would do with them with the heat here. But that wasn't her problem. Not right now. Right now she had men bleeding, needing stitches. Men who needed splints. She had two more prisoners in rough shape with new wounds. They glared at her. She never said a word, just set about bandaging them up.

Finally when she was done, she told the prisoners, "I won't do this a third time. The next time I'll kill you myself."

She turned her back on them and walked away, coming up tight against Ryder's chest.

He grabbed her, tilted her chin up and said, "I do love this kick-ass Caitlyn. How is it so much of your personality is still a mystery to me?"

She blew a few tendrils of hair off her face and smiled. "Ha, not true. You know exactly who I am. And this Caitlyn has always been here. She only comes out when necessary."

"Too bad the rest of you went into hiding and never explained why or what I'd done."

Her gaze softened. "What makes you think you did any-thing?" She hated to think he felt guilty over what had happened. But of course he did.

"If I didn't do anything, why the hell did you cut me out of your life?" His gaze was searching, intent on answers he needed.

She gave him a sad smile. "Not everything is as it seems."

"Ryder?" Devon called from the main entrance. "Let's go, man."

Ryder dropped his arms, took a look around the bloody area and said, "Are you okay here?"

She smiled. "This is my domain. Get lost."

He gave her a crooked grin, the same one that had always pulled at her heartstrings. She thought she'd never see it again, and it brought tears to her eyes. She watched him stride from the tent, the alpha male completely back on the hunt.

He was a damn good man. She just wished to hell he was hers.

HE HATED TO leave her, but, if he understood one thing, it was doing the job. For both her and him. They couldn't allow the enemy time to regroup.

With his unit and an additional four men, Ryder's team headed back out into the night. They were five miles out when a warning sounded. Ryder dropped to the ground and froze. Lying there in the early morning, he heard movement. An ever-so-faint movement.

He crept to the top of a small hill to look over. Sure enough, enemy forces gathered. Not as many as before, but they were well armed. He counted twenty men against their eight. Hours passed. Finally he got word a large rebel group was due in from the east. The military wanted to organize their own attack against the gathering rebel militia.

Even in lockdown, with all the chaos in the medical center, people could be missed. With orders to pull back, he retreated to meet up with the rest of his team. He quickly updated them on the latest orders. "We want to take them out and rescue their prisoners."

The next couple hours were tense as they counted, watched and gathered. As Ryder waited for reinforcements, the numbers of the rebel army swelled to thirty. Still the men he watched didn't appear to be seasoned warriors. It was as if the rebels had gone to villages, armed every available man, trained or not.

Ryder was sorry for all the innocents caught up in this world. When different factions decided to fight, everybody was forced into action. Whether they wanted to or not. There was no saying no. It would just get you a bullet.

Ready finally, Ryder's reinforced team quickly encircled the rebel camp. As Ryder hunched low, waiting for the action to start, he heard Easton and Corey gasp in shock. In the comm in his ear, Ryder whispered, "What's up?"

"Two prisoners, both taken from the outpost."

Ryder narrowed his gaze as he studied the gathering below. The rebels had two vehicles. In the back of one were two prisoners under guard. He caught sight of a white face. "A woman?" Ryder's voice was heavy. And he knew.

"Yes, and Dr. Robertson."

"It's Caitlyn, isn't it?" He closed his eyes. And in his head he started to swear. He never let the sound out as he waited for confirmation. But he didn't need to hear the answer to know.

He would get her back. No soldier down there was capable of stopping him. He just had to get there before they killed her.

CHAPTER 7

CAITLYN GLARED AT her surroundings. She and Dr. Robertson had been forced out of the camp at gunpoint and whisked here. Robertson and she sat on the ground under guard in a rebel camp. She remembered several of her patients had caused a ruckus; then she'd been hit from behind. She reached up and pressed a hand against her pounding head.

She still had stitches from her first head injury. She knew Ryder and the rest of his team were out there somewhere. She had to hold on. Give her captors no reason to kill her. Give Ryder time to get to her as she knew he would. The guards here were laughing and joking but underneath was anger. As if somehow her team had insulted them by capturing as many rebels as they had in the first place.

She wondered how pride and ego could play such a major part in war. And yet, it appeared to. In truth, the world was a mess. Glancing around at the enemy camp, she didn't see any of their badly injured members. She studied their faces carefully, but they appeared to have taken whoever was ambulatory, the others left behind as casualties of war. Or possibility shot so they couldn't talk.

One of the guards nudged her with the end of his rifle. She stood up, Dr. Robertson at her side. Trying to guess what they wanted but not understanding the language, the two were prodded to a large tent.

Inside the tent it didn't take long for her eyes to adjust and to see several men on the ground, obviously hurt. And then she understood. They'd brought the two of them, a medical team, to help their own injured. She rushed to the first man and dropped to her knees. She placed a hand on his neck out of habit yet instinctively knew they couldn't help him, not if she couldn't find a pulse. His chest cavity had taken several bullets. She shook her head, got up and went to the second man. Dr. Robertson bent over the third.

"I have a pulse here," she said quietly.

"This one is going into shock." He glanced around. "We need medicine, bandages, IVs, blood."

She turned to the man with the rifle pointed at her. "Is there medicine? Supplies? We need something to stop the bleeding."

The man shrugged and raised the rifle to her head.

She stared at him. "We can't help them without something. We need supplies."

The man at her side groaned. She returned her attention to him, ripping open his jacket. There was a little bit of blood on the top left shoulder. But that seemed to be a superficial wound. She checked over the rest of him. His lower body was fine, but his head showed trauma. She pulled her cell phone from her pocket, hearing several yells as the men scowled at her.

She pointed to the flashlight on the phone and turned it on so she could check the man's head. As soon as the light shone, the other rebels around her fell silent. She studied the head wound, realizing he'd probably just been knocked out. He would need a few stitches, but she could do little without the necessary tools.

She got up and joined Dr. Robertson who stared down at a man with an ugly abdominal wound. "Gun shot?" She dropped to his side.

He nodded. "Looks like it may have lodged in the spine. He needs surgery."

"We don't have anything to treat him with," she exclaimed. "We don't have any dressings. We don't have any antibiotics. He'll die a very slow, painful death without surgery. Infection is a definite issue."

Dr. Robertson gave her a hard look. "They will blame us if we don't treat these men."

"One is already dead," she said in a low tone, studying his young face not even of an age to shave yet. Her heart aching, she said, "Such a waste." She turned to the two living patients. "The other one is alive with a minor head injury. His pulse is strong and steady. He should wake up soon. This guy, however …" She glanced down at the thirtysomething man with a grimace.

"And that is war, my dear. That is war. This is only one of hundreds they've probably already buried."

She stood and said to the rebels, "He's going to die." She pointed to the stomach of the injured soldier. "We need supplies and medicines."

The man in the doorway holding the rifle on them sputtered a stream of words neither understood. He quickly disappeared from the tent. She didn't even have clean water to wash the wound. Or a sterile dressing to put over it, just to keep the dust out. She glanced down at her dirty clothing. Nothing she wore could be used either.

A few minutes later, two men walked in with boxes they dumped onto the floor. She opened them to see dressings and medicines.

"Yes." Although probably stolen from their camp, she dove into the boxes. The next half hour was painful. She was glad the patient was unconscious but administered morphine to kick in before he woke up. They found the bullet on the spine had missed the spinal cord. Still soft tissue damage could kill him within days as he bled heavily. Thankfully he was unconsciousness. Given his heavy blood loss, she didn't expect him to wake up anytime soon, if at all. Dr. Robertson did the best he could. They had no IVs, no blood and no liquids to give him, but they did administer several more shots of morphine and antibiotics for any infection.

The bleeding slowed eventually. In normal circumstances he'd be flown to a hospital. She didn't think there was such a thing here. Her heart went out to the young man. He *could* pull through; she'd seen it happen, but these were definitely less-than-ideal circumstances. If his wounds became infected …

Sitting beside Dr. Robertson, together they waited, checking often on the two living patients as the hours passed slowly. "Do you think they're coming for us?" she murmured, knowing the doctor understood who she talked about.

"They'll destroy this camp, and hopefully we'll get rescued in the process," he said drily.

She understood what he meant. A lot of priorities came with a war. Retrieving their own personnel was at the top of the list, but they also had to make sure this didn't happen again. At least not again by these particular rebels.

She was so tired. She sat with her head resting on her knees. "Do you think it's safe to sleep?"

"Go ahead and nod off," he said quietly. "I'll keep an eye on the patients."

She didn't want to say anything about the one patient, but they both knew how poor the young man's odds were. She tilted her head to the side and let her eyes close. Wouldn't it be nice if she could wake up to find this was all a nightmare, and she was back in her own bed?

Just as she started to go under, she heard an odd sound—almost a whisper. She lifted her head and looked around. The two injured men still lay on the floor as she'd seen them last. Dr. Robertson had stretched out with his head on his hands, his eyes closed as if sleeping. But his breathing wasn't deep enough. "Did you say something?"

He rolled his head to the side and looked at her. "No."

She frowned. "I thought I heard someone call my name."

When it didn't come again, she dropped her head back to her knees, letting her eyes close. Hearing it again, she bolted to her feet and spun around, but the tent was empty. Then an odd scratch came from behind them. She walked to the back of the tent and said in a low tone, "Hello? Is anybody there?"

"It's Ryder."

And she smiled with relief and joy filling her heart. He'd come after her. *Oh, thank God.*

HE'D SEEN CAITLYN and the doctor forced into the tent. However, maneuvering around to the back to see inside the camp and getting up close to their tent had been nearly impossible. He'd watched as a guard left and two soldiers arrived with boxes. Supplies, he presumed. He couldn't see any other reason to kidnap a doctor and nurse unless their services were required.

Both soldiers came out again without the boxes, meaning Dr. Robertson and Caitlyn might not be guarded inside. But Ryder couldn't be sure. He'd waited, but now that he had confirmed she was in there, she was his number one priority. He needed a way to get those two out.

One guard stood watch in front of Caitlyn's tent, but others were close by. Only a major diversion would give Ryder the opening he needed.

A few minutes later he saw such an opening. Two guards came to the tent and spoke with Caitlyn's guard. The three walked off to the left to speak with somebody in front of another tent.

He slipped his knife along the back of the tent and slipped his head inside. Caitlyn and Dr. Robertson were sitting on the ground, waiting. They bolted to their feet as soon as they saw him. Behind them he could see men stretched out on the ground. He motioned to Caitlyn and Dr. Robertson to hurry. As soon as he got them out, the doctor whispered, "One man will die if we don't help him."

Ryder shook his head and urged them to the tree line. Soon afterward a shout came from the camp, followed by gunfire. Ryder watched as the enemy soldiers spread out. "It's too late to help. They know you're missing now," he continued, watching as two men went into their tent.

The shadows showed the pantomime going on inside. One shot the other, then fired multiple times at the ground as if at different targets. There were shouts, raised voices and then several more shots. Only one man came out of the tent.

"Did he shoot his own men?" Caitlyn asked in a low voice, tucked up close against Ryder.

"Too many bullets were fired to kill just one man," he murmured. "I suspect he not only shot the guard but also the injured soldiers you treated."

"Why would they go through all the work to save them only to shoot them?" Caitlyn asked bewildered.

"It's quite possible that kidnapping you wasn't sanctioned by the rest of the group. Think about it. If someone had an injured family member, he'd need to find medical help. If they had no doctors to treat him, then it would make sense to kidnap you and bring you back to treat their loved ones. However, by kidnapping you two, it guaranteed we'd come after you and rain all kinds of hell down on the camp." He paused, then added quietly, "Now can you see him being punished and the original injured soldiers being shot?"

Unfortunately she could imagine that all too well. "That sucks."

"Yes, it does suck. Welcome to war," Ryder said in low tones. "I wish to God you'd stayed in the States."

He had to get her back to the camp safely. That was miles away. He knew the outpost she'd come from had already been moved. Better if she was back at one of the main Forward Operating Bases—FOBs for short. Any one of the dozens they had here in Iraq would be better than the smaller mobile outposts. "We have a long way to go. Let's move." And he led the way into the hills. Thankfully his orders had been to get her back to the camp she'd been sent from, not the outpost. That meant driving. The rendezvous point had already been changed once. He needed a pickup for these two.

"What about the rest of your team?" Caitlyn asked.

"They're down there," he said. "My job is to get you two back to safety."

There was a whole lot more to it than he'd volunteered. No way would he leave her as a prisoner of war, not when he started to suspect he might be one of the reasons she'd come here in the first place. Out of guilt or to apologize, he didn't know. But the last thing he wanted was to have her injured or killed because of him. She was a hell of a woman, a fine nurse. That they'd fallen out didn't change the fact she was a keeper, and any man she chose was a hell of a lucky man.

Avoiding the main routes, he led them toward the rendezvous point.

They kept to the little cover available, but this was a dry and arid land and didn't offer much protection. They weren't more than a mile away when he heard a vehicle.

And it wasn't one of theirs.

CHAPTER 8

"**G**ET DOWN."

Caitlyn hit the sand a hair before Ryder pushed her down.

"Don't move," he whispered.

With her and Dr. Robertson flat behind a small hill, she watched as Ryder peeked over the top, his head barely visible to the vehicle approaching.

She didn't need to look; the cloud of dust they left behind them showed up for miles. She exchanged a worried glance with Dr. Robertson.

The only one with a weapon was Ryder. But she had no intention of being taken captive again.

She shifted slightly, and Ryder placed a hand on her shoulder. "Don't move."

Her breath caught in the back of her throat, her muscles locking. The sounds of the vehicle raced past. Her breath released on a gust of air. When Ryder didn't move, she whispered, "Aren't we safe?"

"They've driven past, but I want to make sure they don't come back."

She could understand that. But lying in the hot sun on hot sand was deadly. She struggled to stay calm, and, just when she was sure they were safe, Ryder swore.

"Shit."

She turned as Ryder bolted to his feet, swinging his rifle

around. A hard spit sounded, followed by several more shots. He grabbed her by the shoulder. "Let's go. Move. Move. Move."

With Dr. Robertson at her side, she ran in front of Ryder as he kept up a spray of bullets to give them enough clearance to get out of danger.

"Head to the trees," he cried, running at her side, firing at the men she could see racing toward them. Panicked, she ran faster and harder than she ever had before. But running in the sand made it impossible to make any headway. Her feet sank, and her footing rolled under her, giving her no foundation to push off for the next step.

She turned to look at Dr. Robertson beside her. He struggled as well. Suddenly he tripped and fell.

Caitlyn dropped to her knees at his side. "Get up. We have to move." She tugged on his arm, forcing him to the tree line. As soon as they were among the few trees, they both collapsed, gasping for breath. On her hands and knees, her head hanging low, she groaned softly. Her legs burned, and her feet were on fire.

She felt a rifle at her back.

No. Oh, hell no.

She didn't even think about it; she spun, kicked, both hands reaching for the barrel, shoving it skyward as it fired harmlessly in the air.

And suddenly she held the weapon, but the rebel soldier was on the ground, staring sightlessly at the sky.

She spun in a panic, looking for the next attacker, to find the three of them were alone with Ryder holding his weapon on the downed soldier.

"Is it over?" she cried. "Did you kill him or did someone else?"

"I did." Ryder wrapped his arms around her. "It's over."

Dr. Robertson stood up, a little shaky but unhurt and smiled at Caitlyn. "When the chips are down, Caitlyn, you know how to make them count."

She grinned at him. "I couldn't let him hurt us," she cried out.

"Thankfully he's not a problem anymore." Ryder ushered them deeper into the trees. "We have to keep going. They will come looking for their man."

"How many did you kill?" she asked. "How many were there?"

"I took out the two who arrived in the one vehicle, but you know another truck will be along soon enough. We need to make sure we are a long way away before they get here."

With that he pushed them forward. And Caitlyn knew he was determined to get them to safety no matter what.

THEY MARCHED STEADILY, but he knew they would travel on foot at least another hour if not longer. Caitlyn was fading already. After that rush of adrenaline and panic, she'd slowly come down as the shock wore off. But he knew they didn't have time to wallow. They had a rendezvous up ahead to make. If he could contact them to bring it closer he would, but the comm system was down. Casting his gaze to Caitlyn, he slowed his march, so he could walk beside her with Dr. Robertson slightly ahead. "How are you holding up?"

She shot him a look. "I'm fine."

An edge to her voice made him smile. "Good. Glad to hear that."

She shook her head. "I don't understand why they'd shoot their own men," she said, her voice pained. "They were already injured."

"They were a liability. The fact of it is, we are where people do some of the worst things possible to each other."

"If that's the case, I'm worried about humanity," she admitted. "I wonder how we could possibly survive, if we even should survive as a species, given all we do to each other," she said painfully. "There is no need for any of this."

"No, but somebody has to stand up for all the people who have been annihilated by groups like this. The carnage has to stop somewhere, and it takes people like us to stand against them. To let them know they can't just kill whoever they want because they decide to."

She fell silent. And he knew there was really no point in discussing it. Wars happened all over the world. He didn't know a time when there wasn't one somewhere. He was doing what he could. He had to focus on that and to let the rest go.

Another forty minutes passed. He'd been walking between the two, keeping them strong while ensuring they weren't being followed. "We're almost there," he said.

"Thank God for that," Caitlyn said in a fervent whisper.

"About a half mile to the rendezvous." He offered her a drink from his bottle of water, and she took several gulps before passing it back.

"We haven't seen anybody along the way, so I assume we're safe," Dr. Robertson asked, his voice tired, worn out.

"We're safe enough. The rest of the units have taken out the rebel camp."

He watched Caitlyn. She nodded. It seemed she understood that likely dozens of men had just died in the fight behind them. "It's so sad."

Maybe because he agreed with her, or maybe because he was tired of thinking about all the things wrong in the world, his tone was harsher than he meant when he said, "So many things in life should change. We change what we can, and we have to accept it might not be enough."

"And maybe this is as good a time as any. I might never get another chance." She took a deep breath. "I never meant to hurt you."

The doctor walked at their side, slightly ahead. He didn't appear to be listening to the conversation. He struggled to put one foot in front of the other. Still this discussion was personal, and Ryder really didn't want anyone listening in. He let Dr. Robertson get slightly ahead.

"How could you not expect to hurt me? The fact that you just stepped out of my life after twenty years of friend-ship ..." He shook his head, letting his voice trail off. "It made no sense. I told you how I had loved you. Always. And you never talked to me again."

She sighed heavily.

He wasn't sure how much was fatigue or the discussion.

"I was so confused."

He snorted. "Really? That's your excuse?" He shook his head. "There's *confused*, and then there's walking away from a twenty-year friendship."

"And that's why I was so confused," she said, trying for honesty.

At least he thought she was trying to be honest. He stud-ied her face, seeing the fatigue and the earnestness. "Explain."

"What we had was so much more. It was just almost too much. You shocked me. The weekend shocked me, and my feelings were overwhelming. I didn't know what to do, so I ran."

"Ran? Why would all of that have been too much?" He didn't get it.

"Because, up until then, my relationships hadn't the depth I thought they had. Which had also been my ex-husband, George's, complaint. But I hadn't realized it until I spent the weekend with you. Somehow that twenty years of friendship had morphed into something so much more. Yet, I wasn't ready to accept that realization. There was a richness, a complexity between us that added to what we had, and I didn't understand that beforehand.

"At the time I wasn't dealing well with the aftermath of my divorce. Instead of grieving for that relationship, you showed me how that relationship was much less than I thought. That George was actually correct in his complaints," she exclaimed softly. "I see now that what I felt was nothing but a childish infatuation, real enough at the time, but … I felt like I'd hurt him because I hadn't known better. In my defense I thought he was the one for me. I didn't understand that my feelings for George were so … thin. But after I'd seen the depth of the feelings between you and me, I realized I hadn't been there for my husband. I'd cheated him. I couldn't give him a real and mature relationship."

Ryder almost came to a dead stop at her words, but he forced himself to keep marching. Keeping them in the shadows as he led them to safety, he took a deep breath and responded, "That makes no sense."

"I know," she admitted. "At the time it didn't to me either. It took me weeks, if not months, to fathom my way through it all. I felt so damned guilty. I'd been devastated over the breakup with George. And yet, that weekend with you was like a complete paradigm shift. I didn't know who I was anymore. I had to figure it out."

It was not what he'd expected to hear, but it was an interesting explanation to consider. One he had never contemplated for sure.

She looked at him. In a hesitant voice, she asked, "You didn't feel the same?"

"The same as what?" he asked with a quick glance at Dr. Robertson. But the doctor was in front, still putting one foot in front of the other. He could be listening, but, if so, he was keeping his thoughts to himself.

"About your previous relationships?"

He shook his head. "No. I had deliberately kept my relationships light, knowing I was going on more and more missions and one day might not come back."

There was silence after that point.

After a long moment, she said, "So that part was easier for you than it was for me. That slap of awareness was harsh. I didn't like myself much. I felt like a heartless fraud. And no way would I show up in a relationship with you when I was such a mess. I didn't know who I was anymore, and I had to find something inside me that was better."

He shook his head, completely dumbfounded. "So you didn't talk to me again because you felt you weren't worthy?"

There was silence again, and then, with a broken laugh, she said, "It sounds stupid when you put it that way, but I guess maybe that's exactly how I did feel. As if you showed me how much of a fake I'd been. I really hated myself afterward. Maybe I had been too young, like George had suggested. I certainly hadn't shown up for the relationship. Not fully. Not as I would now. If I was less of a person with George, had I been less of a person with you? I really cared about you. But I didn't want to shortchange you, and I couldn't be sure I was 'all in.' You deserved better." She shrugged. "Now that I look back on it, it seems stupid in so many ways. But it was very real to me."

He tried not to keep staring at her, but it was hard when these revelations were not making much sense. "Did you ever explain any of that to George?"

"No way." She shrugged. "I might tell him down the road. Let him know he was right about me. He kept saying things—like he didn't feel we were connected on a deep-enough level, that he didn't think I was there for him. At the time I had been insulted and upset, thinking he was taking my love and tossing it away." She snorted. "But he was right. I had nothing to give because I just didn't realize so much more was inside me to actually give. I didn't even know until I spent that weekend with you."

"Well …" The word clipped out on an exhale. He had no more.

"Is that all you can say?"

"I'm trying," he muttered. "Of all the reasons I came up with about why you never talked to me again, none of this was ever one of them."

"How could it have been? You couldn't have seen the real me because I hadn't let the real me show up in any relationship—including the one with you," she said quietly.

"Not true. I knew who you were inside and out. I watched you grow from pigtails and freckles to a beautiful young woman. I assure you that I understood who you were before and after our weekend. If the *after* person, who put me through hell is the authentic you, I might prefer the earlier model."

She shot him a strange look. "That would be too bad. Because that woman is gone." She hurried her steps and caught up to Dr. Robertson.

He could see the US military trucks racing toward them and guessed this was the end of their conversation.

Still, it would take him some time to figure out how he felt about her explanation. And what that meant for them now.

CHAPTER 9

S HE COULDN'T PUT into words her overall sense of relief as she was welcomed back into the main camp. Even after being picked up at the rendezvous point, the drive had taken hours. She was happy to hear she wouldn't return to the outpost. At the base camp, the other nurses quickly ushered the two kidnap victims into a medical tent where they were checked over. That's when she realized she was covered in blood. It wasn't her blood. It was blood from the man with the gunshot wound in the spine.

She explained how they'd been trying to help one of the rebels, and that's why she was bloody. Still, she was exhausted in more ways than one. Not just from being kidnapped, held hostage and the panicked escape, but also because of a deeper internal exhaustion from the emotional release of finally telling Ryder about why she'd walked away. Something she should have done a long time ago. Although she wasn't sure she had gotten to the bottom of it all even now. It had taken her a lot of personal introspection to get this far. Sometimes answers came as she woke, and other times she found nuggets of illumination at odd times during the day.

With tears threatening, she finally made it to her tent. She'd only been gone a few days, but it felt like a fine homecoming. She stared at her bed with longing. If only she could just collapse, but a shower had to come first. She grabbed her bags, pulled out a change of clothing and walked to the showers. She took close to a half hour under the heated water. Her hair required two shampoos and a lot of conditioner to untangle, plus, she still had her stitches to watch out for.

She was also hungry, but she didn't think she could get anything down right now. As she headed back to her bed, her steps faltered as she looked up to see Ryder standing in front of her tent.

He studied her quietly. "How about food first?"

She wrinkled her face at him. "I'm not sure I can keep anything down."

"Won't hunger wake you in the night?"

Memories of those particular hot nights shared with him flashed through her mind. How well he knew her. How intimately he knew her evenings, at least the three they'd spent together. She took a deep breath and shook her head. "I doubt anything will wake me up." She glanced at her watch and sighed. "Probably have to be up in a few hours anyway."

Which was too bad as she wanted to go with him because time with him was precious.

"I doubt it. Carbs and protein right now will help you sleep better."

She dropped her dirty clothes in the laundry bag, hung the towel at the end of the bed and turned to him with a smile. "All right, let's try to get a little bit down."

He smiled and held out a hand.

She stared at it in wonder. "Does that mean you forgive me?"

He frowned. "I don't know," he said honestly. "I'd like to think so. So how about we take a few steps toward each other and see if we can make this work?"

"Make what work?" She casually reached out and placed her hand in his, loving the feeling as his fingers closed around hers. But she was jerked forward, hard, up tight against his chest. Being in his arms was foreign yet … not. Lord, she wanted to be part of Ryder's life again. His firm body at her fingertips just made her want so much more. She peered up and stared into his eyes. The darkness that told her nothing. "I really didn't mean to hurt you."

He gave her a quick nod. "*That* I believe." Then he turned with an arm around her shoulders, walking her toward the food. "I still don't understand how *any* of what you said caused me to lose my best friend for so long."

She smiled at still being called his best friend. They'd been the best of friends for so long. She wanted to be more. But she'd take what she could get for now. She was so damn grateful for a lot of things in her life, and Ryder was one of the biggest. At the same time, she had to admit to the hope she found in her heart at his words. She had missed him. For more reasons than she could ever have counted. With her arm around his back, she squeezed him close. "Because I'm an idiot. I've hated every day we've been apart."

"So I suggest we turn back the clock and start again." He laughed. "How about it?"

She gave him a surprised smile. "Okay," she said slowly. "That might work." He still hadn't mentioned that weekend between them except in passing. The weekend she could never forget.

"It'll work if we want it to work," he said with spirit. "So fill me in on what I missed. What have you been up to?"

In friendly neutral territory, she slowly brought him current on her life, not that there was much to report. She'd spent a lot of it alone, a lot of it with Mac—platonically—and a lot of it at work. She hadn't had another relationship since him. Although she'd tried. She didn't tell Ryder about that though. At the same time, she didn't want to bring up Mac's name either, not when she and Ryder were on a more friendly footing. "I should have contacted you earlier," she said abruptly.

"It would've been nice if you had," he said quietly. "But it's all good."

And she remembered that about him. That easygoing, laid-back, *everything was always good* mentality. Now at the mess tent, she stopped, wishing she didn't have to go in. She was too tired to eat.

Ryder wrapped an arm around her again and tugged her closer. "It's okay. If you want to take it back to your tent, we'll do that."

Once again memories broke through her consciousness. She shook her head. "No, let's just grab something fast."

In line with a tray in hand, she walked down the short aisle. She didn't think she could handle anything too greasy. A comfort food for her was oatmeal.

Thankfully one of the cooks knew what she had been through, and he asked her if he could get her something.

With a wan smile she asked, "Any chance I could get a hot bowl of oatmeal?"

His eyes lit up. "Absolutely. Back in a minute."

She didn't know where he got it from, but in a few minutes he came back with a very large bowlful, likely two times as much as she could possibly eat.

The top was covered with raisins, nuts and coconut. He gave her a little bowl of brown sugar and a cup of cream. With a smile he said, "This should help fix you up."

She shook her head. "There is enough here for both of us."

The cook nodded toward Ryder and the large tray he'd filled. "Only if he eats that tray full as well. Otherwise, he'd starve on half a bowlful."

She walked over to the coffee corner and stood, staring at it. But her mind was too tired to function. Ryder came up beside her and nudged her away. "Forget about the coffee. We don't want you staying awake."

"Right." She knew that. But, in her state of her mind, she couldn't quite fathom her way through it all. At his urging, she kept going until she reached an empty table. She sat down with a heavy thunk and stared at the bowl. It seemed to get bigger the longer she looked at it. "No way I'm eating all this."

He reached over, placed a spoon in her hand. "Just start," he urged.

She shot him a look, raised the spoon and took her first bite. She added a bit of the brown sugar and the entire amount of cream. She smiled. "It looks so much better with cream on it."

"As long as you can eat it, it doesn't matter what it looks like. You need food."

She watched as he dug into a plateful of protein—sausages and eggs and bacon. She shook her head. "How can you possibly eat that much right now?"

He laughed. "I'm not crashing for a few hours yet." And he picked up a whole link sausage, and, in three bites, it was gone.

She stared. "I shouldn't be surprised. But, for some reason, I find myself shocked."

He tilted his head and grinned. "Don't you remember?"

She flushed. Of course she remembered. They'd spent many a meal feeding each other, teasing each other. All as best friends. Not understanding, at the time, it had really been years of foreplay. She had lots of fun memories. And, when they'd been in bed together, things had been different. They'd raced past friendship and fun into intimacy … and love. Why had she let it get her so out of sorts? Why had she let it drive them apart? Something like that should've brought them together. Instead, she had let it come between them and had rejected him when that was the last thing she'd wanted to do. But he had no clue about that as she'd never talked to him again until now. How horrible. He had bared his soul, and she had walked away, shattered for all the wrong reasons.

She was too tired now to work it out. As if in auto mode she filled her spoon, took it to her mouth and ate. When she slowed down, he urged her again.

She made it through three-quarters of her meal and put down her spoon. "I'm done. In more ways than one."

He'd eaten all his food and sat eyeing her bowl.

She laughed. "Do you want the rest of mine?"

"Nope." He pointed at her bowl. "Eat the last nuts off the top to get a bit more protein."

She groaned. "Damn. All right." She picked up her spoon, scooped the nuts off the top and popped them into her mouth. She laid her spoon back down. "That's it. No more." She stared at his plate. "Do you need more?"

He shook his head. "I'll wait until lunch."

She struggled to get up. "I really have to lie down. I'm almost too exhausted to walk."

He hopped up and came to help. He pushed her chair out of the way and gave her his arm to hold on to. They went out the back, and, within minutes, she was at her own quarters. She didn't think she'd ever had any sense of relief like she did when she collapsed on top of her bed.

"Don't you want to get under the covers?" he asked.

"Too much effort," she mumbled.

He nodded. "I'll grab you another blanket."

Her eyes drifted closed. A blanket soon covered her and tucked up against her shoulders. "Thank you."

She let sleep reach out for her. Just as she went under, she thought a whisper of a ghostly kiss landed on her cheek. But since only Ryder was beside her, she knew she had to be wrong. He was a long way away from kissing her. Unfortunately.

RYDER STOOD AT the end of her bed and watched as the exhaustion carried her under. She'd been a trooper. He hadn't expected her to walk as far as they had to reach their transport. Thankfully they'd met up with their ride for the rest of the trip. She'd been silent after that. Detached. Maybe distancing herself from the heavy emotions that threatened to overwhelm her earlier. You learned a lot about a person when they were in trouble. Caitlyn had never disappointed him yet. She was a good person.

He was still too shocked and astonished at her explanation for their breakup to really analyze it. He wanted to believe it. At the same time, it was hard to consider she hadn't contacted him because she felt he deserved better.

That had blown him away. To him she had always been a bright, bubbly, happy teenager who had turned into a beautiful young woman—confident, glowing, secure in her own femininity and sexuality. He'd always wanted her, but she'd never noticed. She'd always been after some other male.

He hadn't had a chance. Until that one weekend when she saw him as a man and not just a friend. He didn't even know how it came about, but, when he finally held her in his arms, nothing held him back. He'd wanted her for so long. Never would he have thought taking that step would mean losing her. On the other hand, where they were right now was way better than where they had been two years ago. He'd been hurt, devastated that she wouldn't return his calls—which made her original rejection even worse.

Especially after declaring his feelings he'd kept hidden for so long. He was a straightforward guy. If asked a question, he'd give an honest answer. Staring down at her as she slept, he realized nothing had changed. He still wanted her. But he wanted all of her. Not to be just friends. Not a casual weekend. He wanted her to want him the same way. Heart. Mind. Soul. He spun and left her room only to find Corey outside waiting for him.

With a quick assessing gaze, Corey put his hands on his hips and said, "Ryder, you should not be going down this path again."

Ryder gave a headshake. "Not planning on it. We're friends." He emphasized the word *friends*, knowing Corey wouldn't believe him, but Ryder wasn't ready to explain what he was still trying to understand.

"There is no *friends* between you two. Not now. Not after what you shared."

"When did you get in?" Ryder asked, hoping to change the subject as he walked toward his quarters.

"An hour ago. We got word you picked up both Caitlyn and the doctor, got them back safe."

"Are you off duty?" Ryder asked, realizing his fatigue had settled in. It was more emotional and psychological than physical, but one always affected the other.

"We all are until 1300 hours."

Ryder checked his watch, then nodded. "Good." At his quarters he found the others already getting ready to crash. He walked to his bed, prepared to do the same. Just because this particular rebel episode was over didn't mean the team wouldn't be called out again. Ryder hoped not. He'd been on his feet for well over thirty hours.

The last thought as he dropped off to sleep was how he hoped Caitlyn slept soundly. For their relationship it was a whole new day. A whole new beginning.

He hoped it would be a better one.

CHAPTER 10

CAITLYN AWOKE WITH tears running down the side of her face. Were they tears of joy that Ryder was back in her life, tears of release after a horrible night, or tears of relief that, when she woke up, she was in her own bed again? She lay in silence for a long moment, trying to figure out why. All she could think about was the bittersweet relief of having told Ryder *why*.

There just never seemed to be simple answers anymore. She used to think she knew who she was inside and out but not anymore.

She slid her fingers along her scalp, only to get them caught up in her blond curls. Her hair was still damp when she'd gone to bed, and it was now a tangled mess. She should have braided it first. But she'd been too tired to even think about doing that. At least she wasn't hungry, which meant the oatmeal had held her through her sleep.

She sat up slowly, groaning as her body protested. It would be a rough day, but, if she got to bed tonight and slept solid again, she should be fine in the morning. First things first though. She had to check in at the clinic. She stood and pulled on a change of clothes. She was surprised the tent was still empty. The other two nurses she knew well, Wendy and Colleen, should've been around. Caitlyn exited her tent and took several deep breaths.

At the clinic she entered to cries of joy and relief. Wendy and Colleen were both there and gave her big hugs. "You sure you should be out of bed?" Wendy asked.

Caitlyn smiled. "I'm fine." Seeing her coworkers made her feel that much better. "What happened while I was gone?"

"Nothing as exciting as what you went through. As a result of that mess, we have permanent guards now." Wendy rolled her eyes.

Caitlyn turned to look at the men standing at the doorway. One stared at Wendy with adoration. That explained the look in Wendy's eyes. Wendy was a looker and attracted attention wherever she went. Both she and Colleen were happily married to servicemen. "How's Dr. Robertson?"

"He's fine. He was in this morning already. Checked up on the patients and then crashed for a few hours. We haven't seen him since."

Dr. Bruce walked over and said, "You don't need to be here for the rest the day. Go back to bed."

"And I'll be glad to have that time off," Caitlyn said with a smile. "I did promise to check in with you this morning, but I am feeling better. Still, more rest would be good. But make sure you call me if you need me."

With assurances from the others, she turned and walked back outside. As she stood there, she realized her stomach was grumbling again. So much for the oatmeal. It had held her this long and no longer. She walked to the mess tent, this time starting with coffee and then headed to the food. She studied which of the fruits she wanted when Corey stepped up beside her and smacked his empty tray down.

She looked at him with a half smile on her face. "So you're going to be nice too?"

"Not if you break his heart again." Corey's voice was hard. "And don't bother telling me how you're just friends."

She winced and served herself some berries. "We are friends. It's my fault we stopped being friends. But it's not how I want life to continue between us."

"You took everything he had and more the last time. I don't want to see him back in that same space. If you're planning a repeat performance, don't."

She stared at Corey in horror. "I never would've done that if I'd known."

"You should've known." Corey picked up his tray and walked past her, dropped the tray on one of the stacks and walked out, leaving her alone with her thoughts. And the pain. God, she hurt.

But what she was thinking wasn't very nice. With a little bit of food and coffee, she headed to a table at the far side and sat down alone, staring blankly at the room. The one mainstay in her world had been Ryder. Now what the hell was she supposed to do? Listen to Corey and walk away again? Was he making too big a deal out of Ryder's reaction? Even if he was, she knew what she'd done would have hurt anyone. That it was Ryder made it so much worse. Or should she do what she needed to do for herself and make sure she had Ryder in her life in any way she could? And possibly hurt him all over again? Now she understood the adage that lovers should be good friends, but good friends shouldn't be lovers.

Under her breath she whispered, "Talk about blowing it."

Even though she ate her food, she no longer wanted it.

She sat at the mess table, unable to leave just yet. She wasn't sure when she was due to return stateside. She knew it was soon but didn't have the date in her head. She should check to make sure. Nor had she checked in with Mac. Now she really had something to share.

She pulled her phone out and checked for messages, finding none. She sent Mac a text. **Hey, how are you?** She didn't know what else to say. They'd taken him out in a chopper, and she knew he would return to full health, but she missed him. He seemed so far away.

When she got a response almost immediately, it shocked her.

I'm doing well. You?

Not so well. Life sucks. As soon as she sent that, she realized she shouldn't have. The man didn't need to listen to her whining. He had bigger issues. She took a sip of coffee. Before she put her cup back down, her cell phone rang. She looked at the number, realizing it was Mac. She swiped to accept the call and said, "I didn't mean to say that." She quickly looked around the mess hall to see how many people could overhear her conversation.

"Tell me what's going on."

She quickly filled him in on the kidnapping, the escape and the few hours of sleep. "See? I'm just tired."

"And Ryder?"

She sighed heavily and pinched her nose. "Supposedly we're friends again."

Silence hung between them for a few moments. Cautiously he said, "You know you can't be friends again, right?"

Exasperated, she whispered, "Dammit, that's what Corey just said to me too. How I basically broke Ryder and left him on the floor."

"I have to admit Corey's right. Even though I didn't talk to Ryder about it, he was really broken up about what

happened between the two of you. I know it's been unre-
solved for a long time."

"He doesn't fully understand why. Maybe I don't really
understand either," she said before he did. She sighed. "I'm
sorry. I didn't mean to interrupt."

Mac sighed, but his voice was warm with understanding.
"Do you want him in your life, or don't you?"

"I do. What I meant was, not enough time has passed to
heal the hurts," she said. "I tried to explain to him what
happened. I know I didn't do a good job of it though," she
admitted. "It's a little hard when you're walking back after
being kidnapped."

"That's when you told him?"

"Yeah, that's when I told him." She gave a half laugh.
"Obviously my common sense was missing."

"How did he take it?"

"I think he was more stunned than anything." She
smiled at Mac's chuckles. "When I exited the showers this
morning, he was waiting for me. I had a bowl of oatmeal
with him and we talked. He said we were friends again."

"Oh, that's not happening."

"The thing is, Mac, I want so much more."

The silence stretched out for minutes. "You know that
might never happen too, right?" he asked gently.

This time her laugh bordered on hysterical. "I know.
The thing is, that's what I meant about not enough time
passing. It's not enough time for me to have forgotten him.
It's not enough time for me to let it go. It's not enough time
for me to be just friends. I still care."

Overcome by tears, she ended the phone call. Wiping
away the tears from her eyes, she sent a text. **Sorry. I'll call
you when I'm feeling better.**

She stared down at her food. It tasted like sawdust, but she quickly ate her way through it.

She was about to stand when Wendy dropped into a seat across from her and said, "You look like shit. You need to have an affair."

Caitlyn stared at her in surprise. She shook her head. "That's the last thing I need."

Wendy leaned forward and said, "How about Ryder? It's obvious that man's all over you."

Caitlyn felt the last little bit of color leave her skin. "No," she said. "You're wrong. That's the last thing he wants."

Wendy gave her a slow smile. "Nope. I might be happily married but I know men. And that one is stuck on you."

"No," Caitlyn said firmly. She needed to get Wendy off that idea.

"Bull. Something is between you already." Wendy clapped her hands together like a little kid. "Now this is fun."

"Drop it," Caitlyn said quietly. "Please."

Wendy sat back as if insulted. "I wasn't going to say anything to him."

Caitlyn rolled her eyes. "You'd say something to anybody if you thought that would get them into my bed."

Wendy chuckled. "Hey, you just need to lighten up a little bit. If not Ryder, then somebody else. You need to live a little."

Caitlyn sighed. Wendy really did mean well. She just had a very different idea of what *living* meant. And she wanted everybody to be happily in a relationship all the time. The last thing Caitlyn needed right now was a man in her life.

★

RYDER STARED AT his commander in surprise. He hadn't expected to be shipped out so soon. Not that Baghdad was far away. But, then again, his world was nothing if not changeable. Sometimes moves came unexpectedly. Since the SEALs had gotten rid of the last of the rebel camp kidnapping their people and stealing their supplies, the local military here was handling the rest of the cleanup. So no need for him and his team. He just didn't want to leave Caitlyn behind. On the other hand, he could visit with Mac in Baghdad.

Mac was a good man. And if Caitlyn and he were truly just friends, maybe Mac could shed some light on the relationship they did have. And if she'd had anything to say about Ryder at any time.

He couldn't squash his need for more answers.

With a clipped nod after getting his new orders, he and his team turned and left. Corey dropped back to speak with him. "We're not leaving for another four hours."

"I heard," Ryder said. He knew what Corey was nudging at. *Caitlyn.*

"Are you going to tell her that we're leaving?"

Ryder nodded. "I will." How could he not, especially at this delicate stage of their relationship? He quickly packed up. He hadn't fully unpacked, preferring to always be ready to move as fast as he needed to. Then he headed to Caitlyn's tent. He could hope she'd still be off work, but, knowing her, chances were she was in the clinic doing what she could to help out.

Finding her tent empty, he headed back to the medical clinic. Dr. Robertson was there. He looked up and smiled. "She's not here," he said. "She's going to Baghdad for a couple days."

Shocked that she was leaving and at her destination, Ryder raised his eyebrows. "Is she okay?"

Dr. Robertson nodded. "She was due a few days off and decided to visit Mac. She'll be back soon and then will have less than two weeks remaining before going stateside."

Ryder nodded. "Any idea where she is?"

"She should be in her tent packing. If not, she could be on her way already."

Thanking the doctor, making sure he suffered no ill effects from his own kidnaping, Ryder turned to find a couple women standing behind him. "Do you know where Caitlyn is?"

One of them, a tall curvy blonde, said with a wicked grin, "Looking for you."

Inasmuch as he tried to keep his face neutral, he could hardly keep the delighted grin from peeking through.

The women laughed, and one of them said, "I thought so. She said there was nothing between the two of you, but I know better. I've seen the signs before, many times before."

He wasn't sure what to make of that. "Many times before with her?"

The woman shook her head. "No, not with her. Never with her. I thought there was something between her and Mac for the longest time, but she apparently not."

Thanking them, he turned and walked back outside. He headed for the end of the compound and entered the mess tent to see Caitlyn sitting in the far corner with a cup of coffee and a notepad. He grabbed a cup for himself, walked over and sat down beside her. "Saying goodbye in a letter?"

She looked up, and, to his delight, he saw the happy welcome on her face.

He reached across, grasped her hand and said, "I was looking for you."

She squeezed his fingers. "I was looking for you," she exclaimed. "I've got a few days, so I figured I'd visit Mac."

"And Macklin, is he okay?" Ryder asked gently. "We're going to Baghdad too but not sure for how long."

"He is, yes," she said. "I had the time coming and just wanted a change of scenery myself. It feels odd here now, knowing I'm done soon …"

"After what you went through, getting out is a good idea. I wish you were going home today."

"I'm almost done. This could be my last chance to see Baghdad. I figured, why not?"

"You said you were sorry," he said abruptly. "But I never did. And that's an oversight I'm not proud of."

She shook her head. "Please don't apologize for that weekend."

"No, not for the weekend. Never for that," he said with a wicked grin. "I should never have let you walk out that day. I don't know what I could've done, thinking about it now, but I should've done something. We might've gotten to the bottom of it quicker, gone back to being friends without any tension in our relationship." He took a deep breath. "So I'm sorry for not trying harder."

She shook her head. "Not your fault. I didn't figure it out myself for months. So, although you might've convinced me to stay, it wouldn't have brought me to the same awareness. Maybe I needed to do what I did." She shrugged, sighed, then checked her watch. "I have to go." She gave him an awkward half smile and stood.

He studied her and asked, "If I'm staying long enough, do you want to get together in Baghdad?"

Her gaze warmed. "If you want to, yes."

"I want to. I want to get back to what we had."

She tilted her head sideways and gave him a lopsided grin. "How about something new? Maybe better than what we had."

He chuckled. "What we had was pretty special."

She flushed, intensely. In waves. Could only imagine a multitude of red shades coloring her complexion. But she nodded her head as she said, "It was indeed. I have to run." Then she dashed out of the tent, once again running from him.

But she'd admitted what they'd had was special.

Now he had to convince her to go there again. Whistling, he left to grab his duffel bag and meet up with his team.

Life was good for the first time in a long while.

CHAPTER 11

C AITLYN COULDN'T STOP grinning the whole trip. She was headed into a new phase with Ryder. She didn't know what that would mean. She only knew what she wanted it to mean.

At the same time, some major healing was happening inside. She couldn't hear his voice without the same pain as before. She couldn't think of their time together without cringing. She couldn't think of the weekend they'd spent making crazy wild love without slamming a door on the memory because it hurt so much. Even the things they'd done as kids. Movies they'd watched together. His shoulder she'd cried on more than a few times.

When she finally landed at the military base just outside Baghdad, she caught a ride to the hotel, the closest to the base she could find. Baghdad was still on the traveling shit list, but it was a hell of a lot nicer than where she'd been. Besides she was only here for a couple days. After unpacking, she headed to the shower, then would visit Mac.

She didn't know when Ryder would arrive. She hadn't had a chance to ask him. She walked into the medical center and checked which room Mac was in. Following directions, she went to his room to find the door closed. She heard voices inside, and she thought maybe the doctor was in with him. She sat down on a chair in the hallway, leaned back and waited. She pulled out her cellphone and sent several messages to friends and colleagues, letting them know she'd arrived and had checked in.

When she heard male laughter from inside Mac's room, she smiled. It was good to hear Mac doing so well.

The door opened, and a man spoke before leaving the room.

"Okay. I'll check in with you in a couple days."

She recognized the voice. She jumped to her feet and stepped forward, her gaze going from Ryder to Mac and back.

Mac looked at her, frowned and said, "You and I need to talk too."

She glanced at Ryder. He grinned and said, "You at least got a shower. I came straight here."

She frowned, asking slowly, "Why? I didn't think the two of you were good friends."

Ryder gave a crooked smile and said, "We've always been friends."

Mac chuckled. "We'll talk to you later, Ryder. Caitlyn, where is my hug?"

She walked over to the bed, gave him a gentle hug and sat down on the side of his bed. Mac was a huge man. There wasn't a whole lot of space for anybody else on that hospital bed. "What was that all about?" His gaze went to the doorway, and she realized Ryder still leaned against the open door.

She frowned at him. "Don't you have some place to go?" She heard Mac suck in his breath, but her gaze was on Ryder.

He raised an eyebrow and said, "I was going to invite you for lunch."

She flushed. "What is it about you that makes me socially awkward and inadequate at the same time?"

This time both his eyebrows rose. "I have no idea as it's the opposite of the way I'd like you to feel around me."

"I need to talk to Mac," she said quietly. "Would you mind closing the door?"

"Are you going to lunch with me?"

She glanced down at Mac, seeing only encouragement in his eyes. "Fine. After I talk to Mac," she said firmly.

"I'll wait for you out here then." Ryder closed the door with a snap.

She stared at the door for a long moment, then turned to Mac. "What did he talk to you about?"

It was Mac's turn to raise an eyebrow. He didn't answer.

She wanted to shake him. "It was about me, wasn't it?"

"In a small way maybe but not really. It was more about Ryder himself."

She studied Mac's face but only saw a sense of peace on it. "He didn't say anything to upset you?"

Mac shook his head and smiled at her. "No. Ryder is a good man."

"I know." She crossed her arms over her chest and said, "It feels so very different. A little uncomfortable," she admitted. "Like we're strangers but not. Dancing around each other warily."

"Take your time, go slow, make sure there are no more misunderstandings, and you'll do fine."

"What if I want more than friendship?"

"You mentioned that before." A grin whispered across his face. "It might be a lot easier than being just friends. I can't say for sure."

"Men and women can be friends, you know?"

He stayed quiet and stared at her for a long moment. "It wasn't the right time. You both had to get to where that's what you each wanted. I don't know what happened between you two, and, no, I don't really want you to explain it to me. But, going forward, you need to be as honest as you can be. Ryder took a major hit over this. I tried to help you see him again several times, but you weren't ready. Now you are, but this situation's still fragile," he cautioned.

She groaned. "Maybe." She leaned forward, kissed his cheek and said, "Let me know when you're sprung from this place, and we can go have some fun times again."

"That won't be for a while. Not back to active duty for a bit."

"The bullet must have done some real damage."

He nodded. "It embedded itself in my shoulder blade. Caused some deep-muscle tendon damage."

"I'm sorry." She winced. "Stateside would be perfect. Lunch is on me when we both get back."

"You're on."

"You take care of yourself." She walked over to the door.

"And you take care of you," Mac said quietly. "And of Ryder."

Taking his words to heart, she opened the door and smiled at the man waiting. "Ready? I'm starved."

His gaze was intense as he stared at her. "I'm starved too."

Her face flushed as she realized so much meaning was behind his words. Was she ready for that? Hell no. It had changed everything between them before. She didn't think she could do that again. She really wanted him back in her life. But not as a weekend fling. She wanted … more. With a lighthearted voice she hooked her arm through his and said,

"Food. I need to eat real food." Together they walked out of the hospital.

"IT'S GOOD TO hear you laugh." He sat back. He hadn't expected those words to come out of his mouth. In his mind he'd been planning something neutral. Something that wouldn't rile either of them.

She glanced up from her salad in surprise. "I have to admit I haven't done a lot of laughing for a while."

He nodded. "You used to laugh all the time."

"You used to be more lighthearted and fanciful too," she said quietly. "But, when you're hurting, and you're hurting others, there's nothing funny about that."

He reached across and offered her a french fry. "You used to love these too."

She snatched it from his hand, popped it into her mouth and gave him a big grin. "Still do. Especially other people's." She snagged another one off his plate.

He protested. "Hey! How does that work? You're stealing two?"

"Three …" And with her other hand darting across the table, she grabbed the third one.

He chuckled. "You know I can buy you some fries of your own."

She shook her head. "These are enough. Not to mention the fact I can't possibly eat a full plateful."

"You used to."

She glanced at the fries, looked at her salad and said, "I used to do a lot of things. Now I try to eat healthier."

He winced and looked down at his fries and a burger. "Ouch, that hurts. I love my burger and fries."

"But you're also in great shape. I haven't been doing anywhere near the workouts I used to," she admitted. "For a while I became a hermit. Now I'm getting back on track. Unfortunately that means making a few less happy dietary choices."

"Where's the fun in that?"

She chuckled. "You've always been able to eat everything, including the damn kitchen sink, and never had a belly to show for it."

"High metabolism," he said modestly.

She snorted. "No bragging allowed."

He grinned. "Honestly I work out a lot, so I can eat what I want."

"And that brings us back to the conversation we started with. I haven't been working out." She rolled her eyes and grabbed another fry. "But this is making me really want to."

He studied her for a long moment and returned his attention to his plate. He wanted to spend more time with her and help her get back in shape. "How about we work out together?"

She shook her head. "Oh, no. I can imagine how that works. You browbeat me into doing way more than I feel like I can do, and then I can't walk for a week."

He chuckled. "I wouldn't do that. You need to build up slowly."

"When I get home," she said, "I'll start jogging again then. But I'll start gently. Work my way back up."

"We could jog together."

She shrugged but wouldn't commit.

He pressed slightly. "We used to run together all the time."

She nodded. "That's when I was in good shape."

"No, that's when you were in great shape and maintain-

ing. We had a lot of fun on our runs. You need that again."
He offered her another french fry with a teasing look on his
face. "Consider this a bribe."

She stared at the fry, growled in the back of her throat,
snatched it from his fingers and ate it. "That's just mean. I'm
only on holiday for a few days. I don't want to work out
now."

"You used to do it for fun," he reminded her.

"That was before."

"I'll pick you up at six in the morning. We'll just do a
short run."

"That sounds terrible," she said, laughing.

The waitress arrived with the coffeepot. He let her fill his
cup and took a sip of the hot brew. "I really missed this."

"Are you trying to cut back?"

He shrugged. "I meant having coffee with you. Joking,
laughing."

What he didn't want was her to feel so uncomfortable,
so insecure, that she wouldn't run with him. "I mean it
about going for a run. Honestly, we'll take it easy. Figure out
what you need to get back into shape. And approach it in a
manner you can handle." He studied her. "I find it hard to
believe you're out of shape. You walked for miles after your
kidnapping. Plus, you look really good," he said honestly.

But what he didn't say was she was looking damn good.
She always had to him. Something about that fresh all-
American-girl look. She was tall, but she'd always been slim
and lean.

She studied him over the top of her water glass. "Okay.
You've got to promise not to overdo it."

He grinned. "Never."

She rolled her eyes and said, "I know I'll regret this."

CHAPTER 12

S O MANY REGRETS. Not about how she'd actually agreed to go for a run with him but that she'd let herself get out of shape. She was three miles into the run and already flagging. She used to run five miles easily, seven miles on good days, and ten miles for events. Even then that wasn't anything compared to what Ryder could do. But the difference was really showing up now. She'd never felt competitive with him before. She always just accepted they had different fitness levels. But, as he had maintained his, she'd let hers go. And that sucked in a big way.

He slowed down, and she recognized her hotel coming up. He motioned to a park on the far side. "We can cool down over there. You need to walk this out."

She nodded. They came to a stop at the crosswalk and headed to the green grass in the gardens. She bent over and gasped for breath.

"You did great," he said with a big smile.

She shot him a look. "I did *great*? Ha. Only if we forget about what I used to run."

"That's exactly what you should do. Forget about where you used to be. That's history. You can't change it. Today you start fresh. So that wasn't so bad." He grinned a wide infectious smile she couldn't help but respond to.

She chuckled, grateful she'd caught her breath enough to

do so. "How is it you manage to maintain any sense of humor with the work you do?"

"It's about balance," he said. "Without it, I'd burn out. And my friends make a huge difference."

"SEALs don't make it much longer than eight to ten years, do they?"

"After ten years it's tough. It's physically demanding, emotionally difficult, and spiritually … Well, it's just plain hard and almost impossible after a certain point."

As they walked, he pointed out a garden bed of flowers. "That's a pretty spectacular orange."

"It is indeed." The flowers had no smell, yet the tall stalks were stunning. And the color was spectacular.

"Your profession is also demanding," he said.

"Yes, but I'm out soon and not signing back up. I'm considering a small-town setting."

He turned and looked at her in surprise. "Why?"

She shrugged. "A lot of reasons. One of the biggest is, maybe it's time for a change."

He studied her. "And maybe also because your reason for taking overseas positions is no longer so pressing."

She nodded. "That's part of it. I never intended to do this for long. I needed it at the time. Now I'm not sure what to do." She shrugged. "I don't mean to be evasive. I'm just reassessing my future." She watched as he nodded slowly. "Maybe I need to go to a shrink and talk," she said in a half-joking manner.

He surprised her when he nodded. "Even talking with friends helps. You saw a lot of action here. You were kidnapped. Maybe a therapist is a good idea."

In the past he would've been the very best friend she would have talked with. In his absence, she had turned to

Mac. "Point taken."

Ryder nodded. "Just don't run away again," he said in all seriousness. "And, no, I don't mean to bring up the past. You do what you need to so you can move forward." He glanced at his watch. "I also heard rumors I'll be heading out soon. How long is your leave?"

"Two days," she whispered, looking at her watch. So much time had sped by. They'd been catching up and enjoying their time together but at the same time skirting the one big issue. That damnable delightful weekend.

She smiled. "Since we're two old friends who haven't seen much of each other, we need to make the most of the next few days."

He looked up in surprise. "What have you got in mind?"

She chuckled. "Well, one of the things I wanted to do was …" She listed off several tourist places.

He grinned. "Sounds to me like we've got enough to do for the next few years."

She stopped, looked up at him and said, "Unless you have someone else you want to spend some of that time with?"

He shook his head. "I'm spending it with who I want."

She flashed a smile. "Great. So am I."

Inside her heart was light. Could they really get back to where they'd been before? And, if they were lucky, go forward? They had so much potential …

HE REALLY HOPED he could have these next few days with her. They needed what time they could before duty interfered. The world was full of conflict. Still, in order to make the best of it, they would do what they could. Laughing, he pointed out a coffee shop and said, "If we're really going to cram as much as we can into these next couple days, we'll need energy."

She snorted, motioning at her outfit. "I'm hardly dressed for cafés and restaurants. I need a shower first, then a change of clothes."

"Or we can have breakfast first, then spend a few hours doing the tourist thing," he said persuasively. "If we eat now, we can hit several of the tourist attractions on your list before the sun gets too strong. The arid desert atmosphere can be a lovely temperature, but, after a while, it can get to you. By midafternoon you might be ready for relaxing at the pool back at the hotel."

She studied him for a long moment, and he wondered what she was thinking. He had no ulterior motive here. He didn't quite know how to persuade her. Then he realized there really was no need to. She was on vacation and could do as she wanted. He didn't mind. He relaxed and said, "If you want a shower first, that's cool. We can be back here in an hour, have breakfast and then carry on." He shrugged. "So it's all good whichever way you want to go."

Her smile brightened his morning. "As much as your first idea makes sense, I like that second idea better," she said. "You're right about the pool too. And quite possibly I'll need a second shower. She glanced down at her pants and T-shirt and said, "These are hardly the right clothes for what I've got planned though."

He nodded. "Let's do a quick change and get some food."

Laughing and joking like two little kids, they raced back to the hotel while he sat and waited outside for her to change. When she came back out into the hallway looking for him, she stopped and frowned. "You didn't change," she said.

"I have to return to the base for that," he reminded her. "You're on vacation, and you're in a hotel. I didn't want to take the time to go there and back."

She nodded. "Are you okay with what you have on?"

He glanced down at his running gear and shrugged. "I'll be fine."

He held out his arm; she slipped hers through his, and together they walked back down toward the restaurant. "Now that there are options," he said, "do you want to sightsee here at your hotel or where we were this morning or maybe downtown and find something to eat?"

She said, "I'd like to head downtown. I want to experience and see everything I can. The sights, the smells, the noise—all of it. I doubt I'll be back at least in the next decade. So, for the next couple days, I want to see, to breathe Baghdad and all that it means."

He smiled. "In that case that's what we'll do." He held out his hand and said, "Let's go."

CHAPTER 13

THEY SPENT SOME incredible hours as they walked through the main part of the old city. There was so much to see, to absorb. After they picked a spot with an open balcony to sit and have breakfast, they went to the Victory Arch. They then visited the aquarium, the park and places she couldn't even name. She barely made the trip to another half-dozen tourist spots. She didn't think she could lift her feet up one more flight of stairs nor do one more set of crowds. In a park she pointed to a set of benches. "I'm sitting down there, and I'm not moving again," she announced.

And sure enough she sat down and relaxed. He laughed and said, "Stay there. I'll be right back."

He disappeared into the crowd. She wondered what he was up to but was too hot, too tired to really care. The temperature wasn't bad, but, after taking pictures until her fingers were cramped, she realized just what a joy it was to spend a few days experiencing something so very foreign from what she normally did. She was contemplating what she might still have energy left to do when Ryder reappeared with huge ice creams. She gasped. "Oh, my God, they're so huge."

He grinned. "Not that bad." He handed her one and said, "I might be able to finish yours when I'm done with mine."

In the heat the ice cream melted rapidly. When she'd eaten as much as she could, she handed hers over to him and said, "I'm so full. It's all yours."

He snatched it from her fingers, and, in three bites, it was gone. She stared in amazement and started to laugh. "Your face is covered in ice cream." She took one of the napkins and tried to wipe it away, but he was laughing too hard.

The glint in his eye told her she was in trouble. "Do you think your face looks any better than mine?" he said threateningly. "Because you are so wrong." He held the back of her head with one hand as he scrubbed her face with the other. She shrieked with laughter and finally gave up fighting and just rested against his chest as he completed his ministrations. He held her close, dropping his chin to rest on the top of her head.

"It's beautiful out here," she whispered.

"Any place with you would be beautiful," he said quietly.

She squeezed his chest and said, "I'm so happy to be here with you. You were the best part of my life before, and I missed you. I haven't laughed this much in a long time."

"As in several years by any chance?"

She tilted her head back, looked up at him and nodded. "Absolutely. All I did was cry for months." She stared at the crowd that surrounded them. The sounds and the sights here were so much more foreign. But the crowds and the families were the same. Something was very comforting about that.

He hugged her gently. "I'm sorry you were crying."

"I'm not. I needed to. I had a lot of stuff to get rid of. A lot to reassess. It took emotional energy, but it also meant releasing a lot of garbage. And, for women, crying is a great way to release all kinds of stuff," she said with a half smile. "And, if it felt like it was a punishment I deserved, maybe it was something I needed to go through."

When he didn't say anything, she turned to peer at his face, and seeing the sadness, she winced. "I never did say I was a fast learner," she said quietly. "As you remember, some subjects in school were really hard for me."

"Like math, English and science …" he said way too fast for comfort, a lopsided grin on his face.

She sat up in shock. "There was nothing wrong with my math or my English or my science."

He rolled his eyes. "Don't you remember trying to understand calculus?"

"Okay, so anything but calculus," she snapped. "That's not a math. That's just made-up stuff. It makes no sense."

"That was your take on it." He groaned. "Calculus has a flood of applications in the real world."

"Can't possibly be." She shook her head. "It's all gobbledygook."

He chuckled. "And what about trying to figure your own personal horsepower when you were in physics class? That was easy …"

She gasped. "I can't believe you would bring that back up. That was what? Eleventh grade?"

"Hey, you're the one who brought up not being a fast learner," he said in a teasing voice.

She slapped him lightly on the shoulder. "Once I got it though, you have to admit I got it."

He tilted his head and said, "I'll give you that. The trouble was, it took you forever to get it."

"Only with things like calculus," she protested but knew

he was right.

"As I recall there were a few issues in English too."

She groaned. "Any other English teacher and I would've been fine. But Mrs. Dragon ..."

"It was Travon not Dragon," he said, chuckling. "And she did love you so."

Good-naturedly the two wrangled about school from decades ago. "I can't believe you still remember all that stuff."

"How could I forget?"

"I did fine in nursing school."

"You did indeed," he admitted. "Graduated top of your class." He hugged her close. "And you've made an even better nurse. For that I'm really proud of you."

Surprised, she turned to look at him. "Thank you. I really wanted to do something to help people."

"It's part of the reason why, after your tour's up, you're heading possibly to a small town?"

"Maybe. While I'm here, I'm busy. I'm active. I'm helping, but I'm not necessarily building relationships."

"We're back to that feeling of being rootless. As I recall, not having a family of your own was an issue at various points in your life."

"I'm close with my adoptive family, so it's more about not knowing where I came from. I feel like I need to put down my own roots. I was hoping maybe in a small town I could do that. Build relationships with people I'll see more than a few months a year. Where I see people marry and have children and watch them grow up."

"People still move away," he pointed out. "Divorces still happen. People still die. And new people still come in."

"True enough. But they also do it in smaller amounts.

Because it is a smaller population."

"Are you staying in California or moving somewhere else?"

"I'm not sure yet. But I think California. I'd like to stay close to San Diego."

"Good, that means we can still see each other."

She smiled. "And that's one of the reasons I want to stay close. After I walked away, I wanted to head Back East. Spend a few years a long way away where I couldn't be tempted to follow you around, trying to find the words to clear up all the misunderstandings and excuses for my behavior," she admitted. "You should ask Mac about it sometime," she said sadly. "Another aspect of my personality I'm really not fond of."

He frowned and looked at her. "What are you talking about?"

She groaned and said, "If you get me a coffee, we can sit over there by the pond, and I'll tell you."

He hopped to his feet and held out his hand. She placed her fingers through his, and together they walked to the coffee stand. Iced coffee seemed to be the drink of the day. Drinks in hand, they walked to the pond as she thought about how to express what she needed to say.

"Once I figured out what was wrong with me," she said, "why I did what I did, I needed to tell you. I kept thinking, if I could just call you and talk to you, that we would be fine again. And I did call, but, as soon as you answered, I hung up."

Startled, he turned and stared at her. "Was that about six months after our weekend together?"

She winced and nodded. "Yeah, it was. I think I must have called and hung up at least a dozen times."

His jaw dropped as he stared at her. "You almost made me buy a new phone because I couldn't figure out what the hell was happening."

"Yeah, that was me," she groaned. "I used a different phone because I was afraid you wouldn't answer if you saw it was me."

He stared at her in shock.

"You were always in my thoughts, and I wanted to fix things. But the right words wouldn't come out. Every time I heard your voice, I clammed up." She shrugged. "That went on for months."

"All you had to do was arrange to meet me somewhere, and we could have talked face-to-face."

"Exactly," she said in a long-drawn-out voice. "Hence the next thing I did. I started to track you down and figure out where you might be. So I could follow you around and casually run into you and maybe set up a meeting that way." At the look on his face she laughed. "I know it sounds silly now."

"Hang on a minute. You were following me around, and I didn't know it?" He shook his head. "Not possible. I'd have known."

"Well, you might want to talk to Mac about that. It went on for a long time. When he found out, he told me it was really creepy, and I needed to stop."

She watched as Ryder deflated in front of her. "I can't believe it. Several times I felt somebody watching me. For a long time I basically put you in the back of my mind because it seemed like I was seeing your face everywhere. I mentally had to stop or go nuts. Chances were you were there in the background, but I never saw you."

"That was probably around the same time," she said. "I

was trying to find you alone. Mac used to see me every once in a while." She shrugged. "And he often ran interference between us. He wanted me to call you and just get it out. But every time he tried to make me contact you, I would refuse. The longer it went on, the worse it got."

"Mac did that?"

"You told me that he was a good friend." She shook her head. "You have no idea."

"I got that much. But, when you arrived on his arm at the barbecue, I figured you had crossed the line from friends to a lot more," he admitted. "That's why I left when you showed up."

"I begged him to bring me there. I wasn't sleeping well. I wasn't eating well. This was a month after Mac got me to stop stalking you everywhere." She rolled her eyes. "And then I didn't know what to do. I had no way to get a hold of you in person. So, when I found out you and Mac would be at this barbecue, I was desperate to go with him. He was fine with it until he realized I was hoping you'd be there. Then he didn't want me to go."

"Why not?"

She smiled at the surprise in his voice. "Because he figured that, with everybody around, it wasn't the best place for me to see you again. And he was right, but I was being bullheaded and stupid and pressured him into it." She sighed. "And you know the rest. Instead of letting me actually approach, you got up and left."

"Because it was a knife to my heart. You had walked away from me, and the next time I see you is with one of my friends." He shrugged and stared off in the distance. "That was an incredibly ugly day for me."

"And then you were sent on a mission and then another

one and another one, and I realized I'd lost my chance with you. And one of the few ways I could be close to you was to volunteer to be overseas where I knew you would be. Not that working to save our injured soldiers wasn't important, because it was—and is—but I also had the potential to see you."

He sat in shock, thinking. She worried when he remained quiet for so long. Finally he said, "And I thought you hadn't given me a second thought."

"And instead, I couldn't get you out of my mind," she admitted.

"Guilt?"

"Maybe a little but mostly fear. Some was a need for forgiveness," she said quietly. "I just couldn't stand the thought of what we had for so long being stomped on like that, and it was all my fault. But I couldn't for the life of me figure out how to fix it."

"Talk to me about it?" he said simply. "That would've been the thing to do. And from day one, not putting it off like that for things to fester on both sides."

"The longer it went on, the more stupid it got, and the more foolish I acted, and then I didn't know what to do. When you walked out on me at the barbecue, I realized I didn't have a hope in hell."

He shook his head. "I would've met you for coffee any day in the last couple years, except for the day I saw you with Mac. I was so angry, so hurt, and suddenly aware of how much you had moved on in your life, and I hadn't."

She winced. "Well, there is a little bit more truth maybe you need to hear. I've gone out on several occasions since that weekend," she admitted. "And every one of them with Mac. I have not gone to bed with anyone. I have not wanted to."

He tugged her chin gently toward him, and he said, "Now that is the nicest thing I've heard yet."

Tears welled up and slid down her cheeks.

"Oh, Caitlyn, don't cry. Please don't cry."

She sobbed against his chest. "I'm so sorry. Oh, dear God, I am so sorry."

They sat for over an hour just holding each other, letting the newfound peace between them heal what they hadn't been able to heal themselves. As it started to darken, she looked up and said, "Can we go back to the hotel now please? I'm really tired."

"Do you want to take a taxi?"

"No. I'd like to walk, have a hot shower and go to bed," she said quietly. "All this emotional stuff is more exhausting than playing a tourist."

He stood, and, with an arm over her shoulders, they walked back.

Her insides felt like they'd been stomped into the ground and then somebody else slowly rebuilt them. There was joy and a strange disconnect. So much had changed … "For all the pain we have been through, I'm really glad I'm here with you right now." She cuddled up against his chest, her arms locked around his waist.

He dropped a kiss on her forehead and said, "I am too. I'm still struggling to understand how the girl I used to know is the woman I see before me now."

In peaceful silence they strutted the last mile, arms around each other. The time together truly was a gift.

As they got closer to the hotel, he asked, "Are you hungry?"

She shook her head. "Honestly I'm too tired to eat. Besides we've been eating all day."

He led her inside the hotel and took her to her room. She really wanted him to stay with her, but she was so exhausted that she didn't know how to make that happen or if she should even try. He opened her door and waited until she walked inside. In typical Ryder fashion he did a quick search to make sure everything was okay; then he turned to look at her. "You'll be okay here overnight?"

She nodded and smiled. "I will. I'll shower and crash." She hesitated. "Do you want to stay with me?"

He'd been in the act of walking to the door. But he stopped, studied her for a long moment and then said, "I want to, yes. But I don't want to take that step because it caused so much trouble last time. That doesn't mean I wouldn't love to hold you in my arms all night. Except I couldn't leave it at that. I've wanted you for so long. You were my everything. And yet, you just went through boyfriend after boyfriend, then a marriage, and I kept thinking you would get there one day and see me as I really was. But you didn't until that one weekend."

Weary and emotional as she absorbed his words, she sat down on the bed, grimacing. "I guess our relationship was foreplay, building up to that weekend. I just didn't realize that was happening."

He chuckled. "Well, we're back to being friends. It's up to us if we want to move forward into something more. You had a hell of a day, and so did I for that matter. You need to sleep."

"What are you going to do while I curl up in bed?"

He laughed. "I'll have another talk with Mac." And he closed the door behind him.

She sat on the bed for a long moment, thinking of all the

things she'd said about Mac and realized she really needed to warn him. She pulled out her phone.

He answered immediately. "How did it go with Ryder?"

"It was special," she admitted. "We talked and talked."

"Is he there now?"

She knew what he was asking. "He's on his way to you."

Silence followed. "Me?"

"Yeah, I told him about the stalking. I told him about you running interference. I told him about me asking to go to the party with you."

Mac started to laugh. "Wow, it must have been a hell of a good day for you to come clean. I admire you for doing that. That's what a relationship should be about. Trust and honesty. Everything else can come later."

And she knew that was his reference to his ex-girlfriend who'd cheated on him. When he'd found out, she had continued to deny it, believing she'd done such a good job of hiding it that he couldn't possibly know the truth. She hadn't wanted to let him go, and things had gotten ugly. "True enough. Now I'll jump in the shower and wash off a very long day of playing tourist and breaking my heart wide open for Ryder to see so I can do it all over again tomorrow," she said quietly. "Have a good night, and please tell him the truth so he can put himself back together again."

"Oh, I'll tell the truth all right, not that I have all the details," Mac said in a gentle tone. "I wonder if it's the truth as you see it. You always were too hard on yourself."

He hung up before she had a chance to question, and instantly her energy drained. She got up and headed for the shower, getting through it, then readying for bed. After that she figured she'd run out of all the energy she had available.

WHEN RYDER WALKED into Mac's hospital room, he knew instinctively Mac was expecting him. "When did she call you?"

Mark grinned. "The minute you left her hotel she called to tell me how much she'd come clean and that I was to tell you the truth."

Ryder grabbed a chair, swung it around and sat on it backward beside the bed. "So tell me what the truth is. I went through hell these last few years because of her. I don't want to go back there again."

Mac nodded in understanding and launched into an explanation. He ended with, "The stalking stuff was pretty wild."

"I heard a rumor about your ex-girlfriend doing something similar. It sounds like it was really intense," Ryder said. "That must have been rough."

"You didn't hear all of it," Mac said, shaking his head. He told Ryder a few of the more outlandish things his ex-girlfriend had done.

"Jesus. Caitlyn's nothing like that."

"No, she wasn't, but I was afraid she might end up that way when she started stalking you." Mac launched into an explanation of how she would sit outside Ryder's apartment and wait until he got into his vehicle and then followed him. When he was at the gym, she'd go to the coffee shop across the street where she could see him easily but couldn't be seen. She could keep an eye on where he was going, what he was doing. "She did this for months."

Ryder sat back and stared at Mac. "I never knew. I kept thinking I saw Caitlyn's face in every woman around me. I figured I was just so exhausted that I needed to get a life and put her out of my mind. I deliberately didn't look. I stopped looking at all women."

The two men shared commiserating glances. Mac continued. "She was really lost. She felt so guilty for what she'd done and how she didn't know how to fix it. And the hardest thing for her was, she desperately needed to talk to you, but she couldn't seem to call you and set up a meeting even when she did find you. I wasn't going to bring her to the party. I knew you wouldn't want to see her in a public place. I also knew she was really struggling. I tried to get her to call you half a dozen times, but she wouldn't, so I brought her. It never occurred to me that you'd think the two of us were together until you avoided me afterward."

Ryder snorted and stared out the window. "What a waste."

"Yeah, but she's very dear to me. So, as much as I know, she loves you," Mac said. "I need to know you won't turn around and hurt her back."

Startled, Ryder looked at him. "She and I were best friends for twenty years. We would still be best friends if we hadn't taken the step to being lovers. I'm definitely leery about ending up in the same place we were before. That's why I'm here right now and not in her hotel room ..."

Mac nodded. "Yeah, I'd say that's a wise choice. But I do know she loves you, so you guys should get through this fine."

Ryder grinned. "Glad to hear that." He stood up, smacked his hand against the bed and said, "Isn't it time you get off this thing? The world is falling to pieces without you."

"Ha." It was Mac's turn to snort. "I'll be out of here soon. I'm headed stateside in a couple days. It's rehab for me next."

Ryder turned and walked toward the door. "It would probably be good for Caitlyn to see the two of us together."

"We were always friendly. It was only because of her that we stayed apart."

Ryder turned to grin. "Isn't that the truth?" With a wave he walked from the room. His heart was light. For the first time in a long time, the future looked damn bright. All he needed was another few days with her here. And then he knew he could get past all this, and they could move forward.

He just hoped the war would hold off long enough to give them time.

CHAPTER 14

T HE NEXT MORNING Caitlyn woke up with smile on her face. As soon as she got out of bed though, she winced. She stared down at her swollen feet and sighed. "I knew I should've worn sneakers." She headed for a shower, then quickly dressed, expecting to hear from Ryder any moment. She'd been afraid he would be called away overnight, but there had been no phone call, and, for that, she was grateful. Just then her phone rang. She raced to answer it. "Good morning," she cried out cheerfully.

He laughed. "Well, that's the way I like to be greeted."

She sat down on the bed, the towel wrapped around her body and said, "I had a great night."

"Excellent. Then maybe we can start with breakfast somewhere, then visit Mac this morning if you want to see him again. I understand he's heading stateside before you, so this could be your last chance to see him before he leaves."

"Perfect." She glanced around for her clothing, realizing she didn't have much in the way of options. "I can be ready in ten."

"As I'm already in the lobby, make it five." And he hung up.

She laughed, threw down the phone, picked up her sundress and, just before he knocked on the door, was ready. She opened the door, smiled at him and said, "I made it. Let me hang up my wet towels." She dashed back into the room and hung them in the bathroom. Ready, she picked up her purse and said, "Does Mac know we're coming?"

He shook his head. "I haven't spoken to him yet."

"Let's go see him first. I can wait for breakfast."

He had a vehicle from the base and within seconds they were on the road. He drove straight to the hospital. They walked upstairs to find Mac's door closed. She knocked. When she heard his voice, she stuck her head around the door. "You up for visitors?"

His face split into a big grin. And seeing Ryder behind her made his grin widen. "Well, if the two of you are friendly again, I'm definitely up for visitors."

She laughed and said, "We're definitely friends again." She cast a teasing glanced at Ryder and said, "Right?"

Ryder nodded, then spoke to Mac. "I hear you're leaving today."

"I am. They need my bed. A heavy influx is coming from the north." His voice was neutral, but his gaze was not.

Caitlyn looked from one to the other and said, "Our men?"

Mac nodded and looked to Ryder. "Have you been called out?"

"Not yet," Ryder admitted. "But I'm expecting a call."

"It's easy to forget," she murmured. "It's like we're a world away."

He nodded. "It is. But it's always there in the back of my mind."

"Well, forget about it until it happens," she said in a firm voice. She sat down on Mac's bed and said, "What will you do when you get home?"

"See the dogs for one," he said with a big grin. "They'll

be more than happy to have me home for a while."

"Absolutely. How will you make sure your ex doesn't find you?"

"I heard through the grapevine she's found somebody new," he said comfortably. "Are you worrying about me?" He picked up her hand and said, "You've only got a week or so left on your tour, so make sure you stay safe. When are you due back?"

"Tomorrow morning."

He nodded. "Good."

They visited a little bit longer, and then, knowing she might be out of time with Ryder, she stood and said, "Text me or call me when you get back so I know you landed."

On that note they left, and Caitlyn asked, "Where do you want to go for breakfast?"

"I suspect I'll have a couple hours left before I'm recalled."

She smiled. "Then let's go." Just as they drove toward the exit, his phone rang. He pulled off to the side, and her heart sank. "Don't tell me …"

Quietly he said, "Devlin, what's up?"

"Outbreak of fighting in the far north side," she could hear Devlin. The rest of the conversation blurred as she deliberately tuned it out. She stared outside, realizing she was likely spending her last day here alone, without Ryder. Her heart broke at the thought of missing out on another day with him. She knew she should be damn glad to have had the time she had, but she wanted more.

When he put away his phone, she turned toward him. "And?"

"We have two hours."

She looked at him in surprise, her heart jumping for joy.

"Really? I figured you'd be leaving right now."

"I'll be gone soon enough. What do you want to do for two hours?"

"Breakfast on an outside patio and then I don't want to waste time seeing other people. I want to spend the time with you."

His gaze slid her way. "In what way?"

She hesitated, then said, "Maybe at the park where we were yesterday."

He gave a short nod and said, "Coming up."

An hour later they were walking hand-in-hand with some of the local coffee. Every minute disappeared so fast that she wanted to stop time, but there was nothing she could do. Her heart ached. So foolish when she knew this wasn't goodbye. But in a way it felt like it. "I wish you didn't have to go."

"I always have to go," he said quietly. "There is always going to be another mission. At least for a while."

"I know, and I'm okay with that. It just feels like our friendship is still so fragile, and we need more time togeth-er."

"It's mending," he said. "You know I want more. But I want more only if you do too."

She reached out and stroked his cheeks. "I almost sug-gested you stay this morning. But I didn't want our time together to only focus on sex."

"Does that mean you …?"

She placed her finger on his lips and said, "Yes. But not a fast-sex scenario because we're out of time. Next time, when we have hours to be together."

He checked his watch and said, "I have to take you back to the hotel and leave. Damn."

She winced. "I forgot you still had to travel to the base." Arms linked, they walked where his vehicle was parked. "You'll stay safe out there, right?"

He laughed. "Let's just say I won't take any unnecessary chances."

She smiled. "If you don't, then I won't."

"Good point. Make sure your remaining days are good ones." They got into the vehicle and returned to the hotel. Not wanting a long goodbye, she hopped out of the vehicle and stood on the side. "Go," she said. "You need to."

He gave her a shuttered look. "No kiss goodbye?"

She stepped forward and kissed him. Not a kiss of friendship. Not a kiss of passion either. A kiss of love.

As he stepped back, she realized she'd been blessed with a new insight into her feelings, even though she had been determined not to go looking for them just yet.

HE HATED TO walk away from her. But he was relieved they had a promise of getting back together again. Right now he had to refocus. He reached the base just in time to see Mac being helped into a jeep. "You doing okay there, Mac?"

Mac nodded, his face gray. "There's just something about finding out you aren't as healthy as you thought."

Ryder studied his friend and said, "You'll make it. Get home. Get well. I'm heading out right now."

"And Caitlyn?" Mac asked. "Where is she?"

"I just dropped her at the hotel. She's due at camp tomorrow." He hesitated. "You are sure about her, right?"

Sagging back in the seat, Mac said, "Absolutely. She's yours. You should know that by now."

"I know she's my friend," he said. "We just haven't gotten to the next level."

Macklin's eyes drifted closed as he regained his breath. "Well, you should. It's always been about you, buddy, always been about you." Just then the driver arrived, and Mac was taken away.

Devlin and Easton walked up beside Ryder with Corey in tow. "Well?"

Ryder shrugged, knowing what they were asking but not really having a full answer. "Let's just say we're friends again," he said cautiously. "But we didn't get a chance to go any further."

Devlin said, "You will have time for that in the future. Right now we have to kick some enemy ass."

Ryder's face lit up. "Great, I could use the outlet right now. Where are we going?"

"Back to where we came from," Cory said with a smirk. "Chances are you'll see Caitlyn sooner than expected."

Ryder's face split into a big grin. "Even better." And he hopped into their transport jeep. There were definitely some positives to having Caitlin here. Getting to see her from time to time was one of them.

CHAPTER 15

B EFORE SHE KNEW it, Caitlyn was en route to the same camp she'd been at before. She hadn't heard from Ryder since he had left yesterday. But then she didn't expect to. They each had a job to do, and the military always needed good men and women to fill their ranks.

Medical staff was always in short supply too. One doctor with several nurses was often forced to handle multiple life-threatening cases at the same time. When there were just not enough hands, they grabbed anybody close enough to help. As long as the people could follow orders, they were strong-armed into helping.

Hours later, when she walked back into her barracks, her old bed waited for her. She'd only been gone two days but still … Soon she'd be stateside. In a weird sense it was a relief. Something about having a corner in this world to call home made a difference. She dropped her bag and did a quick turnaround. With any luck the medical center hadn't changed much either.

Inside the med center she found everything calm and quiet. Frowning, she walked to the back, only to find the room empty. She stopped and slowly turned. There were no patients and no medical personnel. Where the hell was everyone?

She walked into the supply room and froze. Dr. Carter

had collapsed, unconscious on the floor. Blood poured from a wound to his temple. She dropped to her knees at his side, her hands moving from head to toe, checking him over. His pulse was strong, and he didn't appear to have any other injuries. She found a steel pipe on the floor beside him with blood on the edge. Her heart sank.

She pulled out her phone and made several calls. She had military men pouring into medical within seconds. They took one look and, with grim faces, on her instructions, carried Dr. Carter to one of the beds.

She glanced at the men and asked, "Where is the rest of the medical team?"

The men exchanged hard glances. One stayed behind and stepped forward. "We'll find out."

Just like that three left. One stood at attention at the end of the doctor's bed. She glanced at him, then loosened Dr. Carter's shirt collar. "I just landed. I have no idea what was here before or even who was working. I need to check the schedule to confirm."

He found the schedule and brought it to her.

She glanced through it and said, "Colleen and Wendy should've been here this whole time. Dr. Bruce too. I don't know about Dr. Robertson. We need to find them."

"A search is underway."

She had to be satisfied with that. All too quickly her sense of complacency and calm had disappeared, and panic returned. She had no idea what was going on, but it couldn't be good. What had happened here?

She quickly washed Dr. Carter's head wound, dressing it lightly, happy to see there didn't appear to be a skull fracture. Stitches would help, and she'd do them herself if it came to that. But Dr. Bruce should be the one.

She spoke to the soldier. "Check the supply cabinets. Make sure they're still locked."

He gave a clipped nod, walked into the back and started banging doors. He came around to the front again and said, "Doors unlocked, and cabinets empty."

She swore under her breath. "Which explains the head wound for Dr. Carter. He likely interrupted someone stealing medical supplies. Not an unusual occurrence."

The guard walked to the front of the tent, stepped into the doorway without actually exiting the medical center and studied the surroundings. Then he walked to the rear of the clinic. "How often do you use the back door?"

"I don't," she said. "But, before I left a couple days ago, we were busy. The smell in here was pretty strong. We had both doors open, letting in fresh air. Depending on how much cleaning had to be done, the cleanser itself would add to the smell."

He nodded and didn't say anything.

She pulled out her phone and called the supply desk. "When was the last time supplies were sent to the medical center?"

"Requisition was filed a couple weeks ago. A new shipment came in two days ago. Several more cases came in this morning."

"Well, reorder exactly what was delivered. Plus a whole lot more."

The supply clerk's voice was harsh when he asked, "Why?"

"The medical clinic has been completely cleaned out," she snapped.

She hung up the phone and ran a shaky hand across her temple. Obviously somebody knew the center very well. At least to know when it was restocked. There were often problems like this but never on this scale. Of course after being kidnapped, she had insider knowledge from both sides. Unfortunately she needed supplies here now. Hopefully more casualties would hold off until tomorrow.

When she heard a heavy groan, she turned to see Dr. Carter trying to sit up. She raced to his side and eased him back down. "You were hit over the head," she said. "Lie quietly until the room stops spinning."

He stared up at her, then frowned. "What are you doing here?"

"I'm just back from leave," she said. "Only to find you unconscious in the back room and the other staff missing."

He sighed and lay down. "I reported some people hanging around the clinic the last few days. They were dressed like our soldiers, but I didn't know them. We've had so many staff changes recently that, of course, I wouldn't know them," he said.

"It might not have been any of our men. Just relax. The MPs will get to the bottom of it. First we have to get you back on your feet."

"How much did they take?" he asked, his fingers going to his temple.

"They cleaned the place out," she admitted. "No boxes are on the floor, and all the cupboards are empty. How full were they beforehand?"

He opened his eyes and stared at the ceiling. "They were full. Damn. We're in trouble."

"We'll manage."

"As soon as I can sit up, I'll do an emergency requisition."

It took another fifteen minutes to get him stable and on

his feet. With her help, he walked to the supply area where they did a full count of what they would need.

She held up the requisition sheet. "I'm walking this over to the supply clerk right now. You should have the military police in here any moment to interview you."

He waved at her. "Go on. I can tell them what's happened and let them know where you are."

She nodded and, with a smile to the guard, walked out the front of the clinic. At the supply station, she walked in and handed over the requisition. "This is what we could assess we need immediately. We have literally nothing right now. Do you have any inventory here that's not been distributed?"

"I'll see what I can do, but I don't have very much in stock."

"Understood. But we literally don't even have a Band-Aid."

"I'll put in a special order for supplies. Should be able to do something for you by morning."

She nodded. "If somebody comes in injured beforehand," she warned, "I'll be back here sooner."

"Fair enough."

Outside she headed to the clinic and found the military police arriving to talk to her and Dr. Carter. They asked her a few questions, and she shared as much as she knew. "I'm sorry I don't have more. I literally just landed back at camp again."

"And yet, you were kidnapped earlier and held hostage in one of the rebel camps?"

She frowned but readily nodded. "Yes. The soldiers who kidnapped us were looking for medical supplies and a medical team to help several of their own injured people. But that was miles away from here. And the outpost didn't have the same men or security as this camp does. Still, if they decided to imitate what their other group did and had wounded but no medical team, then I can see the same issue repeating itself all over the country."

She was asked several more questions and then finally released. It was a relief to rush back inside to Dr. Carter. He sat in the same place she'd left him, but now he sipped water and had a cup of coffee in front of him.

"Where did you get the coffee?"

He pointed to a fresh pot he'd made, sitting off to the side.

"That's new." She smiled. "Nice."

He grinned. "Working is one thing. Working without coffee, well, that's a whole other story."

She spent the rest of the day keeping an eye on Dr. Carter, who kept pushing her away, insisting he was fine. Of course there was still no sign of Dr. Bruce or the two missing nurses, Wendy and Colleen. Thankfully she found out Dr. Robertson had taken a few days off himself, like she had. So he was safe.

It was hard for her to understand how three staff members could've been snatched away. But she had no doubt it did happen as it was exactly what had happened to her and Dr. Robertson. She knew teams were out looking for them, but, as she'd been saved by Ryder, it was hard to imagine anybody else being quite so good.

She winced. Just where was Ryder? Was he searching for the missing medical team? She hoped so. He was one of the best. And, if he wasn't out there hunting, he should be.

As darkness settled in, she sat in the clinic with Dr. Carter for another few hours as a familiar figure walked inside. She looked up at him and gasped. "Ryder?"

He gave her a grim smile.

She raced toward him. At the last minute he opened his arms, and she threw herself into them. "Oh, my God. What are you doing here?"

"I'm heading out after the missing medical team. What do you know about it?"

She quickly filled him in on what she knew. "There are no signs of them."

"There will be," he said gently. "We'll get to the bottom of this."

She nodded but knew so much time had gone by that her colleagues could be a long way away.

"Stay here and stay safe," he said in a stern voice.

She beamed a smile up at him. "I'm fine. Dr. Carter and I appear to have missed out on this kidnapping. And Dr. Robertson isn't here."

"It does not mean they won't come back for you. Depending on how long this goes on, they also know you will be restocking the supplies, and that means they could return for more."

"They took everything we have."

"How did they get into the cabinets?"

She shrugged. "I can't say for sure, but I imagine they got the keys off one of the staff."

Ryder nodded.

Corey walked in and asked, "You okay, Caitlyn?"

She stepped back slightly from Ryder's arms and nodded. "I am. I just got in a few hours ago. Dr. Carter sustained a head injury but will be fine. I hope you find our missing people quickly."

"We're on it."

At that they both gave her hard smiles, turned and left.

RYDER COULDN'T BELIEVE it when he heard the medical team had been kidnapped. It was one thing to try something like that at the tent outpost where the enemy had taken Caitlyn and Dr. Robertson, but this was a military camp. It shouldn't have happened here. Thankfully it wasn't Caitlyn this time. That the enemy had also taken supplies made a lot of sense. But it wasn't something they could continue to allow.

What they really needed right now was intel. Hence his trip here. By morning they'd have a rescue in place. If they got a chance to retrieve the medical team tonight, they'd take it. But they had to find them first.

Suited up, they were already on their way out of the camp, and he was breathing more dust than he cared to admit. There'd been no rain in weeks. Every step they took raised a cloud. Not good and not easy to keep the enemy in the dark as to their whereabouts.

As he read the tracks the enemy had left behind, Ryder could see the women hadn't done much fighting back, but Dr. Bruce had. Ryder's team caught up with the other mobile military units within an hour. With the updated information, his team split off from the rest and circled around to one of the suspected rebel militia's camps. There were three known locations. The question was, which one held the US medical team?

With his unit high on the hill looking down below, Ryder could see a white man sitting outside, leaning against the building. He had a bottle of water in his hand, but he didn't look too good. On closer examination he could see the man's legs were tied. That confirmed he was one of the prisoners.

Ryder tried to see his face but it was hard from this distance. In his heart he knew it was Dr. Bruce. But the women? White women alone out here? That was not good.

He heard a scream from one of the tents. Dr. Bruce jumped to his feet and hobbled a few steps before one of the armed rebels forced him back down again. And Ryder realized their window had just closed.

This rescue had to go down, and it had to go down now.

CHAPTER 16

CAITLYN WOKE UP on one of the cots in the clinic. She sat up slowly and looked around. Dr. Carter slept beside her on the next cot, his breathing, although low, was even and deep. So why had she awakened?

In the distance she could hear sounds of troops returning. She bounded to her feet and raced to the front entrance. There she stopped to listen. It looked like a group of men, maybe a dozen, and they were coming toward the camp on the far side. She heard the *wup-wup-wup* of the helicopter blades racing toward her. She was about to get busy.

Thankfully an emergency supply run had come in, and the clinic was partially restocked.

Dr. Carter sat up and asked, "What's going on?"

Caitlyn turned and glanced at him. "We've got injured coming in."

He nodded, straightening slowly. She watched his progress with a critical eye. But he appeared to stand strong once on his feet, and his gaze was clear. "How are you feeling?"

"Like I'd rather be in Hawaii. But considering we have injured men and women coming, this is where we need to be."

As soon as she heard the *pop-pop* of the helicopters, she checked for the wounded every few minutes. Afraid Ryder might be one of them.

She knew he'd scoff at her worries and say they were the best men for the job. And that might be true. But she'd also seen more than her fair share of men with good, solid, healthy egos come up against bullets, IEDs and a million other weapons that would rip them apart.

She stopped and assessed the trauma center, making sure she had enough compression bandages and IVs ready and the rest of the supplies were within easy grasp. Were her coworkers returning? Had they been found? She and Dr. Carter stood ready when the first gurney flew through the center. The patient had stepped on an IED. There was a bloody stump where his right leg used to be. Shit.

She knew what that meant. All of a sudden they didn't have enough hands. The two of them worked fast, in a musical coordination they'd reenacted so many times before. "Is the helicopter ready to take off again?"

"Yes. They are fueling up now."

The second man who came through was breathing steady and his pulse was slightly more stable. But his bleeding was just as bad. He'd taken a bullet to the side and a second one to the elbow. There wasn't much left of the joint. Short on hands, they enlisted the soldiers to keep pressure on his wounds as they worked on both men. They needed transport to Baghdad now.

She shook her head. "Both of these men need surgery."

Together they slowed the bleeding, set up IVs and started pumping fluids. The second man needed blood, and she had none.

It seemed like hours but was only minutes before the emergency vehicles raced the now slightly more stable men out to the helicopters. As she turned around to clean up the blood, she saw a second vehicle coming in. Even from where she stood, she could see the head bandage on the man in the front. She called to Dr. Carter, "More coming."

And that's how it went. The second helicopter went out less than an hour and a half later with two more heading to Baghdad. She had three in beds under watch right now with a steady stream coming through her doors.

"What the hell happened out there?" she asked one of the soldiers.

"The unit hunting down the kidnapped medical crew were caught by surprise. The rescue went okay, but they were ambushed on retreat."

"And the medical crew?" She hoped they were safe.

"One's injured, but she'll be fine. A couple soldiers were taken out."

"Dead?"

He nodded and gave her a hard look. "Two of them."

After that she stayed quiet. Her frayed nerves threatened to overtake her, but she didn't dare let them paralyze her. She worked steadily, doing what she could and staving off her fear deep inside. She cleaned and bandaged wounds, set up IVs and opened airways for many who came through her door. Dr. Carter worked madly at her side. She didn't have enough hands to do what needed to be done, but they had no one else to call in.

They were shipping out men who needed further care almost as fast as they were coming in. She didn't know what time it was when she straightened from covering up a patient. Hearing a sound, she turned around to see Corey step through the entrance. Her eyes lit up at the sight of him. And then slowly fell away as he stared at her steadily.

"Ryder?" she asked, her voice soft, gentle, so afraid to hope. Her stomach clenched, holding back a pain so deep, so intense, she couldn't move.

"He's coming in. He's alive, cranky and injured."

Her gaze lit up. "If he's cranky that's a good sign."

Corey snorted. "As long as you're the one looking after him."

Sure enough Ryder came through the door on his own feet and swearing a blue streak. A point of pride she knew because he sure as hell wasn't holding himself up. Easton and Devlin had him on either side, helping him to a bed. The only bed she had left. She was at his side immediately, her hands and eyes checking him over, looking for the trauma. He had all four limbs, and his head was bleeding, and his arm had a bad gash. She shook her head. "What the hell happened to you?"

"Nothing." He glared at her.

She smirked. "You better become my best patient, or I'll ship you to Baghdad right now."

"Like hell," he roared, trying to pull himself off the bed.

She smacked him down hard. "Listen up. You stay in bed until I'm done, you hear me?"

He glared at her even harder but subsided.

She caught the short gasps of the men at his side. She gave Easton and Devlin a hard look. "He can be a hard-ass all he wants," she told them, "but this is my domain. If there's anybody harder and tougher than me, it's Dr. Carter."

Easton smiled. "I gather not too many men give you grief in here."

"No time, no energy, no patience." While she talked, she checked Ryder's vitals. His blood pressure wasn't anything to be unduly alarmed about. He was angry; adrenaline still ran through his injured body. She hooked up an IV, completely ignoring his protests. With the heat his body was already dehydrated.

Then she turned her attention to his head wound.

"I'm fine." Ryder glared at her again, not willing to give an inch.

Fine, she could be that way too. She glanced at Corey. "What happened?"

"I don't know," he said. "It's likely he doesn't either. The first I heard was him swearing."

She cleaned the wound. "He needs stitches." She tilted his head to the side, studying how deep the wound was. "It's not too deep. Although it's bleeding badly. Typical of head wounds."

Dr. Carter walked over. He took a look and said, "We can put in a couple stitches. It will speed up the healing. How's the arm?"

Together they assessed the arm and realized Ryder had a dislocated shoulder she hadn't noticed at first glance. The gash was ugly in length but not deep.

"You're lucky. We can stitch this and reset the shoulder. But that arm needs complete rest or it'll become a much bigger issue."

His smile fell away. "Damn it. That means I'm off work."

"You're off work anyway for a few days," Devlin said. "Don't be such a hard-ass. Let her fix you up properly."

Ryder relented, closing his eyes and groaning in frustration.

"Did you even say thank-you to the men who brought you home safely?" she chided.

"Don't need to say it. They know how I feel."

"That doesn't mean it's not the polite thing to say." She

turned to the men. "Thank you for bringing him home alive."

The men grinned at her. "He was screaming at us pretty good to make sure we didn't bring him here."

She narrowed her gaze, hating the instant hurt she felt inside. "Why's that?"

"Something about not wanting to come back less than perfect," Easton said with a snort.

"Of course he'd think that." She glanced down at him to see him glaring at his men. "You're an idiot, Ryder. You know you're welcome in my world no matter what shape you're in." She motioned to the door. "You guys can go. Get some food and a shower. We'll need him for the next few hours. After we get his shoulder popped in and his wounds stitched, then you can see him."

The men nodded. Corey patted Ryder on his good shoulder and said, "Take it easy."

Ryder nodded and then winced at the movement.

She exchanged glances with the doctor. "Maybe we should start with the stitches on his head."

"No. Shoulder, then stitches."

Several hours later she took a bowl of hot soapy water to Ryder who was now sitting up bare chested, his arm in a sling and bandages around his head and forearm. "You can't have a shower. This is the best I can offer you."

He glanced at the bowl, surprise lighting his face. "Thank you. That actually would feel great."

She dipped her hand in the water and pulled up a large washcloth and wrung it out.

When she went to wipe his face, he said, "Whoa. I'll do it."

She handed it to him with a smile. "Stubborn. When

you're done with your face and chest, I'll do your back."

That was as far as she would let him off the hook.

THE WARM WATER felt good as Ryder washed his face and neck. He healed fast and generally went through any injuries with just a bounce to slow him down. The problem was, this time he'd been brought back before the mission was done, and that pissed him off.

Stepping around in front of him, Caitlyn removed the bowl and returned a few minutes later with another one. She picked up the washcloth and gently cleaned his face a little better than he had. Then she worked on the fingers of the hand he couldn't access easily because of the sling and the bandages. When she was done with that, she walked behind him and wiped down his back. He had to admit it felt damn good. He hadn't realized just how dirty and sweaty he'd become.

When she was done, she picked up the bowl and dumped it outside. It was so intimate having her bathe him. Naturally his mind moved in a different direction. When she returned, he watched as she checked several other patients, making sure they were all okay.

He motioned with his hand. "Any reason I can't go back to my own bed?"

"Except for the fact I'll miss you?" She smiled, then shook her head. "No, you're good to go as long as you aren't dizzy and you promise to go to bed and rest. I'll see you back here in the morning to get the stitches checked and to make sure the swelling in your arm is okay. Don't forget to take your antibiotics."

He slid off the hospital bed and then paused. He reached

out with his good arm, wrapped it around her shoulders and tugged her close. And he held her, just held her. In a low voice he said, "For a moment there I thought I wouldn't see you again."

She tilted her head back and smiled. "I'm glad you did."

He stroked her chin with his thumb, then leaned down and kissed her. Just a gentle, light *hey, I missed you* kind of kiss. When he lifted his head, he almost kissed her again when he saw her eyes half lowered and slumbering. "If you keep looking at me like that, I'll have to kiss you again. I'm sorry I had to leave you in Baghdad." He watched her lips quirk.

"Me too," she said softly.

His thumb moved along her lower lip, gently caressing her soft skin. Feeling like he was on the precipice again of another change in their relationship, he dropped his head and kissed her a little bit harder, a little bit deeper, a little more passionately. Then pulled back. There was an audience, whether they were conscious or unconscious, and Dr. Carter was here somewhere. In a husky voice, he whispered, "Hold that thought."

He grabbed his belongings and strode from the tent. He wished to hell he could go back out in the field but knew that wouldn't happen today. Not with his injuries. He might have gotten away with the stitches in his head but not with his arm injuries.

He entered his barracks, tossed his bloody clothing on the end of his bed and threw himself atop the blanket on his bunk. His skull was splitting. The painkillers he'd been given only muted the pain.

Corey found him there a few minutes later. "Good news. The medical team is on their way in. They don't appear to be any worse for wear. We'll call this a successful mission."

"Like hell." It was never a successful mission if he got hurt. On the other hand, the mission had been accomplished. He was good with that.

"So what happened with you and Caitlyn?"

"Nothing," Ryder said quietly. "I said 'Thank you,' kissed her goodbye and left."

Corey nodded. "That's a good thing."

Ryder thought about it. "I've never felt that way with anybody else. Just with her."

"This is you being unsure of her. You're scared to make the wrong move and have her walk out of your life again."

That was just a little too damn true. "Not a whole lot I can do about it if she does."

Corey walked out of their quarters, calling back, "I might take her a coffee. Have a talk with her myself."

"Maybe you shouldn't," Ryder called out but was too late. Corey was gone.

Corey had been hard on Caitlyn since he'd learned what happened between them. Ryder hoped Corey would ease up.

The more Ryder lay here, the more he worried. He trusted Corey, but Ryder also knew how edgy Corey was right now. Really, Ryder should be the one who took Caitlyn a coffee. Or maybe he could follow up with a meal.

As he lay stewing, Devlin and Easton came back in and updated him on the rest of the team. By the time they were done, Corey returned, and Ryder realized he'd missed his chance.

Corey smiled at him. "She's doing fine."

Ryder rolled his eyes. He glanced at his watch. "I need food."

The men got up. Corey asked, "Are you coming, or do

you want us to bring you back something?"

"I'm coming." He stood and wavered. Then on guts alone he said, "Hold two places at the table. I'll see if Caitlyn is hungry."

With knowing grins, the men walked out.

Ryder struggled into a clean T-shirt and slowly walked to the clinic.

She looked up in surprise, then bounced to her feet. "You shouldn't be up and walking around," she scolded.

He chuckled. "I came to see if you have time for a meal. Can you leave?"

She shook her head. "I can't. There's no one else to cover for me."

"Can I bring you something?" he offered.

Surprise lit up her beautiful chocolate-colored eyes, making her smile all that more real. "That would be very nice." She handed him her empty coffee cup. "Corey brought this for me. If you wouldn't mind taking it back, that would be great."

He nodded and said, "I'll bring you a tray and more coffee."

She grinned. "Thanks."

As he was about to leave when he realized something felt unfinished. He turned to look back at her. She was staring at him questioningly. He sighed. "It seems like I can't leave without doing this anymore." He leaned down and kissed her. This time he left with a smile.

She wore one too.

HE WAS STILL smiling when he walked into what passed for a dining room. After years of being in the military, he'd eaten in some strange conditions. But this was clean and quiet, and his head appreciated that. Plus, it was nice to have a lighter heart. Right now it was just a joy to know he had Caitlyn back in his life, and they were sharing a few kisses here and there. Her tour was almost up, and she'd be back in California soon. That would provide them both more time off together.

At the table, the guys looked at him strangely. He dropped the smile and said, "What's the matter? Not used to seeing me happy?"

All three shook their heads.

Leaving them, he collected food for himself. As he walked down the line, he tried to assess what Caitlyn would like. He knew her food tastes as well as his own, but there were only so many choices.

Finally, he sat down with the rest of his men, where the discussion quickly fell to work and the missions. While they sat, Mason entered. Along with him were six other SEALs who Ryder knew. The discussion moved to the day's mission as they hashed and rehashed what had gone down.

Dinner was over soon enough, with groups breaking up. Ryder excused himself from the table and said, "I promised Caitlyn that I'd take her some food." She wouldn't leave that clinic until she was relieved from duty, and he wanted to make sure she had enough for the night. He had coffee, water and a juice to go with the food. The challenge was to carry it with his bad arm.

Caitlyn took one look and bolted toward him. "You know you're not supposed to be using that arm yet," she scolded. "It's bad enough you're up at all but to be using your arm like you are …"

"I'm barely touching the tray," he protested. "Besides, I

didn't want to see you go hungry."

She took the tray from him and carried it to a desk at the far end. The lights in the center were turned down, and he could see many of the men were sleeping. A couple more were lying in bed, resting.

"How's everything here?" he asked.

"It's fine. Dr. Robertson is back from leave. He came to check on me, but I sent him off to get dinner. When he returns, I'll take a few hours downtime myself."

"What about the rest of the medical team? I heard they were back safe and sound."

She nodded. "Yes, but they are going to Baghdad for several days." She smiled. "More staff is coming to relieve them."

"When is your tour up?"

"One week." She gave him a smile. "One week and then I'm home." She glanced at his arm. "How long will you be off work?"

He shrugged. "It's too early to tell. A week maybe. Then I'm on partial duty after that."

"Stateside?" she asked hopefully.

He grinned. "Maybe. I can't wait. I'd really love to spend more time with you there."

She glanced around the room, knowing others could hear them. In a low voice she said, "Yeah, me too." She patted his cheek gently and said, "Now go to bed and rest."

He gave her a wicked grin. "Not sure I want to go alone."

She flushed bright red. "Nothing else is an option right now. Not with that arm like it is. Besides, are you sure you want me now that you know what I did and why?"

"It's only you I want, warts and all," he said with a smile.

"It's always only been you."

She gave him a startled look, and her jaw dropped. "Really?"

He nodded. "Really. If you take away only one thing from this, know *that* is the truth."

She allowed a beautiful, breathtaking smile to cross her face.

CHAPTER 17

AFTER RYDER WALKED out, she studied the tray of food. She hadn't been hungry before, but now, seeing the bounty before her, she was dying to dive in. But Ryder's words fired through her mind. She wanted to believe him. Lord, she really did. Was it possible? Was she ready? Well, of course she wasn't, but she wanted to be.

More guards came in to keep an eye on the place, so hopefully there'd be no more problems. But the medical supply issue worried her. The enemy had cleaned out their inventory, which meant the rebels had a great need themselves. Of course medicine and supplies were easy cash on the black market. But still, it didn't feel right.

Just then Dr. Robertson walked in. His phone rang as he greeted her, and he sat down to answer it.

She only half heard the conversation as she plowed into her food. Something about roast beef and mashed potatoes made everything feel like home.

When Dr. Robertson bolted to his feet and looked at her, she stopped chewing and stared back. As he continued to speak into his phone, she resumed eating but kept an eye on him. She didn't know what was going on, but something obviously was. She might not get much chance to eat more, so she attacked the rest of her plate with a hearty gusto.

When he got off the phone, he walked over to the chair

and sat down in front of her. He watched as she swallowed water to clear her mouth.

"What's going on?" she asked as soon as she could.

"The rest of our team has been interviewed, and some of the information was a little disturbing. It took a bit of time for the information to make its way down to us, as of course we don't have clearance," he said with an eye roll and a grin. He turned and nodded toward a couple guards at the entrance. "And explains why we are heavily guarded."

"Why?"

"Apparently your name was mentioned several times, as was mine, to the rest of the medical team."

She sank back with her coffee cup in her hand and stared at him over the rim. "What? Why would they care?"

"They were angry we weren't part of the second group kidnapped." His face grim, he added, "Apparently the team was roughed up a little bit until the enemy could understand why we weren't there."

"This is bizarre. Why do they care?"

"The brass thinks we may have seen somebody or something we shouldn't have."

She stared at the doctor in shock. "We didn't see anything in the area."

"But what we did see might've been important." He glanced toward the opening of the tent as he heard approaching footsteps. "The brass is hoping we can tell them what might be so important that we were supposed to be kidnapped again."

Bewildered she watched as several men came toward her. Not military police but special investigators. She cleaned up her place, removing the half-eaten meal, and set the tray off to the side. And then the questions started.

"Did you see anybody you recognized?"

"No."

"Did you see their leader?"

"How would we know who their leader was?" she asked, then shook her head. "No."

"Have you had any contact before, during or after with any of those men?"

She shook her head. "No. I don't understand all these questions."

"We're trying to figure out why they want you back."

"Because we escaped? Pissed them off? They had too many injured?" She could only hazard a guess, but the expression on the men's faces didn't change.

"Okay," she said. "They took us because they had injured we were supposed to help."

Dr. Robertson nodded. "One man was already dead. The second man survived with a head injury. The third man was shot. We treated him as best we could, but it was rough."

"Even if he survived, they shot both of them anyway," she said. "It didn't make any sense that we were kidnapped to administer medical aid, and then they turned around and killed them and our guards."

The taller of the two men turned to look at her. "Who shot who?"

She frowned. "A different man. He came in with a rifle, fired downward at the injured men, then shot the guards."

She turned to look at Dr. Robertson. "Isn't that right?"

He shook his head. "I didn't see it all. I was already moving ahead." He glanced at her. "You didn't mention all of that."

She shrugged. "After Ryder cut the tent and we left, I

looked back several times. There was a kerfuffle, and then the man closest to the opening shot them all. I figured he did that because the guards failed to keep us secure. Ryder saw it too."

"But there was no need to kill the men already hurt," one of the interviewers said. "What were the ages of the injured men?"

"The one with the head injury was older, maybe mid-forties." She gave a brief description of what she could remember. "The other man was not as old, maybe early thirties."

A few questions later, they realized the two men who'd been alive and most likely shot were officers in the rebel group. Leaders. "Are we assuming that, because I saw this one man killing everybody in that tent, he's now after me? Why would they care?"

Silence followed.

"Because," Dr. Robertson said slowly, "maybe they don't know for sure who shot their leader, and they want you to identify the killer."

Everybody stared at her. "I can't possibly identify anyone. I saw the shooting because of the shadows. I could recognize the two men who stood outside the tent, but then so could you. But it's not like we knew the men."

"It's not just you they want. It's also Dr. Robertson."

Dr. Robertson and Caitlyn exchanged glances. At the same time they turned to look at the interviewers. "Is the rest of the team coming back?"

The men shook their heads. One of the interviewers said, "No. This camp is being decommissioned."

Caitlyn nodded. "I have one week left. Then I'm shipping stateside."

The men nodded. "And you might be leaving earlier. What we want to avoid is a third incident."

In a firm voice she said, "I trust you guys to take care of me and everybody else here. Two attacks is already two too many."

The man gave her a hard look and a clipped nod. "Indeed." They got up and left.

She stared at the doorway, then turned to look at Dr. Robertson. "Are we really in danger?"

"The military is moving everyone out. The camp will no longer be used as a base for military operations, at least until this last year of action has been reviewed," he said quietly. "At this point it's best if the enemy sorts themselves without involving us any further. They are changing leadership every five minutes it seems. Somebody kills off the leader and takes his spot, with another dozen eager men to take advantage and move up. So best to leave them to their own system of infighting."

"Oh, I agree with that." She nodded.

"I imagine we'll have our orders within a few hours."

She snorted. "Good. Our supplies that came in are long gone. It's all bizarre." She eyed him carefully. "Where will you end up?"

He tossed her a grin. "I'm kind of hoping for the FOB just outside Baghdad. I'd like to finish the next few months there."

"That would be nice for you." Still she was happy to have the guards and the extra sense of security as she checked on their patients. The last thing she wanted was to experience any more of the ugly side of life.

THE MILITARY WAS a well-oiled machine. Setting up and pulling down a camp was nothing but good practice for them. Organized chaos was what Ryder called it. But there was a method to it. As everything moved swiftly around him, he jumped in to help where he could. He refused to sit around and do nothing while everyone else worked, even if he was using his arm too much. Thank heavens for the painkillers. Easton and Devlin were having a lot of fun at his expense. If it wouldn't make his arm worse, he'd have punched them out.

Easton said, "Ryder, you should be resting somewhere."

"Like hell," he responded yet again. "Not going to lie down. Or rest or anything else you think I should do."

A severe urgency inside him wouldn't let him sit back and relax. He wanted to make sure they all got the hell away from this place. He'd heard the rumors about an enemy coup in progress, somebody looking for Caitlyn to confirm who shot who. He'd been interviewed himself soon afterward. He'd confirmed what Caitlyn said but hadn't been able to add much. There was no winning in this situation. It was also very hard, if not almost impossible, to identify all the various players in a fast-moving game like this. The best thing they could do was get her the hell away. And fast.

With that uppermost in his mind, he walked to the medical tent to see how it was progressing. He found the tent already down, boxes and supplies stacked off to the side, men all over the place. But of Caitlyn … there was no sign. He glanced around and frowned.

Catching one of the soldiers beside him, he asked, "Where's the medical team?"

"I think they were shipped out early," he said, lifting a box, placing it on another. "Shouldn't you be leaving too?"

He motioned at the sling and bandages on Ryder's arm.

Ryder shrugged. "In theory, yeah." He took another look around. "I'm looking for Caitlyn, the nurse."

"Good luck with that. Most of the phones aren't working right now either."

Ryder nodded. "I noticed."

He walked the small area but didn't see any sign of Caitlyn. Several trucks had already pulled out, and helicopters had flown in and out. If the enemy knew what they were doing, it would make them happy. Out of the corner of his eye, he saw somebody with a white coat. He raced after him. "Dr. Robertson, wait up."

The doctor turned. "Hey, Ryder." He glanced at his arm. "You should be resting."

Ryder waved his concern away. "Where's Caitlyn?"

Dr. Robertson turned and looked around. "I have no idea. We were packing up this morning. Somebody called to talk to her." He shrugged. "Honestly, it's chaos here."

With a sinking feeling in his heart, Ryder asked, "How long ago was that?"

"I don't know," Dr. Robertson frowned. "Do you think something happened to her?"

"I don't know, but answer the question so I can find out," he said in frustration.

"At least an hour I'd say. I know she was talking about getting some food."

"The mess tent is gone. No food until we get to the new base."

"It's down to rations again?" Dr. Robertson grimaced. "I'll wait for mess tent food. As for Caitlyn, she's got to be here somewhere."

Ryder watched as the doctor argued with somebody

stacking up bags. Presumably Dr. Robertson's own. Swearing under his breath, Ryder pulled out his phone only to realize he still didn't have any reception. He couldn't contact the rest of his team. He picked up his pace.

He found Corey first. "Have you seen Caitlyn? Nobody has seen her in the last hour."

Corey shook his head.

Ryder explained what one of the soldier's had said in his interview.

Corey slowly stopped what he was doing and stood up. "You think something's happened to her?"

"I have no idea." Ryder raised both hands in frustration, followed by a grimace of pain. "Why would they take her and not Dr. Robertson?"

Just then there was a harsh crack. Ryder glanced around. "Was that a gunshot?"

At the uproar behind him, he spun and saw Dr. Robertson collapse to the ground. "Shit." He raced back toward the doctor.

With several people helping Dr. Robertson sit up as he arrived, Ryder could see fresh blood across his shoulder. Dr. Robertson caught sight of Ryder. "I don't know what the hell happened," he said, "but you need to find Caitlyn fast."

Corey was already veering away from the crowd. "The shot came from the left, the trees up on the far side."

The whole camp was now on high alert, weapons ready, as they raced to finish the move. Dr. Robertson was injured but holding his own as they prepped him for the next helicopter ride.

Easton showed up behind Ryder. He yelled, "We have to go. They must have Caitlyn."

Easton said, "Can you be sure of that? I'm all for going

after her, but we have to make sure it's not a wild goose chase."

Ryder shook his head. "I don't know where she is. I just know she's not here."

"Damn it, Ryder." Easton shook his head, activated his comm unit. "Ryder and Easton on the move to retrieve possible kidnapped victim Caitlyn. Corey and Devlin, let the brass know so a full headcount is done before we lose someone else in the chaos, before rendezvousing with us in the far east section of the trees."

Ryder and Easton raced through the woods, heading in the direction where the shot had been fired. Teams formed down below, and another team was on guard as the rest of the men packed up the last of the camp. They'd be out of here in fifteen minutes.

But Ryder wasn't going without Caitlyn. And as long as the teams knew they were out looking, somebody would stay behind. The dust was in his face, the sun beating down over the treetops. He didn't slow his pace. If Caitlyn was up ahead, the rebels would be moving fast. Sure enough, a plume of dust rose ahead of him. They had wheels. Dammit, he didn't have any.

Just then he heard an engine. He turned around to see Corey and Devlin driving one of the jeeps toward him. He waited until they were beside him before he and Easton joined Corey in the back. It didn't take long to update them. The plan was rough, but it was to get ahead and cut off the kidnappers. It was the only way they could stop them from disappearing into the hills. Once that happened, it would be hell to find her again, particularly since the rebels had wheels and could move fast. They had places to hide which Ryder's team didn't know about. He'd track her down, but speed was paramount.

He'd never give up searching for her. As soon as the rebels were done with her, the men would shoot her and bury her in the sand. Mother Nature would take care of the rest.

Leaning forward, he urged Devlin to drive faster.

Devlin said, "Hang on, Ryder. We'll get her."

Ryder sat back and caught sight of something moving to the left. He stood up in the back of the open-air jeep and studied the plumes. The other vehicle was escaping. "We have to go faster. We can't come in ahead of them at this rate."

Corey handed Ryder a long-range semiautomatic rifle. He picked it up with his good arm and awkwardly put it into position. This was much better. If nothing else, this gave them a little bit of a chance. Taking a shot at the driver while moving was not the same as a shot when he was stationary, but it was all Ryder had.

Just then they hit a rock. Devlin lurched to the side, pulling the wheel hard. Ryder grabbed on but was still tossed from one side to the other. His arm jarred, sending shards of pain up his shoulder.

"Sit down," Corey urged. "Calm down. We'll get her."

Ryder's fingers locked on the weapon in his hand as he kept telling Caitlyn, *Hang on, girl. Hang on. I'm coming.* Inside his stomach knotted tighter. But adrenaline kicked his blood to pump faster. He just wished he was driving.

The jeep rounded a corner, came up over a crest, taking to the air before landing hard. Ryder wasn't sure where Devlin was going. As they came around the corner, they saw the other vehicle catch sight of them and yanked to the side, gaining slightly. Immediately Ryder stood, took aim and fired. But his vehicle bounced, and his shot went wide. He could see a woman in the back of the vehicle and knew they had Caitlyn. But it would be hard to get close enough to get them. What they needed to do was stop the vehicle without making it flip; otherwise Caitlyn could get hurt in the crash.

There was also a chance the vehicle ahead was riding toward a rebel army. A group of trees were coming up where the road split. The enemy went to the left, Devlin went to the right. With his heart in his throat, Ryder tried to see through the brush, but there was no visibility. Devlin flattened out the gas pedal and poured in as much effort as he could into making up time and moving faster and faster. The huge dust cloud rising around them made it impossible to see where the other vehicle was. Ryder knew they were in danger of coming up against an entire army, and they could be picked off easily.

Finally the road curved to the right, but, instead of taking it, Devlin took a turn to the left and drove cross-country. There was a little bit of a rise up ahead. He hit the brakes hard, and everybody swept from the vehicle, weapons ready. A second enemy vehicle came racing forward. But the men were ready. The first shot took out the driver; the second shot took out his passenger riding shotgun. Several more shots took out the wheels. They had it surrounded within minutes.

Only to find Caitlyn wasn't there.

The vehicle was empty except for the dead guys.

"Shit." Ryder stared in anger and frustration. "Where the hell is she?"

"They had to have met up with someone."

"Or they dumped her out."

At that the men bolted back into the vehicle. "That's why we managed to get ahead of them. They stopped."

Devlin jumped into the driver's seat a hair faster than Ryder. He drove, following the other vehicle's tracks. Ryder's biggest worry was, if this enemy vehicle had been a diversion, another rebel vehicle carried Caitlyn farther away even now.

They couldn't go as fast this time because they needed to see where the other vehicle might have stopped. The slower pace chafed at him. Ryder realized another problem. Fuel. They were almost out of gas.

CHAPTER 18

CAITLYN OPENED HER eyes, and terror slammed into her at the sight of an enemy soldier sitting beside her. Her body was being jostled from side to side; pain drummed through her skull. It seemed like every part of her had been pounded into hamburger. She had no idea what had happened or what was still happening, but panic coursed through her, and hot acid fought to escape her mouth. She was in the back of some kind of vehicle. Although she wasn't tied up, she wasn't alone. Soldiers sat beside her. But not in uniforms she recognized. She'd been taken prisoner again.

She closed her eyes so nobody would know she was awake. But they yelled and screamed at each other and made gestures. She desperately wanted to lift her head and see if somebody was following, possibly already searching, but didn't dare. There was a reason her head hurt now. There was a reason the rest of her throbbed. She doubted anybody had given a crap as to how gently they had treated her. And all the yelling made her head pound even worse. She wanted to cry. She could feel the hot tears burning the corners of her eyes. But letting them drop would mean they would know she was awake. And that couldn't happen at any cost.

Finally the noises quieted. The men reduced their tones to something more like shouting instead of screaming in a mad panic. She took that as a bad sign. She was quite happy to share what she knew, but it wouldn't make anyone happy. She expected a bullet to the back of her head, followed by a shallow grave somewhere in the sand. But she wasn't giving up yet. Not now that she had Ryder back in her life. She didn't know what it would take to stay alive, but there had to be something she could do.

Through her lashes she studied what she could see without moving a muscle. The man beside her leaned forward and talked to somebody, pointing between the driver and passenger. The sun wasn't high yet, so it was still morning. She was supposed to be out of the camp. How long had she been gone? At least one, maybe two, hours. Hell, it could be three or four. She wasn't very good at navigating and still couldn't get east and west within a city straight. She understood when the sun was high, but other than that she was lost.

The man seated beside her held a rifle. It looked like a semiautomatic and was pointed in her direction. But he wasn't paying attention.

Just then the vehicle slowed, and her heart jumped to her throat. The brakes were slammed on, and she was covered in a blanket of dust. Doors opened, and she was dragged out, tossed over somebody's shoulder. She was jostled, her head smashing, and the pain …

When she woke up again, she was trussed up under a tree. She rested in place, figuring out exactly where she was. She was hot, tired, her throat clogged with dust, and she could barely get enough saliva to moisten the inside her mouth. The hot tears refused to be held back this time. Instead, they ran in rivulets down her cheeks. She blinked, furious at herself. She wanted to sit up and look around, see if she was under guard. Find a way to free herself and get the hell out of here, but she was too scared to move. She listened intently.

Was she alone? Had they taken off and left her to die? God, wouldn't that be brutal. How far could she get without water? The answer didn't really matter because it would not be enough regardless. She slowly twisted and turned to see where she might be. She was grateful for a little bit of shade, but it wouldn't last long.

Her hands were tied behind her. She managed to shuffle until she sat against the tree trunk. She studied her surroundings. This was not how she'd planned her day. She could see footprints leading her here, and then they walked away. A single set only. The tracks headed off to the left. She studied them. They climbed over a rise and disappeared. It wasn't like she had much of a chance of getting away, but they hadn't even left a guard with her, which was both good and bad. It was great they didn't consider her a threat, but it was also incredibly scary to consider she had been abandoned. Or was left for bait to ambush Ryder's team. Or was left without food and water to lower her resistance before the leader came to interrogate her.

The rebels could come back and get her at any time … That thought spurred her on. Or they planned for the desert to kill her, after they got what they wanted from her. She struggled to free her hands and could feel her blood making her wrists slippery, but still it was useless. She did manage to hook her arms under her butt and, after much struggling, got them in front of her. She then started working on the knots with her teeth.

It was just an old frayed rope. Surely with time she could untie her hands. She just didn't know how much time she had. And then there were her bound feet to deal with. An hour later, frustrated and angry and so damn alone, she took a break and bowed her head against her arms. She caught her breath and asked herself what Ryder would do in a situation like this?

Of course the answer was Ryder wouldn't be in a situation like this. And, if he did find himself in the unlikely position, he'd get himself out of it. So why the hell couldn't she? She stared down at the ropes on her feet and realized they weren't tied as tightly as the one around her hands. Using her fingers, she quickly untied the knots around her ankles. With her feet free, she bounded to a standing position, and, with her arms still tied in front, she stared out in all directions, but saw nothing but dirt and sand and brush for miles.

There were the footprints that had retreated and had to lead to vehicle tracks. They were, however, tracks made by her kidnappers, which were the last people she wanted to find. But those tracks were the only ones she could see. And they had to lead somewhere.

Somewhere was better than being nowhere.

She took off at a dead run. She hadn't gotten far when she realized she had to slow down. Her throat was dry, and she was burning through her energy too fast. But the tracks had led her down and around one hill already.

There was still no sign of anyone. Up ahead she could see what passed for a road. Or at least tracks the vehicles had traveled.

That was her goal. Her biggest problem would be if the enemy came upon her first. But she heard no sounds of a vehicle. Nor was there a plume of dust as far as she could see in any direction. She kept putting one foot in front of the other. She'd heard of tricks like putting rocks in her mouth to keep the saliva flowing to stop the parched sensation, but it offered minimal relief at best.

The heat beat down on her, baking her face and scalp. A grove of trees was up on the far side. She headed toward it, needing the coolness of the shade. When she reached it, she slumped down, waiting for the heat to ease and for her breathing to calm. There had to be a way to contact somebody. She had no cell phone, no matches, no gun, no knife … She had nothing. She'd never felt so unprepared for the reality of where she found herself. She studied the tree line and realized more trees were farther up a hill. Maybe at least there she could find something to signal someone.

Taking a chance with a bit more of her energy, which she was running quickly out of, she raced up the hillside to the trees. There, hidden deep inside the grove, she studied the ground below. On the far side she could see a vehicle approaching. But she didn't know whose it was. She also didn't think she could catch it in time. If she'd stayed where she had been, she would have. With her heart in her throat she watched as the vehicle came to where she'd gotten off the path and gone to the first grove of trees.

It wasn't until it passed that she realized the skin color of the people in the vehicle was white.

"Help," she screamed. "Help." And she raced down the hill, but it was too late.

The jeep was long gone.

"STOP. THERE ARE tracks heading off to the side."

The vehicle was going so fast they were already up and over the hill before Devlin had a chance to register and hit the brakes. Ryder was out of the vehicle and racing back to the tracks. He motioned to the others coming behind him.

There was no guarantee it was Caitlyn they were following, but the tracks belonged to a lighter-weight person with small feet. With the sand filling in the footsteps, he couldn't confirm what kind of shoe the person wore.

Once again he raced up to the first set of trees and saw the tracks going to the far side. As he sat here hidden, he let his gaze wander, trying to pick up the proof of someone, anyone, up ahead. Going from one group of trees to the next would leave him open.

And then he saw her. She'd collapsed under a tree. With her back against the trunk, she stared at the sky. But he could see her face. He signaled to the others, watched as their gazes lit on her, and he took off. He had his water bottle out of the side holder before he'd even reached her. He dropped to his knees. "Caitlyn, can you hear me?"

But she didn't respond. He could see the blood on the side of her head, but a quick search didn't show any other injuries. With the water spout open, he poured water gently into her mouth, trying to revive her. She coughed and choked, but it was music to his ears. He eased her into a sitting position.

"Caitlyn, it's me, Ryder. Take it easy." She coughed several times and then reached for the water bottle. He had to hold her back or she would have drunk it all in one go. "Take it easy. You can't have too much right away."

She pushed it against him. "Oh, my God," she said, her voice a hoarse whisper, followed by a cough. "I thought I was done for."

"I'd never leave you here," he reassured her. "We just didn't have a clue what happened."

"Neither did I." She coughed again, as if clearing the

sand from her throat. "I stepped out of the way while they took down the tents"—she forced a swallow, then grimaced—"and somebody called me. … That's the last thing I remember."

He nodded. "With all the vehicles in the area and everybody taking down camp, snatching you and secreting you away wouldn't have been hard. Particularly if more than one person was involved." He held up the water bottle, and she grabbed it again, drinking greedily. By the time she returned it to him, she was half a bottle down, and he'd had a chance to assess her newest head injury. "Looks like they hit you over the head and knocked you out."

"My head's hurting," she admitted. "But I can't tell if that's the heat or my injuries. All of me hurts, in fact," she admitted. "I really want to go home."

He gave her a gentle hug and then helped her to her feet. "Soon," he promised. "We need to get back to the vehicle and out of here before they come looking for you." He glanced around. "Have you seen anyone else?"

She motioned in the direction she'd come from. "No, they dumped me back there, and then they took off. I didn't want to be there when they got back."

"Good thinking." He cut the ropes on her hands, and she cried out as her arms fell to her side. He picked them up and clutched them across her chest.

"Oh, my God, that hurts," she gasped, trying to adjust them.

He squatted, picked her up in his arms and headed back toward the men already almost upon them. "We have to get Caitlyn out of here in case they come back for her."

Back at the vehicle she filled in the men on what little she knew.

"Did anybody say anything to you?" Devlin asked.

"I have no idea. There were lots of voices, but I didn't understand the language," she admitted. "Sometimes they were yelling and screaming and getting very excited, and other times they were just talking quietly. I drifted in and out of consciousness. I'm sorry I don't have much to offer."

"It's all good. You survived. That's what is important."

In the far distance he could see a plume of dust, and he knew what that meant. The rebel group was coming to collect her. How and why they'd dumped her in the first place he didn't know. This time Corey hopped into the driver's spot, and Ryder kept Caitlyn tucked up in his arms, Devlin beside them. Corey hit the gas, and Easton was at his side, his rifle ready as he kept watch. More of their men should be coming up behind them. If they could get close enough to the enemy, they could take them out and put a stop to this. Of course, with the camp moving miles away, it wasn't likely worth the effort from now on. But somebody was pretty determined to grab a hold of Caitlyn. The rebels had lost her again, and that would cause more chaos.

Ryder glanced down at Caitlyn, but her eyes were closed. "You awake?"

"Yes," she said, not opening her eyes. "But I wish I wasn't."

He hugged her close.

"We'll be fine."

A startled sound came from Devlin, and Ryder spun to look back. A second enemy vehicle had joined in following them on one of the many cross-country paths that riddled the area. "Caitlyn, I'm moving you to the footwell. I want you to stay tucked in as small a ball as you can. You hear me?"

She stared up at him, twisted in his arms to look behind her, gasped at the sight of the enemy on their tail and sank into the footwell.

Ryder grabbed his weapon and turned, using the back of the seat for protection as he waited for his chance. The rebels were still too far out, and, with Ryder's vehicle hitting ruts like it was, it would be too hard to get off a decent shot. These assholes weren't going down easy, but he'd be damned if he'd let them get back up again.

Not when they'd come after Caitlyn for a second time.

The first shot sounded and missed.

The second hit their vehicle.

By the time they recognized a second vehicle coming from the left, Ryder instinctively twisted to shield himself and started firing.

Like hell he would die today.

<h1 style="text-align:center">CHAPTER 19</h1>

CAITLYN HUDDLED AS low as she could go while the men returned fire. They were outnumbered, but it didn't seem to bother them. She just hung on mentally and emotionally. They needed a little bit of luck to get farther ahead of the men chasing them. She hoped Ryder had a plan.

Another shot hit the vehicle. She winced, cringing lower. Ryder fired several more times, then cheered. She raised her head, looked up at him. "Did you get him?"

He chuckled. "I got him. We disabled the vehicle at the same time, so that group isn't coming after us anymore."

She shifted upward, but Ryder grabbed her shoulder and gently pushed her down again. "They might have another vehicle. And they are still firing at us. It remains dangerous up here."

She glared at him. "I could help, you know."

He glanced down. "Sweetheart, I hope you don't have to. If we need your help, that means one of us is hurt."

He was right. But she felt so helpless. There had to be something she could do. "If you need more men to handle the guns, I could drive."

"We got this," Corey said. "You stay down. You stay alive. Otherwise this would be all for nothing."

The jeep hit another series of bumps, rattling her right

through to her teeth. It was a good thing she didn't have broken bones or bruised ribs or a gunshot wound right now as her body would really be screaming at her. Although she was sore and achy, it wasn't as terrible as it could have been.

Just then the jeep took a hard left. She was thrown against the back of the front seats. With a hard right she was tossed against Ryder. "I'm so sorry," she screamed.

"Don't worry about it," Ryder said. He swore and started firing again.

It seemed to go on forever. There was a haze of dust and confusion and noise and, threading through it all, fear. But not from the men. No, they showed control and determination as they did what they did best. She had to admire anybody who could hold his cool in a scenario like this. She thought she'd been doing really well overseas. But, as she watched these men perform, she realized she was just barely getting by. And Ryder was right; they didn't want her particular skill set to be needed right now as that would mean one of them was injured.

The vehicle took another hard left. She watched tree branches overhead as the vehicle raced underneath. The road was rougher here. She bounced and slammed into the back of the front seat again and so did the men with her. There was nothing really to hang on to. She had her arms wrapped around one of the seats in the front, but it didn't help much. She was trying desperately to stay out of the men's way, but it was hard.

Just as suddenly, the jeep braked. In a harsh voice Ryder said, "Stay down, Caitlyn."

All around her the men stood up, and she could only listen in to their conversation.

"Let's see if we can pick off the ones coming behind us."

"They'll be here soon, but we don't want these men setting up an ambush for our guys."

She could hear the rifle fire in the background. She focused on her breathing, wishing them all to stay alive and healthy. Life was too short and, right now, too dangerous. Anything could happen.

It was that thought that made her look up at Ryder and say, "I never stopped caring, you know?"

For a moment she thought he hadn't heard her, but finally he glanced down. "I know. That's why I found it so very hard." His voice was soft and gentle. "I knew how you felt inside, but you turned away from me and wouldn't let me help."

She stared at him in surprise. What could she say to that?

"Stay down," he said.

Instantly, her ears felt as if they'd been blasted, and gunfire hit right beside Ryder. She curled up into a ball as he shifted to the side of the jeep, changing his angle. From where she was, she could hear the approaching sound of another set of wheels. "Incoming," she yelled at him.

He nodded. "They're ours."

She wanted to whoop with joy.

Then he swore, raised his weapon and fired. And again, then again. Huddled down in the relative safety of the footwell, she waited for the gunfire to slow down. And just like that it stopped. She listened intently but heard only silence.

She slowly raised her head and looked at him. "Is it over?"

He held his fingers to his lips and whispered, "We're checking now."

When he relaxed, she realized it was really okay. She smiled and shifted up to the seat. And the smile wiped off her face. There were bodies, several of them. "Let me go check on them."

"No." He shook his head.

She watched as Corey, Devlin and Easton went out and checked on each of the men. She knew as soon as they glanced their way, all the enemy men were dead.

She turned and sat back on the seat. "How horrible. I'm glad we're alive but still … If only they had just walked away."

"That would have been nice. But it rarely happens that way."

"What do we do with the bodies?"

"The cavalry's arriving now." He pointed down the road. She could see several vehicles racing toward them. "They will take care of this. And they have spare gas cans so we can get back."

"What about us?"

"We'll join up with the rest of the team moving to Baghdad," he said. "We're done here."

But it was a somber trip back. Everybody was safe; nobody was hurt. Although it should've been a trip full of rejoicing, the loss of life hung heavy.

"Why do I feel guilty?" she asked.

"Because, in your mind, they died because of you. That's wrong. They didn't have to kidnap you in the first place."

"What'll happen to the group they were part of? Will they still come after us?"

"I doubt it. I recognized several of the men," Easton said. "When we came and rescued you the first time, they were the ones hanging around your tent. I highly suspect that now, with these men gone, the leadership will shift yet again."

"What a life."

"Not a fun one for anyone," Corey said. "It's hard to instill peace in a country that breeds war."

By the time they made it back to where the camp had been, it was gone. Only the disturbed sand showed a camp had ever been here. After a good wind, that would disappear too.

"They are good at this."

Ryder wrapped an arm around her shoulders, nudged her next to him in the jeep and said, "They are. But then so are we. Let's go. We have places to be."

KNOWING HE HADN'T been there to watch over her just ate at Ryder. That they found her when they did would be stuff for his nightmares for a long time. He'd like to think it was skill. It was to a certain extent, but it was also blind luck. Nobody knew that better than he did. But they had rescued her, and that's what he had to focus on.

So much of his work ended up taking a life. It took time to deal with the aftermath. By now he'd had a lot of practice. But he knew it wasn't the same thing for her. He wrapped an arm around her again and tucked her close against him. "Sleep if you can. We have a few hours to go."

She nestled into his chest and arms. He raised his gaze and caught Corey's steady look. With a half nod Corey smiled and turned away to talk to the others. Ryder leaned his head back. He didn't want to suggest she needed to head stateside, but it was in his heart. He knew that was where he wanted her. She'd done her time, unless she felt she needed to be here. It would have to be her choice though, and he'd stand by it. As she'd need to find peace with his work. He wouldn't give up his job, and that meant she'd have to wait, knowing what he was going through. After this, she'd have insider knowledge of what Ryder went up against.

And that couldn't be easy for her either. For the first time he admired all the wives who stayed at home while the men went off to war. Sure war was difficult on the men, but he couldn't imagine staying home, taking care of business and raising families without knowing if the men would come home again. And he wasn't sure he could do it. That double standard again.

He held her close to his chest until she lifted her head a long while later and stared around in confusion. He loved the cloudy look in her beautiful eyes. "Take it easy. You've been napping. But you're safe."

She wiped the strands of hair off her face and smiled up at him. "Thanks to you and the others."

He shrugged. "It's the least we could do."

She snorted. "Did you even think about your injured arm?"

He glanced down at the bandages, at the sling still around his neck but no longer on his arm. "No." He shrugged. "Why would I?"

She changed her position.

"How are your injuries?" he asked.

She reached a hand to her head and smiled. "Still hard-headed as always. I have a couple scrapes and bruises, and I'm very thirsty. But I'm fine."

"You're more than fine." He handed her his bottle of water and watched as she drank.

"Oh, that's good." She took several deep breaths. He

could see the stress slipping off her shoulders. "It's a very unforgiving land in so many ways."

"And yet, other parts of it are beautiful and nowhere near as desolate or difficult to live in."

She nodded. "I believe you. I did see pretty bits and pieces, just enough to forget the uncomfortable places." She looked up and smiled at him. "Thank you for the second chance at life."

He reached down and kissed her just off to the side of her stitches. With a tender smile he said, "You're welcome."

"You know you shouldn't be working with your arm, right? Are you coming back stateside?"

"I should be," he said cheerfully. "I was not leaving without you. Especially not for something so minor."

She snickered. "Why? Is there a law against having weak, injured SEALs?" She paused, then whispered, "Thank you."

Ryder cuddled her close.

"You can't have both *weak* and *SEAL* in the same sentence," Corey said in mock outrage. "*Injured,* maybe. But not *weak.*"

She smiled. "Isn't that the truth? And you are definitely men of honor."

Devlin chuckled. "*SEALs* of honor. *SEALs* of honor."

She glanced at Ryder and said with a wicked smile, "So you have time off, and I have time off. Any chance we can spend some of that time together?"

Corey glanced from one to the other, raised one eyebrow. He started to say something, then thought better of it and twisted around to face the front of the vehicle again.

Ryder glanced down at her and said with a big grin, "Tell me more."

"Well, it involves"—she leaned closer to his ear—"lots a

hot water, room service and a whole lot of resting in a bed with clean sheets and no sand." Then she added with a grin, "After all, I should keep you in bed until that arm of yours heals."

He tilted her chin up, leaned down and gave her a real kiss. "Now that's my kind of keeper."

Her gaze narrowed at the term, and he remembered she knew Mason and his Band of Keepers.

He lowered his head a second time, just to make sure she understood exactly what he meant by that. As she sagged against his chest, he tilted her head toward him so he could look into her eyes.

"I know I'm the one who walked away the last time. I was wrong. I can't imagine ever doing it again. I was in such torment. Please don't ever do that to me. You're way stronger than I am. I wouldn't survive."

He stared down and shook his head, whispering, "I couldn't. Ever. It'd be like leaving half of me behind."

Tears came to her eyes. She stroked his face. And in a voice that he could barely hear, she whispered, "I love you so much."

He crushed her against his chest and just hung on for the ride, knowing that finally, after all this time, he'd come home again.

CHAPTER 20

THE DOOR CLOSED behind them. She stopped, spun around and stared at Ryder. They were a banged-up pair with multiple sets of stitches and bandages between them.

And he'd never looked more beautiful to her.

He studied her with that warm and caring gaze she'd come to depend on these last few days. But there was also just that hint of a question. That hint of fear. Insecurity and uncertainty that she'd been responsible for placing there. She gave him a tremulous smile and said, "We're alone."

He nodded. "With a big bed, room service, plenty of clean sheets and lots of hot water."

She laughed, remembering her words to him twenty-four hours earlier. "What a couple of days it's been." She walked to the double glass doors of the London hotel and stared out at the lights. "This is a world away from where we've been."

"And that's one of the joys about doing what we do. We see the world, both the good and the bad parts."

She smiled. "You could've stayed with your unit."

He chuckled. "Not one of them would've thought I was in my right mind if I had. It's all good. They have friends around. We have a couple days in London to regroup. Then you and I head back to California. What's not to like about that?" He wrapped his good arm around her.

She smiled and snuggled close. "Is this really the start of our new life?"

"I think it started a while ago," he said cheerfully. "This is yet another step on our journey. Hopefully one that will be a little easier moving forward."

She turned in his arms and stared up at him. She desperately didn't want to cry, but the moment was so emotional it was hard not to. "It's my fault the journey was difficult."

He shook his head. "There's no fault here, no blame to place. Besides it all worked out in the end. And that's what matters." He stroked her along her jaw and cheekbone. "Although your reasoning took a bit to get my mind wrapped around it, I can see how, for you, that's the way it was."

She dropped her head against his chest. "I feel like such a fool."

He tilted her chin higher, dropped a kiss on her forehead, then on the space between her eyes, down on the tip of her nose. Gently he brushed his lips across hers. "I don't ever want you to feel foolish over something like that. But it would be nice if you talk to me as soon as you get as confused as you were back then."

She chuckled. "If we had talked immediately afterward, everything would've been a lot easier." She slipped her arms around his neck.

He lowered his head, and, just before he took her lips for his own, he whispered, "And I suggest we revisit that weekend. I'm sure it's time for you to remember."

She thought he would kiss her. But instead, his hand dropped lower. Then he scooped down, swung her into his arms, turned and walked a few steps to the bed. He tossed her lightly into the middle of the big cloud of bedding. She shrieked with laughter and tried to bounce back onto her feet, but he was over and above her, his legs pinning her in place, his good arm pulling her arms over her head.

He glanced down at her and whispered, "You remember this?" And he ground his pelvis against hers.

His erection prodded at the heart of her. She could feel her body softening, warming, welcoming—waiting for him. And she moaned.

"Do you remember this?" He clasped both wrists with his injured arm and slid his other hand down to cup her breast, his fingers automatically testing the weight, the plumpness, the firm peak between his fingers. Then he slid his hand lower, then under her shirt to sweep across her soft smooth skin, his fingers dancing along the edge of her pants. "You remember this?"

Her breath came out in harsh gasps as she twisted in his arms. "I remember this all too well," she groaned, her body arching under him. "I remember threatening you if you didn't let go of my wrists."

He chuckled and gently released one of her hands. "And I remember doing exactly as you requested." He slid his hand down her hip, around the back to her cheeks and gave a gentle squeeze of her jeans-clad butt. Slowly teasing, he slipped his hand farther down her thigh to the back of her knee, skimming the space where she was so tender and ticklish, all the way down to her ankle. He slipped her shoes off and followed them with her socks.

Within seconds his hand was at her jeans, opening the zipper and undoing the button. She'd been amazed back then at his skill in removing her clothes. Now she was damn grateful. Her jeans went flying to the floor almost without her noticing.

Now that she was clad in a narrow thong, his breath caught in the back of his throat as he dipped a finger under the elastic to the tiny swath of curls underneath. "Jesus, you're beautiful."

He lowered his head, placed a ribbon of kisses across her ribs, her collarbone, her arms and the inside of her elbow. He pushed her shirt higher and higher, making a path for his kisses, for that sensitive trail that drove her nuts. He'd always been able to do that to her. Their passion had been instant. Once they had given themselves permission to go that route, nothing had ever been the same again. And she knew nothing ever would be again.

This was the man for her. This was the man she'd always loved. She didn't know why it had taken her so long to figure it out. But now that she had, she didn't want to waste another moment. With her shirt pulled up against her chin, and her chest exposed, he quickly loosened her bra around the back, letting it slide up over her breasts. He drove her wild as he suckled each in turn.

She tried to release her other hand to get his shirt off, but it was so damn hard. She couldn't reach more than his shoulders, a little bit of his back, his head. She stroked her fingers through his curls around his ear, trying to pull him up higher, but he wouldn't let her. He was doing this his way, in his time, and she was helpless to resist. Nor did she want to. She twisted beneath him, moaning as he lit a fire deep inside. Finally he released her, and her shirt flew off her back to the floor. He straddled her and slipped the bra up her arms to join the rest of her clothing.

As she lay there before him, beneath him in just a thong, she watched him as he studied her. Her heart thudded in her chest at his flushed skin and the hot gaze as he grasped her hands, tugging them against his mouth, where he kissed her fingers one by one.

"Dear God, I never thought I'd get here again."

She stretched out her fingers to stroke his cheek, her body arching, and whispered, "Come to me. Come to me now."

He released her fingers and pulled his shirt off over his head. Her fingers slid down his chest to his jeans, opening the button, sliding down the zipper over the hard ridge underneath. Her finger slipped inside, searching, stroking and aching to grasp the erection she knew all too well. And yet, not well enough. He groaned, rolled to the side, and within seconds he was nude.

His right hand closed around hers on his shaft, and he squeezed gently for a moment, shuddering. The fingers of his left hand slid in long strokes from her shoulders over her breasts down to her small waist. "Your skin … it's so delicate … soft."

His fingers stroked, soothed and teased her skin. Tiny mewling cries escaped her throat. She barely recognized the sounds or her body movements as she twisted under his ministrations. When his fingers teased along the edge of her thong, her lower body both retreated and arched into his caress, wanting so much more but barely able to stand his sensuous touch. He lowered his head and kissed her navel, his tongue sliding along the elastic of her thong, his mouth dropping kisses on the curls below. She reached out and grabbed his head to pull him up, her legs widening and stretching, making room for him.

"I need you now," she whispered. "I want you inside me. As a part of me. One with me."

He shuddered at her words, and the triangle scrap of material was suddenly gone. He slid his hands under her hips, lifted her up, opened her even wider and then, sitting back on his knees, he placed himself at the heart of her.

She opened her eyes and smiled. "Yes," she whispered. "Yes."

And he thrust home. She arched, crying out. He stilled, a question in his eyes.

She shook her head. "So good. So damned good."

Then he started to move. Gone was the control. Gone was the restraint. He pounded into her, driving hard for the release they both needed. And she reached it, crying out, before collapsing down to hold him close. He drove once, twice, three more times, and unbelievably she could feel the tension inside her twisting harder, tighter, stronger yet again. Finally he groaned, and a long cry, guttural and deep, released from his throat as he rode through her.

She splintered apart again. He collapsed beside her and held her close.

When she could, she whispered, "I don't think two days will be enough."

"I don't think our lifetime will be enough."

Tears burned her eyes as she realized just how much she'd almost missed out on. She tilted her head back and said, "Welcome home."

He rolled over and kissed her. And she knew neither of them would ever be alone again.

MACKLIN

SEALs of Honor, Book 15

Dale Mayer

PROLOGUE

"THERE THEY ARE," Macklin said to Corey as they sipped coffee at a popular coffee shop in Coronado. He watched Caitlyn and Ryder park outside the café and enter. He stood and waved. Caitlyn caught sight of him, and a big smile broke out across her face.

Macklin opened his arms, and Caitlyn raced into them, laughing.

Then she jumped back and exclaimed, "Oh, your shoulder. I'm so sorry."

It was his turn to laugh. "Oh, no, you don't. No way an injury will stop me from accepting a hug from you. Besides, I'm doing just fine. I'm heading back to work next week."

She squealed. "Oh, that's excellent news."

He hugged her and stepped back. "I'm glad you think so." He nodded at Ryder who stood behind her. "And I have you to thank for saving my life."

Ryder shook his head. "No need to thank me. Besides, you can return the favor sometime. Although I hope the situation doesn't arise."

"It better not," Caitlyn said. She spun to glare at Ryder. "That would mean you were in a really bad place." She slugged him gently. "And I won't have that. Not anymore."

Ryder's smile quirked, and he wrapped an arm around her, cuddling her close. "I'll be fine."

Corey motioned them to the seats at their table.

Mac was happy the two of them had settled their differences and appeared to be on a smooth path for the first time in years. They looked like they'd make it this time.

He, on the other hand, was avoiding all relationships. He was happy to be around his friends, but not one of them had had the horrible experience he'd had. And no way would he repeat it.

Marsha had been a bad mistake—but he'd chosen her. So what did that say about the decisions he made? It said, he was shitty at them. And the last thing he wanted was to make another bad one.

So it was abstinence for him.

Something he never thought he'd say.

A commotion at the entrance had the diners turning to look. A police officer accompanied by a woman—another officer, maybe a detective—stepped inside and surveyed the patrons. The officer closest to them stood tall, her posture commanding, powerful. Macklin had seen that in men but not so much in a woman. Despite himself, he was intrigued. For the first time he considered softening his stance on abstinence.

Ryder took one look and said, "Uh-oh, I hope she's not coming over here."

"Why?" Caitlyn asked. "I've seen Alex at the gym several times. She's really nice."

"She might be, but she's also the hotshot new detective who just arrived at Coronado PD. She's an ex-CID special agent from back east." Ryder shifted slightly in his chair.

Macklin studied the tall slim woman who even now walked toward him. "I don't think I've met her."

"I have." Caitlyn jumped to her feet as the agent approached. "Hi, Alex."

A warmth lit up the thirtysomething woman's eyes. She acknowledged Caitlyn's greeting, but her gaze was locked on Macklin.

He raised his eyebrow and waited.

"Macklin Princeton, I need you to come with me, please," she said in a low but firm tone.

Macklin frowned at the others at the table, then turned back to her. "Sure. Can you tell me why?"

"We need to ask you some questions down at the station." She waited quietly. No pressure but not relenting. He would go with her one way or the other.

"Questions about what?" He pulled out his wallet and tossed a few bills on the table. Lunch was obviously not happening.

"A young woman. I believe you know her. Marsha McEwan?"

He froze. Caitlyn and Ryder's gasps echoed in the café. Corey jumped up from his chair. "I'll come with you, Mac."

Macklin stared at the agent, hating that he wanted to drown in her clear-mountain-lake blue eyes, and stood, instantly dwarfing her. In no way did she appear intimidated. "I'd be happy to come," he said calmly. "What's the problem?"

"She's dead."

CHAPTER 1

AT POLICE HEADQUARTERS, Mac was ushered into a room with two chairs and a small table. In a strategic move, Mac casually sat in the first chair, placing his back to the door. It showed he didn't care who came and went, and forced others to walk around him. He didn't have a clue what his involvement in this murder case was supposed to be but knew he'd be questioned based on Marsha's death alone.

The tall woman sat across from him. She dropped her folder on the table and looked at him for a long moment.

He stared back. It was the oddest time to recognize a woman's attributes, but he was male and had been celibate for long enough, and her mesmerizing gaze was the deepest, darkest midnight blue he'd ever seen. He opened his mouth to mention it to her, then snapped his lips closed. That comment would be foolhardy at best.

She raised an eyebrow. "Is there something you want to say?" she asked quietly.

He quirked a grin at her. "You wouldn't believe me if I did."

"Try me."

He chuckled, settled back, crossed his arms over his chest, and said, "I was just thinking how you have the softest midnight-blue eyes I've ever seen."

He knew he'd surprised her, but she was quick to mask

it. The woman was all about control.

She shook her head, opened the folder in front of her, and said, "Before we begin, please state your name."

He leaned forward. "It's hardly fair for you to know my name and to not share yours."

She flushed. "I'm sorry. I should've introduced myself. I'm Detective Alex Carson."

He reached out a hand to shake hers. "Nice to meet you. I'm Macklin." Despite herself he could see her fighting a smile. "I'm harmless," he said gently. "I would never kill Marsha. I haven't seen her in at least six months—and it was just a glimpse of her—and all our meetings before that were unpleasant for several years. Not from me hitting on her but from her hitting on me."

Alex settled back. "Can you explain?"

He launched into as honest an accounting of the strange relationship he had had with Marsha as he could. "Originally I invited her out on a date. We ended up in bed, an incredibly hot, wild weekend, but it only took until Monday for me to realize she was a crazy woman. As in, something was not quite right."

Alex frowned. "Meaning?"

"I had to go to work that Monday. I needed her to leave so I could lock up." He shook his head with the memories. "But she had no intention of leaving. Although she made it look like she did. We left together. I went to work. When I came home, I found her moving in."

Surprise lit Alex's face. "After one weekend?"

Macklin nodded. "Right? It made no sense. I was quite pissed off. I like my space."

She nodded. "Most of us do, particularly if it's a new relationship."

He nodded. "She had her vehicle packed full and was unloading. Instead of going to work that day, she had gone home and packed up everything."

"What did you do?"

"I told her that, as much as I had enjoyed the weekend, I wasn't ready for a commitment." He winced. "If I had been smart, I would've just ushered her out the door and left her like that. But it wasn't to be quite so neat and clean. She broke into tears, said she'd made me a special dinner, and the least I could do was be nice about it. I felt like a heel. I kept going over our weekend, wondering where she would have gotten the idea we were moving in together, but I don't think she needed any encouragement. The fact that we went to bed together was enough for her."

"Did you talk about commitment in any way?"

"Hell no. That's not really on my agenda, at least not for a while." He stared around the small room, hating all the memories filling his head. "We had her special dinner. I managed to get her packed back up and out of the apartment. And then I had to go to a meeting. I had sent a text to one of the guys in my unit. Between us, we found somebody who could come that night and change the locks."

She frowned. "You mean she got into your locked apartment?"

He nodded. "And, no, I don't have a clue how she got back in. I didn't want to take the chance she'd picked the lock, so I added a bolt on top. I know it sounds stupid, but I was paranoid."

Alex nodded. "Carry on."

"After that she seemed to back off a little, acting more normal. I was still wary, but I really wondered if I had made a mistake. Maybe I'd been the one at fault. ... I didn't really know or understand what I might've done, but she didn't pressure me or try to move in again. All my friends told me to get the hell away and just forget about it. But I didn't listen. I didn't want to hurt her. I was also just beginning to realize what a drama queen she was. Anyway, we saw each other off and on for a couple weeks, and finally I broke it off. We were out one night, and I told her that I was heading overseas. I was letting go of my apartment, and I was starting a whole new phase of my life, and that was the end of us."

He winced. "But of course it wasn't the end. I went back home that night. It was true I had let my apartment go, but I still wasn't due to fly out for a couple days. I woke up in the middle of the night to somebody trying to get in my door."

Alex leaned forward and grabbed a pen and jotted down notes. "Was it her?"

He nodded. "It was. And I didn't open the door. I could see her through the peephole. But she seemed to sense I was there and pounded on the door, screaming, kicking, and waking up the neighbors. The cops were called—I didn't call them though. She was given a warning, but I would still be there for another two days. I woke up the next morning, and she was trying to get in through the living room window."

He shook his head. "I told her through the window it was over, and I was leaving. The apartment would belong to somebody else. She started crying. I tried to calm her down and went to have coffee with her. I thought maybe it would make things a little better." He shrugged. "But it was extremely uncomfortable as she made a big scene. I got up, walked out in the middle of it, and went back to my apartment. I finished my packing and cleaning. All I had to do was move my stuff outside to the truck coming to take it to storage. That's when she arrived again." Just thinking about what he'd gone through made his stomach boil all over again. He shook his head. "This time I had several buddies helping me. They knew about her. But she acted crazy. She said it was *our* stuff going into storage. That we were looking for a place together. By the time we were done, several of my friends took me aside and said, 'Buddy, you need to get the hell out. Something is clearly wrong with her.' I was just grateful I was leaving."

"Where did you go?"

"Germany for eight weeks of training. And then another program I had deliberately requested in Iraq, so I would be gone for over three months. You can check my file. It's all there. And my stay was extended several times. By the time I returned, about eight months had gone by, and, no, I can't tell you exactly how many months it was. This was four, five years ago, remember? But, when I came back, she was not on my radar. I'd had a good time while I was away. It had been a nice break for me. New scenery, people, and activities. I ended up getting another apartment on my own off base and was going on missions steadily. I was in Iraq and then Afghanistan doing some training. I was up in Alaska for a while." He frowned. "Then I came home from a long trip. I was tired and cranky. I went to my apartment, parked my vehicle in front, got inside, threw down my bag, stripped, and headed for the shower. When I walked into the bedroom, she was there in my bed."

Alex's face hardened. "Can any of your friends verify this?"

"All of them can," he said in an equally hard voice. "Do you know how many times every one of them has told me to watch my back and to get the hell out?"

"What did you end up doing?"

"I picked her up, grabbed her bag sitting off to the side, put her out into the hall. I shut and locked the doors. I took a kitchen chair and jammed it up against the door so she couldn't open it. I hadn't slept in thirty-six hours. I was beyond exhausted. But I sent a text to several of my crew and my unit leader to let them know what was going on. And that, as soon as I caught six hours, I'd get back in touch."

"What happened when you woke up?"

"She was gone, and I thought I was in the clear." He shook his head. "But you know stalkers never leave that easily. She started emailing me. I changed my email account. Then I got letters in the mailbox. I was getting phone calls and little presents left on the front door. I did at one point entertain the fact that maybe it was somebody else, but I couldn't think of anyone else who might've done something like that. It made no sense why anybody would. I did not have another lady friend at the time. I was not busy partying and having sex with nameless partners either. Since Marsha, I've been extremely circumspect and have not had a relationship."

Alex's hand flew across her notebook as she took notes. He appreciated her efficiency. "When did you see her again?"

"When she followed me."

At that Alex looked up.

He nodded. "Yes, you can talk with my team members. They all saw her. She followed me to the gym, followed me through the coffee shops, followed me to the grocery store when I went shopping. She even followed me to a party. Several friends told her that she needed to back off. She came with the same sad story, that we'd had a fight and she was just making sure I wasn't mad at her."

"That's hardly a tiny fight."

"And I was mad at her. But I also didn't know what to do. Over the course of my career I've bumped up against a lot of law enforcement, and some of them gave me insights and some tips as to how to avoid her. But she was determined. Anyway, it all came to a head when she followed me to a second party. I was sitting with a woman on each side. They happened to be partners of two of my friends, and we were celebrating engagements among the group, and Marsha lost it. She threw alcohol in my face and broke glasses. She threw furniture and bottles. Anything she could. It was just bad news.

"She ended up getting arrested, and we filed a restraining order against her. She broke it on the very first day. She was tossed in jail overnight. Somebody bailed her out. I don't know who. Maybe she bailed herself out. I didn't want to get involved. And it seemed like maybe she understood she had crossed the line, and this wasn't getting her anything. So she backed off."

"Totally?"

He shot her a look. "Hell no. After that, she got ugly."

The detective settled back and said, "Ugly in what way?"

"Instead of love letters, she sent hate letters. Then copies of hate letters cut into tiny pieces were stuffed into an envelope. Then she progressed to broken glass parcels. A wineglass was in the first one—not exactly sure what was in the second one because it was just shattered. A number of packages were delivered to my apartment, each containing something shattered."

"Did you call the cops to let them know? Did they take any fingerprints?"

He shook his head. "I just wanted it to be over with. But then she went after my Jeep."

"What did she do?"

"She keyed it," he said, his voice hard, angry. "And then she put sand in my gas tank. I went out another morning, and all four of my tires were flat."

"At that point did you contact the cops?"

"Yes, again she was charged, but somehow she ended up with a misdemeanor—apparently by pleading she was bipolar or something, and had forgotten to take her meds. She claimed she was back on her meds, and she was fine again."

He shook his head. "When I saw her, I didn't have much to say to her. The bottom line is, at the end of the day, she finally disappeared from my life. And I have been very low profile because of her. I have not seen her since. And, until you came to the restaurant this morning and said she was dead, I hadn't seen her in six months."

"When exactly was the last time you saw her?"

"I caught sight of her in a coffee shop six months ago. I turned around and walked out."

She nodded. "Do you know anybody who would have a reason to kill her?"

He snorted. "Except for me, any other lover she's done this to. She was dangerous as hell. I don't know how she was killed, but there is a good chance the other person killed her in self-defense. Believe me when I tell you—she was nuts."

ALEX FOCUSED ON the man across the table from her. She was sure his name gave him nothing but hell as he grew up. Similarly his size, compared to that of the Mack trucks, would not have gone unnoticed by kids intent on sending jabs to the most painful emotional spots. She'd asked Caitlyn about him only days ago. Caitlyn had gushed with joy as she expounded on the man Mac was. When Alex had asked Caitlyn about Mac's girlfriend, all humor and joy had left her face, and she had explained just how psychotic Marsha had been in her treatment of Mac. Caitlyn had ended it with "We were really worried about him. Mac seems to be unconcerned, but she kept coming around. She'd go under for a couple weeks and pop right back up, like a bad penny." Alex remembered Caitlyn's last words because she had stared off in the distance and told Alex, "This can't have a good end."

She dropped her gaze to the folder on the table in front of her, realizing how prophetic Caitlyn's words were. "What about your relationship with Caitlyn?"

She watched as his body language settled and opened. The grin that came across his face was incredibly endearing. "Caitlyn is a sweetheart. She got a little bit lost, but now she's back where she belongs. She's with Ryder, and, as far as I know, her world is completely rosy."

Alex had heard the same from Caitlyn herself. Alex nodded and said, "What other girlfriends have you been involved with since Marsha walked into your life."

Macklin snorted. "I now live by a couple rules. One of those is, don't if you think they're crazy. Because obviously I've lived that."

She barely held back a smirk at his first comment.

"The second is, I don't go out with girls unless I know them really, really well."

The second surprised her. She studied the man carefully. "No one-night stands? No short-term weekends? No girls overseas?"

At each question Macklin shook his head. "No," he said

flatly. "When you're up against somebody with a serious problem like Marsha's, it makes you very hesitant to move forward."

She nodded. "Do you know any of her friends? Relatives? Enemies? Who might've hated her?"

Mac's response was instant. He shook his head. "I've never met anybody else in her circle. I never met any family or other friends. The fact that she's done this to me means she very likely did it to somebody else, which would make that other person a likely suspect."

"Which also puts you exactly in the suspect seat as well."

He nodded his head in acknowledgment. "Which is why I'm here. But I did not kill her."

"Something else makes you a whole lot guiltier than you may like."

He leaned across the table, his sheer size intimidating. But it was the cold clarity in his gaze that made her swallow hard. "Explain," he said in a very soft voice.

Rather than explain, she pulled one of the crime scene photographs from the file and placed it in front of him. Written in blood at the site of Marsha's murder was his name. He leaned back, swore, and said, "Wouldn't it be just like that bitch. The last thing she does is incriminate me. As if she couldn't make my life bad enough while she was alive, so she has to make sure she keeps the torture on after she's dead."

He turned his gaze to the far corner of the room, his mind occupied with what he'd seen. His shoulders sagged, and he turned to look at Alex and said, "I shouldn't have said that. I think she was probably mentally unstable, but maybe that wasn't her fault. I'm sorry she's dead. I'm sorry that, in her lifetime, she couldn't get the help she needed. But I still didn't kill her. And whoever wrote my name could've been her killer."

"Which is why I'm asking the next question."

He waited, his gaze unwavering.

"Who hates you enough to see you get charged with murder?"

He pinched his lips and stared for a long moment, but she didn't drop her gaze. She searched his eyes for the truth. She didn't see any deceit. She saw no lies. No hesitation, no searching for answers or a plausible excuse.

"I don't know. I've been in the military a long time. I was off on medical leave for three months this year. I don't think I have anyone personally who hates me. However, if a terrorist happened to be on American soil who knows about me, he could easily have targeted me. The problem is, he would've been after everybody else in my unit too."

She tapped her finger on the folder, thinking about that. "Give me the names of the men in your unit. And who else met her."

Mac gave her six names without hesitation.

"If you think of any more, let me know. I'll run down these names, verify your story, and take it from there."

He looked at her and asked, "Am I free to go?"

She nodded, and then her smile fell away. She knew he wouldn't appreciate the next hit. "I need you to stay in town for the moment."

A thundercloud swept across his face.

She expected that and looked for any sign of loss of control.

But instead he groaned and said, "Fair enough. But please hurry up. I'm finally cleared medically to go back to work next week."

She stood and said, "I'm working on it." Alex shook his hand and walked him back to the waiting area. Caitlyn caught sight of Alex, lifted a hand, and waved. Alex let her guard drop, and she smiled at her friend and waved back. She stood for a long moment and then realized she was attracting attention. She turned and headed back to her office.

Why the hell did the most interesting man she'd seen in over a decade end up being a murder suspect?

Just her bloody luck.

CHAPTER 2

ALEX LEFT HER car in the Coronado PD parking lot and walked into work the next morning. She was still getting used to the California weather. The mornings were lovely, but, by the afternoons, she struggled with the heat. She was from Delaware originally, then moved across the country. California was by far the nicest state she had lived in, but it was also the most crowded, and it was hard for her to acclimatize. Things were different here. More casual. No longer being in the military had opened up Alex's lifestyle completely.

Then, with her new job, she just might be feeling the pressure a little more. In past years, the Coronado PD had five to six detectives. Now there was one—her. And, true enough, there hadn't been a murder in this city in over a decade, and the budget hadn't allowed for officers whose mandate wasn't being utilized so … But having come from a department with dozens of other detectives and officers to this one, where everyone looked to her to solve the issues on her own, was intimidating. Empowering. Challenging. And she loved that, but it also pushed her buttons. She had no one to turn to for help. She missed bouncing ideas off her peers. She had supervisors and a chief here of course, but that wasn't the same as having a partner.

She also had to rely on the local police officers in a way

she hadn't had to before.

As such she hadn't found her comfort level yet. But then she'd only been here for a month.

As usual, she sat at her desk to see papers and messages tossed on top. She booted up the computer and logged in. First thing she did was check her emails. She was waiting on the autopsy report for Marsha, but it still wasn't in.

Neither were the lab tests back.

In other words, things were operating at the normal slow pace they always did, no matter what part of the country she lived in. She went through her phone messages until she came to one, a caller who wanted to speak to her about the McEwan case. Alex picked up the phone and dialed the number. There was no answer. She frowned and let it continue to ring, hoping for voice mail. But there was nothing.

She wrote a note to call back and stabbed it onto the spike she kept on her desk. It was an easy way to keep track of pieces of information she'd lose otherwise. They often had people calling in, wanting to say something about a case, then getting cold feet.

Those were messages or notes she couldn't afford to forget. She had to go through the pieces of paper on that spike every day before she left work. That was the only way she didn't miss anything. Details were the devil. But, without them, everything fell apart.

She continued to work steadily that morning. She had Macklin's interview typed up and in the system and checked on a couple more people to interview.

For the rest of that afternoon she made phone calls to get the contact information of the men from Macklin's unit who were overseas so she could back up his statement. She'd have to arrange to make those calls through formal channels. Depending on where the men were, what they were doing, confirming Mac's story with them could take a few days, if not longer. Unfortunately Marsha's murder wasn't Alex's only case. There'd been several break-ins at Silver Strand Housing, the military housing complex—three so far, all in the last week. In each case but one, a woman had been home alone. In each case the intruder had been chased off.

But what really bothered Alex was, in each case, the intruder got a little farther. The first case, he managed to get into the front door before the woman screamed. He'd bolted, and she had raced onto the front deck, screaming for the police, and he'd escaped into the shadows.

The police had done the usual interviews and filed reports, but they had not found anything helpful. There were no footprints outside, nor fingerprints on the door.

The second case had been similar, but he'd made it all the way through the kitchen and into living room, where the homeowner was coming down the stairs. In that case, she had a dog. The dog started barking, and the intruder bolted—getting away again.

In the third case, however, the intruder was caught upstairs. He tried to get downstairs, but the woman's boyfriend was there. Blows were exchanged, and the assailant managed to escape again.

Now Alex had three breaking-and-entering cases, and, in each one, the intruder had been more successful than the last. She highly doubted that getting caught by a boyfriend would stop him from trying again. Having successfully circumvented any problems, she knew he would feel proud of himself for getting that far. The trouble was, she didn't know what his end game was.

She was stuck, waiting for him to make his next move. She had officers out canvassing the community and warning the locals to beef up their security and to be extra vigilant.

In the meantime, she lacked any forensic evidence for when they did catch him. They had a visual from the boyfriend, but, outside of basic traits—young, tall, brown hair, and white—the boyfriend couldn't give them any further details.

The woman with the dog had added he was slim built and fit. But he'd worn a black hood, black gloves, black athletic jogging pants, and a black jacket zipped up in the front.

The intruder had gone into the houses around the same time, which was early evening. So he was casing the victims, either assuming they were away or assuming he was in the clear, and had gone in when it was still daylight but just as darkness settled.

That was an interesting time because a lot of people were still moving about then. She'd have expected him to go around midnight or the early hours of the morning. So either he did a crappy job in assuming nobody was home, or he did not care. His next attempt would tell her which way he was going.

If he continued as is, he not only was okay with the confrontation but he was possibly looking for more. And she knew that would bring an escalation of violence.

"Alex?"

She glanced up to see Lance, one of her senior police officers, standing in the doorway. She smiled. "Good morning."

He frowned. "I thought you'd be at the house."

Her heart sank. "What house?"

He crossed his arms over his chest. "We had another one last night."

She stood slowly. "I wasn't called."

He nodded. "I realize it's awkward with you just taking over, but you got to go hardnose to get the respect you deserve. And you gotta do it now. Don't give them any leeway, or it'll just get worse. You know you'll have to deal with that, right?"

She drummed her fingers on the desk for all of ten seconds and then gave a clipped nod. "I thought I had, but apparently I wasn't clear enough." She grabbed her bag. "You have the address?"

He handed her a small sheet of paper.

She glared at it, then him. "When did you find out?"

"Several hours ago," he admitted. "It never occurred to me to call you because I assumed you'd already been there."

She didn't say anything, just brushed past him. "Any report in yet on it?"

"It happened in the wee hours of the morning."

She spun to look at him and said, "When?"

"Initial reports say somewhere around three o'clock in the morning."

She nodded. "Who were the responding officers?"

"Wilson and Owen."

Under her breath, she murmured, "Interesting." She didn't have a beef with either officer. As far as she knew, they were on board with her arrival, but she'd jumped over several internal applications. However, the bosses had their reasons for bypassing those people in lieu of Alex. Still, that didn't make it any easier for those who had applied and were rejected. Now by her vehicle, she took a moment to look up the address. She recognized it to be in the same military complex area, just slightly to the left of the other houses, but still in the Silver Strand Housing complex, according to the map on her cell. Getting in her car, she drove to the house.

When she pulled up and saw an ambulance, her heart sank. She hadn't asked if there had been any fatalities. By going in during the middle of the night, the attacker had assumed either the house was empty, the inhabitants were asleep, or maybe he didn't give a damn but knew he would be in the power position. After the altercation at the last break-in, it was quite possible he didn't want to have another one.

When she arrived, one of the officers stood outside taking pictures. She stepped to his side.

He smiled. "There you are. We wondered when you were getting in."

"I wasn't called," she said, her voice hard.

His smile fell away. "Oh."

Everyone knew what that meant.

"Good enough." She walked in the front door, careful to stay clear of the men and their equipment. It didn't take her long to figure out this case had not only been an escalation but it had been bad.

Officer Sandra Mellon stood on the far side of the living room. She looked up and smiled. "There you are."

Alex made her way over and repeated, "Sorry. I wasn't called."

Sandra's eyebrows rose. "Really? I assumed you were busy." She glanced at her wrist. "But it's been hours. I should have called you myself." She glanced around and frowned. "Owen called me after Wilson had to leave."

Officer Owen caught sight of Alex and said, "I got the call at ten to four. Wilson came in right behind me. But he had to leave, so Sandra came in."

Alex stared at him in disbelief. "Five hours? Five hours later and nobody called me?" She didn't bother asking what they were still doing here at this point. An hour—two, max—was all that should have been required. Still it wasn't her problem. Thankfully.

The two officers looked at each other and then shrugged. "At least you're here now," Owen said. "I don't have a formal report written up, but I can give you the gist of it. The perp broke in about three this morning. The owner… the resident is Melanie Schaefer. She was sleeping alone. She heard a noise downstairs. She has no security in the place and no dog. She got up to investigate and was grabbed from behind. A fight ensued. She took a bit of a beating but not bad. She was knocked out. When she woke up, he was gone."

"Was she raped?"

Owen shook his head. "It doesn't look like it. We're still figuring that out."

"So she was fully dressed?"

Owen nodded. "Yes. She called the police soon after waking. We were here within fifteen minutes. But of course he was gone. She doesn't know how long she was unconscious. She's currently at the hospital being checked over. She did a quick examination of the house but didn't recognize anything missing."

"Right. I'll do a walk-through." She was still miffed but needed to focus.

Turning her attention to the house, she did a careful walk-through, checking how the intruder entered, which appeared to be via the backyard.

And then he went up the stairs to the bedroom. Nothing

seemed to have occurred while the owner was out cold. It was almost as if, when the intruder came in, the woman woke up right away, came downstairs, a fight ensued, and then he took off. But, if the woman was unconscious, he was free to do what he wanted, at least until she regained awareness. She had no camera system inside or out, no security on the doors or windows. Which was typical of all the houses in this area. The intruder picked the lock and just walked right in.

Alex stopped in the kitchen and stared at the backyard. A short fence surrounded the yard, but there was no back gate, no entrance or exit coming in from the other properties. Short of jumping the fence, that was certainly possible. She'd seen it happen. These cookie-cutter homes and cookie-cutter backyards were fenced to give each person a little bit of privacy and a little bit of space. But, if someone wanted to, it was easy to hop between houses.

He likely came in over the fence to hide the true direction he had traveled from.

She turned back to Owen. "Did she hear a vehicle?"

He shook his head. "The first sound she heard was him accidentally kicking a kitchen chair. She has no pets so knew she had an intruder."

"So she came downstairs instead of calling the police? Even though we've put it out everywhere on the news we have a rash of break-ins?"

Both Sandra and Owen nodded.

"Send me a report as soon as you've got something written up." She stepped outside the back door and surveyed the small porch. No clear footprints could be seen in the grass as it had been trampled by law enforcement.

She turned back to Owen. "Did anyone find tracks out

here before it was trampled?"

"There was bent grass but not necessarily footprints," he admitted. "We have photos."

"I want to see those images to confirm how he approached the property."

Owen brought out his phone. "I have a few here." He flicked through his cell phone and then held up one of the snapshots.

She studied the backyard. The trail came from the corner. "We need to check the other houses in this area."

"I can do that," Sandra said. "Several officers are going door to door, to see if they heard or saw anything. But no one has spoken with these adjacent owners."

"Let's get on that. This guy will hit again and soon." Alex turned to the light yellow-toned house. "But I don't know what he's after. I need to know that," she murmured. "He was interrupted here too. But then he knocked the woman unconscious and had the entire house available to pore over and steal what he wanted with no more interference… and yet he didn't."

Owen nodded slowly. "At least not that the owner's seen."

"The TV is too big for him to carry away for a long distance," Alex said. "The owner's purse is still here. Her wallet with money and cards are still inside," she mused. "Did she have any expensive jewelry?"

Owen shook his head. "No, she was quite puzzled when she realized he hadn't taken anything. But, as you look around the house, not a whole lot is a quick snatch-and-grab."

"How about a laptop?" Sandra asked. She turned to view the house. "I don't remember seeing a laptop."

Owen checked his notes. "Yes, it was still there."

"There has to be some reason why he was here," Alex said. "All these women were alone in their homes at the time of entry, except one. I'm concerned he's getting up the nerve to do so much more."

Sandra and Owen winced.

And Alex knew they understood what she meant. "Sometimes people need several trial runs to prepare for what it is they really want to do. But I would have thought an unconscious woman was a perfect opportunity. Maybe he thought he'd killed her?" she said a bit absentmindedly. "Maybe, when she collapsed, he thought he'd hurt her worse than he had, and he took off, scared?"

"That makes sense," Owen said. "There's got to be some reason he left."

Alex walked back inside. "Where did she wake up?"

Owen led her into the living room. "She woke up here, on the floor in front of the couch."

"And that's where she'd been fighting with him?" That made no sense. The coffee table was still perfectly straight in line with the couch. "They didn't have a fight in here. Nothing's shifted. Nothing's moved. Nothing's broken. The lamps are perfectly fine. The tables and everything are lined up as if nobody had even been in here."

The two officers stood aside and surveyed the living room. "No, you're right. That doesn't make any sense." Owen checked his notes. "I just have down that she was in the living room. But I don't know exactly where they were fighting."

"Or the intruder straightened the furniture. But why?" She turned to him. "Find out where they'd been fighting and ask if she straightened up the furniture herself. I especially want to know if she was laid on the couch itself because that would show a different level of compassion for an intruder."

Owen snapped his notebook shut. "I'll head to the hospital now and get a few more details."

"No, on second thought, I'll go to the hospital," Alex said. "You guys finish this up. Check with the neighbors and see if they heard or saw anything, particularly the three that are kitty-corner to this property. And make sure he didn't hit two houses last night. For all we know, this house was an afterthought with the real hit being somewhere else."

The others nodded and broke away. Alex returned to her car and stood for a long moment. She also had to deal with the problem of why she hadn't been called. She pulled out her phone and called dispatch.

After one ring, dispatch answered, "Good morning, Alex."

"Why wasn't I called when the break-in came in?" she asked.

"We have a call logged to your phone at the same time as Owen and Wilson were called. Are you saying you didn't receive one?"

"No, I didn't receive one."

"We have a call logged in though."

"And did you speak with somebody?"

"I didn't make the phone call. I just have it down that the call was made. Oh, it says *no answer*."

"Okay, that needs to be checked. Because I was never called," she said, her voice sharp. "I can't have that happening again." Alex realized she should be talking to the supervisor, not the woman on the line. "Don't worry about it," she said quickly. "I'll sort it out."

She ended her call and quickly checked her phone history. Although it was stupid, she was relieved to see she hadn't missed a call. That would be too embarrassing. She couldn't think of any time in her career that it had happened, but there was always a first.

Back in her car, she turned it around and headed toward the hospital. When she got there, she found the woman had already been released. Alex growled quietly and said, "Do you have forwarding contact information for her?"

The nurse pulled up a file and brought out a sheet of paper. "She said she would be staying with her friend Kimberly Lane. This is the address. This is the phone number."

"Did she have her cell phone with her?"

"Yes, her number is this one." The nurse took a moment to run through the file and then jotted down the injured woman's phone number.

"So she wasn't badly hurt then. Just how severe were her injuries?"

The nurse smiled. "She got off lucky. She was just shaken. She had a small head injury, which would account for her being unconscious. She also had a few bruises and was shaken up, that's all. She was in shock more than anything. But a friend came to collect her, and they went to have breakfast." The nurse gave her a name of a popular local hotspot.

Alex nodded. She took the piece of paper and stepped outside. When she dialed the woman's number, nobody picked up right away. She let it ring several more times and then decided she'd head to the restaurant herself. If the women were having breakfast, it would be a good time to catch both.

She walked into the restaurant, but there was no sign of

two single women at a table. Feeling like an idiot, she turned and headed toward the front door as she called the woman's cell phone again.

MACKLIN WALKED INTO the gym. If ever there was a day he needed to work out, this was it. He barely had the bar set up with weights when he heard a shout behind him. He turned and grinned when he saw a group of his teammates walking toward him.

"Hey! You could have at least told us you were alive and well," Ryder said.

Mason and the other guys all clustered around. Mason commented, "I wasn't sure they would let you out so fast."

Macklin shrugged. "She just asked me some questions." But he knew they didn't believe him.

They stayed and waited.

He sighed. "I'm trying to get used to the idea myself. But unfortunately it looks like somebody's setting me up."

And, typical of his friends, they all continued to wait, arms crossed over their chests. They wouldn't let him go until they had the details. Not because they had morbid curiosity but because they wanted to know how bad things really were.

He explained, finishing with, "And, to top it off, somebody wrote my name in blood at the crime scene, as if Marsha had named her killer."

Corey whistled. Ryder's face was almost comical with the anger twisting up his features.

It made Macklin feel good to know they were behind him all the way. "I think the detective believed me, though I certainly had no alibi for the night Marsha was murdered. I was home alone."

"We've been saying you should have another girlfriend," Corey said with a big grin.

Macklin shook his head. "Remember that adage about, if you keep doing the same thing repeatedly, how do you expect a different outcome? Well, I don't have any intention of repeating the Marsha scenario."

"You do know not all women are like Marsha?" Mason asked seriously. "Still, this is bad news. Did Alex Carson have any other evidence pointing to you? DNA evidence, forensic evidence? A name is one thing that could be just a bitchy woman making sure she stabbed you once again in the back as she died," he said. "I know that sounds terrible, but we've all met people who are so soured on life and so angry at everything that they'd do anything, including blaming the wrong man."

Ryder interrupted. "Any chance she committed suicide and made it look like murder?"

"Not unless she smashed her own head hard enough to knock her out and gave herself a skull fracture."

"So then could she even have been alert enough to write your name in blood?" Corey asked.

Right. Macklin's gaze went from one man to the other. He liked that about these guys. They didn't question his guilt. They already knew instinctively he was innocent. They were just figuring out the how and the who. Anybody could have made this look like Marsha had done it.

"I'm not exactly sure. Maybe I need to talk to Alex… Detective Carson, a little more about that," Mac said slowly. "I wonder how long Marsha had been in her place? How many people would have known she was there?"

"Don't get involved," Mason said quietly. "If you're too

interested, it'll look bad."

"But I don't have a choice," Macklin said. "I'm not sure anybody else in the department will fight to clear me. If I look too damn good for the job, you know they'll just charge me with it, so they can close the case and move on."

"Caitlyn said Alex isn't like that," Ryder said. "They haven't known each other all that long, but Caitlyn says Alex seems to be fairly straight up."

"But we've seen lots of people who are on the up-and-up. But, when the pressure is on to close a case, they must do what they must do. Not necessarily in the best interests of anybody else around."

"What do you think is going on?" Mason asked.

Macklin looked at him. "I think Marsha pissed off the wrong person."

"But apparently you pissed them off too," Ryder said quietly. "There was no need to write your name in blood, except to point the finger at you."

"Are we absolutely sure there's no way she could have written that?"

Macklin looked at Corey and shrugged. "Anything's possible. For all I know, she lay there bleeding out, wrote the name, and somebody came and clunked her on the head. Does it make any sense? No. Is it a working theory? No. I'm grasping at straws. There was something wrong with her. She was fixated on me. She was a stalker and just two steps away from a full-blown psychopath. But the bottom line is, she didn't commit suicide. And that means, whoever killed her used that moment to point the finger at me."

"So the next question that must be answered is, who hates you enough to do that?"

"I don't know." Macklin stared moodily out the windows. "Since I saw the crime scene photos, I've been wondering the same thing."

Corey's tone was hard. "We all know law enforcement officers who took the easy way, not the right way."

Macklin admitted it was a concern, but he had no way to judge Alex's performance based on his interview. He shrugged. "It's too early to tell."

"The problem is, I think they are also short-staffed and overworked."

Macklin got a short bark from Mason. "Isn't it always that way? There's a rash of break-ins and not enough law enforcement. It's not good news."

Macklin glanced at him. "I haven't heard any details."

"They have been warning everyone on the Silver Strand Housing complex. Four houses in about a five-block radius have been hit in the last week. One of them was early this morning."

"Just break-ins?"

"Whenever he's come across a resident, he's had an altercation but only with the intent of escaping. We have an awful lot of hotshots and hotheads here. So that could account for the temperament on both sides of the law."

"So high potential for the suspect to have been military personnel as well."

"Certainly the odds are there. It doesn't mean it's a fact though. We have an awful lot of supporting staff here as well. And a lot of service people who are not military."

"Any connection to Marsha?" Corey asked thoughtfully. "She was living alone as well. Didn't she live in that area?"

Macklin pondered that. "A couple blocks away from the housing complex."

"But definitely close enough to be possible. They may

have to widen that grid soon."

"But how does that make any sense? It was my name written in blood. It's not exactly a common name and not exactly one to be mistaken for somebody else's."

"It could easily be that the break-ins were a cover-up," Ryder said. "Completely distracting the investigation away from the murder."

"The problem is, it's all a guesstimate now. We don't know anything. And unfortunately I don't think the police do either."

"Do we know any of the people who have been targeted?"

Corey walked a few steps away and brought up his phone. "Ryder, what about Caitlyn talking to Alex?"

"I don't think they're that close of friends. And, if Alex is any decent law enforcement officer, she won't talk out of turn."

"The news will have updates on where the homes were. We can always take a drive through the area and see if we see anybody we know there. I don't believe I know any of the people targeted."

"That's a very valid word," Mason said. "*Targeted.* Just like you were."

Macklin looked at him strangely. "You're thinking there's a link between Marsha and these houses that were broken into?"

"Or there's a link between you and past men of these other women. All single women. Likely all with relationships in their history. What's the chance someone in that history is connected to you?"

"*Huh.*" Macklin shook his head. "I hadn't thought of that. The trouble with that theory is, I've lived here for a lot of years. We've been working here for many more. My life will have intersected with these women who obviously have ties with the military, given they live in military housing."

"Exactly. And the men they were associated with. So the question is whether that association is something somebody might hold against you."

"I've made a ton of enemies, but I would have said they were all overseas. No terrorists should know my name, but we've been on a lot of missions and stepped into some government coups." He shook his head again. "It's kind of hard to believe it would be somebody close to home. If you'd asked me even last week who hated me, the only person I could have said was Marsha herself."

"And, for all you know, this is still her doing," Corey said quietly. "It's never quite so straightforward. And, when we're dealing with somebody like Marsha, it's even less so. First off, let's find out more about her psychological problems, if she had any suicide attempts, anything that could possibly lead to the idea she may have hired her own murder, a suicide made to look like you did it."

Silence.

Macklin looked at Corey with respect. "That's a hell of a theory. It fits more in a horror novel than in my life, but it is a theory."

Corey grinned. "I told you that I like writing fiction on the side, right?"

Everybody laughed.

Mason smacked the weight bar in Macklin's hand. "Are you just going to stand around and talk, or were you planning to get some work done here?"

At that, the serious conversation dissolved, and joking took over. The men went through their workouts, helping each other, pushing each other, working against and for each other, until they all sat dripping in sweat and exhausted. But Macklin's grin was bright. Fierce.

"The only good thing about doing a workout like this is it revives that sense of fighting. That sense of 'I won't let this beat me.'"

Mason chuckled. "In that case, it did its job. Not to mention you're getting stronger, faster …"

"Uglier," Corey interjected.

"Than ever," Mason finished triumphantly.

The men headed off to the showers. But for all the levity and the fact that he did feel much better, Macklin knew it wasn't over. This was just the beginning.

CHAPTER 3

ALEX HEARD THE cell phone ring in her ear. She'd called again in case she'd misdialed. Then she heard it ringing in the large dining area, coming from the far side of the room. She walked over and saw four women sitting at one of the tables. She double-checked the faces and brought up the woman's picture on her cell phone. She was at the right place. She stopped at the table, introduced herself, and asked to speak with Melanie Schaefer for a few minutes.

Melanie swallowed and said, "Can this wait until after breakfast?"

Alex considered the issue. "How about in half an hour?" she compromised. "Make it forty-five minutes, if you want to meet me at the station."

With the woman's assurance she'd be there in forty-five minutes, Alex turned to the front counter, ordered a coffee to go, and stepped outside. She studied this corner of town. She'd felt like a stranger for a long time, but Coronado was settling into her soul. The city was like any other large city, with the exception of this one being full of servicemen and women. Still, the people here had motivations and reactions, the same as anyone else.

Wherever there were people, there was trouble, and that was her specialty.

She got back in her vehicle with her coffee and slowly

drove past the other three houses that had been broken into. She stopped at each, took pictures of the front with her cell phone so she could compare them. Then she took her time driving back to her office.

Instead of heading to her own cubbyhole, she walked around the building to dispatch and headed for the boss's office.

Somebody else was in his office, but she didn't wait. She knocked and opened the door, stepping in. Barry looked up and glared at her. She glared right back. He made a motion to his visitor and said, "Come up later, and we'll go over this then."

The woman got up, smiled at Alex, and left quickly. Alex stormed in, sat down on the vacated chair, and said, "Why the hell wasn't I called?"

Barry pounded the desk in front of him. "I don't know what you're talking about."

"That's because your people don't do their jobs," she said smoothly. "If I get missed on a call-out again, it'll go down on paper."

"Don't threaten me," Barry roared. "I already talked to them. You should have been called."

She pulled out her cell phone, opened it up to the calls from that day, and tossed it in front of him. "I didn't get called. The fourth break-in in a week, and I didn't get called."

He frowned, tapped his desk, and said, "That's not good."

She raised an eyebrow. "You think?" She grabbed her cell phone and walked out without another word.

She didn't know what was going on, but the locals sure didn't like the fact she'd taken over this job. And of course they expected those already here to get promoted first. But that hadn't happened, and they all needed to deal with it. She admitted that her predecessor had been on the job for ten years and had been the kind to walk around and hand out chocolates and flowers to everybody.

That wasn't her style, but she didn't expect to be stabbed in the back over it. To not be kept informed when crimes occurred was inexcusable. She kept hoping they could work it out without bringing all the brass down on top of everybody. Because, in that case, when heads rolled, they would roll long and far. She didn't want to cost anybody their job, but no doubt the person deliberately keeping her out of the loop deserved it.

As she pondered that, she wondered if it was possible the person doing so was protecting whoever was responsible for the break-ins. It was a huge leap in her own mind as she couldn't imagine anybody being that obvious. But it didn't mean it wasn't possible.

She stopped in the outer office and looked around. That thought wouldn't leave her alone. She strode back into Barry's office, stepped inside, and said, "I want the names of everybody working from midnight to eight this morning."

He shook his head. "You don't need that."

"If one of your staff is covering up for whoever is doing these break-ins, I do need that. And I'll make it official if I have to."

His glare turned stern. "You can't be thinking somebody else is involved?"

"What else am I supposed to believe when I'm deliberately kept out of something like that? I want those names, and I want them on my desk by this afternoon."

She turned and this time strode straight out of the outer

office. She hadn't closed the door between her and Barry, so she knew some people would have overheard the conversation.

Offices like this thrived on gossip, and that was okay. She'd bust those asses down a grade or two. It just wasn't acceptable, and she was still fuming when she got back to her office. She took the lid off her take-out coffee, poured it into her mug, and sat down.

There had to be some way to track this asshole.

Traffic cams were set up on the main streets, but so far there had been no indication this person was driving a vehicle. Chances were good he was on foot, and that made him a local. He'd picked that neighborhood for a reason. Quite possibly it was his own stomping ground.

In that case, she wanted to know exactly who lived in every one of those houses, and that involved a lot of canvassing. She needed to narrow it down so she wasn't wasting man-hours, her own included.

As she sat here making notes, her phone rang. She lifted the desk phone to find out Melanie sat in the lobby waiting for her. Alex got up, walked through to the main entrance, motioned for Melanie to join her, and led the way back. After they were both seated, Alex said, "I'm sorry to make you go through this again, but I need to know exactly what happened."

Melanie was anything but cooperative. "Why don't you just ask your other officers?"

"Because I want to hear from you personally," Alex answered smoothly, her gaze narrowing as it settled on the young woman. "So, from the beginning please." She kept her voice strict and stern, giving Melanie no leeway to not comply.

As if realizing that, Melanie slowly spoke. "There's not much to say. I was sleeping soundly. I woke up when I heard a noise downstairs. I went down and found the intruder. I screamed at him, told him to get out of my house. He turned around and whacked me one. I fought. My head hit something, and I fell. When I woke up, he was gone. I called the police for assistance, and it was a damn long time before they got there."

"How long was it exactly?" She had her pen over a sheet of paper, taking notes. When the woman said fifteen minutes, Alex looked up at her.

"I'd have been dead if the guy hadn't been gone already," Melanie snapped.

"You don't know where the officers were at that time, who they were already helping. Just because officers are on duty doesn't mean they aren't already busy," Alex said shortly.

Melanie stood. "Can I go now?"

"No, I have a few more questions." And she proceeded to work through the list of questions she had in front of her.

Melanie remained standing through them all.

"Did you hear a vehicle at any time, arriving or leaving?"

Melanie shook her head. "No, I didn't hear a vehicle at all."

"When you heard the first noise, was it coming from the back of the house or from the front of the house?"

"I have no idea. It came from underneath me."

"Is your bedroom in the front of the house or the back of the house?"

"My bedroom is in the front of the house. So, are you asking if he came in through the front door or the back door?"

"Partially …" Alex waited for Melanie to answer.

Melanie thought about it. "I assumed he came in the kitchen door because, if it had been the front, somebody could have seen him." She shrugged. "I had both doors locked, so it doesn't really matter."

"It matters if somebody else might have seen him."

"Well, if they did, I doubt they'd say anything."

"Had you heard the media coverage warning everybody in your area to be careful, to watch out for an intruder?"

"Sure, I heard about it, but I didn't think it applied to me. Why would he come after me?"

"That's the next question I was going to ask," she said. Melanie was looking a whole lot less belligerent now. "I wonder why he targeted you."

Melanie shrugged. "I figured because I was a female at home alone. But that would mean he knew that. Which means he either has been watching my house or following me." At that, the look on her face was stricken as if she hadn't really understood just how personal this attack could have been.

"Do you have valuable items in your house?"

Melanie shook her head. "No. The most expensive thing I have is the TV, but it's wall-mounted, and it is still there."

"It's probably too heavy for him to have moved on his own."

Melanie gave a short, hard laugh. "Well, that's one good thing about being extravagant. I always wanted a large TV. But it never occurred to me it would be too big to steal."

"I presume you only saw one man?"

Melanie nodded. "Yes, but that doesn't mean there weren't more."

"Is there anything you can tell me about him?"

"He was wearing a black mask, dressed all in black, and I never heard him say anything."

"So, you didn't hear his voice, couldn't recognize his face?"

"No. But he had a slight build. He wasn't one of those big, solid, chunky guys, and he certainly wasn't fat. He was very lean, tall and wiry-framed."

"Good to know." Alex continued to jot down notes as she kept questioning Melanie. Finally, when she figured she had everything Melanie could offer, she asked, "What are your plans now?"

"I'll stay with a friend overnight. My sister is flying in," she said. "But she won't be here until tomorrow." After an uneasy silence, Melanie asked, "Do you think he'll come back?"

Alex looked up at her. "He hasn't returned to the others yet. However, that doesn't mean he won't." She watched as Melanie deflated like a balloon in front of her.

"I really hope he doesn't come," Melanie said fervently. "It was bad enough the first time around. I can't imagine a second time."

"I hope he doesn't too. The problem is, now he knows the inside of your house. He knows what you have for security, or rather that you don't have any security. He knows you live alone. All things that he assumed before, but now he knows for sure."

"What did he want?" Melanie cried out. "I don't have anything worth stealing."

Alex tossed down her pen, leaned back in her chair, and studied the small woman. "And that's my concern too. In each of the houses he entered, he didn't take anything."

Her face blanched. "Do you think he meant to rape

me?"

"It's a possibility. The question then is, why he didn't while you were unconscious."

Melanie's hand went to her throat. "I screamed. I was screaming as loud as I could just before he knocked me out."

"And that's probably what saved you," Alex said gently. "If you screamed loud enough, then he'd be afraid somebody else would raise the alarm, and the police would come. If you hadn't done that, he might have considered there would be enough time to do what he wanted."

In her head, that reassured her about his motivation for not having touched the woman while she was out cold. There was nothing like a good set of lungs to warn the neighbors.

"When your sister gets in tomorrow, feel free to go back to your home. You might want to invest in a security system."

"I never bothered before because everybody told me it was too easy to bypass them."

"That's quite true. It is easy to do. But, if you get one, you have somebody at the end of a phone. As soon as the alarms are cut or set off, they will contact you to make sure everything is okay. And you can also have a panic button linked directly to them. There are all kinds of options. What you don't want to do is treat this as a one-off that never happens again."

Melanie shook her head. "No," she said. "That's not going to happen. I never want to experience this again. I just have to find the best way to do that."

Alex stood. "Thank you for coming in."

Melanie smiled. "I really didn't want to talk about it over breakfast, and I didn't want to have to go through it with all the women there beside me. They are friends, but I knew it would just make it worse. It's bad enough to know others see you differently. But when they hear all the details, well …"

"That's an interesting way to look at it. Most people would tell their friends so they would have their support and understanding."

Melanie shrugged. "I guess most aren't that good of friends." She turned and walked off.

Alex watched Melanie head outside into the sunshine and get into her vehicle. She made a very good point. We have friends, and then we have friends. She herself would only tell her best friends. The others, she wouldn't want them to know. There'd be too many questions, and Melanie was right; they'd look at her differently. But, in this case, nothing had happened. She'd had an intruder; she fought him off, and the intruder ran away, scared. The end.

At least Alex hoped so.

She headed back to her desk. No matter how many assholes there were in the world and how many they caught, the number of files on her desk grew.

MACKLIN HAD SEARCHED the internet, looking for any insight into Marsha's last years. There were a couple of mentions of a Marsha with different last names and variations on the spelling of her first name but no exact hits. When they'd spent time together, she'd enjoyed coffee shops and walking on the beach, but he didn't really know much more about her.

And that made it difficult to figure out what she'd been doing. She used to work as an office clerk, he thought, but whether she had until her death, he wasn't sure. Yet that little bit of information made no difference to the damn case.

Just because bits and pieces came up from the depths of his memories didn't mean anything at this point.

His phone rang. He picked it up and grinned. "Hey, Caitlyn. How are you doing?"

"I'm doing fine, but it's you I'm worried about. How did the meeting go with Alex? I'm sorry that I couldn't wait until you were done, but I had to go into work."

"Not a problem. She just asked a few questions about Marsha, where I'd been the night she was killed. What kind of relationship we had. You know—things like that."

"She's a good person, and she doesn't know you like I do."

Macklin chuckled. "She wasn't mean to me. She was professional. I answered her questions like I would for any other officer."

"Good. She'll get to the bottom of this. I know she will."

That was his cheerleader best friend. She always tried to believe the best in everyone.

"I know she will," he said calmly. "Don't worry about me. I didn't do anything. And the evidence will show that."

"I know it will," she muttered. "But it's frustrating."

"These things take time so not to worry." They spoke for several more minutes; then she had to run to meet Ryder.

Mac smiled as he put away his phone. Caitlyn and Ryder were good together. He wondered if Alex had someone in her life.

CHAPTER 4

ALEX SPENT THE rest of the day tracking down known associates, neighbors, going through videos, searching through traffic cams. The break-ins were not her only cases; there was still Marsha's murder. Not that that was a secondary case, but it was more confusing than anything.

They also had no damn leads and no forensic evidence on the murder. Macklin had no alibi for the night Marsha was killed, but neither did he have a motive. It didn't wash with Alex that, out of the blue, several years after their relationship had broken off, he'd decide to kill Marsha. Alex was waiting for the coroner to tell her if it was possible Marsha did the writing in blood herself.

Alex was also looking for forensics to see if they could have caught a fingerprint within the blood smears. It hadn't been considered at the time, and the opportunity was now most likely lost. But she had to ask anyway.

She got in her vehicle and drove to the hospital. She wanted to talk to the coroner himself, to see exactly what was possible with the injuries Marsha had sustained. Alex walked into his office, after giving a clear crisp rap on the door.

She introduced herself and sat down.

He looked up and smiled. "Nice way to get settled into your job, isn't it?" He stood and reached over to shake her hand.

"I don't know about a *great* introduction," she said with a laugh, "but it's definitely an interesting case."

"Oh, tell me more." He sat back down, crossed his hands on the desk, and waited for her to continue.

"Marsha has a long history of stalking one man. Several restraining orders had been served on her. Her behavior improved and deteriorated, improved and deteriorated."

At the first mention of the victim being a stalker, the coroner's eyebrows rose straight up. "Well, this is a twist on an old theme. Normally we have a male stalker killing the female victim. In this case we have a female stalker who ends up dead. And is the male victim the killer, do you think?"

She leaned forward, pulled her file out of her bag, and said, "That's the obvious question. Yet, at this point, I'm not sure it's the correct answer." She pulled out one of the crime scene photos, showing the blood. "The victim of the stalker has his name written in blood." She pointed it out on the photos. "He has no alibi for the time, and he also had no contact with the victim for the last six months, and only then because he saw her and left the establishment to avoid her. He's the one who took out the restraining orders. Not to mention there'd been no actual contact for more than two years. Why would he kill her now? At this moment, the motivation is beyond thin."

"And yet the dying words of a dead woman speak far louder," the coroner murmured, staring at the crime scene photo.

"Or is it just what we're expected to think?"

The coroner's eyes sharpened with interest. "What is it you think happened?"

"That's why I'm here. Given her injuries, was she even capable of writing that name in blood? Or is it possible the killer did it to throw the guilt onto her long, well-established fixation?"

He leaned back, his fingers drumming on the top of the desk, and smiled. "That's an interesting theory."

He turned to a stack of files on his desk, picked up a couple, checked the names, returned them to the stack, and pulled out another one below. "You're correct in the sense her injuries were extensive. The initial blow was on the top of her head—which was a direct downward blow, as if she were sitting on a chair or couch at the time. The weapon could potentially be a hammer or something of equal size and force. It broke the skull and pretty well rendered her unconscious from that moment on."

"The throat slitting was after that?"

He nodded.

"So then the victim couldn't have written the name in blood." She sat back, wondering at the relief that flowed through her. "That's good to know."

He picked up the photo and looked at it. "The hammer did crack the skull and penetrated into the brain matter, so it's unlikely."

"Is it possible she was still conscious afterward or she woke up later?"

He shrugged. "I've seen cases where it was certainly *possible*." He stressed the last word. "It's not probable though." He tapped the photo. "Her hand is lying right in the blood, as if she wrote those words."

"Of course. But then that's just one simple movement, isn't it? The killer only had to write the name, place her arm in the appropriate position, turn around, and walk away."

He frowned. "I see what you mean. And it certainly would have been easy enough to do. It's too bad we can't get fingerprints off those bloody marks.”

"I wondered about that, and I had to call forensics on it. Although the letters were clear enough to read—maybe too clear for a dying woman to form. She'd been dead, I would say, at least two hours before the Coronado PD got there. Possibly longer." She looked over at him inquiringly. "Do you have a time of death for me?”

"It would have been in the wee hours of the morning. My estimate is between two and four a.m." He was looking through the papers in the file. "We're still waiting on the tox screens to come back. The cause of death was blood loss from the slashed throat. However, what would have rendered her incapable of fighting back, leaving her an easy victim at that point, was the blow to the top of the skull.”

"So, you're saying it's quite possible she didn't write that name.”

"Yes," he admitted. "In fact, given that blow, I would say it's most likely that the killer wrote that name. And that changes your investigation entirely, doesn't it?”

Feeling happier, and yet she had no justification for it, she stood with a small grin.

"You're happy about that?" he asked shrewdly.

"I had no reason to pin anything on him. Just because a man was alone at the time that somebody he used to know was killed shouldn't be motive enough for charging him. I need forensic proof, and none was found at the scene.”

"Just the name in blood, huh?”

"Yes. But I can think of a lot of reasons why somebody might do that. And first and foremost is to throw suspicion onto someone else. In this case this person was an easy victim because of his history with Marsha.”

"Glad I could help. I'll let you know when I get the tox

screens back."

"Thanks for taking the time to talk with me." She walked out, her mind buzzing.

She needed to shift this investigation in a new direction. The trouble was, she had no other direction to go. She needed to talk to Macklin.

She pulled out her phone, called him, and said, "I need to ask you more questions. You want to come down to my office, or you want to meet somewhere?"

"Meet somewhere. I'm just finishing up at the gym and was about to head home. How about coffee?"

She gave a half dance step of joy, grateful she was alone, and looked around to make sure she really was.

"Sure," she said in a deliberately neutral voice. "Let's go to the coffee shop beside the gym. I'm only about five minutes away."

"I'll go in and grab us a table then."

He hung up, and she stared down at the phone. She was way too happy to be meeting somebody she needed to question. Still, this was good. If he was in an amiable mood, he might be more open to giving her information that would lead her in the right direction. Because only one person would know who hated him enough to pin a murder rap on him, and that was Macklin himself.

At the coffee shop, she stood in the open doorway. It was the same coffee shop where she had asked him to leave with her. The noise in the room muted. She hated that about her job. It was never considered a good thing to have the police walk in. As she walked over to Macklin, she could feel dozens of pairs of eyes watching her. As she sat down, she gave a wide grin. "That will get them all gossiping."

He gave her a startled look and then chuckled.

She liked that about him. He had a sense of humor even amid this very difficult time. But then, if he was innocent, there was no reason for him not to be happy. Only the guilty had something to hide.

Just then the waitress walked over. Macklin ordered coffee for two. And nothing else. When the waitress asked Alex if she wanted something to eat, Alex shook her head. "No, I'm fine. Thanks."

Once the waitress left, Macklin turned to look at her. "What kind of questions do you need answered?"

"If you didn't kill Marsha …"

"I didn't."

She nodded. "If you didn't," she repeated, "then somebody is throwing the investigation in your direction. So the question really is, who do you know who would do this?"

He sat back, his huge arms and shoulders making the chair childlike in comparison. "I've been thinking about nothing else. I just haven't come up with anybody who would hate me so much."

"A man like you must have enemies."

Macklin pinned her with a stare, all humor gone. "A man like me?"

She realized how much she had insulted him. "I don't mean that in any negative way. But you do a lot of dangerous work, difficult missions. And you're obviously a ladies' man. It's possible you've pissed off a husband, an ex-boyfriend, some of Marsha's friends?"

"No, I'm not a ladies' man. I *was* a ladies' man, but Marsha was a huge wakeup call. I don't go in that direction anymore, thank you." His tone, although quiet and level, was a rebuke. "I already told you all this."

And she didn't want to feel ashamed of asking the questions she needed to, but she had made a judgment call, and that was unfair. She nodded. "Any other people who might have done this to you?"

"I have no idea. There's no reason to have singled me out versus anybody else in my unit. I'm not a paid killer who picks off well-known people, like a mercenary or a money-for-hire assassin. I work as part of a unit of the military on highly classified missions. There was no reason to single me out."

"What about here on your home turf? Did you get a promotion that somebody else thought they should get? Do you know someone who didn't make it through BUD/S training and is holding a grudge against you?"

As he heard mention of the BUD/S training, his eyebrows raised. He leaned forward and said, "I hadn't considered that." He turned to look out the window. "A lot of people didn't make it. Only three of us did." His fingers drummed the tabletop. "But I can't say I knew any of the others. I met them through the training program, and we weren't friends before I went in."

"I have to ask, were there any sexual indiscretions, any affairs with married women? Anything like that, that somebody maybe held a grudge for?"

He stared at her in bewilderment. "That's not who I am. Your comment about the BUD/S training would be closer, in that most of the men are incredibly competitive. And maybe not always thinking some of the tests were fair. It certainly wasn't an easy or a comfortable training, but those of us who survived and passed know we accomplished something tremendous. But of course those who didn't pass had failed something they had really hoped to achieve. But again there was no need to target me. If they were to target those who passed, then they would have to target the three of us."

"Who were the other two men?" She pulled a notebook from her jacket pocket, opened it to a clean page, and looked up at him.

"Jim Burgess and Bill Toronto."

She wrote down the names. "I'll check into them and see where they are now." She turned to look up at him. "Do you know if the men are stationed in Coronado right now?"

He frowned. "I thought Bill Toronto was, but I haven't seen him around in a couple years. As for Jim, I think he went back east."

"I'll find out."

The coffee arrived just then. She smiled and added a little bit of cream, thanked the waitress as she left and said to Macklin, "That's good. That's a start. What about other areas of your life? How about your current missions? Any problems with any of the other team members?"

He gave her a hard stare and said in a flat tone, "No, no, and no. It won't be one of my teammates. It won't be one of the other unit members either. We're a close-knit family here. And much of what you're asking, I can't speak about."

"Understood. So let's hope what you can give me is enough," she said, her voice cool. "If it's not, I will go through the proper authorities. I know you don't want to think about it, but I can't knock these people off the list until we discuss it. So, I agree, it's not *likely* to be any of your teammates, but getting your back up when I ask questions won't help you or me. What I need is their names on a list and then to put a line through them." As she watched, he backed down as if understanding her thought processes.

"You're still barking up the wrong tree."

"That's fine. I'm happy to climb back down again, but I

won't leave any stone unturned until I get to the bottom of this." She turned to a clean page. "Let's go through the men you've worked with."

"Have you got the rest of the morning?" he joked.

She gave him the stare that she used to intimidate all kinds of men. "Absolutely."

It didn't take quite all morning, but it was ninety minutes later before they got through every name he could remember.

She made detailed notes. He looked tired, annoyed, frustrated when she was done. Her tone was calm when she said, "Now, what about service people?"

He looked at her. "What are you talking about?"

"The pizza delivery man? The nurse at the dental clinic? The receptionist at the garage you take your vehicles to? All those kinds of people."

He just stared at her.

"Yes, I'm serious. Like I said, *every* person in your life."

He raised both hands in mock surrender. "I have no idea."

"Then that's your homework. I want you to go home and think about where you've been, what you've been doing, and who might have served you, who might have seen you with Marsha, who might have known she was a difficulty in your life."

"Then go look at the court records. I've had two restraining orders. That involved an awful lot of clerks, lawyers, judges. Plus it's public record. Any nosy body could find it online if they were so inclined. There are so many people who could know about that." He leaned forward on his arms. "Are you going through her life as intently as you're going through mine?"

"Yes, I am, but I don't have her to ask any more questions of."

He glanced at her. "Look. I'll think about it. Can I email you the list?"

She wrote down her email address, ripped it off the bottom of her notepad, and handed it to him. "You do that." She stood, pulling money from her pocket to pay for the coffee.

He held up a hand. "I'll get the coffee," he said, his tone implacable.

She glanced at him for a moment and studied the look on his face. "Thanks. Maybe next time it won't be such a chore."

Before he could get an answer out, she turned and walked out. He was right in one sense—she had to focus on Marsha, but she knew Macklin could be called away on a mission at any time. And that meant catching him while she could. Unfortunately for Marsha, she wasn't going anywhere.

MACKLIN SAT AT the table. He couldn't believe how drained he was. Her questions had been in-depth, intelligent, and she had been extremely meticulous in working his way through every man in his unit, not only the current unit, but every one previous. She'd done her homework before meeting with him. He appreciated that, but, at the same time, having his life turned upside down like this was not fun. And once again, Marsha had to be laughing her fool head off, wherever she was.

He didn't know what made a person like her become what she'd been, but he wished there was an early warning system. It had completely ruined his view on relationships. Yet, he was petrified of having the next five years of his life ruined by somebody else. Even though Marsha was dead, she was still causing him trouble. He stared out the window, watching as Alex got in a vehicle and drove away.

She was very intense, very focused. He'd seen that look in several other women. Mason's partner, Tesla, for one, and Bristol, Devlin's partner. They had that same inclination to shut out the rest of the world, focusing on whatever they were working on. Tesla was an IT specialist; Bristol, an inventor of all things cool and astonishing. He'd been lucky enough to meet her a couple times. And he realized that was who Alex reminded him of. She was tall, unlike Bristol, but Alex had that same drive, that same focus in her eyes, that same sense that she would be relentless in getting to the bottom of this. He appreciated that because he still didn't want to see Marsha's killer go unpunished.

And he really needed Alex to turn that intense attention of hers away from him. He hadn't done anything wrong, and he didn't want to get caught in the crossfire any more than he had to.

The waitress walked back over with the coffeepot and refilled his cup. "You okay?" she asked in concern.

Macklin drummed up a smile. "Yeah. Just not one of my better mornings."

The waitress chuckled. "Welcome to my world." She turned and walked back to the front reception area.

He thought about that, realizing how many people had crappy lives, crappy jobs, crappy days, and how many of those he might have intersected with off and on over the last couple of years in particular.

He thought of the few places he'd been with Marsha, both good and bad. And then realized Alex was right. There could be any number of people who maybe not so much hated him but saw him as an easy scapegoat. He searched through his pockets for a piece of paper. Not finding any, he snatched a clean napkin and jotted down the places where he and Marsha had gone.

There were a couple restaurants and a coffee shop where she'd thrown fits. If anybody had seen Marsha blow up, it would be easy to believe he'd been such an asshole that he had turned around and killed her. The problem with any of this was the fact that all those incidences were years ago. So somebody had to have been hanging on to that occasion in their mind and had to have known who he was.

His phone rang just as he finished adding in one more notation to his list. He pulled out his cell and smiled when he saw Corey's name. "What's up?"

"I was just thinking we should do some investigating on our own," he said. "This is too big a deal to leave to the police to figure out."

"I hear you. I just spent all morning being grilled about my associations by Alex," Macklin said. "Honestly I wouldn't have a clue even where to look."

"I do. The first house that was broken into. You know who lived in it last?"

"You mean before the woman who lives there now?"

"Yeah. It was Bill, the guy you graduated BUD/S with. He lived there for two years. He moved out about five weeks ago."

Macklin stared at his phone and shot back, "No shit?"

"You interested now?" Corey laughed. "I will meet you back at your place, one hour." And he hung up.

Macklin could do nothing but stare at the list on his napkin and think about the massive list Alex had taken away with her. Maybe she was on to something after all.

CHAPTER 5

WHEN ALEX MADE it home that night, she had to admit her nerves were frazzled around the edges. She'd been in meetings all afternoon. Her boss had pushed to know what progress she'd made. It was a little hard to choke out *zero progress* in front of a group of Coronado HP officers *and* Barry. But, when she had explained what they had so far, nobody had any answers as to how to move forward. Looking at the houses, looking at the people, looking at the relationships in each person's history took time.

She spent another hour plus on the phone talking to each of the tenants, asking questions about relationships and how long they lived there, where they'd lived before, and if they knew Macklin. Everybody had said they didn't know who Macklin was, and, as she filled up a whiteboard full of charts, she realized just how little was in common among any of them. It made no sense. She stared at the board for a long time, until Lance walked over and said, "Time to call it quits, boss. Go home, and think about it."

She shot him a shuttered look. "The trouble is, while we're sitting here figuring it out, he's already scoping out the next house."

Lance entered her office. "That's likely very true. But we don't have any way we can catch him right now."

"Did you set up extra patrol cars around that area for the

night?"

He nodded. "We have indeed. It's not just one block though. Silver Strand's huge. And, if he spots the black-and-whites going by, he'll widen his hunting ground."

"I know. It's a bitch." She tossed down her pencil, snatched her jacket and purse. "Hopefully we'll be lucky enough to sleep through the night. I'll see you in the morning."

He gave her a wave as she walked out the door. Only as she stood outside and looked at how low the sun was did she realize it was well past quitting time. The last thing she wanted to do was go out to eat, but she had very little food left at the house. It was a dilemma. Go grocery shopping and pick up something, or go out to eat. Or she could follow her usual pattern: go home and not bother eating much. But sandwiches were her catchall.

She needed to sleep tonight and should at least eat something to keep up her energy.

She pulled into the grocery store, did a quick trip around the aisles, picked up stuff for sandwiches and a salad. When she got home, she made herself a sub sandwich and a salad to go with it. Feeling smug about her food choices, she walked over to the table and sat down to eat.

Her mind still buzzed between the two separate cases. She hadn't found any link to connect the four break-ins to Macklin. That Marsha had lived alone and was close to the chosen area was a concern as her case resembled the other break-ins but differed on the rest of the details.

But none of the other victims had been killed. That was a massive difference. And they didn't even appear close enough in MO to be used as a cover-up. In her mind she couldn't see they were connected. At least not yet. Maybe if they got more facts, there would be more answers. But, for the moment, it was a wait-and-see game. When she finished washing the dishes, she had a quick shower, changed into her civilian clothes, and stood outside to take several deep breaths of fresh air. She stared in the direction where the four break-ins had occurred.

They were a couple miles away from her. She hadn't found any traffic cams that revealed anything of interest. But then this was a suburban area, residential. Cams were only on the main intersections. She was pretty sure the assailant was walking to his chosen targets. What she didn't know was if any of the neighbors had a surveillance camera and if he had parked his vehicle a block or two away.

She'd hoped to leave one of the unmarked cars parked with a camera set up on the street to see if any traffic came during the night.

But at the meeting earlier today, it had been vetoed. She'd be guessing where the intruder would be walking. Seeing strangers in the cameras wouldn't give her a clue as to whether they were guilty or not. She needed to continue to delve in, drill deeper into the intruder's life to see if this was a random choice or whether each of these people were targeted.

As she sat here, she picked up her phone and looked at the picture she'd taken. Each of the houses looked so similar. What made one appear a better bet than the other? How would this intruder have any idea who lived there or who didn't? And, if he was keeping a close eye on them, where could he be that he wasn't observed?

He could be someone out walking a dog, looking inno-cent, but at the same time she couldn't interview everybody out with a dog. And yet, it wasn't a bad way to find out if anybody had seen anything suspicious.

The police had spoken to several neighbors, and, so far, nobody had said anything helpful. It always amazed Alex how little people noticed anything in their neighborhood. She set aside her cell phone with the images for a moment to clear her head.

She reached for the bottle of wine she brought with her and the empty glass. As she poured the liquid, she winced at the bright red color. There'd been a lot of blood in Marsha's place. It would take Alex a long time to forget those images. Outside of the death of the woman, there didn't appear to be anything stolen. The TV was still there; her purse was still there. If something small and personal had been taken, it was hard to know what. Marsha didn't have any other friends who stepped forward to say they knew what was going on in her life.

The police had gone through Marsha's address book, but it had been damn empty except for one name. The name with multiple scratches and corrections was Macklin's. Marsha had written down every house he'd lived in since they'd met.

As she sipped her wine, Alex wondered what it would be like to be the object of such a fixated person. It'd be damn scary—that sense of being watched, knowing something was wrong and somebody really ill was targeting you. He had gone the legal route and hadn't had much luck.

But then it wouldn't matter if the victim was male or female, stalkers were hard to stop in the best of times. Anybody who was dedicated enough could find a way to get to somebody. Alex pondered that concept. Had Marsha herself been a victim? Had somebody stalked her?

Alex quickly checked to see if Marsha had filed any restraining orders herself, but couldn't find any. Neither could she find any other restraining orders filed against her, except for Mackin's. She'd talked to Marsha's boss, but the conversation had been short and simple. Marsha worked as a clerk for a shredding company. She showed up on time and left on time. Other than that she kept to herself, and got along with her coworkers but wasn't unduly friendly.

The apartment block where Marsha lived was within walking distance of the Silver Strand Housing complex, and Alex had canvassed most of Marsha's neighbors, but nobody had seen or heard anything. Although Alex still had several more to contact. Nobody wanted to get involved until it was their own life involved. One of the women she'd talked to hadn't even known Marsha lived there.

When Alex had knocked, a woman opened the door nervously. Alex quickly reassured her that she was a police detective, and the Coronado PD was investigating the woman's neighbor's death. The woman still hadn't wanted to talk. She'd closed the door and snapped the locks closed. Fear did that. Murder hit a little too close to home.

Her phone rang beside her. She picked it up, looked at the display, and winced. "Hello, Mom," she said, her voice deliberately neutral. Give her mother an inch of emotion either way, and she pounced, looking for every dirty detail.

"How are you, Alex?"

"I'm fine."

"Stop saying you're fine. You're not fine. You've taken on too much. You should come home to the family. I'm sure you could get a nice job here."

"A nice job? Why? I wouldn't get to deal with thieves and murderers that way," she said, her tone a hint above mocking. If her mother thought something would bug her, she'd be all over it.

"You need a safe job. A safe place to live. Obviously the job you're doing isn't safe."

Alex gave a bark of laughter. "It should be safer here than anywhere. I'm surrounded by servicemen and women who go out and bleed for our country on a regular basis. We're all here to protect each other."

"And yet there you are, considering things like murders and break-ins," her mother scolded. "How good are the people there, really? They are just like everyone else."

"I know that," Alex said quietly. Unfortunately she knew it all too well. Every day she walked into work, she was faced with the fact some of these honorable men and women were much less honorable human beings.

"No way I'm walking away and letting the victims not get the full benefit of my investigative abilities. And I say, *I'm fine*, because, if I say anything else, you don't give me an option. You don't stop digging until you get all the details."

"Of course I do. You're my daughter."

"Being your daughter doesn't mean you have the right to know all the details of my life," Alex said with exasperation. "We've had this conversation before, many times."

Her mother chuckled. "I figure, if I work at you a bit at a time, like water on a stone, eventually you'll give up and let me into your life a little more."

Like that's ever going to happen. But she didn't let her mother know that. "Any boyfriends yet?" she asked her mother. "That always takes you out of my personal life."

"You have a personal life, do you?" her mother slid in smoothly.

"None I'm talking about, Mom. What about your personal life?"

"Well, I did go out for dinner last night with a lovely young man."

Alex winced. Her mother had this penchant for men a good ten to twenty years younger than she was. The last one had only been a few years older than Alex. That had been awkward. "Nice. Where did you go?"

"He took me to a lovely fish restaurant downtown. We had seafood on some special pasta dish. It was really quite lovely."

"And did you go home alone?" Alex asked in a humorous voice.

"I'll tell you if you tell me."

"I don't need the details, thanks."

"Chicken!" her mother said. "I wish there were questions to ask," she said in exasperation. "You can't stay alone forever, Alex."

"I can if I want to."

"It's not healthy. I get that Brad hurt you, but he wasn't a nice man. The two of you weren't meant to be together, and he proved it by sleeping with somebody else."

"You know loyalty and honor are qualities that are important to me. Why is it so hard to imagine I don't want to have a boyfriend who sleeps around?"

"The thing is, if he's still sleeping around, he's just a boy. Men grow up. They make a decision, and they stick with it."

Alex stared moodily out at the night slowly darkening around her. She took a sip of the red wine and thought about her mother's words. "I don't want a boyfriend anymore," she said. "But I might be interested in a man friend."

Her mother chuckled. "Whereas I am looking for boyfriends. I really don't want any kind of permanent relationship. And, if he sleeps around, that's fine by me. Because then I can sleep around too."

Alex didn't want to know so much about her mother's love life and tried to change the subject. "How's work going?"

"The same as always. You know how much I hate being in the office. But it's the busy season for us."

Her mother was a buyer for one of the large retail stores. But nothing as glamorous as clothing. It was paper supplies. And she spent a lot of her days contacting suppliers, looking for deals.

"But you know you love it. You get to wheel and deal and save the company lots of money."

"Maybe, but that doesn't mean I want to do it for the rest of my life."

Alex frowned. She'd heard her mother express distaste for her life before but not lately. "What would you like to do instead?"

"Retire and travel," her mother said promptly.

"So, do it."

"You know I can't. I can't afford to yet."

The phone call with her mother ended abruptly when her phone beeped, signaling another call coming in. "Mom, I've got to go." She quickly switched over to the other call and realized it was dispatch. "What's up?"

"There's been a second break-in at the first house, the one that went down four days ago. Two units are on their way."

"What's the address again?"

Dispatch rattled it off, confirming it indeed was the first house.

"I'm on my way."

Relieved to have been called, hoping that her problems were over from that department, she headed out. In the back of her mind she stewed on why that house? She highly doubted it was the same person who had already been there once. There was no need to go back again. But, if it was the same perp, it certainly made her wonder if he was looking for something specific. Something they hadn't considered yet.

What if he had some connection to these women, and/or their partners, and was looking for something specific? It was a troubling thought, considering four houses were already involved. But what if one of them had something he wanted? What if he was going through each house to make sure it wasn't there? And, if he hadn't found it on the first run-through, would he go back and check the houses again?

She grabbed her sweater, purse, and keys, and headed out the door. Dusk was just setting in. The light was that half-light. It was great for skulking through the shadows. But less so for seeing clearly. It took her ten minutes to get to the address. Two vehicles were already on the scene. She hopped out. "Who called it in?" she asked.

"The neighbors." Lance pointed to the house on the right. "These guys did."

"Nobody here?"

"No, the house was empty when we got here."

"I'll talk to the neighbors."

"Are you going into the house as well?"

She called over her shoulders, "Absolutely. I'll go through it with a fine-tooth comb now."

The neighbors stood on their front porch. Alex introduced herself, shook their hands, and asked, "Can you tell me exactly what you saw?"

She put her phone on Record, let them know what she

did, and said, "Now please tell me."

The man said, "I saw what appeared to be a young male, tall, slim, dressed all in black, approach the house from our side. I was doing dishes in the kitchen when I looked out and saw him come up against the side here. He turned to the side of the house, went around to the back, and I thought I saw him sit on the deck for a little bit. I went outside myself, banging lots of doors, hoping he would disappear. And he did. But he went inside the house."

She stared at him for a long moment. "How long was he inside the house?"

"I called as soon as he went in because I knew he didn't live there. That's Kathleen's house. And I know she hasn't been around since the break-in. She's been living with her mother in San Diego."

Alex nodded. She knew that too. "How did he act?"

"Assured and yet furtive. As in, he kept looking around, but he walked with a calm, straightforward walk," his wife added.

Alex turned to look at her. "You saw him as well?"

The wife nodded. "Yes, I did. He was dressed in all black. It was kind of creepy."

"Did he have a hood over his face?"

Both shook their heads.

Her interest piqued. She leaned forward slightly. "Did you get a look at his face?"

Both shook their heads again.

"Did you get a look at the color of his skin?"

This time they nodded. "He was white, but his complexion wasn't pure white. He might have been a mixed race. He might have just had a heavy San Diego tan," the husband said. "It was really hard to tell in this light."

Having made a comment about visibility in that light, she understood what he meant. "So he walked inside the house, by way of the back door, but first he sat on the deck for a moment, looked around, and then went inside?"

They both nodded.

"Did you see him leave?"

The husband said, "I went out front to see if he left that way while my wife stared out back."

"And did either of you see him?"

Both shook their heads.

She studied them carefully. "Any idea how he left?"

Again they both shook their heads. "Honestly I thought he was still inside the house. I figured when the cops came, you'd catch him. But you're saying he's not in there?"

"Apparently the officers have already done a sweep of the house, and he's not there. Correct." She turned and looked at the house in question. "I'm about to go over, but I wanted to hear what you had to say first." She thanked them and went down the porch steps.

She stopped at the sidewalk and looked in the direction the intruder had approached from. He'd just been walking down the sidewalk and then deliberately stepped up to this house and around the back. He might have assumed the house was empty or took a chance on the house being empty, so he could have just come in looking for anything he could pick up quickly. Burglars were opportunists. As soon as they knew a house was empty, they cased it out. And that could have been what this was. Being dressed in black was, in a way, just a smart outfit to be wearing if you were to break into a house. The fact that the news advertised they were looking for a man dressed in black added to the perception this could be a copycat.

She walked back to the house in question. "Nobody saw the man leave?"

Lance shook his head. "Not since we arrived. I did speak to the neighbors and understood, as far as they were concerned, he was still in there. But we did a sweep, and nobody's there."

"I'll go look myself." She walked up the sidewalk to the porch and stepped through the front door. One of the officers stood off to the side.

He nodded respectfully.

She asked in a low tone, "Have you been all through the house?"

"With the initial sweep, yes. But I haven't moved from here since."

She nodded and did a very careful walk-through of the main floor and then headed to the stairs. She passed a front closet, but both doors were open. She stepped inside, took a quick look, moving all the jackets aside, searching for any kind of a trapdoor, attic access, or anything else. But came up empty. She headed to the stairs and swiftly moved up.

At the second floor she stopped and listened. She couldn't hear anything. She moved into the spare bedroom, checked under the bed, inside the closet, checking for a trapdoor again, and then stepped out. As she walked past the hall closet, she stopped and looked at it. She pulled her weapon, opened the door, but found it empty. Yet oddly enough the shelving had collapsed or been placed on the floor instead of in their slots. As if somebody made space to stand. Using her cell phone, she shone the flashlight at the top of the closet to look. But again found no trapdoor or attic access.

She'd lived in enough places across the country to know

some locations had no attics, and some had no basements. She closed the door to the hall closet, did a search in the main bathroom, still finding nothing. She headed toward the last bedroom.

The master bedroom door was open. She assumed her men had already searched here. But she followed suit and checked the area as well. The master bedroom had double windows with a view over the front street. She opened the window and stuck her head out.

There was no place for an intruder to have gone but straight down. She walked to the rear of the master bedroom and realized this window wasn't latched. She slid it open to see a small roof over the top of the back porch. It would have been easy for him to have climbed out, stepped onto the rear porch roof, gone to the far side of the house, jumped down, and carried on without the next-door-neighbor's wife seeing him.

Satisfied that she understood how he left the house, she turned and walked back downstairs and spoke to Lance. "He probably left within minutes of the police sirens."

"I never thought to look at the small roof," he said. "Which direction do you think he would have gone?"

"The only way he would have left," she said, "is either through the backyard of either neighbor or around the front of the neighbors in such a way that the husband out in front didn't see him. So please confirm with him that he stayed out in front on the porch and didn't leave at all, and then I think we can safely assume the intruder headed in the opposite direction than he arrived."

"Do you want us to send out a search?"

"He'll be long gone, but we have to canvass the houses in this direction—see if anybody might have seen him leave, and then we need to check the houses on both sides of the street to see if anybody saw him arrive. What we're looking for, of course, is where he has been and where he's going." She turned, looked back inside, and said, "I'll see if there's a specific reason why the same guy might have come back. Otherwise, I think we're looking at somebody taking advantage of an empty house for easy pickings."

Lance agreed. "That's what I was thinking too. Even in this type of housing, with so many families, not everyone knows who is around all the time."

Back in the house, she went through each room again, looking to see if something specific would have brought the same intruder back. Yet that theory felt wrong. But, as she hadn't explored the concept that somebody had to be linked to the four people whose houses had been broken into, she couldn't let it go yet. The living room was bare of finishing touches. No shelving, no pictures on the walls. There was a TV stand that held electronics, but the TV itself was older. She took a quick glance behind it, behind the cabinet, and then moved into the kitchen.

Kitchens were always a pain. So many cupboards and items in the way. She didn't even know what she was looking for. She suspected USB keys or something valuable, like jewelry. But she didn't dare keep her mind closed to the fact a lot of other items were valuable. Keeping to a systematic approach, she went through each of the kitchen cupboards and drawers.

At one point, she turned around to find Lance in the doorway. She shrugged. "I can't let go of the idea he might have come back for a specific reason."

She walked over to the broom closet, carefully went through the contents, shifting aside brooms and mops and cleansers on the shelves, rags and packages of dish towels sitting on the side. Again nothing looked suspicious to her.

With the downstairs fully looked over, she went upstairs, checking the stairs as she went. They were wooden, but she didn't feel any were hollow along the way. She rapped on the walls as she carried on up the stairs.

Lance called out from the bottom, "Are you really serious?"

"Can't mark it off my list until I've checked it out."

She knew they all studied her methods and thought she went way too far all the time. But when something niggled at the back of her head, she wouldn't let it go. She'd been wrong before, but she'd rather waste the time looking and not finding anything than not to look and miss something important. And, being new on her job, she felt like she couldn't afford to mess up. As if she had to prove herself. Not to herself but to everyone watching her performance.

She went through the second bedroom first. Not only was it smaller and easier, but it was the avenue he chose as his escape. The dresser in there was empty, and, when she moved it out to look underneath and behind it, she found nothing as well. She did the same treatment to the night table, also empty. The closet was empty, so it really was just a spare bedroom—nobody stayed in here. It was made up, ready in case she did have company though. Knowing she'd hate to have it done to her own bed, but needing to know for sure, Alex quickly stripped the bed, checked between the mattresses and under the frame. Nothing. She stacked up all the bedding on top and walked out.

At the hall closet she stopped and stared again. "Why would you take all the shelving off your closet walls and stack the shelves on the floor like this?" she asked Lance.

He stepped up behind her. "No idea."

But she also got the feeling he didn't give a damn either. She took a photo of it and closed the door.

Stepping into the bathroom, she found a few toiletries, shampoos along the bathtub, but nothing major, nothing hidden, nothing secret. She did lift the toilet tank lid to make sure. Nothing to find there.

The master bedroom was a different story. It was stuffed. She carefully made her way through the room. She turned to find Lance just standing in the doorway again. "Either help or go do something useful," she said in exasperation.

He raised both hands, palms up. "What is it you want me to do? I don't even know what I'm looking for."

"Anything suspicious, anything that somebody would want to hurt somebody over. Look for a safe. Look for envelopes full of dirty photos. Look for blackmail material. Look for signs of a secret lover. I don't know," she cried out. "But, if this was the same guy, he had a reason to return here, and it had to be a hell of a reason to come back to a place he knows the police are now watching."

"But we aren't watching it specifically anymore," Lance argued. "It was broken into. The owner left. Finished. Amen."

"So you think it was just another guy casing the joint?"

"What else could it be? It makes no sense for the burglar to come back."

"Unless he came looking for something specific ... How many times have we seen the perpetrator return to the scene of the crime?"

"Fine," Lance muttered. He walked over to the bed. "Do you want me to strip it?"

"Yes, I want you to strip it."

She finished with the closet and headed to the dresser. She took out one drawer, placed it on the floor, carefully went through everything inside it, went to the next drawer, and the next drawer. When she was done, she found nothing there either. She picked up the first drawer and carefully tried to fit it back in again, but it wouldn't go. She reached underneath and froze. Putting it on the floor again, she carefully upended it to find an envelope taped to the bottom. "Well, well, well. What do we have here?"

Lance was at her side immediately. "What do you think that is?"

"No idea but I suggest we find out."

She ripped the envelope off the drawer bottom, opened it, and took out the contents. Inside were photographs. Lots and lots of photographs. The problem was, they were all of the same person. "These are all Marsha," Alex whispered.

"Marsha?"

"The woman who was murdered." She laid them out on the bed. "The stalker was being stalked."

MACKLIN COULDN'T SETTLE down. He rattled around in his small place, hating the feel of not knowing what to do. He understood the person who had lived in one of the targeted houses was also one of the guys who had graduated from BUD/S training with him. He didn't know if that was important, but at least it was a connection.

He just didn't know how and why it mattered. He tossed ideas back and forth as to whether he should contact Alex and let her know. He figured, if it was nothing, she'd knock it off her list damn fast. But she'd been emphatic about him making a list and giving it to her.

He hated to write anything further down and pondered the concept of giving her a quick call. Finally he snatched his phone, not wanting to look too closely at why he wanted to contact her personally. He could have just as easily sent her an email. But he had her card, and he dialed her number. When she answered, he said, "It's me."

"Hi, me," she said in a dry tone. "My display did say it was you. Macklin, what's up?"

"One of my buddies found out one of the houses in the four break-ins … kind of …" He stumbled to a stop, organizing his thoughts. "One of the guys who graduated from BUD/S with me used to live in the first house up until five weeks ago."

"So he finished the BUD/S training?" she asked in confusion.

"Yes. It's a connection, but I don't know how tenuous. I know it sounds stupid, but you seemed to want to know everything, so that's the only thing my team came up with."

"Interesting," she said quietly. "Do you happen to know a Kathleen Matron?"

"Not off the top of my head. Why?"

"Hers was the first property broken in to, where your guy once lived," Alex said. "We had a second incident at the same house tonight."

"Is she hurt?" Macklin asked in a sharp tone. He wondered when this nightmare would end.

"No, she wasn't there. The property was empty."

"So chances are, it was just a bunch of kids then?"

"I don't think so. The description matches the first intruder, without the hood over his face."

"The only reason not to do that is because he doesn't expect anyone to see him or to recognize him."

"Thanks. I had worked that out for myself," she said drily.

"Look. I'm not trying to tell you how to do your job. I just called to let you know there is a connection, however slight, between me and those break-ins."

"Noted. I'll pull the records for every one of these houses."

"Okay." He was about to hang up when she spoke again.

"Wait. Any idea if Marsha might have known this Kathleen Matron?"

"No idea. I tried to stay away from Marsha as much as I could."

"So, you don't know any of her friends?"

"No, I told you that I didn't." Macklin frowned. "Why? Did you find a connection between the two of them?"

"We found pictures of Marsha in that house."

Macklin walked to his big easy chair and sat down heavily. "This was the first house of the four break-ins?"

"Yes."

"So that's also the same house Bill Toronto used to live in."

"Yes."

"Damn, how does all this fit together?"

"No idea." she said, her voice low, determined. "But, if there's one thing you can be sure of, I will find out." And she hung up.

Macklin quickly sent out a text to his buddies, giving them an update on the photos Alex had found. He'd barely sent out the last notice when his phone went off.

It was Corey. "What the hell is going on, Macklin?"

"I have no idea. But the only reason for the intruder to go back into the first house was if he's looking for something."

"And the detective found pictures of Marsha in that same house?"

"Apparently. Alex didn't say where they were hidden, just that she found photographs."

"Any chance the intruder wasn't there to take anything, but he planted something?"

"I hadn't considered that." Moodily Macklin stood in the middle of his living room. "Nothing makes sense."

"But it will. It will. Unfortunately it'll probably be too late to be of any value to anybody."

"Isn't that the way of things?" Macklin shook his head. "I'm going nuts here. I want to get out, but I got no place to go."

"You want to go out for coffee? Go for a run at the beach?"

"You're not doing anything?" Macklin asked.

"No, I'm not. I was watching TV, but it's not holding my interest. I keep pondering what the hell is going on in your world."

"Yeah, me too." He made a sudden decision and said, "You know what I want to do? I want to go walk the neighborhood. Are you up for it?"

"Sure. What are we looking for?"

"I won't have a clue until I see it," Macklin said.

"Good enough. Pick a place to meet, and we'll walk the area together."

They set up a place within two blocks of the first house hit in the Silver Strand complex.

Within ten minutes Mac pulled off the side of the road, parking behind a small pickup, noting its license plate number and general description to share with Alex later. Mac couldn't tell if Corey had arrived or not. The light made it hard to see at this time of night. He shut off the engine, hopped out, and stood on the sidewalk, looking around.

"Macklin?" Corey was on the opposite side of the road, waving at him.

Mac crossed the street, noting it was quiet, calm, with no sign of traffic anywhere. Together the two men slowly walked the outside perimeter of the crime area, memorizing the blocks, the layout of the properties, and sorting through the viability of the break-ins.

"They don't even have to be professional burglars. The way the windows are lined up creates blind spots on the sides for anyone to walk in and out unseen. It was set up that way for privacy, so one house doesn't look into the windows of the second house."

"Exactly," Macklin said. He motioned at the houses, one after the other. "Once you know the layout of one, chances are you know the layout of at least half of them here." Macklin laughed. "Makes it much easier on intruders too."

Corey snorted. "Absolutely. The thing is, it's still brazen. And either he knew if anybody was home or he didn't give a shit. The fact is, he's met tenants almost every time. So he obviously isn't bothered by witnesses."

Macklin nodded again. "We're two unknown men, walking down the street together at dusk. Yet we're not drawing any attention, and no one is peeking at us from behind curtains. Essentially it's just a small-town road. Nobody cares."

"I doubt any traffic here would bring attention either. A loud party might raise some eyebrows, but nobody's going to be too bothered."

"Do you think that's the standard across America? Nobody wants to get involved? Nobody wants to see anything because then they may have to make a judgment call or do something about it? Or they're just not interested in their neighbors anymore?"

"Probably a little bit of all of it," Corey said quietly. "Think about it. If you see an intruder, you'll have to phone it in. If you call it in, they want your name, your number, your address. They pretty much want to know everything about you. Nobody wants to give that much information anymore. If there's an anonymous tip line, that's a different story."

Macklin pointed out a house as they passed. "That was where the woman was beaten and knocked out."

"That was the fourth on the list?"

"Yes. The second house that was hit is up in the next block."

They approached that with the same attitude as all the rest, looking for angles, looking for options. If they were an intruder, how would they approach the problem? And, if they were on a security detail, how would they look for threats?

When they walked past, Corey shook his head. "It's the same layout, the same look. Once he's made it into the kitchen of one of them ..." He let his voice trail off.

Macklin didn't need to say anything. It had all been said before. But it was a good reminder this really wasn't a hardship for anybody who knew what they were doing.

After they passed the second targeted house, they walked to the end of the block, took a right, and headed toward the third house. This layout looked to be slightly different. As in, the door was slightly off-center, the living room in the front, still the kitchen in the back.

Rather than stopping and staring at the house in question, they made their observations as they went past. "No alleyway in this part of the world either, is there?"

"Not here. Land values and the increasing population don't give room for something like that," Macklin said. "In a way that's nice because it stops the intruders from having that kind of ingress and egress. The thing is, if the guy had approached like we are, it's a simple thing to slip in between two houses and come around the back."

"Exactly. No skill required."

Macklin realized how futile this was. He wasn't sure what he thought this trip would produce, if anything. All it showed him was how easy these break-ins were for anybody to do.

They continued walking, moving two streets over. As they got to where the first house was, he could see several police vehicles still parked at the curb.

Corey looked at him. "You sure you want to head that way? Alex's likely to be there."

Macklin shrugged. He hated that, inside, he kind of hoped she was. In any other circumstance, he might have asked her out, but, given he was a suspect in a murder case, it wasn't a good idea. But that twinge inside told him that she was around.

Corey gave him a sideways look. "This is the most interest I've seen you show in anybody in a long time."

Keeping his face straight, Mac said in a laughing voice, "Hey, I'm not showing any interest in her. I just want to ensure my neck is not on the chopping block."

Corey chuckled. "Tell yourself whatever you need to, buddy. But, no doubt, some sparks are flying here."

"Yeah. It's the chink of the chains as they close the

shackles around my legs," he said. "I'd do a lot not to go down for a murder I didn't commit."

"No worries there. We will make sure that doesn't happen."

If nothing else, Macklin had good friends; he had a support system. He was also innocent, and he'd like to believe that meant something, but he'd heard enough about cases of innocent men being charged and convicted. "Thanks. Appreciate that," he said with a head nod toward Corey. "Plus I can give her the details on that truck I'm parked behind. It may be nothing, but …"

"By the way, Tesla is checking out Marsha's history and looking to see what she can find."

Macklin grinned. "I keep forgetting about her skills."

"Don't. She's pretty amazing."

Macklin nodded. "She's a good person to have on our side."

"Everyone is. Marsha was a fruitcake right from the beginning, and I know you don't like it when we refer to her as such, but the fact remains that she was off-balance. Honestly, I know it's not nice, but I'm glad it's her that's dead and in the morgue, not you."

Macklin had to agree.

Just as he walked past the house, he heard a voice call out, "Macklin?"

Beside him, he could feel Corey's shoulders shake in mirth. Mac turned to look at Alex striding toward him, a serious look on her face, her gaze narrowed. He smiled. "Hi, Alex."

"What are you doing here?"

The suspicion in her tone got his back up. "Going for a walk," he said pointedly. "Is there a law against that?"

"No, but you don't live here. We all know that people like to come back to the scene of their crimes."

He let his breath out quietly, anger stirring inside. "I'm pretty sure not one description of the intruder would match my physical form."

She took a long look at his face, not even bothering to check out the rest of the form he'd referred to. He wasn't sure if that was a good thing or not.

She nodded. "True enough, but that doesn't mean you're in the clear with regard to Marsha."

Corey stepped forward, his body now vibrating.

Macklin grabbed Corey's arm to hold him back. "But, since I had nothing to do with her murder, that doesn't apply to me."

At that moment Corey stepped closer to Mac.

Alex switched her focus to Corey. As he glared at her, her jaw locked down while she studied him. "You can be as pissed off as you want to be, Corey, because I'm not here for you, and I'm not here for Macklin. I'm here for the woman who had her throat cut. So deal with it."

She turned and stormed off. Several feet away, she spun around and said, "It's probably a good idea if you gentlemen go home."

"What? No neighborhood watch?" Corey said in a mocking tone.

Her gaze locked on his as she said, "No, not tonight."

CHAPTER 6

"**F**OOL," SHE WHISPERED under her breath. Didn't he realize what it looked like to have him walking the crime area? If he was smart, he'd have stayed home. She turned around to make sure the two men were moving on, and they were. But their heads were together as they discussed something. Dammit. Given their skill set, she wished she knew what it was about.

If they had any working theories, she wanted them; she wanted it all, because this needed to stop. She knew a lot of people were watching her to see how she would handle this case. She had already been the target of enough negativity upon her arrival as it was. She got into her vehicle and headed toward her office, her mind churning too much to go home and sleep.

At the station, she quickly logged in the photographs they'd found, then made digital copies of all of them. It wasn't that she believed the evidence would go missing, but she believed a backup was just smart on all sides.

She'd also learned the hard way how sometimes evidence went missing by accident and then, on occasions, when officers were less-than-honest. She added the photos to the box with the rest of the evidence. Back at her desk, she sat down and brought up the photos on her computer screen. She reviewed each one in turn. They were all of Marsha.

Marsha happily smiling, Marsha staring at something, Marsha angry.

She named the collection The Moods of Marsha. She needed to talk to the woman who lived in that house. Had she taken the photos? It was her dresser. How much of this was just a photography student's project? "But then why tape them under the dresser drawer?" she muttered.

She brought up her notes and quickly typed in the name Macklin had given her earlier. It didn't make sense that another man who had been in the same BUD/S program would have anything against Macklin. They'd both successfully finished that year. Still, it was a name she needed to check out. Any connection to Macklin was important.

The cases had obviously dovetailed. She just couldn't imagine how they fit together. It didn't make any sense. She thought about the fact that Marsha had lived alone too. It didn't mean Macklin was in the clear, but neither did it make him the most suspicious person on her list. She did a quick search for Bill Toronto. He'd transferred back east five weeks ago. The house had been empty for a week before Kathleen moved in.

Alex leaned forward to review the other files. She checked Marsha's residential history, remembering something was odd about it. She moved like every six months—except for a few months' gap in the housing record. Maybe she'd been forced to live with a relative until she found a new place. According to the managers of the various apartments, one move was due to a neighbor bothering her—Marsha didn't feel safe. Another one was due to too many fights with the neighbors, and another one was because the apartment *felt* wrong. Alex raised her eyebrows at that. Marsha had rented five places in a period of three years. Alex's fingers ran freely over the keyboard as she typed out her thoughts, confusions, and questions.

She needed answers, and she needed them fast. She checked her watch; it was ten p.m. The woman who had been at that location when it was broken into was currently visiting her mother in San Diego. Taking a chance, she quickly dialed the number she had on file. When Kathleen Matron answered, Alex identified herself. She let the woman know the house had been broken into a second time tonight.

She listened to the woman's cries of shock.

"Do you have any idea why either the same intruder or a second man would enter that house?"

"No," she said. "My God, I've only been there for a month."

Alex already knew that because she had the records for the house in front of her. "Did you bring the dresser in your bedroom with you?"

"What do you mean?" Kathleen asked.

"The dresser in your bedroom," Alex asked patiently. "Is it yours?"

"No, it was there when I moved in. I was pissed at first because I didn't want to have anything left in the house. Who does? Somebody leaves their junk, and you must deal with it yourself, but I'd requested to have it moved out. Then, in the move, my own dresser had been broken. I intend to get a new one, but I haven't yet."

"Do you happen to know Marsha McEwan?"

"I don't. Why?"

"Just part of another case. She was murdered two nights before your place was broken into."

A stunned silence seemed to take over the other end of this call, and then Kathleen said, "That's terrible."

"Yes."

"You can't think it has something to do with me?"

"No. But since we found photographs of Marsha taped underneath one of the drawers in the dresser, I needed to know if you knew anything about it."

"Photographs in my dresser?"

"Yes."

Alex could understand how the woman felt. Nobody wanted to think anybody was in her bedroom or, even worse, invading her dresser, her own space. "I'm sorry, but I did have to go into your home and search to see why the intruder would come back."

"It doesn't matter," Kathleen stated firmly. "I'm not spending another night in that house."

"I do have the photographs but didn't take anything else."

"They weren't mine, so I don't care." Kathleen hesitated, then added, "Were they nasty photographs?"

"No, just of Marsha's face. They were taken at various locations around the city."

More silence. "Like somebody was stalking her?" Kathleen asked slowly. "I really don't want anything to do with that dresser now."

"That's fine. We might very well need to take the whole thing in and get it fingerprinted."

"You can have it. Take one of my bags from the closet and pack all my personal belongings first, please. I'm not sure I want to come back at all."

When Alex got off the phone, she updated her notes and sat in front of the monitor for a long moment. It was the wrong time to phone back east to confirm with Bill that he'd left the dresser behind. It wasn't new; it wasn't terribly nice.

But it was functional. It was also large and heavy, making it tempting to leave behind for someone else to deal with. She also had to consider the fact that the second intruder might not have come back to steal something but to plant something.

Like that envelope. She wondered if the lab would find Macklin's fingerprints on the photographs. It would be a good way to frame him since he'd never lived there. According to him and Kathleen, they didn't know each other. So no reason for something with his fingerprints to be here.

She picked up her phone, called Macklin, and asked, "The house I was standing at when you walked by, have you ever been inside?"

"No, not that I can remember," he said slowly. "Why?"

"Because that's where the photos of Marsha were found." She waited for any response from him. Got none. "Can you tell me honestly if I'll find fingerprints of yours in that house?"

The air between them thickened when he said, "I can't tell you that, no. I've been based out of this area for a long time. I've helped many a buddy move in and out of plenty of military residences in this area. But I can tell you, to the best of my memory, I have never been in that house."

"Why would I find your fingerprints there?"

"Because someone is obviously framing me. I doubt they stopped with writing my name in blood at the crime scene. It follows that they would plant evidence. My fingerprints could be on a book. They could be on an envelope. They could be on a cup."

"An envelope?" She stared at the digital photos on her monitor. "Interesting you would say that."

"Why?" he snapped. "What did you find?"

She groaned. "That's how we found the photographs of Marsha. In a large envelope."

There was silence between them for a long moment.

"Well, it was an accidental turn of phrase from me. Did you find any fingerprints on the pictures or the envelope?" His voice was more curious than worried.

"I haven't gotten the results yet."

"Well, I'm sure you'll get back to me if mine are on there." His voice thinned with frustration. "I know it's useless to tell you again I'm innocent. But, if somebody's planted an envelope in that house, it still doesn't do anything to move the investigation forward. It's just churning up the water so you can't see clearly."

"Well, believe it or not, I can figure that out myself," Alex said. "Just make sure you stay out of trouble."

"I stayed out of trouble right from the beginning," he said wearily. "The only thing I did wrong was date Marsha."

She chuckled. "Sometimes that's all any of us have to do."

More silence followed.

In an awkward tone she said, "Okay, that's all I need for the moment. Have a good night." She hung up.

But he was right. The only thing finding an envelope at that house did was muddy the waters. And that just pissed her off. Somebody was out to cause trouble. The question was, was it for Macklin or was it for her? Only time would tell.

HOW ODD TO consider someone hated him enough to set him up on a murder charge. Mac had done a lot of things in his life as a SEAL, but hurting some civilian or deliberately being an asshole weren't part of who he was. Sure, as a callow youth, he might have been a jerk once or twice but never in a big way.

Marsha had terrified him. But how did he prove he didn't do something when he had no alibi for the time of her murder?

He wanted to call Mason and ask him for advice, but, before he got a chance, his phone rang. It was Corey, checking up on him.

"Why don't you come stay the night with me? If there is another B&E, you'll have an alibi. If you're not getting a girlfriend anytime soon, then let's at least make sure Alex can rule you out."

"Not too interested in a girlfriend right now," he muttered, seeing the sense in Corey's suggestion but hating it all the same. He glanced at the clock. "It's only ten."

"I suggest we hit the pub and shoot some pool. Anything to take your mind off this shit. Then crash at my place and carry on tomorrow."

"I was trying to figure out who killed Marsha," Macklin said quietly.

"I know. And that's why you need to get out. Be visible and take this off your mind. While covering your ass." He gave a half laugh. "Let's make it easy for Alex to knock you off her list, so you can ask her out."

"Getting my name knocked off her list—now that's an idea I can get behind. Asking her out... I'm not so sure about."

"You're already planning on it, just haven't gotten your head wrapped around it fully yet. Doesn't matter at this point. Not until we clear your name. So get your ass over here."

CHAPTER 7

ALEX WOKE UP early the next morning, feeling like she hadn't had any sleep at all. Her dreams were filled with break-ins and bodies with throats slashed. A life filled with carcasses.

Still groggy she stepped into the shower and turned on the water cooler than normal. She needed something to blast her back into reality. As she stepped out to dry off, she could hear her phone ring. Swearing, she raced into the bedroom, grabbed her cell phone, and said, "Hello."

"How about we meet for breakfast?"

Macklin's voice was quiet in her ear. She turned to stare at the mirror, seeing her dripping hair, the damp towel barely hiding the lean body she had been complaining about since she was a child. "I'm not sure that's a good idea."

"I think it's a great idea. Maybe the more you get to know me, the more you'll realize I had nothing to do with this."

"You are still a suspect in a murder inquiry. Getting friendly is not cool."

"Find a way to knock me off the list so I'm no longer a suspect. I don't know what you need to do that. But surely we need to do another interview over breakfast," he said in a warm, persuasive voice.

She smiled despite herself. "I could question you anywhere. A restaurant in full public view is hardly the best location." But she could feel herself giving in.

"Well, I want to talk over some ideas I've had since you told me about those photographs."

"That's a different story."

"Exactly."

She rolled her eyes. "I'm not that easy to manipulate."

"Sure you are," he said with a big smile in his voice. "Pick the place. Meet you there in fifteen."

"And if I can't make it in fifteen?"

"Then I'll meet you there in twenty."

She chose a restaurant between the two of them for a convenient location. "And I'll try for fifteen but no guarantees." She tossed the phone back on the bed and got to work. Her hair was soaking wet; she braided it to stop most of the dripping. She didn't have time to use her hair dryer. Pulling on a pair of jeans and a clean white T-shirt. Once dressed, she picked up her weapon, wallet, purse, and keys. She walked outside into the heat and took several long deep breaths. It was probably the coolest it would be all day. Plus the air had a freshness to it this morning that she hadn't noticed last night. She got into her vehicle and drove to the appointed spot. She checked her watch as she walked in the front door. She was exactly three minutes late. She stood in the center of the restaurant and looked around and then grinned when there was no sign of him. Had she beaten him?

A waitress asked how many for her table.

"Two please. I'm meeting someone here."

"Macklin? He's expecting you."

"He is?" Her grin fell away. "He's here already?"

The waitress nodded. "Follow me."

She followed the waitress to the back of the restaurant

where the private rooms were. Macklin was inside with his laptop on the table, a cup of coffee beside him.

He looked up and smiled. "I figured, if this was a working breakfast, we should work."

"Don't you have a job to go to yourself?"

"A conference. I return to active duty in a week." He lifted his cup and had a sip, twisting to study her face. "That's why the early morning call."

"I like early mornings," she admitted. "But I prefer them after a good night's sleep."

"Hard to sleep with everything going on."

"True enough but last night it was calm." She understood what he was asking, even if he didn't come out and say anything. She noted the look of relief on his face. "So, did you get some sleep?"

"I bunked in with a friend last night. I wanted to make sure if something happened, I had an alibi."

She sat down slowly, her gaze focused on his features. "That's very smart of you. Unless, of course, he's such a good friend he'd lie for you."

His eyebrows rose to his hairline. "He's a good friend, but honor is very strong among us. He would never lie for me."

"I didn't think so, but you never know."

"Isn't that something husbands and wives do for each other? Parents and siblings? Do buddies do that?"

"More often than you think," she said shortly.

He slipped a piece of paper across the table to her.

"What's this?"

"When I was walking the Silver Strand neighborhood, I parked a couple blocks away behind a small truck. It may be nothing, but I thought I'd share that info with you."

She nodded, looked it over, then folded it, and placed it in her purse. "I would like any theories you and your team might have. Otherwise, butt out of my investigation."

But she had said it with a smile.

The waitress arrived just then. She brought not only a fresh cup of coffee for Alex but also a pot she put on the sideboard heater.

After she left, Alex looked at the pot and said, "I never thought to arrange a backroom meeting like this. It's a good idea."

"If we're going to talk business, we need privacy," he explained. "There's an awful lot we need to discuss."

"Unless you have anything new, there's nothing I can add," she said smoothly.

"An IT friend of mine looked closely into Marsha's background, specifically for friends, since you keep asking me about that element. Even given the current social media climate, she found very little. But the same individual kept coming up as a contact person, both for Marsha's rental agreements as well as her medical insurance records. A cousin."

Alex tilted her head. "I already have that name and spoke to her. They are not close."

"Seems to be the pattern with Marsha." He leaned back and smiled. "So have you found the intruder?"

She just raised an eyebrow. "You know we haven't."

Macklin nodded. "You haven't. Have you considered maybe it was a woman?"

Alex felt the color drain from her face. She leaned forward, her gaze locking on his, and said, "No. I hadn't. Why?"

"Tall, lean. Dressed in a way to not define the sex of the

intruder. Plus, he did not rape the last woman, even though she was unconscious."

Alex tapped her pencil on the tabletop as she processed the suggestion. Even those who saw the intruder had said it was male. "If she was very tall, she might have passed as male," she said slowly, still thinking about it. "Yes, it does help explain the reason why the last woman wasn't raped. Not all intruders are rapists, however."

"No, that's very true. But it might also give you another connection to the four women. ... What if Marsha knew them?"

"Well, that's a possibility I hadn't considered. We have no forensic evidence, no fingerprints or DNA to say either way." She turned her head to stare off in the far corner. Even the neighbor had said it was a male. Tall, slim, white skin, but he could only see so much in the gloom. No way to tell male versus female. "If she didn't have a curvy build and was wearing a jacket ..." She slumped back in her chair and thought about it. "No reason it couldn't have been a female, let's put it that way."

"But there are a lot of reasons for it to *be* a female. She might very well have known all four women."

"Possibly, but it could be a male for the same reason. One of the women's boyfriends did have a fight with the intruder. I'll have to contact him and see if he felt it could be a woman."

"Particularly because she took off. If it was a physically fit male, it would have been an equal fight, and he might have stayed to pound the guy into the ground a little farther. But instead the person ran away. Correct?"

"Correct," she said. She pulled out her notepad and jotted down a note. It was an interesting concept.

"Was Marsha a lesbian?" Alex asked.

"If you mean, did we have sex? The answer is yes."

Alex nodded. "But that doesn't mean she didn't have sexual relations with women in her life too."

The waitress returned a few moments later. She carried two plates heaped high with waffles.

Alex stared down at them. "I didn't order these."

"I ordered them," Macklin said with relish. He rubbed his hands together. "No problem if you can't eat all of yours. I'll finish those too."

She stared at the size of them and at the number of them on each plate. "These are big, even for you."

"Like hell," he said naturally. He shoved the paperwork to the side and moved his plate in front of him. He attacked it with a vengeance.

"Hungry by any chance?"

"Yep. By the time we got back to my friend's place, and I settled on the couch for the rest of the night, it was the wee hours of the morning. I didn't sleep well because I wasn't in my bed."

She nodded. "Still, it's a smart idea to have somebody with you right now."

"Yep. Safety in numbers." He took another bite, and she watched love wash over his face. He settled back with a happy sigh and chewed.

She couldn't even look at her own plate because she was too busy watching his face. "I don't think I've ever seen anybody enjoy food quite the same as you are now."

When he could, he chuckled. "I do like my groceries." He cut another piece, forked it up, and chewed it slowly.

She surveyed the plate in front of her: three big waffles covered in fresh strawberries and whipping cream all over the top. Her stomach was growling already, but she couldn't imagine putting all of this down, even if she was famished. She had gotten into the habit of not eating enough, and what she did eat was crappy when it came to nutrition. She cut her first bite and tasted it. The waffles were fresh, crisp on the outside, soft on the inside, and incredibly flavorful. Often waffles themselves were just a carrier for the fruit and whipping cream. But these had a hint of cinnamon and a little bit of vanilla in them. She swallowed and said, "These are delicious."

Macklin nodded, but he didn't waste any energy talking.

She grinned at his focus and singular determination to enjoy his meal. It was a pleasure to watch him. He was the kind of guy her mother would have loved cooking for. Her mom hadn't done any cooking in a long time, but, back in the day, when Alex was young, her mom had enjoyed cooking and taking food to the office.

By the time she was halfway through her waffles, she slowed down. After a few more bites, she put down her fork and moved her plate aside. One full waffle and one-third of another were left. But the strawberries and whipping cream were long gone. She reached for her coffee and realized her cup was empty. Pushing back her chair, she walked to the sideboard and filled her cup. "Do you want a refill?"

"Yes, please."

She brought the pot over and saw his plate was empty. "Do you want the rest of mine?"

He looked at her plate and smiled. "Oh, yeah. Thank you."

"Sorry about the lack of cream and berries."

"Not a problem." He finished her plate off in what seemed like four or five bites.

When he stacked the empty plates out of the way and rubbed his tummy, she had to laugh. "I guess it takes a lot of food to feed somebody your size."

"It does. Lots of it and often." He looked at the rest of the paperwork as he dragged it toward him. "Is there anything else here we need to discuss?"

"There's nothing we need to discuss. This is my investigation," she said, adding a cool note to her tone. It wouldn't do him any good to think he was involved in this investigation. "I need you to stay clear of trouble while I get to the bottom of it."

"Okay. I'll continue doing what I can on my side, and you do what you do officially." He lifted his gaze and gave her a hard smile. "Just don't tell me to back off."

She sat back in her chair. "You're going to be difficult, aren't you?"

"It's my life. Wouldn't you want to consider the aspects of a murder investigation if somebody was trying to pin it on you?"

She frowned and mentally gave him a point for that one. "If you don't interfere with my investigation, it's fine."

"I have no problem with that. I spoke to Bill this morning."

She growled. "He was on my list to call."

"Well, now he's expecting your call."

She shook her head. "And that's interfering with my investigation."

MACKLIN LOOKED AT her. He'd hoped she'd ease up on him if he had arranged breakfast. And it seemed to work, at least for a while. He leaned forward. "Come on. Bill is a friend. Once he understood what the problem was, he had no hesitation talking to you. I needed to know for myself if he thought someone was against me when we were in BUD/S training. He was the logical person to ask." He added in a low voice, "So don't get mad at me. I need to know if anybody might have had a reason to do this to me. He was just one of the people I contacted to look for information."

He watched as she calmed down slightly. She was fun to get riled up, but, at the same time, she could turn snippy. He liked that about her. He also liked the fact she was pushing back inside her investigation. He liked women with back-bone. Of course she couldn't be easygoing and deal with criminals all day.

"Would you like to go out for a drink one night?" He froze. He hadn't expected that to come out. But it looked like she was even more shocked than he was.

She narrowed her gaze as if accessing if there was a true sense of attraction or if he was trying to be manipulative.

He settled back and grinned. "I didn't expect that to come out," he admitted. "But it's a great idea."

She continued to stare at him. "Remember the part where we shouldn't be spending time together while you're a suspect?"

"Remember that part about clearing me so I'm no longer a suspect?" he countered.

She chuckled. The sound was joyous as it rebounded around the room. "Yes, I do remember. You're certainly sliding down the list, but you're not off it completely."

"The only time it's a good thing not to be at the top of the class," he said, laughing.

"What else did Bill have to say?"

"He said some of the guys who didn't make the cut were angry. They felt my size gave me an advantage in some of the endurance tasks."

She chuckled. "Everybody will always have an excuse as to why they haven't done as well as somebody else. They just need to look to themselves first and foremost instead of looking for excuses."

"I agree with you," Macklin said. "Too often people look for outside reasons, not inside reasons. BUD/S training was more than about size and fitness. It was all about internal strength. That I've got in spades." He watched as she picked up her coffee cup and took a sip, her gaze never leaving his face. He liked that about her. "I like you," he said, surprise following his words. "I hadn't expected to."

"Oh? Why not?"

"After Marsha, I didn't like very many women," he admitted. "But you're different."

That tumbled a laugh out of her. "In what way?"

"Intelligent. Driven. You don't take flak from anyone. And of course that spark of chemistry is there."

She didn't say anything for a long moment.

But he'd been around enough women, had had enough relationships to know what he felt. He also knew it was reciprocated. Whether she wanted to admit it or not.

But how she reacted would tell him a lot about who she was.

She gave him a small nod and said, "Yes, I feel it. That doesn't mean I'll do anything about it."

He leaned back and said, "And that's why I like you again. You've got enough self-confidence to step up and say, *Yes, there is that same attraction, but it's not the time or the place.* Not that I agree with you," he said with a smirk. "But

I understand your reasons."

"Then don't push me," she said quietly. "Please."

He gave her a quick nod. "Only until the investigation is over."

"Talk about being focused and dedicated," she said. "I should take lessons from you."

"Nope. But, when I really like something—someone," he said, "I go after it."

And damn if he didn't watch color come up her face to match the heat she felt there. She glanced at her notes and asked, "Don't you have somewhere to go by now? It's almost nine."

"Shit." He stacked his notes and said, "You're too much of a distraction."

"Another reason we shouldn't meet like this," she said smoothly.

He rolled his eyes at her. "Nice try." But he was grinning.

CHAPTER 8

SHE CHUCKLED AS he walked out with a multifinger wave. He really was something. She wasn't exactly sure what she wanted to do about it, but what she'd said was right. No relationship should occur until after her investigation was done. She didn't want to get him into any more trouble. Neither did she want to go down that path to find out she'd been very, very wrong. That would leave her with devastating consequences—both professionally and personally.

The waitress returned, collected the empty dishes, and asked if Alex wanted more coffee.

She nodded. "If you don't mind. Does anybody else need this room, or can I stay here?"

"You have another thirty minutes without any pressure."

"Excellent. Thank you. I'll sit here and do some more paperwork then."

After the waitress left, the table cleared now, Alex brought out all her documents and organized her notes. Everything was convoluted. She needed to update her timeline. What she really wanted was to know who had lived in which house when. The fact that Macklin had theorized the intruder may be female was very interesting.

And she was quite pissed at herself for not having thought of it herself.

It did give her a completely different angle to tug and another possible connection to these four women. Speaking of which, she had the boyfriend who'd fought off the intruder to call. She pulled up her notes, and quickly dialed the number. Luckily the boyfriend was there. She asked him several questions but he wasn't helpful. His tone was cautious, as he said, "Yes, it's possible but it could just as easily been a slight male. I didn't sense anything feminine about him."

She thanked him and hung up.

She entered her notes into her digital files. She wanted everything organized before her meeting later this morning. Her superiors were looking for results. Realizing she still had a few more minutes, she picked up her phone and called Bill. After introducing herself, she said, "You spoke with Macklin earlier."

"Yes, I did."

Bill's voice was warm with intelligence shining through. She liked that. "What's Macklin like?"

"He's everybody's best friend. He's loyal. He's not the type to stab you in the back. And I know for a fact, he's the kind to give you a hand-up. In one of our endurance tests, I wasn't going to make it. I was done. But Macklin wouldn't let me go. He hassled me. He bugged me, and he swore at me—cursed me out—anything he could to make sure I made it through the test. I was so mad I didn't realize it when I completed the test. That's the kind of man Macklin is."

"So you don't think he could have anything to do with this case."

"No. I don't know Marsha myself, but, if she was anything like Macklin told me… I can see a hint of anger in any man if a woman did something like that to him. But to set it up, hit her over the head, and then slice her throat? No. One must wonder why it was done that way. The blow to her head would have rendered her unconscious. Why slice her throat too? To make sure she was dead? Maybe. But then why not hit her over the head again?"

"What's your theory?"

"I think she was hit over the head so she'd be unconscious. But then, while she was unconscious, why didn't anything else happen?"

"Something else did happen," she said drily. "Somebody slit her throat."

"Sure, but no strength was required for that. When Marsha was already subdued, no force was required to kill her."

Getting an inclination of what he might be saying, she said, "Meaning, it could have been a woman who did this?"

"Absolutely. It could have been a woman. Marsha could have been sitting on a couch. The blow could have incapacitated her, and the woman could have dragged her from the couch, slit her throat, written Macklin's name in blood, and left. Nobody would be any the wiser."

As soon as Alex got off the phone with Bill, she updated her notes and considered the other residential properties and their previous owners. Through the housing files, she went through each of the addresses one by one, wrote down the names and the contact information.

Then she followed up with each person whose house had been broken into. Checking how long they'd lived there, if they knew either Marsha or Macklin or any of the other three women who had had their houses broken into. Each time she came up blank. Each time the homeowner had lived there long enough that Alex discounted previous residents as being an issue.

Shaking her head, frustrated at the complete lack of pertinent information, she got up, poured herself another cup of coffee.

After finishing up at the restaurant, she drove to her office. She had the autopsy back on Marsha, but then she'd already talked to the coroner. Nothing new there. The tox screen was also negative. She sent Macklin a quick text, saying she'd contacted Bill, and he had confirmed everything Macklin had said. She left it at that, short and sweet.

The response was almost instant. "So am I off the hook? Does that mean we can do lunch?"

She shook her head. But knowing she was grinning like a silly fool, she quickly replied, against her better judgment, but unable to ignore the need to see him. "Sure. But you're not off the hook yet."

"I'll pick you up at noon."

"No. I've got interviews. Pick someplace close to my office." She didn't know why she was being contrary, but she didn't want to be gone too long, out of the loop, in case anything blew up here. Not that anything was likely to blow up anywhere. She had a meeting shortly with the rest of the team.

She walked in to see she was already late. She wasn't running the meeting, so she grabbed a chair at the back and sat down. All the murder evidence on Marsha had been discussed, and Alex added the last bit of information she'd gleamed that morning.

Lance asked, "So we're now thinking this could have been a woman?"

"It *could* have been a woman, but we're not sure either way, and we can't confirm that the same woman did the

B&Es. The killing was extremely vicious. But it wasn't a crime of passion. It was well laid out."

"But that blow to the head opened up the field to it being a female killer?"

Alex nodded. "That's exactly true. We have to keep all options open. What we don't have is any idea why those photographs were underneath the drawer in Kathleen's bedroom. Bill said he did leave a dresser behind. His buddy was supposed to drop it off for charity somewhere but forgot. Bill assumed the housing complex managers removed it.

"I'll call her doctor today to do a follow-up on her medications. According to Macklin, she was on and off medications all the time he knew her."

"I bet she was. The problem is, when they don't voluntarily take them, all kinds of hell breaks loose."

"Theories? Strings to pull? Anybody have any suggestions as to where to go from here?"

"We were hoping something would show up on the lab tests, but the tox screen was negative," Lance said slowly. "She doesn't appear to have had any friends. And yet, I think we need to dig further into the relationship between Marsha and these other women."

"They didn't know her," Sandra said from the back.

"I came to the same conclusion, but people lie all the time. Let's dig deeper into that, and see if we can pull any threads. It's possible they met, but it wasn't important enough to remember."

The meeting concluded soon afterward. Alex grabbed her bag and keys, and headed for the hospital to talk to the doctor. She had tried to make an appointment, but that was almost impossible. So she planned to walk in and spend five minutes of his time, whether he liked it or not.

As she walked into his office, she found a full waiting room. The receptionist looked up at Alex, and her smile dropped. "He's really busy."

Alex nodded. "I understand that," she said gently. "But we have a murder investigation."

The receptionist looked nervously at the full waiting room. "Just a minute." She walked into the doctor's office. When she came back out, she said, "He'll fit you in between a couple appointments. If you could come through here please."

She led Alex down a hall in the opposite direction and into a small room that was more like a boardroom. Assuming it was for staff lunches, possibly for meetings, Alex sat down and waited. She pulled out her notepad and jotted down some questions she wanted to ask. A few minutes later, the doctor raced in, looking harried and in a hurry. "What's this about?" he demanded.

She lifted her head. "Marsha McEwan."

Confusion crossed the doctor's face, and then it lit with understanding. "What's wrong with her?"

"She's dead." She watched shock, then horror, and finally understanding change his expression.

He sat down, clicked on his phone, and asked the receptionist for the file. "I can't say I'm surprised. Was it suicide?"

"No, she was murdered."

His gaze widened, and he swallowed hard. "I'm sorry to hear that. She was extremely unstable. She was committed for a period of six months for testing. But, on the right medication, she did really well and was released." He stopped talking when he heard a knock at the door. "Come in."

The receptionist entered, handed over a file, and left quickly.

"When were those months she was committed?" She quickly wrote down the dates, realizing it matched one of the periods when nobody had very much information on her. "That explains what she was doing during that time. Was she released into someone's care?"

"Yes. She had a cousin who signed for her. Marsha got a job and moved out within a few months. The cousin was off the hook, and everything returned to normal." He looked up from his file, frowning. "I really thought she had turned the corner because we had the right medication for her."

"How much do you know about her life?"

"As much as anybody," he said. "I suppose."

"Were you aware of her fixation and stalker tendencies toward a certain man?"

He groaned. "Marsha did speak of it a couple times. He was one of the problems we had tried to get her to deal with. To get her to understand this person was not her partner, not the love of her life. According to her, they were not only married but he cheated on her. She was pretty angry about it."

That settled into Alex's brain. "Do you remember the name of the person?"

He nodded. "It was an unusual name, but she'd showed me a picture of him. He's a big guy. His name is Mack. Like the big Mack trucks."

"He filed two restraining orders against her several years ago," Alex said. "She became violent and extremely disruptive."

The doctor sighed. "She was certainly focused. I have all kinds of clinical terms for that type of thing. But she wasn't my patient other than for her medical needs. I checked in to make sure she was doing okay physically, but, other than that, you'll have to see Dr. Sherman. He was her psychologist. He's the one who helped get her committed, ran her through the testing, and then released her."

"Do you have Dr. Sherman's contact information?" She asked a few more questions, but nothing seemed to pop. "Any idea if she was ever pregnant?"

He flipped through the file and said, "Doesn't look like it." He lifted his head and looked at her. "Does it matter?"

She shook her head. "No. I'm just checking if she had other relationships and how involved they were."

"The last time I saw her, she was alone, I believe, but I don't know for sure," the doctor admitted. He stood. "I really do have to get back to my patients."

Alex nodded. She rose and said, "Thank you very much." She packed up her notebook and walked out, thanking the receptionist with a smile as she walked outside. When she was on the street, she phoned Dr. Sherman's office. He was in San Diego, and she could see him in the afternoon.

She checked her watch and realized she had just enough time to meet Macklin. If she was a little early, that was fine. She'd rather be a little early than a little late in this case. If she was honest, she'd rather he was a little early as well, so they could spend a little more time together. She really liked him; she just knew it was a hell of a bad deal to get involved now.

She knew better …

Macklin pulled in beside her as she parked and got out of her vehicle. She waited, uncharacteristically happy to see him. Even when she tried to stomp down the joy surging through her at his big smiling face, telling herself she was being silly, she knew it wouldn't be that easy. He was right;

there was an attraction between them. It was just shitty he was on her suspect list. But she had found no serious motive for him, so she couldn't charge him.

As far as she was concerned, he was wiped off her list. However, he was the only one who had any real connection to Marsha. It just made no sense he would have waited all this time to do something about her.

She knew her mother would be horrified, telling her to get away from a killer. But Alex felt absolutely nothing but calm, control, and comfort when she was around Macklin. He slung an arm around her shoulders and gave her a quick hug.

She stepped back and frowned at him. "We don't have that kind of a relationship," she scolded.

He chuckled. "Yes, we do. You're just hiding behind your files."

"I am not," she retorted. She let him nudge her ahead into the restaurant. They took a table at the far back corner. "How was your morning, Macklin?"

"Busy. Any news?"

"Nothing that makes a big difference," she confessed. "Filling in the background on the various players in this game. But nothing major. It's hard in Marsha's case to find anyone who knew her."

"The only things I knew about was that Marsha was a big yoga fan. She belonged to a yoga club for a long time." He frowned. "And I know she went afterwards with a few of the women but that was years ago and I don't think she went often."

She stared at him. "Interesting."

He shook his head. "It's pretty common. I often go for a beer or coffee with the guys. It could have been the same idea." He shrugged. "I honestly don't know. And don't forget that was a few years ago. I have no idea what she might have done in the last couple years."

"I haven't tracked down anything she was involved in yet."

"Have you checked her credit cards? The way everybody is switching to subscription services these days, it's possible her yoga classes involved a fee, and, if she belonged to a social club, possibly fees were charged there too."

Alex stared down at her notepad, pissed at herself for not having checked it. "I checked her credit card for purchases in the last month, but found nothing. Her purchases appear to be normal."

"That's the problem with subscription services. They can be monthly, but it can also be bimonthly or quarterly. Some of them might even be annually."

She added *credit cards* on her notepad and beneath that she wrote *subscriptions*. "That's a good suggestion." She dropped her pen and looked up at him. "Any talk of upcoming missions?"

"Lots of talk about the situation in the Middle East. I could be heading out soon on a training mission." He leaned forward, stared her straight in the eye, and said, "Unless I'm not allowed to go."

"As far as I'm concerned, you can go," she said candidly. "I'll know where to find you, if it's a military mission."

"That you can." He stared around the restaurant. "It's hard. Everybody knows. Everybody talks. Nobody has any answers."

"You appear to be good friends with Corey."

He glanced at her. "I'm good friends with men from several units. ... We're like brothers."

"That's the way to have it. My job usually pits me against everybody. It's hard to have the same sort of camaraderie."

"What about the guys you work with?"

"In my old office, yes. But, since I moved here, hell no." She gave him a chilly smile. "That's the problem with being the boss. Nobody wants to get too friendly with you."

"Must be lonely."

"Same for you. It's not like you've had much in the way of relationships for the last few years."

His grin flashed. "I was saving myself for you."

Inside, her tummy fluttered, and her heart smiled. "But who said I was saving myself for you?" She laughed at the look on his face.

"You're a cruel woman."

But he said it in such a joking tone that she knew he didn't mean it. She really enjoyed the banter between them.

Just then the waitress arrived, and they ordered lunch. Knowing her afternoon could be busy, she ordered a healthy salad with chicken, then watched as Macklin ordered a double burger and fries.

"You know all that cholesterol will kill you one day."

"You know a bullet could kill me a whole lot earlier too."

She thought about that. "I guess that's something you have to think about when you head off to these dangerous missions."

"Hell no. That will get you all twisted up in knots. The last thing I want to do is think of how short my life could be, and I might not come back from any of these missions. There's enough to worry about besides the *ifs*. I enjoy life, and I try to live it on a day-to-day basis, not worrying about the things I can't change. Enough is going on in the world right now."

"So your health isn't an issue?"

"It is, indeed. And normally I watch the food I eat. But occasionally it's nice to have food you want, even if it isn't good for you."

After that there was a lull in the conversation. Yet it wasn't awkward. It was peaceful and calm. She really liked that. "If you do go overseas, when do you come back?"

He shrugged. "It could be anywhere from four to forty days. It depends on what's happening."

"We both have jobs like that. Lots of times I can't talk about cases too."

He rolled his head toward her and grinned. "Now that we've got some of those boundaries established, I think you should let me take you out for dinner."

"We haven't even finished lunch yet," she protested.

"Well, we could jump into bed instead." The grin that flashed on his face was knowing and full of mischief.

She didn't know if she should take him seriously but figured he was ready to go whichever way she responded. "Not a good idea."

He said, "Actually it's a hell of a good idea. But I can understand needing to take a little more time. Can't say I'm all that smooth at this anymore."

"Good. Enough smooth males are around. I'd rather have natural and real."

At that, he chuckled.

The waitress arrived, and they dropped their conversation. Alex settled back as her food was placed in front of her. The interruption was well-timed because she was confused at her feelings inside. And, if she went with her heart, she'd have said, "Bed now."

But, if she went with her mind, it told her to back off and to stay backed off. Because of the investigation. If nothing else, it would make her look bad to the rest of the company if she had a relationship with one of the murder suspects.

That thought alone made her uncomfortable as she realized they were already in a public place, and this time it wasn't to ask questions. To counter that, she brought out her notepad and placed it beside her, then pulled out a pen. She considered the notes from the doctor this morning. "This afternoon I'm meeting Marsha's psychologist." She glanced up to see he was studying her carefully as he ate. "I remember you saying she disappeared for a while?"

He nodded.

She said, "She spent six months in a mental facility, going through a series of tests. When they finally stabilized her medication, she was released."

He froze for a long moment and then nodded. "That fits. Like I said, she had troubles with her medication all the time."

"Troubles in what way?"

"Troubles in that sometimes she forgot to take it. Sometimes she did not know how many to take—they confused her. Or maybe she just didn't care enough to get it straight in her head."

"Or maybe she couldn't. I feel like I must give her the benefit of doubt that her mental problems made more than just one area of her life difficult."

"That's because you're a softie," he said quietly. "But you wear it well."

Flushing, she turned her attention to her salad and then

attacked it with a little more force than necessary. It was kind of easy for him to say so, and, at the same time, it was a little awkward. She couldn't remember the last time she had anybody quite as interested in her. It was funny he had never asked about that.

As if reading her mind, he said, "How long since your last relationship?"

Startled, she glanced up. "I was just thinking about that."

"And what were you thinking about?"

"It ended several years ago," she hedged.

He read her expression for a long moment and then shook his head. "Nope, there's something behind that."

She glared at him. "What if I don't want to talk about it?"

He shrugged. "That's your choice. Chances are the guy slept with somebody."

She nodded. "Yeah. He wasn't faithful, and I decided I didn't need that or him."

"Good. He wasn't ready to settle down, and you needed something different. That's what relationships are all about, finding what works and what doesn't."

She stared at him for a long moment. "Most people don't have that attitude."

"I'm not most people," he said quietly. He again studied her. "And neither are you."

She could feel the blush warming her cheeks. She lowered her gaze and continued to eat.

"So, about that dinner …"

She shot him a look. "You're very persistent."

"I am. Because I really want to get to know you."

"I don't have a problem with getting to know you. I do

have a problem having a relationship with someone who's a suspect in an active case. No, I don't think you killed Marsha."

"Thank you," he said quietly. "I know the paperwork still hasn't cleared me because you haven't found the guy who did it, but I appreciate you saying that."

She gave him a small smile. "But I'm new in my job, and the rest of the office will not look on this favorably."

He thought about that for a long moment. "Now *that* I can see. And, because it makes sense to me, I'll accept that as a reason. So we'll take it a little slower than I would like. But we can work toward getting to know each other better." He stared at her for a long moment. "Deal?"

She laughed. "Deal."

Just as she lay down her fork, her phone buzzed. She glanced at it and frowned. "I have to return to the office. Somebody's there to see me."

"So why the frown? That could be a good thing."

She nodded. "It just means work intrudes once again."

Hearing that, he gave her a bright beam of a smile.

She stared at him in confusion. "What, that work intrudes?"

"No, that you consider this lunch not work. That means I've gone from being part of the job to something personal."

She rolled her eyes and laughed. "Don't let it go to your head."

He leaned forward and whispered, "Never. It has already gone to my heart." He chuckled when he saw she was flustered.

She shook her head, stood, pulled out her wallet.

He grabbed her hand. "Lunch is on me."

She hesitated, but she was already late. "Fine, but I'm

paying for the next lunch." When she saw the cool satisfaction in his eyes, she said, "You did that deliberately."

He chuckled. "Sure did. Where do you want to go for dinner?"

She groaned. "No idea. But I've got to run." She snatched her keys off the table and walked out.

Alex couldn't stop chuckling inside. Macklin might have manipulated her into another date, but it was hard to get angry. She really liked him; she loved their banter, the lighthearted attitude. Physically there was a hell of a lot more to love, but that was just because he was a huge man.

His sense of humor caught her the most. She hadn't realized how dry and boring her life had become. He added some sparkle.

The traffic was much heavier on her way back to the station. She only had a few blocks to go, but it seemed like forever. She parked, strode into the station, and headed to her office. She barely had time to check her emails to make sure nothing else drastic was coming down on top of her before Lance poked his head in the door and said, "Are you ready for her?"

She looked up and nodded. "Who is she again?"

"You'll see. This could be big."

He disappeared only to reappear a few minutes later with an older woman—mid-fifties, maybe early sixties—in tow. She clutched her handbag nervously.

Alex rose and motioned to the visitor's chair in front of her desk. "Have a seat please."

Lance left them alone, closing the door with a sharp *snick*. The woman made a jump at the sound. Alex walked around the desk and hitched her hip on the corner. In a gentle, easy tone of voice, she said, "I'm Alex. What can I do for you?"

The woman took a deep breath. "I'm Betty. My last name is Kroger. And I live on Wagner Road."

"In Silver Strand's?"

The woman nodded. "Yes, but I've been away for the last ten days. I don't spend a whole lot of time here now, as I lost my son in active duty three months ago, and I just can't stay here. We don't have to move out for another nine months, but I want to move out earlier, only I'm still too emotional to pack up his stuff."

Inside Alex winced. "I'm so sorry. That's extremely devastating for anybody."

Betty's shoulders shook, but she regained a bit of control after a moment. She took a deep breath again, let it out, and then tried for a third time.

"Whenever you're ready, just tell me what's going on."

Betty shot her a grateful look. "I think my house was broken into," she said in a rush.

Alex turned her gaze to the map. She had to get up and walk closer to find Wagner Road. It was within the area she had marked off for the B&Es. "What makes you think that?" She turned to face the woman who, now that she'd gotten the words out, seemed to be calmer.

"Well, that's the thing. See? That's why I didn't want to come in. My daughter told me that I should. She says there's been a lot of break-ins and that you needed to know about my place."

"Why didn't you want to come in?"

"Because I can't see that anything is missing," she said in frustration. "I don't know how to explain that I know somebody was in there, but it …" She lifted her hands in appeal. "It feels different. It feels like a stranger was there.

For all I know, he stayed there."

"Interesting. As in, you're afraid he stayed in the spare bedroom? Crashed on the couch? Moved into your room?"

The woman shrugged. "I don't know, but potentially yes to all of it."

"Okay. Start from the beginning. You got home from visiting your daughter …"

Betty nodded. "Yes. I've been spending a lot of time there with her in San Diego. I'm moving to a house on her street," she confessed. "I have to move anyway, and the sooner the better, after this."

"Completely understandable. Now what happened when you got home?"

"The door was locked. I unlocked the door, and I walked in," she said and then retraced her steps. "But it was like being hit almost immediately with a sense of wrongness. I stood in the front entranceway, and I just didn't know what to do. Now I know I'm very emotional about that property. I spent a lot of time with my son there. I get that. But this just didn't feel right."

"Okay. So tell me what felt wrong."

"The smell for one." She held up a hand. "I know you'll say the house had been closed up, and of course it was stuffy smelling with no fresh air. But it was cigarette smoke. I swear to God it was cigarette smoke."

Alex settled back on the desk, her arms crossed over her chest as she questioned the woman. "And you don't smoke?"

"I hate cigarette smoke. My son never smoked either."

"Friends of yours?"

"I can't stand being around anybody who smokes. It clings to them. It's in their hair. It's in their clothing. It's just terrible."

"And how strong an odor was it?"

She slumped in the chair. "That's the thing. It wasn't that strong. So of course I thought I must be making it up."

Alex smiled at her gently. "Sometimes our instincts are right. Don't always knock them."

Betty managed her first smile. "Thanks for that."

"What happened afterward?"

Betty seemed to pull herself together, thinking for a long moment, then said, "I took off my jacket and hung it up in the front closet. And that was also off."

"Off?"

Betty nodded. "All the jackets were pushed to one side. But they weren't pushed to the side that was easily accessible. They were pushed to the far left, so I had to open both doors to get my jacket. I never open that door because it's behind the front door so it's awkward to get at. I only open the right-hand door, grab my jacket, and leave."

"This time you're saying, all the coats had been pushed to the left?" At Betty's nod, Alex walked around the desk, sat down, and grabbed her notepad. "This is good. What else do you remember?"

"I hung up my coat, went to the kitchen, and put on the teakettle. I dropped my purse on the table there, and that was a sign I wasn't feeling very secure. I normally put my purse right away in the entryway closet."

"So you thought maybe you would need to grab it and run?" Alex asked out of curiosity.

"I don't know. It was just one more thing that was off." The woman shrugged. "I guess it was ten nights and eleven days I was gone, so I knew no food would be in the fridge." She shook her head. "The thing is, I opened the fridge, maybe out of habit. I normally have milk in my tea, and of course there was no milk. *Shouldn't* have been any milk. But I was so rattled at this point, that it was automatic to open the fridge. And milk was there."

Alex sat back slowly. "The same brand of milk you use normally?" She studied the older woman, wondering how much of this was memory, how much of this was an intruder, how much of this was a friend who maybe took advantage, and how much did the woman not recollect, given her state of mind before she left.

"Well, yes. And it was a half-gallon. But it was also open. I wouldn't have left milk for that long in the fridge. And that was the other thing. It was still good … after ten days?"

Her tone was almost apologetic, as if she was sorry she'd had to come and say these things.

"Okay, so let me get this right. You got home. The closet was not the way you'd left it, but the kitchen was the way you'd left it?"

Betty nodded.

"The fridge held fresh milk or at least milk not past its due date. And if you were gone ten days …" Alex nodded. "Okay, so what else?"

"I was a little freaked out over the milk, and I kept looking around to make sure nobody would pop out at me from behind the counter. I told myself that I needed to learn to live alone and not be so scared. And I didn't have any reason to be scared. It's not like my son was murdered in his house or anything. And I just didn't have any reason, but I was jumpy, so I did a quick search of the downstairs. There's not very many places anybody could hide, behind the couch maybe, but it's sitting in the middle of the living room, so I could very quickly verify nobody was there. I couldn't hear anybody, but I found the kitchen door to the backyard was unlocked."

"And you normally keep it unlocked?"

"When I'm there, yes. But I know I locked it before I left." Betty started to shake. "There are a lot of little things here, and I know they could be attributed to memory loss because I was upset. But I think, when added up, maybe they mean something other than that."

"Well, let's not worry about potential memory loss issues now," Alex said. "What happened when you found the kitchen door unlocked?"

"I stepped out on the back porch and looked at the backyard."

"And?"

Betty shrugged. "Nothing was obviously different or wrong. Nobody was there. Nothing had been added or taken away that I could see. It's just a simple backyard with a couple lawn chairs and a table."

"Were those chairs and table still in the same place?"

Betty nodded. "Yes, they were."

"Okay. What did you do next?"

"I went back in and closed the kitchen door. I did not lock it, but that was a deliberate decision."

Alex understood. Betty was not only giving herself a chance to grab her purse but she was giving herself an exit. "And then?" Alex prompted.

"I walked around to the front stairs and made it to the second floor. At the top landing, I saw my bedroom door was closed."

Alex tapped the notepad with her pencil. "And I presume that's not something you would normally do?"

"Not when I'm there. The only time I would close it would be if I was getting changed. That's just out of habit."

"Do you have any other bedrooms?"

"Yes, one. That door was open."

Alex didn't like where this was going. "Did you check out the spare bedroom?"

The woman nodded. "I checked out the spare bedroom. I checked out the bathroom. And honestly I was terrified to open up the master bedroom door."

"With good reason. All right, you should've called us then."

"And have you laugh at me? I've had just about enough of people telling me how I should feel and shouldn't feel, and what I should do and shouldn't do for the last three months."

Alex could relate. Nothing like a disaster to have the world give an opinion about how you should handle things—with very well-meant personalities attached. But those words were not always welcome. "And did you open the door?"

Betty nodded. "I did. I told myself to stop being a baby, that I had nothing there anybody would want, and it was my home, and I needed to deal with this."

Alex settled back and waited. Betty would get through the story on her own time; pushing wouldn't help.

"I opened the door, and there was no sign of anyone. I stepped in. It looked the same, except for one thing." She winced. "I swear to God, it wasn't the same bedding I had on my bed before."

MACKLIN PAID THE restaurant bill and headed off to work again. He was attending a series of computer security seminars, and they were all on base. The military was good at constantly upgrading the men's skill sets. It seemed like the criminals of the world were split in two—those who used muscles and guns to get their way, and those who used computer hacking skills to get their way. Mac was strong on the assholes who liked to shoot and cause mayhem that way—but knew he could never become complacent with his IT skills. The good news was, it meant every one of these seminars was fascinating. There were always new ways to hack systems, new ways to bypass authentication systems, and new ways to hack into bank accounts and government databases. There was just no end to it.

He'd often wondered about going into that field as a specialty, but he wasn't quite ready to stay at a desk. That really was a different way of life. Now he got to get the hell out, and he got to visit places all over the world. He was active; he'd always been a bit of a field junkie. But he had to admit that he was fascinated with this whole computer-hacking stuff too; he just didn't have the innate talent for it. He worked at it. He knew other guys who were unbelievably good. And then of course there were the women he knew, like Tesla, Mason's girlfriend, and Devlin's girlfriend, Bristol, both of whom were brilliant.

But then they both used computers as an adjunct to their actual design work. They were big thinkers, global thinkers. They could see systems helping people when others were stuck considering how their inventions would work on a smaller scale. Those two women were special that way. He was grateful for the hours he got to spend with them, but he always walked away in awe of just where their brainpower took them. And they were both so damn normal. That really made it nice.

When the seminar ended, Corey smacked him on the

shoulder and said, "You want to go for a run?"

Mac looked at him in surprise, then thought of the burger and fries he had for lunch. "Yeah, I do. You got a place in mind?"

Corey nodded. "I heard through the grapevine there could have been another house broken into."

"How did you hear that?"

"The woman who lives there—her son died in the accident overseas. She's been visiting her daughter in San Diego instead of staying alone at the house. The daughter is friends with an airman buddy. She told him, and he told someone else. … You know how it is. Apparently Mason heard about it. He'd planned to talk to you about it, but he's in a meeting. It looks like we could be heading overseas pretty quick, and I figured, in the meantime, we should maybe take a run and assess the location of that house versus the others."

The two of them walked out, notebooks in hand. "We could just look on a map too," Macklin said in a dry tone.

But Corey was a physical guy too. Any chance he had to do things with his legs, he did them. "Yeah, but I could use the exercise," Corey said with a groan. "And, if we are heading out soon, you know what that can be like. It will screw up our fitness routine completely."

"And sometimes these trips exhaust us to the point we need a week off before getting back into doing anything."

"Exactly what I meant." With a big grin, the two headed off to get changed. Just before they separated at the parking lot, Corey said, "Ten minutes."

"Where do you want to meet?" Macklin asked.

Corey looked at him with a smirk. "At your house, bro. We're going for a long run today."

Once home, Macklin raced up the stairs. Corey would

be here in less than five minutes. He was up for the run, but at the same time, he was stressed and frustrated. Maybe that was why Corey had suggested a longer run, to do something to wear all that stress down.

He was dressed and back outside when Corey ran up to him. He tapped Macklin lightly on the shoulder and said, "Let's go for it," and he bolted.

Sprinting and laughing at the same time, Macklin raced to catch up. "We don't have to sprint, do we?"

"Nah, just for the first couple minutes to get really warmed up. I feel like we haven't had a good run in weeks."

Macklin groaned. "Are you telling me that we're settling in for something really big?"

"I figure we could do 10k easy."

Relieved, Macklin picked up the pace, and, as he caught up with Corey, he smacked him on the shoulder and said, "You're it." And raced past him. Corey swore, gave a great big shout, and picked up the pace again. Macklin could hear his footsteps pounding behind him. But no way in hell would he let Corey catch up.

Making a game out of it made the 10k easier to get through. Nothing like a little friendly sibling rivalry to make them all happy.

After about 6k, Corey said, "We're taking a right up here."

Macklin turned to look around the area and said, "We're pretty close to the other break-ins."

"Exactly. There's also something weird about that latest break-in."

"What? You're not exactly giving me details here."

"There's a chance the intruder might have moved in for a few days."

That almost brought Macklin to a stop.

Immediately Corey raced ahead. "Got you."

Swearing, Macklin caught up with Corey. "So did you mean that, or was that just to set me off my stride?"

"I meant it. Apparently the bedding had been changed and there was milk, potentially food, in the fridge—as if the guy decided the house was empty, and he should have a place to stay."

"So that was likely his base of operation."

"Maybe, but the mother's home now. So what the hell will happen when he finds out?"

Swearing once again, Macklin pulled out his phone and dialed Alex. He was running, so he tried to stabilize his breath so he didn't sound like he was a complete moron when she answered. But instead her phone went to voice mail.

Corey looked over at him. "She already knows. Mason will have contacted her. Plus the daughter said she had convinced her mother to talk to the police."

Relieved, Macklin put away his phone. "I want to see this house."

"I think everybody does."

"But, more important, we need to know if that was his base. And if he made those four hits from there. We still don't know why he entered those places, and what we really need to know is what his plans are."

"If she doesn't go home again, he might go back on his own."

"Well, I've already heard about it, and you know the police have heard about it, so what's the chance this guy has heard it too?"

The two men exchanged glances.

"Somebody needs to make sure she's not going back to her house," Macklin said. "We've already had enough women injured and killed."

"Do you really think Marsha's death is involved in this?" Corey asked.

"It's hard not to. Just think about it. How often do we have this many crimes in this area? Serious ones, like this? They've got to be connected. Nothing else makes any sense."

CHAPTER 9

A LEX HEADED HER car toward Betty's house, Betty in the passenger seat. Alex wanted to see the layout and all the issues Betty had pointed out. Betty's daughter would meet them at the coffee shop and take her mother back to her place. Alex wanted to make sure this was done quietly. If the intruder was still around, watching, she wanted him or her to not realize the cops had found out about Betty's house. It was the perfect opportunity to go in, set up cameras, and see if they could find out what the hell was going on. There was also a good chance this person had already left the area. But she'd take whatever opportunity she could.

Betty pointed out the house. Instead of parking out front, Alex parked down the street. She really didn't want anybody to know they were here or which house they would enter. She pulled on a jacket from her trunk and, with Betty at her side, they walked toward the house and passed it. She went into the neighbor's backyard and around, as if going to a different house, then slipped behind to Betty's house. With Betty safely behind her, Alex pulled her weapon and stepped inside. She listened but couldn't hear or see anything.

From where she stood, she could see two officers in the opposite backyard. They hopped the fence and joined them. They went in ahead of Alex and did a quick sweep through the property. When clear, she let Betty in. Grabbing the bags and jacket Betty wanted, Alex turned to her and asked, "Do you need anything else right now?"

Betty shook her head. "No. I just ... I just want to leave."

With the men now installing cameras, Alex walked casually with Betty back out front to the street to the car, talking animatedly. Thankfully she was driving her own car, not one of the cruisers. With Betty at her side, she drove to the coffee shop where they met her daughter. As soon as they arrived, the daughter rushed toward her mom.

"Are you all right?" she demanded.

Betty nodded and patted her daughter's hand. "But you were right. I needed to go to the police."

The daughter turned to look at Alex. "Do you know anything about the intruder?"

Alex shook her head. "No. But we have four other cases like this. We're installing cameras in Betty's house, and, if he returns, we'll catch him. He might already know she's back though, and that's something we can't do anything about."

The daughter nodded. "Is it okay if I take her now?"

"Absolutely." She turned to Betty. "I'll let you know if we find out anything."

Betty gave Alex a grateful smile and let her daughter lead her away.

Alex watched them back out of the parking lot and turn onto the main road. This was a huge break in the case for so many reasons. The trouble was, they might not have had enough warning to make the best of it. If the intruder had seen Betty return, then he'd spook and take off. If he hadn't seen her, he could return. However, if he did come back to her house, and they had the cameras installed ...

She pulled out her buzzing phone and saw Macklin was calling. "What's up?"

"We just ran past the house, the one whose place was broken into while the resident wasn't there," he said calmly. "Don't go getting wild. Gossip around the place travels quickly."

"That's really bad news," she snapped. "Do you realize that, if the intruder finds out, he won't return to that house?"

"You do have cameras set up for him, don't you?"

"Of course I do. I'm not a fool."

"Never thought you were. But, if you placed a marker on all the houses on a map, do you realize they are all on the right side, forming an irregular semicircle? Chances are good he'll swing around and try some of the houses on the other side."

"If he is staying at Betty's house, however, he may have to go to another location now if he knows she's back. And that could completely shift his demographics," she said. It just occurred to her that Mac was extremely out of breath. "Why are you breathing so hard? Are you hurt?"

He chuckled, even as he gasped for breath. "No. We've been out for a long run."

"Of course you just had to run past the house in question. Correct?"

"Yes, of course I did. None of us like to know someone is preying on women."

"I just don't know what it is we're looking for," she said with a hard sigh. "It'd be good if I didn't have to trip over you every time. Did you see us?"

"We were there. I saw you walk out with an older woman, presumably the woman who lived there. But you didn't see us."

She cast her mind back, frowning as she realized that, in her need to make it look natural, she had deliberately avoided looking around to see if they were being watched. "What if the intruder saw you?"

"It doesn't matter if he did. We were out for a jog. Totally normal and natural. On any block, on any given day, at any given hour, you can find someone jogging around here. These residences are all for military personnel, remember?"

She hated to say it, but he was right. Everybody, military or not, was into fitness, and running was one of the cheapest and easiest forms of exercise. "I sure as hell hope you didn't blow my case wide open."

"I sure as hell hope we did," he corrected. "But I doubt it. I just hope you have a ghost car or somebody who can sit out front and keep watch."

"That's what the cameras are for." And she hung up on him. She was pissed he had gone to look, even angrier the gossip had picked up on the latest news. She slowly headed back to the office. She wanted to see the map for herself. Way too many houses were still in that area.

She also wanted to find out if body-recognition programs were available—similar to facial recognition. She glanced at her watch and decided she should head there first. She didn't have an appointment, so when she walked into the security office, nobody was expecting her.

Surprised welcome flashed across their faces. She walked over to the man in charge and said, "Greg, I have a few questions regarding the camera systems in town."

He motioned to a chair beside him. "Fly away."

"I understand we have facial recognition, so if somebody catches a face on one of their gates, the camera will take a photo of their face. Do we have any cameras set up where we can use a body-imaging program?"

He looked at her in confusion.

"Let me be a little clearer. I'm looking for a tall, slim, fit person, but I don't know if it's male or female."

He considered her for a long moment. "No. There's not enough identification points mapped on the human body to do a comparison. The facial recognition program has multiple points identified on each face so, once it has analyzed a person's facial features, it can search through the video feeds to look for a match. There is no such program for the entire body."

"Right. I didn't think there would be ..." She smiled. "I can always hope technology has moved faster than expected. So you have hours and hours of video feeds I would have to sit here and go through and potentially never see the person I'm looking for."

"Possibly, yes. We can't capture everybody, but, when you consider the traffic cameras and all the security cameras, I highly doubt anybody could have come and left without having been caught on camera somewhere."

"I was thinking the point of recognition will still be visible. Hip bones, thighs, height, length, things like that."

"If you give me a body, I can give you their height," he offered. "And a few other characteristics. But there are no body-type matching programs to streamline the matching-up process."

"I knew it was a long shot, but I figured I wouldn't know if I didn't ask."

"Are we talking about all the break-ins?"

She nodded. "We just set up cameras inside one house, in case the guy comes back."

"Comes back? Why did you do it in one and not the others?"

"We had no reason to believe he would return." She frowned. "Maybe you haven't heard about that one yet." She was kicking herself at not having filled him in initially.

When she explained, he asked, "And the neighbors didn't notice anything off?"

"No. And, if we set up any alarm by talking to the neighbors or have the neighbors react unnaturally, then it'll chase him off."

Greg tapped the desk thoughtfully for a long moment, thinking. "I don't have cameras anywhere close to that area. The closest intersection is over two blocks away."

"So far, we're assuming he had approached the house on foot. It's either that or he's parking a distance away or he's living close by. In fact, I ran a plate on a suspicious truck, but the name doesn't match anything in our fingerprint database and isn't an obvious match to our victims. I'll have to dig deeper on that. However, if you look on the map, Betty's house has a unique location to the others."

The two of them got up and walked over to the big wall map. She pinned spots on the map where the four break-ins had occurred and then added a pin where Betty's house was.

"They're all on the 12-to-6 side of the circle. Why hasn't he gone from the 6-to-12 side?" He turned to look at her. "You need to answer that question."

"I had assumed the women were the targets. That he was going to each of those addresses specifically for the women."

"Sure. Everybody will be assuming that, because it's empty or a single woman lives there alone, or the people involved know each other."

"And sometimes intruders don't need to know anything

but that these women know each other."

He turned to her. "What do you mean?"

"Well, imagine this guy sees a group of five women at a coffee shop. He can't forget about them, so he goes and could, in theory, check out every one of their homes, mentally making plans to 'meet' them for something much different. But, so far, we can't figure out why he's gone into any of the houses," she said. "Nothing's missing. Nothing has been stolen. He got into an altercation with a boyfriend in one and an altercation with the homeowner in another. She was knocked unconscious, but there was no sexual assault."

"Nice for her, but it doesn't exactly clarify what he's looking for."

"We're wondering why he went back to the first house a second time if it was the same person. A neighbor noticed a tall, lean, potentially male individual entering. I searched the house, looking for some clues, but he was no longer there, and, as far as I can tell, he went out the window on the second floor, landed on the roof of the small porch, and took off on the side of the house in the dark."

She stared around the room filled with equipment. "It's so frustrating to think you have eyes in so many corners, and yet this guy is slipping in underneath the shadows. Somehow we have to ID him."

"And now, with everybody hearing about this many break-ins in this one area, everybody should be careful and take extra precautions."

"The fourth woman woke up in the middle of the night to the intruder in her house," Alex admitted. "Even though she knew about the B&Es."

"Did she have security?"

"No." She gave him a wry look. "Yet you and I both know that most security systems can be disabled easily."

"Especially the affordable systems. However, there's still a certain skill required to bypass them."

With a final smile, she turned to leave. That security center was incredibly well-run. A quick call to the Silver Strand housing manager confirmed there were no cameras—traffic or security—on the housing complex. For her own sake, she did another slow drive past Betty's house.

There was no sign of movement. There were traffic cameras on the main intersection several blocks away from the complex's main entrance, but poring over days of video would eat into a lot of man-hours and could be useless. She could give the neighbors a quick call, but she was afraid they'd start looking around and peering out their windows, looking for whoever had been at Betty's house.

She continued to drive up and down the street, wondering how she could find out who was away. Obviously she knew to look for the usual things, like a pile of newspapers in the driveway, but most people didn't even get newspapers delivered to the door anymore. Honestly, the standard mail system itself had declined with the advance of emails. And there was no need to stop emails because you could access them from anywhere in the world.

Back at the office, she walked in to find several of the officers standing around talking. "What's up?"

"We're just discussing Betty's house. The cameras have been installed. Now it's wait-and-see time." Lance pointed out an office to the side that she didn't think she'd been in yet. "These monitors are connected to the video cameras. We also have a van outside fully equipped for stakeouts."

"*Hmm.* Being mobile could be a big help." She walked

into the room to see one of the officers in front of the monitors. "Anything yet?"

He shook his head. "I just finished running all the tests. Everything is live. Now it's a matter of waiting."

She nodded, turned, and walked back into the squad room. "Anybody got any bright ideas as to how we can tell who's away on vacation?"

The gathered officers turned to look at her in confusion.

"I want to know which houses are empty in that area."

"We can check with the management company, but tenants aren't required to check in or out for holidays. It's a regular rental contract. They could tell us if any houses haven't been rented, but I doubt they would do so without a warrant. Although we could ask."

"That's a good idea. Do you want to follow that up for me? Make sure that includes houses that might be undergoing renovations."

Lance nodded. "Yes. There could be one or two in the complex, but they're pretty efficient at filling them up as fast as possible."

"Makes sense. How do we tell who's on holidays and may have left their property empty?"

Lance frowned. "Outside of having some access to payroll, none, but, even then, they're still getting their paychecks if they're on vacation."

"Not to mention some people take a few days off, and they just stay at home," Lance said.

Alex nodded. "Think about it. We used to stop the newspaper service. We used to stop milk delivery. Just for while we're away. And that was always something you could check up on. I used to call the newspapers and see who stopped service for a week or two. And I will still do that.

But it seems like less people read physical newspapers now."

They racked their brains.

"Outside of asking people to report friends or neighbors who may have left on vacation or left their properties empty, I don't know if we could find that out," Lance said.

"And, if we do that, we also alert the intruder what we're looking for."

The other two nodded. "Exactly."

Still thinking, she wandered back into her office. She didn't want somebody else to get hurt. She'd already warned the public about the break-ins, told people to be vigilant. What she probably needed to do was put out a warning and request anyone to contact the police if they knew of any vacant houses. The intruder would go underground for a period after hearing that, but maybe, in the meantime, they'd get a heads-up on him.

Lance walked in. "I still think we should contact the news."

"I agree. I was just thinking that. If we could wait until tomorrow, we might have a chance to see if this guy returns to Betty's house first."

He nodded. "I agree. Let's hope we can get through the night without another break-in."

"Assign someone to check the feed from the security on the intersection outside the housing complex." She wrote the instructions down on a notepad. "It's a long shot, but we might spot our intruder walking about."

He took her note and left her office.

It was almost time to leave. She stayed back and took care of a mess of paperwork that always seemed to clog up her desk. The more she had risen in the ranks, the more reports and paperwork she had to do. And still had to verbally report to her superiors. That didn't help her mood.

By the time she was done, she was grouchy and tired. She walked into the sun and smiled. Talk about a mood changer. The weather was dynamite here.

She'd had enough winter back east that she appreciated all good weather. And right now, it was typical California sunshine. She looked down at her jeans and T-shirt and thought maybe it was time for a jog on the beach.

She headed back home and quickly changed. She hadn't been on a run at least since last week, and that wasn't good. It was part of her job to stay fit.

She went through physical training and testing on a regular basis. But, anytime she got busy like this, it was almost impossible to maintain a routine. Just thinking of Macklin running past that house was enough to put her on edge again. That damned fool.

He might be smart and know what was what when it came to his job, but he wasn't a pro at hers. She laced up her sneakers and headed outside. She had gone for leggings, a sports bra, and a tank top.

She had a headband wrapped around her wrist several times. With her hair in a ponytail most of time, she was fine without it. But sometimes, when the heat and humidity got to her, it was all she could do to stop the sweat from running into her eyes. She started off on a nice loose jog. She didn't know why she decided to run locally and not at the beach, except she wanted to people watch.

Every time she saw somebody super tall or lean now, she had to study them. She kept up her steady pace for a good twenty minutes. Up ahead was the park. She steadied her breath to speed up and raced around it, laughing and cheering herself on. When she got to the far corner, she slowed her pace again and jogged through several more blocks. When she came to a familiar house, she realized, to her horror, she'd done exactly what Macklin had done. Like a homing pigeon, she'd jogged through the neighborhoods that were broken into.

She was on neighborhood watch, she told herself. The fact that she was a police officer gave much more credence to her trip but not enough to make her feel any better. She hadn't intended to come here. Still, she could see Betty's house up toward the end of the block. She surveyed the area, seeing groups of people walking, some walking home from work, others driving, parking their cars, and getting out.

She knew the ghost car with a camera setup was somewhere ahead. She casually jogged down the road. The last thing she wanted was to be hassled when she went into the office in the morning.

As she passed Betty's house, she thought she caught a movement out of the corner of her eye. She glanced toward the house to see a face staring back at her. She smiled casually and kept going. But in her mind, she was like, "Who the hell was that?"

One house away, she pulled out her cell phone and called Lance. "I just jogged past Betty's. Check the cameras. There was a face in the front window."

She heard his startled exclamation as he raced toward the camera room. She could hear the raised voices.

Lance said, "He didn't see anybody. He's been sitting in front of the monitors the whole time."

"Any chance it's not working? Could the intruder have done something to the cameras?"

"He shouldn't be able to," Lance said. "Are you sure you saw someone at the house? It wasn't just your imagination?"

If he had been in the same room with her, she would have cut him down for that comment. But even then, she had to wonder, *Had she imagined it?*

IT WASN'T A good idea. Mac knew it wasn't. He stared down at his phone, his finger itching to call her. He got her to agree to lunch. He knew he could push it to dinner. But how many times could he see her or contact her in a day before it became abnormal? Of course he always had Marsha on his mind. The woman had driven him nuts. Is that how Alex would feel if he called her? But he couldn't stop thinking about her.

He poured himself yet another beer from the growler on the counter. He and Corey had split the first half. Now he was working his way through the second half on his own. He walked out to a small deck and slumped down into the chair, kicking his feet up over the railing.

There were a lot of good things about his life right now. And a lot that could be a whole lot better. His days were normal—training, upgrading his skills, learning. The IT seminar had been fascinating. But no matter how hard he tried, he couldn't keep his mind off his problems right now. All the break-ins and Marsha's murder had to be connected. That one of the houses had been one Bill had lived in surely was a coincidence. But Mac didn't know how this all worked together. Trying to sort it out was a circle that didn't seem to stop. And not having access to the information he needed was frustrating.

He let his mind freewheel as he sat here, holding his cold beer. Thoughts flowing in, flowing out. With Betty now gone from her house, he wondered if the asshole would return. If the intruder had any decent instincts, he'd avoid it like the plague. Unless he had a way to disengage the cameras or keep them on an endless loop. Macklin frowned as he considered that. If you wired the camera to do an endless loop of the last hour or so, then, in theory, the intruder could stay there all he wanted, and the police would eventually give up on that concept.

How hard would that be? Not hard if the intruder was good with electronics—or even if he was just good at research. The internet had step-by-step instructions.

Knowing it was a slim excuse, feeble at best, Macklin hit the Dial button. When Alex answered, her tone was wry. "Macklin? Pretty sure I had lunch with you already today."

"Is there a law against calling you?" he asked, dry humor mixed with a little bit of hesitation.

She chuckled. "No. Not at all. But was there something specific or were you just checking to make sure I'm eating dinner?"

At that, he laughed out loud. "I was thinking that, just because you have the cameras up in that empty house, it doesn't mean you'll catch him."

"Of course it doesn't mean that," she said. "Just think about what you said. He may not even return to the house. So of course there's no guarantee we'll catch him."

"Or he'll return to the house, switch the camera to an endless loop. And all your cameras will pick up is the exact same scene repeatedly in the house, and then you won't know he's in there."

Dead silence was on her end. "How hard is that to do?" she asked, her tone hesitant. "I went past there today, jogging. And, I swear to God, I saw somebody in the house staring at me."

"What?" He bounded to his feet. "Are you serious?"

"Yeah. But there's no sign of anyone on the security camera feed," she said. "They are running a check on the system now, and two officers are doing drive-bys. The lights were off, and curtains were partially closed, so they hadn't recognized when daylight darkened."

"I've just come out of a seminar on hacking and IT fraud. And it occurred to me, while I sat here on my deck, that it's quite possible to put that camera feed on an endless loop. You'll never know."

"Which means, I have to go back into the house."

"Not alone," he snapped.

She snapped right back at him. "I'm a cop, remember?"

"Well, I'm not a cop, but this is what I deal with often," he said in a low tone. "You also have to go in undercover. As soon as he makes you, this operation is a bust."

"I do know how to do my job," she reminded him, but there was less heat in her tone.

"I don't want any more women hurt. There is a killer out there."

"Remember that whole thing about me being in law enforcement? I'm the one people call when there is this kind of trouble."

"No. You're who gets called afterward," he reminded her. "I'm the one they call all around the world before this part happens." He couldn't help himself. "I'll meet you there."

Then he hung up without giving her a chance to respond. He slammed back the last bit of his beer, changed to his running shoes, and headed out. His phone rang before he even hit the street. He pulled it out and answered it. "I'm in my running shoes, and I'm jogging. You can drive a block away and meet me at the corner off North Wallington."

She groaned. "You don't take no for an answer, do you?"

"You won't go out for a real date, will you?" Then he hung up. She was still spluttering, but it was music to his ears. It wasn't necessarily a bad thing to keep her off-center. But there was something going on around this place, and, if he could help, he would.

CHAPTER 10

FUMING, ALEX THREW on her sweater to prepare for the cooler night temperature, grabbed her purse and keys, and headed out. She knew the corner Macklin spoke of. Even for a fast sprinter, it would take him a bit.

She thought she saw him ahead. His was not a physique to miss. He waved at her. She parked and walked toward him. She didn't want to look at the house in any obvious way, but, at the same time, she needed to know. Her quick glance in that direction showed no face at all. But then what did she expect? It was not like he would sit there and stare out the window forever.

When he was close enough, Macklin opened his arms, picked her up, swung her around, gave her a great big hug, and dropped her gently back on her feet.

She gasped as she tried to stabilize herself. "Don't do that," she scolded.

He chuckled. "I figured we needed a nice greeting to show we were long-lost friends."

She rolled her eyes at him. "And the truth of the matter is, you really just wanted to pick me up."

"Anything to get my hands on you," he said with a big smirk.

She sighed. "Did you see anything?"

He shook his head. "No, I didn't. That means absolutely

nothing though."

She stood there, undecided. "I'd like to go in," she said suddenly.

"Good idea. But not from here. Let's go to the far side, coming over the back fence."

She shook her head. "No. The back fence is visible from that entire wall of windows. We have to go in from the side." And she thought about it for a little longer, adding, "From the left side."

"Why the left?"

He wasn't questioning her judgment, she realized. He was interested in knowing her reasoning. "Because only one window is on that side, on the second floor. I think it's a bathroom window, and it's frosted."

He nodded. "Then let's continue down the direction I'm traveling. We'll go past your car, come around the far block, come up that side, and whip in."

She grinned. "That's a plan."

"Unless you'll get into trouble having a civilian with you?"

"We're just going for a walk. If we see something, of course I'll check it out. Nobody would have anything to say about it."

He nodded. He jutted out his elbow slightly and said, "Then tuck your hand into my arm, and let's just go for a nice walk as if we were meant to be together."

"You really like to push that, don't you?"

"I'm just acting out what I'd really like to be doing. I was sitting at home, wondering if it was too early to call you."

That startled a laugh out of her. "Are there rules to this stuff?"

He gave her a lopsided grin. "Marsha made me very leery. I was just figuring out if a phone call tonight put me in stalker category."

"No, you're not in stalker category." Then in a mock-threatening tone she added, "At least not yet."

They continued to talk, getting to know each other as they walked around the block and back up the other side. As they approached, she could feel her body tensing with awareness.

"Stay calm," he said in a low voice. "Act natural. We're two people, out spending time enjoying each other's company."

"I thought that's what I was doing."

"Well, you were. Then you tensed as we got closer. If he's watching, he's watching. There's no help for it. Like you said, there's got to be a reason for him to be looking."

"He's probably looking," she said. "And he might see us from the front and then wonder where we went."

"No, he won't. The neighbors on the left just got into their vehicle and drove away. Two kids, two adults. So I suggest we go up their sidewalk and then step around the back. Think of us as having been out for the evening."

"Which, in a way, we have," she said drily. But she kept her arm crooked against his as they detoured to the house.

Flattened against the wall, she said, "It's hardly dark enough for this."

"It's just about perfect actually. In this half-light, everybody mistakes objects. Most of the time, their gaze just glances right over them."

She followed his lead around the house and crept up the porch steps to the kitchen door; he slipped back so they were hidden against the wall. From there, he could peer into the kitchen.

"There's a light on." He turned to look at her. "Did you guys leave it on?"

She frowned. "There shouldn't be a light on."

He held up a finger, warning her to be quiet as he tilted his head.

She watched him go into full predator mode as he peered forward, considering the kitchen. Even from where she was, she could hear his jaw click in anger.

He slipped back down, shot her a hard look, and said, "You need to call in your men. There's a dish towel on the table and a dishrag, wet on the tap. He may not be in residence now, but there's a very good chance he's living here again."

In a low whisper, she said, "Then I'm going to back out of here so I can get the team together."

He looked at her hard for a moment and then gave her a quick nod.

Good. He would let her take over. As he crept back to the other house, she realized he was in control always, and that was damn good to see. It also made a mockery of thinking he might have killed Marsha. It didn't suit who she was coming to realize Macklin was.

Several houses down, leaning against a tree, she called up her men and said, "I've just checked in on the house. There are signs of someone having been in the house. There's something wrong with your feed."

Lance gave a startled exclamation. "Really?"

"Yes, really. We need the team, and we need them down here fast." Then she hung up. Macklin joined her. "It'll be a few minutes."

He gave her a grin. "Deputize me. I'd be happy to do

this job for the cause."

She shook her head. "Even if I wanted to, I couldn't. You're still part of an active investigation. What I can't do is compromise the case."

His jaw tensed in frustration, but he nodded. "I'm not leaving," he said. "I'm staying right here and keeping watch."

She tossed that concept over and then shrugged. "Fine. But you stay out of the way. And don't make it look like you're my date for the night," she warned. "That'll just muddy the waters even worse."

"I understand that. But another set of eyes won't hurt." He pulled out his phone and said, "Maybe I could even bring Corey down. We can watch the area and observe any one leaving or entering the area."

With a hard look to make sure he stayed where he was, she then watched the vehicles coming around the corner.

"That green car is one of my men. You can bring Corey in but make sure you stay the hell out of my way." Then she turned and walked toward the car. She waved when Lance got out.

As she approached, he said, "It'll take another fifteen minutes to set up. We need men in uniforms coming in on all sides."

She nodded. "We just have to make sure he doesn't see us."

"No way to know if he's in the house?"

"No. I'm sure I saw him earlier, but he could be out prowling for his next victim right now."

Lance looked down the block at the house. "It's so frustrating. I want to walk in to see if he's there."

"How do you think I felt earlier?"

"True enough. I didn't believe you, and I should have. I

never thought about the feed looping so that we wouldn't see anything."

"It's a good idea though. Apparently not hard to do."

He turned to look at her. "Was that your idea?"

"No. Macklin called me and said he thought that was way-too-possible. He's been in an IT seminar for the last couple days."

Lance's gaze narrowed, but he didn't say anything for a long moment. "I presume you considered that implication?"

"I have. Believe me. I'm not getting involved with him. At least not until he's cleared as a suspect."

"Which you already have, haven't you?"

She nodded. "I have. But, until we find Marsha's killer, he's not off the hook completely."

"No. But as long as he's a reasonable doubt ..."

She sighed. "Relationships are never easy. And, as far as my experience goes, they're almost always at inconvenient times."

"True enough," he said. He stared at a point past her head. "Don't turn around."

"What do you see?"

"A man approaching from the far side."

"As in, crossing the road?" She studied the area in front of her. But of course she couldn't take a chance of turning around to look.

"Yes. He came up the opposite side of the road. Looked like he was about to cross, but he dashed back to his side again."

She watched as Lance tracked his movements.

"He's going past the house now. But he's watching it."

Instinct kicked in. "We should nab him."

Lance shook his head. "Nab him for what? Walking past

the house?"

"Can we get a picture of him?"

"From here, no. He's too far away." He pulled out his phone and called one of the other men. "Is anybody in position? We have a suspect walking right past on the opposite side of the road. We're hoping to get a photo of his face."

She turned to look around. Macklin and Corey walked down from the far end of the block. She didn't know how they had circled around and got here in time. She grabbed her phone and dialed Macklin. "A man is approaching you," she said in a rush. "We need a picture of his face."

She watched as Macklin dropped the phone in front of him, chest height, and started clicking buttons.

"Macklin and Corey are coming from the far end. I've asked him to try to take a photograph."

Lance turned to look at her. "Can he do it without being caught?"

"If anybody can, he can."

She could see Macklin's jaw working, as if talking to Corey. It was easy to make it look like they were setting up plans. Texting was a hell of a cover these days too. Knowing the two of them, they were both doing something. They stopped to talk, half facing each other, and both with their phones in their hands. The man approached them, skipped around, probably apologizing as Macklin and Corey stepped back to give him space. Then Macklin laughed and said something. She watched as Corey snapped some more images.

"They got it." She couldn't stop the cool sense of satisfaction inside her.

"What do you want to do about the house?" Lance

asked.

"I want two men to go in from the back and do a full sweep."

Lance relayed the order as they kept an eye on the man who disappeared around the block.

Macklin texted her.

We've got several photos and a video.

You're in position. Do you want to follow up?

You think he's the one?

Can't take the chance he's not.

Mason is driving toward us. We've tagged him. He'll pick up the tail as we keep walking.

She read that last bit, then said to Lance, "Mason's picking up the tail."

"Is that a smart idea to bring someone else into this?"

"It'll be hard for anybody to prove Mason had something to do with these break-ins. The fact that we have multiple well-respected military men, sitting here, ready to help, is not an offer I'll turn down."

Lance thought about it for a long moment and then nodded. "That works for me." Lance's phone rang. He answered it on the first ring. "What did you find?"

He turned to look at Alex. "Definitely signs of somebody living in the house. It is currently empty."

She nodded. "Have them fix a camera, the one in the least obvious place he'd check."

Lance shook his head. "He's checking them all."

"Do we have another camera to put in that he won't know about?"

Lance listened on the phone as the officer on the other

side said, "Two of the cameras have been disabled, one was on a standard loop."

"Two have been disabled?" She turned to look at him. "Were they all showing on the monitors?"

"We could never get one of them to work."

"Then have it fixed. If you can, make it so he won't know it's working."

The conversation continued. Finally Lance put away his phone. "They think they've got it."

"We need surveillance on that property. If he thinks he got away with it, he'll be back. Otherwise, he'll be looking for a place to stay."

"The men are out of the house now. It's clear on the other side."

She nodded. "Good."

"But that doesn't mean he isn't backing around and crossing over to that block. So have them pull away. We'll set up surveillance."

She motioned to the car. "Let's change position."

At the vehicle Lance turned on the engine, slowly pulled the vehicle back out onto the main road. "Where do you want to go?"

"There's a coffee shop two blocks down. Let's park there and walk back."

MACKLIN WISHED HE could see where Alex was hiding, but he and Corey were slowly strolling. Mason had already confirmed the suspect would be coming around the corner any moment.

As they watched, the suspect made a right and went back down the same block he'd just come up. Corey smiled and said, "This is good."

Macklin agreed. Because any time a suspect just went around the block, one had to wonder why. The fact that he, Corey, and Alex earlier had been doing the exact same thing added to that. They were up to something. They'd been looking for this guy.

Macklin watched as Mason made a left and headed down the street a couple blocks behind the suspect. He was the tail again. "We should walk toward the coffee shop, maybe grab coffees, and head back toward the house. See how Mason's doing."

"He can only go so far. He'll overtake the suspect in seconds."

"I know. We can pick up the surveillance ourselves down a couple blocks."

They turned on the next block and headed down. There was no way to see from where they were if the suspect was still moving toward the house or toward the coffee shop. Mason would drive down a couple blocks, turn around, and come back, as if he was looking for an address. With any luck they could pick up the tail again before Mason had to do too many U-turns.

"No word from Mason yet."

"Which is good. That means he's on it and still has the suspect in his sights."

In fact, Macklin was pretty sure he had seen Tesla, Mason's partner, in the vehicle beside him. A couple was less conspicuous than a single man when undercover. Up ahead he could see the lights of the coffee shop. "I wonder where Alex went."

"She should be around the house still."

Macklin wasn't so sure about that. It depended on what

her men had found inside.

There was still no message from Mason as they arrived at the coffee shop. Macklin stayed outside while Corey went inside and ordered two coffees to go.

Timewise that should be just about right to catch the suspect coming around the corner to the coffee shop, and, sure enough, just as they crossed the street, he came down, looked at the coffee shop, like he had decided to go in, and then took a right.

As they stood in the parking lot, Macklin's phone rang. It was Mason. "I see him. He's just heading away from the coffee shop."

"Good." Mason said.

"Corey's inside getting a drink." Macklin chuckled. "I'm standing in the parking lot, waiting on my coffee right now."

Mason's voice was full of humor as he said, "I can see you. That's why I called. You get to pick up the tail from here. And, by the way, is this a good suspect?"

"Looking better every minute."

"For Marsha's case?"

"If they're connected, yes. But, even if they aren't, it looks like the suspect from the break-ins."

"Good. Let's get that bastard. Tesla knows both Kathleen and Betty. Not well but enough to smile and say hi in passing."

"Not to mention the fact that, when you're not there, Tesla is home alone."

There was silence for a long moment, then Mason's voice turned even harder. "Make sure you get that bastard tonight."

At the odd note in Mason's voice, Macklin wondered if they were all heading out on a mission or if Mason was.

Because that would leave Tesla alone for weeks. Tesla had already been attacked several times in the past. Mason had a very low tolerance for anybody hurting what was his. Macklin and the rest of their unit felt the same.

Only cowards went after women.

Mac recognized a green car off to the side that he had seen earlier. Deliberately not looking directly at the vehicle, he could see Alex and her cohort inside. They were both busy on laptops and cell phones and that meant they were focused on something. That was good too.

When Corey came out, the two walked back up the block Mason had driven down. Now the question was whether to continue watching to see if he went back toward the house or not.

As they strolled down the block, they watched in delight as the suspect made a turn to head back up the block toward the empty house. They stayed behind him all the way, letting him get farther and farther ahead.

When Macklin's phone rang again, he smiled to see Alex's ID.

"Any idea where the suspect is?"

"Mason just handed him off a few minutes ago. The suspect is currently one block away from the house, heading in that direction."

She gasped. "Now that would be lovely."

"Have you got a team in place to nab him if he goes in?"

"Everybody is on standby. We fixed one of the cameras."

"When did they go out?" he asked curiously.

"It could have been a couple hours ago."

"Did your guy take a break or leave the room at the time?"

She sighed. "Quite possibly. Nobody was there to relieve

him so he could get a meal."

"Surely in a case like this they aren't allowed to walk away?"

"Not sure he was in the loop on that memo," she said in a dry tone. "Don't worry. That's my problem, not yours."

He grinned. "True enough. I just want to make sure my girl is being looked after." And he hung up.

Corey looked at him. "*Your girl?*"

Macklin chuckled. "Maybe. As soon as I'm off the hook, that is."

"You do like to live dangerously, don't you?"

Macklin nodded. "I sure do. That girl can tie me up and handcuff me to a bed any day."

Corey shook his head. "On the other hand, at least she doesn't appear to be another resident of crazy land."

"She's as sane as you or me," Macklin said in all seriousness. "It's been a long time."

"I know, man. Marsha was a hell of a lesson."

"She was a scary lesson. I just hope she's at peace now. I never wished her ill. I just wanted her to leave me alone."

"And that's why you're such a good man. Somebody killed her, and it was probably because she pissed him off."

"And yet, what reasons are there for murder? Power, money, revenge?"

"Yep, that's pretty much the trio. Power? I don't see how killing Marsha would give anyone power. I mean, yeah, death as the ultimate power over someone, but that's power on a small scale. One on one. And Marsha didn't have any money. She might have been blackmailing somebody, but I don't think your detective found any unexpected money in her bank accounts. So the last one, revenge?"

"Revenge definitely. And often love and revenge go hand

in hand."

"That's possible. While she was fixated on you, somebody else could have wanted that attention for herself or himself."

"I didn't know her at all, so I have no way to gauge that. But currently anything goes."

"I keep coming back to that head wound. It was a downward force, so she was sitting. That means, Marsha had to have trusted this person. Somebody was inside her house, and Marsha just sat there. Either they were having a meal on the couch, watching TV, or doing something like that."

"And that usually means a friend."

"Yeah, it's not like you would let a stranger into the house and go back and sit down at the TV, would you?"

"But we never found any friends."

"No. Which also puts it down to either revenge or possibly a scorned lover. Somebody who really wanted Marsha, but maybe Marsha didn't want them in return."

"But was still friendly enough with to let in the house." Macklin stopped and turned to look at Corey. "Did anybody check Marsha's neighbors—her current neighbors—to see if they were in a relationship with Marsha?"

Corey shrugged. "Who the hell knows? Don't ask me. I had nothing to do with it."

Instantly Macklin pulled out his phone again. He didn't bother texting and went straight to calling Alex. "Did you check out Marsha's current neighbors?"

"Yes, why?"

"Because Marsha had to let somebody in for them to have attacked her. And it had to be somebody she trusted enough for her to sit down while they were in her house. Because the coroner said the blow on the top of the head was a downward force while she was potentially sitting, correct?"

"Yes, that's what he said," Alex said slowly. "But why a neighbor?"

"Because you and I didn't find any friends."

Alex's breath slowly let out on a long sigh. "I'll look up the records tonight and do a follow-up in the morning." She hung up.

He looked over at Corey and shrugged. "She has this habit of hanging up on me."

Corey grinned. "Dude, you keep jumping into her case. You're lucky that's all she does. If it was my case, I would have smacked you into tomorrow."

"Nah, she wouldn't hit me." Macklin smirked. "She likes me too much for that."

<h1 style="text-align:center">CHAPTER 11</h1>

A LEX RAISED HER head from the laptop in front of her. She contemplated Macklin's logic. It wasn't that there was anything faulty with it, she just wasn't sure it was strong enough, but it was easy enough to check out. He'd emailed the photos and video he'd taken when she'd asked him earlier. She filed the material away with the rest of the case files.

Lance's gaze came up. "Now what does lover boy want?"

She shot him a look of mock disgust, liking the camaraderie and gentle teasing developing with him. It made for a much nicer working relationship—as long as he respected her position, it was all good. "Remember, we're not lovers."

"*Yet.* You're not lovers *yet*," he said with a smile. "Besides, he's had some good ideas so far."

"And he might have had another one." She quickly explained.

"I can see what he means. If you haven't found any friends, and no lovers, who are the people in her life? Obviously there's at least one because somebody killed her."

"Unless it was a random act."

"No, I don't think so. But it was somebody who knew her if that blow on the head is indicative of her being seated when the person hit her."

"Somebody who came over to do her hair?"

Surprise hit Lance's gaze. "Wow, that's not a bad idea. Except there was no hair or anything else around to indicate she might have been getting a haircut."

"Maybe they hadn't started to cut her hair. It could just be they let her believe they were getting ready to do so." She stopped to look at him again. "I need to talk with her neighbors who I missed before—at least the ones on her floor." Alex checked her watch. "It's nine o'clock."

"Call them instead."

She thought about that and shook her head. "No. I really like to see people's reactions and get a feel of who they are from their facial expressions."

"You want to take a drive over there?"

She shook her head. "I'm not leaving here until we know if we've got this guy or not."

"But it's being handled," he said. "We've got good men on it. Having you here right now, not to insult you, but it won't make a bit of difference. How many neighbors did Marsha have?"

"She was on the bottom floor. I think seven apartments were on that floor."

"So, six doors to knock on. Chances are, they could be home right now. Check in with me so I know you're safe. Because, if there's a killer out there... they've already killed once—and a woman at that. They won't balk at killing a second one. Cop or no cop."

"Give me a ride back to my car. I'll head over there and see who might be home."

Ten minutes later she was in her own vehicle with an update of what was happening at the house. They were still waiting for somebody to enter, and, so far, their suspect was out walking the blocks. She really didn't want to leave, but, at the same time, she felt like she needed to check out Marsha's neighbors.

It meant two separate people were involved, and that made more sense than anything because murder versus break-ins weren't the same level of crime at all. Making a sudden decision, she pulled away, barely noticing she passed Macklin. From the startled look on his face he'd seen her.

She drove to Marsha's apartment building and parked. She had a key to Marsha's place, and, on impulse, she opened the door and walked in. It had occurred to her after the news coverage that maybe this guy was staying in Marsha's empty place too.

But it was empty. Bloodstains covered the living room floor and the couch.

Back in the hallway she headed to the first neighbor and knocked on the door. An older man came out with his wife peering over his shoulder. Alex quickly identified herself, asked a few questions as to whether they'd ever seen anybody coming or going in Marsha's place. Both were horrified to find out their neighbor had been killed. Apparently they hadn't heard the news or seen the police activity. Alex understood keeping to themselves, but, to this level, it was dangerous.

"We never really saw her. We don't get out much."

They both were apologetic.

"I couldn't even tell you what she looked like." The older lady turned to her husband. "Isn't that a terrible thing to have to admit?"

Alex moved on to the next apartment. Two young men were living there. From the looks of them, they were in a caring relationship. She asked similar questions and was told they'd seen Marsha coming and going but never saw anybody else there.

No one answered at the third apartment, which happened last time and wasn't helpful right now. Alex wrote down the number, figured she'd check it out as soon as she got back to the office.

The fourth door opened to a neighbor she'd spoken to earlier. The woman smiled and said, "Did you find anything new?"

Alex shook her head. "No, sorry, not yet. I'm just back double-checking that nobody has seen anybody around the apartment."

The woman's face twisted in confusion. "You mean, now that she's gone?"

"Sometimes killers come back to their hunting grounds," Alex explained.

The woman gasped and shook her head. "Honestly I race past that apartment these days."

"Do you live alone?"

"No, I don't. My sister lives with me."

"Is she here now?"

The young woman shook her head. "No, she's out with her boyfriend."

After writing down her name and her sister's name, Alex thanked her. "Is there somebody living next door to you? Nobody's answering the door."

"I believe they moved out a couple weeks ago."

"Any idea if they knew Marsha?"

The woman lifted her shoulders. "I'm sorry. I don't know anything about my neighbors."

With an apology for disturbing her so late, Alex moved on to the next door. She got no answer here, but she had spoken to a young woman earlier this week. She'd try once more before she left.

Moving on to the last door on this floor, a young male opened the door, looked at her, and started flirting.

Alex held up her ID. "I'm here about the murder of your neighbor."

His smile fell away, and he held up his hands. "I didn't have nothing to do with it. I wasn't even home."

"Where were you?"

"Back east," he said. "I have my flight itineraries to prove it."

"I wasn't here to accuse you," she said with a half smile. "I'm wondering if you knew her. If you ever saw her with anyone? Anybody coming or going out of the apartment?"

He nodded. "I saw her occasionally. She wasn't terribly friendly, but she did have one visitor who I saw more than once." He looked down the hall. "I thought maybe the woman lived here too because I saw her coming from that hallway. But I don't know."

"What did she look like?"

"She was tall and slim and easy on the eyes. She had a really short haircut. It looked good on her." He grinned and shook his head. "I don't think she swung that way. I did put the moves on her a time or two." He went silent. "I have been striking out a lot lately."

"Maybe you shouldn't try to strike. Maybe let things happen a little more naturally."

He chuckled. "Nah. Life's too short. You've got to make a move or miss out."

Despite everything, she liked his youth and humor. He wasn't old enough to be jaded by relationship troubles. After getting his name and seeing a copy of his airline tickets, which he swore he'd scan in an email to her, she left him alone. She walked back to the previous apartment and knocked on the door. When the door opened this time, the woman had a harried look on her face.

"I had just gotten into the bath," she explained, wrapping the bathrobe tighter around her neck. "I wasn't going to open the door, but I saw it was you again."

"Sorry. I didn't mean to disturb you a second time, but I was just speaking with one of your neighbors."

The woman frowned. "Which neighbor?" she asked suspiciously.

Alex pointed.

The woman rolled her eyes. "Yeah, him. He's flirty with all the girls. He should be able to tell you something about Marsha. It seemed like he was chatting her up all the time."

"He also said he saw another young woman with a short haircut at Marsha's apartment."

The young woman before her shook her head. "Doesn't sound familiar to me. But that's the back entrance hallway at that end. Lots of people come and go from there."

With a sinking heart, Alex realized that was quite true. "So, in other words, she could've parked in the back lot, come in through that entrance, straight through to Marsha's place?"

The woman nodded.

"Okay, I'm sorry for bothering you," Alex said as she stepped back.

The door was closed firmly in front of her, and the bolt shot home. Good afterthought. It wasn't smart to go to bed with the doors unlocked. Not given the intruder these days.

Out of curiosity, and just on pure instinct that she was missing something, she walked back into Marsha's apartment and strolled around. It was so strange to be in here. Only a few days before a vibrant young woman had picked up the coffee cup and sipped from it, used the water from the taps, and dried her face and hair with the towels. Alex wandered around. They'd gone through everything, fingerprinted the place, and had yet to find anything useful. There was just no forensic evidence.

She stood in the middle of the empty room, hoping something would jump out at her. After a moment, she shook her head and said aloud, "I'm sorry, Marsha. I will get to the bottom of this. I promise."

She walked back out to the hallway, locked the door, and headed out to her car. As she buckled her seat belt, her phone rang. "Lance, how are we doing?"

"We've got him in custody," Lance crowed. "He's on his way to the station right now."

She grinned. "Now let's just hope it's the right guy."

"Well, he resisted arrest pretty damn good. At least this way we can fingerprint him, get some DNA, and see if he was maybe the guy who the neighbor saw. He had his driver's license on him, so we'll do a full check to see what pops."

"Now that you've got him, let's get that house checked over too. We need fingerprints that match. At least let's prove he's the one who's been in the house. It'll still take a bit to prove he's the intruder from the other houses, but it's a damn good start."

"Are you coming in?" Lance asked.

"I'm about five minutes away. One of the apartments here is empty, but I've spoken to everybody else on Marsha's floor."

"Any news?"

"Not really. As usual nobody knows anything about anyone."

She closed her phone, put the keys into the ignition, and turned it on. It was good news about the intruder, but she couldn't stop worrying that maybe it was just an innocent man out for a stroll after all. It would take a lot of police work to put that asshole away. If it wasn't this guy, she was back to square one, and that was not where she wanted to be.

"DO YOU WANT to go to the coffee shop again?" Corey asked. "Or head home?"

They were still standing on the corner after the suspect had been picked up.

"Home. Although I'd rather go to Alex's house."

Corey shot him a sharp glance. "Is that wise?"

"I don't know. No way to know if she caught her man or not. She caught one, but is it the right one?" He shrugged. "I'm just saying what I'd like to do."

"Better to stay away until this is done," Corey advised. "I know she's a *Keeper*, but you don't want to do anything to jeopardize her job either."

"*Keeper?*" he asked, a note of humor in his voice.

Corey stared at him. "And you know it. She doesn't maybe, but I haven't watched a dozen friends find that special someone to not recognize one when I see one."

"So?" He was right but that didn't mean Macklin felt like listening. It was odd waiting on someone else to fix something in his life. Normally he was out there fixing things for other people. Still it was nice to hear Corey's evaluation. And he was right. They'd both seen a lot of their teammates find the right woman. Hence the joke about Mason's Keepers. "You looking for yourself?" Mac asked.

"Nah, I'm hoping I'll trip over her, like you guys did."
Corey walked backward as he spoke. "Coming or staying?"

"I'll head home," he decided, "and maybe call Alex later." He wasn't going back to Corey's. There was no way to know when another break-in would happen. He didn't want to impose on his friend for days, weeks possibly.

"You sure?" Corey turned toward his vehicle. "Do you want a lift?"

Macklin lifted his nose and sniffed the fresh air. Now that they'd caught the suspect, the air was lighter, fresher. It held hope that this could be over soon and also joy that he could see Alex openly.

"Nah, it's a nice night out. I'll walk." And, with a wave, he turned and headed home, his footsteps lighter than they'd been for days.

CHAPTER 12

OVERJOYED AT THE news, Alex quickly headed back to the station. She wanted to get a look at the intruder. After she parked, she strolled in with a light step. Excitement bubbled through the station. Several people looked up and smiled at her.

"Looks like we got him, Alex."

"Let's hope so," she said. "Now we need proof."

Lance stepped out of the office. "A full team is doing forensics right now."

She nodded. "Outside of picking up this person, do we have anything that places him at the scene of the crimes?"

Lance smirked. "I'm just about to head in and interrogate him. Do you want to come?"

She shook her head. "No, not yet. I want to observe though."

Surprised, Lance agreed. "No problem." He picked up his notepad and pen off his desk. "I'm going in right now."

"I'll grab a coffee and step into the observation room." She also wanted to give them a little bit of time to settle in. She didn't want Lance thinking she was watching his every move. What she really wanted was to get an eyeful of the person they'd picked up. So many things just didn't make any sense. What, if anything, did the guy have to do with Marsha? That was one of the biggest issues for Alex. She knew in her heart that Macklin had nothing to do with Marsha's death, but, until she could close that file and find out who had killed her, that question would always be hanging over his head. And she wouldn't wish that on anybody.

With her coffee, she stepped into the observation room. She listened as Lance asked his questions. She studied the man as he answered. He was young, maybe twenty-five, could be as old as twenty-eight. Long and lean as many people had described him. Very short hair.

He stretched back and kicked his legs out under the table. "I was out for a run and then a walk. There's no law against that. There have been police crawling all over the place. I heard about all the break-ins, and, just like everybody else, I'm out wandering around, trying to figure out what the hell is going on."

"So have you ever been in the house?"

The young man's face twisted. "Maybe, I don't know."

"How could you not know?" Lance asked.

"There are a lot of parties around here. I've been to a lot of house parties over the last few years. There could've been one there. How am I supposed to know? I used to come out so drunk I couldn't remember anything."

Alex had to give him points for that. If they found prints in the house, they could easily be tossed off as being from one of those parties. Given his age, he could have been there. Betty's son had lived there while she'd been traveling. Who knew what he might have been up to. There were a lot of parties. And there were any number of reasons why his fingerprints could be inside the house. She considered the suspect more closely. He had long fingers, striking high cheekbones. She wanted to know how much of his persona was based on ego. There was certainly a lot of casual confidence and a twitch of arrogance, as if holding back how brilliant he was.

Lance seemed nonplussed. "C'mon, Andy. If you didn't have anything to do with it, then answering these questions won't hurt you in any way."

"Sure. That's what you cops always say." Andy shook his head. "No way in hell you can place me in that house anytime recently because I wasn't there."

"Do you know anybody staying there?"

"Graham Kroger was there, but I haven't seen him for a while."

"Graham was killed on an overseas mission."

Andy froze. "Really?" He turned and stared off into the distance, and then he shrugged. "That sucks, man."

"But it doesn't involve you in any way, right?"

At that, Andy's gaze zeroed back in on Lance. "If you mean, did I have anything to do with his death, then obviously the answer is no."

"Where do you live, Andy?"

"Nowhere in particular." He flashed a grin. "I've been staying with a girlfriend for the past couple months. But apparently she's moved out and didn't bother to tell me. So, when I went back to the place after an all-night party, it was empty."

"Where was that?"

He rattled off an address.

Alex wrote it down. She didn't know what game Andy was playing, but it wouldn't make sense to give an address if he couldn't back it up. Still, she'd get one of the officers to check it out.

"And how long did you stay there?"

"It was her place. She was there for probably three or four years. I was only with her for a couple months."

"Do you happen to know Kathleen Matron?" Lance went through a series of names. All the residents of houses that had been broken into. Each time Andy shook his head. "No. No. No. No."

Lance leaned back, tapped his pencil on the tabletop. "What do you do for a living?"

"Currently I deliver pizzas."

"Interesting," Alex said to herself. That was a great job for getting around, scoping out houses. Keeping an eye on empty houses. Knowing where single women might live.

"How long have you been doing that?"

"Two years."

Lance continued the same line of questioning. But there wasn't a lot more that was useful. Either Andy had nothing to do with it or he was an excellent liar.

Alex was voting on the latter. She hoped some evidence came out of Betty's kitchen. She left the observation room and headed to her office. There she phoned Candice, the head of the crime scene team. "Did you find anything?"

"No fingerprints of any kind."

"Shit."

"I know. We are looking for DNA, but the food boxes were tossed and dishes were in the dishwasher, and it was turned on."

"Therefore, sterilizing everything."

"You did pick up a suspect, did you not?"

"Sure, but we don't have anything to hold him on."

"So, let him go, keep the tail on him. He'll slip up soon enough." And with that, Candice hung up.

Alex sat there, wondering. It wasn't a bad idea.

At a scuff at her door, she looked up to see Lance.

He held up his notepad. "I can go over this with you."

"I was there for the most part. He's either a very good liar or he had nothing to do with it."

"He's the type we tend to love to hate in the first place," Lance said. He was fatigued, which showed as he crashed down on the visitor's chair across from her. "He's got that arrogance we all want to pound into the ground. As if he's above the law. As if he thinks he's smarter than all of us."

"And, if he's done this, he's certainly been smart so far. His job is something that gives him access to all the houses. We'd have a hell of a time tracking through the pizza deliveries to see if he ever delivered to any of the houses on those streets, but I'm sure he has."

"Chances are also good it was an easy way to keep an eye on the women and the empty houses." Lance echoed her thoughts from earlier.

"Exactly. Forensics found nothing."

Lance stared at her. "Nothing?"

She shook her head. "No fingerprints. Nothing they see so far. Obviously they are doing some testing, but you know it'll take forever."

"So I've got no reason to hold him."

"No. I imagine he has a lawyer on the way. The only thing we did was pick up somebody suspicious off the streets. Candice did suggest we turn him loose and keep a tail on him."

Lance nodded. "I was thinking of that when I was in the interview room. It's not a bad half-measure. He'll slip up. We just have to be ready."

"I know." She stared at no point in the room, thinking of her options. Her pencil automatically drew circles on a piece of paper as her mind spun equally around and around. "Then let's do that. Take his fingerprints. Ask him for a DNA sample and see what he says. Then release him. We need to check out that address he was staying at. He says he doesn't have one now, so where is he going for the night?" She wasn't looking for an answer. "We want him to stay in town, and we want him to come back tomorrow morning."

"Why come back tomorrow morning?"

"If he doesn't come back, he becomes a suspect, and, if he does come back, we can confirm where he slept, in case we lose him, or he lies to us."

"I like that." Lance hopped up from the chair. "I'm about to release him then."

"Who do we have to run a tail on him?"

"I thought to put Wilson and Owen. They're out in cruisers right now."

"Then put them on him."

"He's on foot."

"Then they'll be on foot."

He chuckled. "Owen will love that."

After he left, she sat back and thought about that. There were more fit men and women per capita here in Coronado than any other place in the world most likely. They should give chase for a good mile without even catching their breath. Keeping a tail on some young male on foot should be second nature to them all. If it wasn't, they needed to up their training. She knew there hadn't been much money set aside for things like that. But, if this case was ever a good one to bring to the bosses and show they needed more budget money, she'd use it.

Tired and frustrated, she got up and headed to the squad room to assign an officer the job of checking the address in

Andy's statement. With that taken care of, she headed home.

Her phone had gone off when she'd been busy at the station. She hadn't even checked to see who it was. Now she realized it was most likely Macklin. She pulled it out as she unlocked the door to her apartment and stepped inside. *Macklin.* He'd left a voice mail. "Call me."

She snickered. "Like hell." She tossed her phone on the kitchen table and dropped her purse beside it.

However, just as she was headed for the shower, her phone rang again. She picked it up, saw it was Macklin.

"You didn't call when you got home."

"How do you know I'm home already?"

"I didn't, but, since you didn't call me, I'm calling you."

"Are you stalking me?" she asked incredulously.

"Of course not." He sighed. "You do realize you're a single female living alone, though not necessarily in the same grid that we were looking in, but you're not far out."

She straightened and frowned. "So? Hundreds of us are here."

"True, but I can't say I'm terribly comfortable with the concept of you living alone right now."

"That's probably just your line to get into my bed."

"Oh!" His voice piqued with curiosity. "Will that work?"

"Hell no."

"Because, if it will, I'll be there in a heartbeat."

She sat down on her bed and raised her hand to her forehead. "Did you hear that part about *hell no?*"

But his voice turned serious again. "Would you object to somebody sleeping on the couch?"

She frowned into the phone. "You can't be serious."

"I am."

"Why?" But something in his voice got her nerves going.

She stood and looked around. She'd walked in, assuming the place was safe, and had been completely relaxed. Her bed, closet, everything appeared to be the same. Feeling foolish for even questioning it, she walked out and back through her living room, then into her kitchen.

"What are you doing?"

"Well, you made me nervous," she snapped. "So I'm checking out my apartment."

"You didn't do that first?"

"No. I didn't. Besides, I'm on the second floor. Everybody else had a house."

"Not Marsha."

"But she was on the ground floor. And that may not be related in any way to the break-ins."

"Maybe not but it's still not safe for women right now."

She stared out into the night. It would be so wrong to bring him over.

"Please." His voice was very quiet. "I've been lying here, trying to sleep, but I can't because I'll worry about you all night."

"What about all the other women living alone in the area?"

"I can't worry about everybody."

It was a good answer. And one she would use herself. "You know I'm the one who people call to protect them, right?"

"We've been over that. Right now I don't think you should be alone."

"Right now I don't think you should be spending the night." A heavy pause suddenly turned sexual. She shook her head. "Don't even think that."

In an all-too-innocent voice he said, "Think what?"

"About sex."

"Well, the only reason you wouldn't want me to stay there is because you're afraid you might succumb to my charms," he said in a smooth voice. "I promise I'll stay on the couch… unless you drag me to the bed."

"Well, I won't be dragging your fat ass anywhere, will I?"

"No, but you can join me on the couch," he said suggestively. "I'm on my way." And he hung up.

MACKLIN DRESSED QUICKLY, threw a change of clothing and his shaving gear in a small bag he used for the gym, grabbed his keys and wallet, and walked out. He didn't know what was wrong, but, ever since he got back to his place, he had this nagging sense of something not being right. And every time he tried to think about what direction it came from, all he could think about was Alex.

And that was good enough for him. He didn't know who or what, but no way in hell would he leave her to the same fate as Marsha. He wasn't to blame for Marsha's death, he knew, but at the same time, he'd known her. He'd known she was a very sad young woman. He just hadn't been the right person to help her. And sometimes that was enough to make a person feel guilty. He didn't know any of the other women whose houses had been broken into, but, if the guy was still out there …

Then that was an issue.

They had picked up the intruder. Great. He was kind of hoping he would get some details from Alex. But, even if she couldn't give him very much, she might tell him if it was the guy they were looking for.

He drove the short distance to her apartment, climbed

up the stairs, and stepped into the hallway. Another door across the hall clicked shut. He strolled down and knocked on her door. She opened it almost immediately, a snarl forming on her face. He grinned. "Pizza?"

She opened her mouth and snapped it shut.

He leaned forward to kiss her briefly. Though she was spluttering—again—he pushed her back and stepped inside, then closed and locked the door. He smiled. "Now that I know you're okay, I'm hungry." He pulled out his phone and asked, "Do you like anchovies?" He tried to keep his voice light, conversational.

She was mad, and a part of him could understand that. At the same time, she needed to get over it—and fast. She stalked to her living room, as if gathering her thoughts or maybe just holding back her temper. He really appreciated her control. At least until he was off the phone. He hung up. "Two pizzas are on the way, one with the works and one just anchovies and pepperoni."

At that she spun and stared at him. "Who the hell puts anchovies on a pepperoni pizza?"

He gave her an innocent look as he sat on her couch. "I do."

She raised both hands in frustration and threw herself down on the couch beside him. "You are so damn irritating."

"I love you too," he said in a flippant tone.

She shook her head. "You don't love anybody."

He slanted a hard gaze her way. "I love my family. But I don't spread myself around thin. And when I love, I love deep, and I love long."

"Have you ever really been in love?"

He nodded. "But not for a lot of years."

"Well, love hasn't been on my list for a long time either.

Not for several years."

"Good." He smiled at her. "So can you tell me? Did you get the guy?"

"We picked him up, took him in for questioning, but we're not sure he's the guy."

"Damn."

"I was so hoping that too," she said. "Even worse, no forensic evidence has been found at the house yet. Whoever it was wore gloves, and, even though the food was left out, the dishes were put in the dishwasher, and it was turned on."

"So no DNA off the dishes or fingerprints off the counters?"

"Apparently the intruder was a neat freak." She nodded. "Life's like that sometimes."

He settled back and stared at the ceiling. "But it's interesting because it means a lot of planning and thought went into this. The clean house. No forensic evidence. The video feed. It all points to someone who's either very detail-oriented or has OCD."

"And I'm wondering how much of all that was just a red herring."

"In what way?" He rolled his head to look at her.

"We have extremely limited resources, very limited manpower. These break-ins have achieved nothing, in that nobody has stolen anything. The whole town is on edge. It has used much of our man-hours to track him down. And, therefore, the investigation has turned away from Marsha."

Mac gave a silent whistle. "That's ..." He was at a loss for words. "That's very smart." He leaned over, picked up her feet, and laid them across his lap. "And that would show the same kind of planning I'm talking about. Harmless and at the same time with a purpose."

"But I still have no way to match that person to Marsha. There is no connection I can see yet."

"And I suppose you had a hard time leaving the station because of it."

"I was planning on working from home. I brought my laptop to track down this person's history and to see if I can connect him to Marsha at any time."

"What does he do for a living?"

At her silence he turned to look at her.

Reluctantly she said, "He delivers pizza."

"That would be a perfect cover."

"That's what we were all thinking."

"Where does he live?"

"No stated address," she said sarcastically. "According to him, he and his girlfriend just broke up, but he didn't know she had planned to break up. It was the end of the month yesterday. She pulled out, leaving him with no place to go."

"So why not just say he was staying at Betty's house?"

She shrugged. "Who the hell knows?"

"Of course it might not have been him." Mac stared off in the distance, his mind plugging all the pieces of the puzzle into place. But they still wouldn't fit. "He'll be looking for a place tonight, right?"

"He said he would stay at a hotel. We wouldn't release him without an address."

"What hotel is that?"

Just then the doorbell rang. The two of them hopped up.

"That'll be the pizza," Macklin said as he strolled toward the door.

"Wait," she hissed. "Stand behind the door. Let me deal with this. Don't let whoever it is know you're here." He raised his eyebrows and took a step to the back of the door. She opened it to see the damn suspect. He held out her pizzas.

Struggling to keep her face neutral, she hoped he didn't recognize her. She hadn't been in the interrogation room, but she had been in one of the offices when he was led out. She hadn't thought of it at the time but realized he could have seen her then. She accepted the pizzas with a smile, paid for it, gave him a tip, and, when he left, closed the door.

Her hands were clammy. Macklin watched the whole thing. "That was him, wasn't it?"

She nodded. "How did you see him?"

"Through the crack," he said, his tone short. "And he recognized you."

She turned to stare at him. "Did he?"

Macklin gave a slow nod of his head. "Oh, hell yeah."

"Well then, I guess it's a good thing you're staying tonight," she said quietly. "Just in case he decides to come back."

"I hope he does, that little bastard. Because I'll be waiting."

She shoved the pizzas into his hands. "Down, boy. Let's get you fed. Otherwise you might eat him."

"I didn't like the look in his eye," Macklin said as they walked to the table. "There was a hell of a lot of anger in that gaze."

She turned to look at him. "I know. I saw it too."

CHAPTER 13

MACKLIN SEPARATED THE two boxes and opened them up. She stared at the hot cheesy pie and sighed. "He's coming back tonight, isn't he?"

"Not if he is smart, he won't."

She looked over at him. "Set a trap?"

"Hell yeah."

She picked up a hot piece of cheesy deliciousness and took a bite.

He motioned to the dining table chairs. "He won't be back right this moment, so sit down and relax."

"No way I can relax. Not with that thought uppermost in my mind," she said. "Still, if it were me breaking in, I'd wait until tomorrow or another day when I'm relaxed and not thinking about it."

"Which is why I'm not leaving until this guy is caught."

After she started on her third piece, her stomach protested. She handed it off to him. "I don't know how you can eat so much. You've eaten half a pizza by yourself already."

He accepted her portion and grinned. "You don't eat enough."

She rolled her eyes. "I do eat, you know?"

"Yes, but do you eat healthy?"

"Nobody in their right mind would say pizza was proper food." He looked at her in such horror she had to laugh. "I'd love a cup of coffee, but I'm so tired I'm better off going to bed."

"Go to bed then," he urged. "I'll stay up for a while. Besides, I have more pizza to eat."

She looked at him, uncertain. "You're really staying on the couch?"

"Hell yeah. That's what I promised."

She smiled, got up, walked over to the front closet, and pulled out blankets and a pillow. She dropped them on the edge of the couch and said, "It's a bit warm tonight, but maybe you want to be covered up." She turned and headed toward her bedroom. "I'll shower and crawl under the covers."

"Have a good night."

"You too." She closed the door of the master bedroom, stripped, dropping her clothes everywhere, and stepped into the hot shower. It felt good. It had been a long day. She gave her head a good scrubbing. When she was done, she stepped out, wrapped up in a towel, and plaited her hair in a braid. Finally dressed in a camisole and boxers, she lay down in bed. She pulled the light cover and sheet over her.

The sliding glass door was open, but there was only a small Juliet balcony. Meaning, nobody could get in this way. She'd always felt safe sleeping with it open, until now. But she was so tired, and, with Macklin in her living room, she relaxed.

She surprised herself. Her nightmare of the day wasn't carrying through to her night; she could feel sleep reaching up for her. She took several deep breaths, yawned, and sank gently under the surface of consciousness.

Just as she was about to drop off, she heard an odd noise. She froze, sat up, and listened. *What the hell?*

But the sound didn't come again. She got up and put her ear to the door, but there was nothing, not a sound coming from the other side. She stepped out into the living room.

Macklin was stretched out on the couch, his eyes closed. He was only in boxers, and she couldn't help but stare. The moonlight played across the muscled planes of his body. He was a stunning male animal in his prime. She could still see scars from old wounds on his body, but it just made him more of a warrior to her.

He opened his eyes and stared at her. "Problems?"

She shrugged. "I heard something."

His gaze warmed with understanding. "You'll find that happening a lot for the next while."

She crossed her arms. "I'm not normally so jumpy."

He opened his arms. "You want to cuddle?"

Unwillingly her feet took a step forward.

His gaze warmed.

"This is really a bad idea. I don't think you cuddle well."

He gave her an injured look, but the gleam in his eyes shone bright in the darkened room. "I cuddle very well."

She snorted. "You may look cuddly, but there's very much a predatory appearance in that gaze of yours."

He smiled. "I promise I won't pounce unless you want me to."

She rolled her eyes but found herself standing beside him. He grabbed her wrist and gently pulled her down so she sprawled across his chest.

"This is still a really bad idea." But her heart wasn't interested in getting away. She knew what she wanted. He was no longer a suspect, but they still hadn't caught the killer. She also knew what he wanted.

He tilted his chin, lifted his head, and kissed her gently. "Sometimes bad ideas turn out to be the best ideas of all."

"There speaks a male."

He chuckled. "I am that," he said. "But remember, I won't pounce unless you say I can."

She sighed and laid her head down against his chest. "Feels weird to be like this."

His hand gently stroked up and down her long spine. "Why's that?"

"It's been a long time."

"I hear you there. It has been a long time for me too," he admitted. "But it's kind of nice. Makes it special."

She traced his square-cut jaw, high cheekbones, and prominent forehead. If their positions were reversed, he would completely dwarf her since he was so big. And yet, at the same time, she knew he'd never let that happen. She shifted on top of him, getting a little more comfortable, and realized something else. She froze.

He chuckled. "I'm a man, not a boy. Of course there'll be a reaction when I have a beautiful woman, basically nude, lying on top of me. I'm human. I'm male, and you're absolutely gorgeous."

She had to consider that he had a point. She'd been asking for trouble by even coming over to him. And he was right; lying on top, it wasn't just his body reacting to her presence. Her body had warmed up considerably too. She stroked a finger across his lips and smiled. "You're the one that's so deadly."

"I'm deadly? Look who's talking?"

She chuckled, tried to pull herself slightly forward, leaned down, and kissed him. Instantly his hand cupped the back of her head, and he held her there longer.

She broke free and said, "You're also a very good kisser."

"I've hardly even kissed you," he protested. "Now if you really want a kiss …" He reached up with both hands, tucked her against him, and this time he laid it on her.

She hadn't been kissed like that in years. Hot, luscious, in control, but with so much passion her body was softening, readying for him. She broke free and pushed her head back. "This is stupid."

"What's stupid?"

And she decided. She sat up and held out a hand. "It's stupid we're on the couch when I have a bed."

A light came into his eyes. He sat up slowly; then the two of them stood. He looked down at her. "Is that permission to pounce?"

She chuckled but the chuckle turned to outright laughter as he scooped her up in his arms and strode to her bed.

He tossed her down in the middle of the big mattress, the blankets still tussled from her lying in them. He covered her body with his.

And she was right; he completely covered her. But he held his weight on his elbows. Her body shifted and moved, lining up planes and angles for the best fit. She wrapped her legs around his hips and pulled him in tighter.

His gaze heated up, and he lowered his head. Just before his lips took hers, he whispered, "You are dangerous."

This time when he kissed her, there was no holding back. There was no control for her to crack. It was already sliding them both toward fulfillment. She curled her arms around him as he took her to a place she didn't remember ever going. Hands stroked; lips teased and coaxed; tongues tangled and soothed. Teeth nipped, only to have lips kiss once again. She felt so right beneath him, her body hot, steaming, and looking for so much more. She wrapped her arms tighter around him and tried to tug him down to her. But he was too busy exploring her ribs and breasts. He lowered his head, took one nipple in his mouth, and tugged it in a deep sucking motion. Knots and tingles started in her lower belly. She shuddered in his grasp.

He raised his head, lowered himself into position, and whispered, "Lady, I wasn't kidding—you are deadly."

She grabbed him by the ears, pulled him to her, and kissed him hard. "You're all talk. Isn't it time you really showed me what you're all about?"

He caught his breath, set himself into the right position, and plunged deep. She gasped and stilled. He froze. She smiled and held him close, letting her body adjust, stretching until fully accepting him inside. She took a deep breath and let it out.

He pushed himself up on his elbows, looking down at her, and whispered, "You okay?"

She smiled. "I am. It's just been a while."

He slid a hand slowly down her ribs and belly to her hips. Sliding just underneath her, he held her in position as he started to ride. "It is for both of us. That makes this all the sweeter. We'll take this together."

He was true to his word as he lifted and plunged deep, again and again, taking them both to the edge. Just when she didn't think she could stand it anymore, he tossed them both over. Her cries rolled free only to be followed by his guttural groan as he sank heavily down on top of her.

When he finally rolled off, he tucked her close against him and wrapped his arms around her. His breath was heavy and shaky against her ear. She was still shuddering in reaction. She looked up at him in wonder. He lowered his head, kissed her gently on the nose, and whispered, "That was so much better than I imagined."

She wrapped her arms around his neck and held him tight.

And fell asleep.

MACKLIN HELD HER close, pulling a sheet over them both. He really hoped the asshole didn't come back tonight. He wanted this time with Alex. He didn't want just half a night; he wanted the whole thing. He wanted to wake up in the morning and be the first thing she saw when she opened her eyes. They had the start of something stunning, and he wanted every moment he had available to explore the possibilities and see where they could go.

He hadn't been kidding when he had said it had been a long time. He'd watched his friends meet the women of their dreams, had watched the hook ups, the ups and downs, and they finally settled into something he couldn't imagine. That Marsha had tainted his love life was something he'd let happen, but, at the same time, he'd been so unsure of his ability to make the right decision, to pick the right person, he had stepped back from the whole dating scene. He'd missed sex. But he'd missed this—this closeness, the cuddling more than anything. Just to know somebody special cared about him as much as he cared about her. There really was no substitute for that.

He let his mind drift back and forth, wondering how long before she caught the asshole who killed Marsha. Because, only after that, could they really have an open relationship. He'd never do anything to jeopardize her career. And he'd seen just how unfair it was sometimes being a female in a power position—how vulnerable they were. They had to hold themselves up to a higher standard than their male counterparts. It wasn't fair, but it was a fact of life. And he would hate to be responsible for her getting into trouble. He knew he was innocent of Marsha's murder. He knew she believed he was innocent, and that meant so much, but that didn't mean the rest of the cops at the station did.

He let himself drift off toward sleep.

A cool breeze flowed across the bedroom, and he wondered what still bothered him about this scenario? He'd caught a good look at the man who had delivered the pizza. But it was hard to imagine that same person having been involved in all the break-ins.

Just as Mac was about to go under, he wondered at the fresh air again. She had the window open obviously. But as he watched the long curtains blow in the wind, he realized it was a sliding glass door. And that meant it was open, hopefully just a little bit. But he couldn't relax enough to let it go. He hopped up and walked over to the gauzy white curtains and looked closer. The door was locked open about four inches. Outside was one of those little tiny balconies, just big enough to stand and stare at the outside. He'd never really seen the purpose of them. He'd much rather have a balcony big enough to put a chair on. At least then you could sit outside and have coffee. If she wanted to sit anywhere, she'd have to sit half in and half out of the door.

As he checked the door, he saw a form sneaking across the grass. He flattened himself against the wall and waited. When he heard an odd scrabbling noise below, he went back to the bed, put on his boxers, and gave Alex a shake.

Her eyes opened instantly.

He placed a finger against her lips and whispered, "We

are about to have company."

Understanding slammed into her gaze. She bolted out of bed, took one look, realizing she was nude, and scrambled into her pajamas. He watched appreciatively. She was long and lean, small-breasted, extraordinarily fit. He never thought he'd go for the athletic type. But there was absolutely everything to go for with her. And dressed in what she would call pajamas was like teasing any male. The camisole hung just on the edge of her breasts. The shadow between her legs barely showed through the pale pink material of the boxers. As she walked, her rounded cheeks were enough to give any man wet dreams. But, when she pulled out her service pistol and slid to the other side of the glass door, he realized she was all business.

He had to appreciate that. He had no weapons with him but was a pro when it came to hand-to-hand combat. On either side of the glass door they waited. After a few minutes of silence, she looked over at him in question. He held up a finger as a signal to wait. And, sure enough, a hand appeared at the bottom of the deck. The little bastard found something to climb up on, and he was climbing up over the little balcony now.

Macklin considered the position of her apartment and realized her balcony faced the backyard. So, unless anybody else was standing outside, they wouldn't have seen him. There were houses across the way, but this was a small green space for the apartment residents. Nobody could look directly into the apartment, so it was all too easy for this guy to access her place without being seen.

Within seconds the intruder had climbed up the railing and onto the small balcony.

The two of them watched and waited as he tried to open

the glass door. Macklin understood the lock on the sliding door, and it wasn't hard to disarm. Unfortunately anyone could research that information on the internet. He waited and watched.

The guy went to his knees, got out some tools, and silently popped the lock. He slid the glass door back and waited.

Macklin looked at the bed and realized they should have made up the bedding to look like Alex was sleeping. Because, as soon as the pizza guy stepped in, he would know she wasn't there. Then again, he would have a hard time going anyplace. It was either straight into the bedroom or over the balcony. And it was a decent jump. He'd probably make it without any broken bones, particularly if he'd done it a time or two. But he wouldn't get far with Macklin right behind him.

A hand reached out for the gauze curtain as if to pull it back and step in. But he froze. Macklin forced his breathing to stop, and he waited. Sirens sounded in the distance, coming closer. He could hear their uninvited guest whisper, "Shit."

There was an odd tone to the voice. One he didn't quite understand. And his mind, although cataloging the differences, didn't see it immediately. The hand withdrew. And the intruder stepped back on the little balcony and leaned over, as if to see where the sirens were coming from. He couldn't see if they pulled into the apartment complex lot because it was on the other side of the building. What he couldn't know was if he'd been seen or if Alex knew she had a visitor.

The big question right now was whether he would slip away or enter the bedroom. Macklin didn't want to take a chance of him escaping. Yet he couldn't see the intruder well from his position.

Just then Macklin heard noises on the far side of the apartment. Likely on the next balcony or one or two over.

Macklin could hear laughing and talking. Their visitor was now flattened against the outside of the sliding glass door, his back to the gauzy curtain as if hiding from the neighbors. After a few moments, the neighbors went back inside, their laughter and hilarity going inside with them. Macklin could almost feel the tension ease off the intruder's shoulders. Just then the gauzy curtain was flung back, and the intruder stepped in. It took a moment to assess the bedding. As soon as he took another step, Macklin was on him. The man turned, tried to fight him off, hands swinging, feet kicking, but in control.

"Oh, you might have some self-defense moves, asshole," Macklin muttered, "but you're a hell of a long way from being smart enough, big enough, or fast enough to beat me." And he dropped the intruder and pounced on him. He could feel the slimmer form fighting beneath him in desperation.

He looked at Alex and said, "Hit the lights."

She raced to the bedroom light switch, turned on the overhead light. The intruder was wearing a full-on mask. She bent down, pulled it off, and laughed. "Hello, Andy."

Andy glared up at her. "Bitch."

Macklin stared down at Andy and realized what was wrong with the voice. With Andy's hands pinned, Macklin sat up for a closer look and said, "If she's a bitch, then so are you."

Andy's gaze pivoted to look at him. "What the hell are you talking about?"

But this time Alex heard it too. She walked up to stand

behind Macklin. "Well, well, well. Now that changes things entirely."

She bent down to take a closer look at Andy's face. "So, what's Andy short for?"

But at this point Andy fell silent. She just glared up at the two of them.

Alex looked over at Macklin. "There's no real doubt, is there?"

"She wears one of the best androgynous looks I've seen in a long time," Macklin admitted. "But look at the clothing."

And they both stared down at the T-shirt material twisted tight, showing a very soft faint female form.

He looked over at Alex. "Your Andy is definitely female."

CHAPTER 14

ALEX STARED DOWN at the woman struggling on the floor, spitting and hissing like a cat.

Finally she stopped struggling and glared up at the two of them. "You don't know anything," she said in a broken voice.

Alex squatted down beside her. She needed to call this in, but she wanted answers first.

"Then explain it to us. Right now, before we go to the station and you're in a whole different environment. You explain it to us. I promise we'll do our best to understand."

"I'm Andi with an i, but prefer Andy with a y." Andy stared up at the two of them. She looked over at Macklin and said, "She was obsessed with you. Had a bunch of pictures of you. At the coffee shop. At the gym. At a restaurant. Walking down the street. She had them hidden away. But I saw her once going through them, over and over again."

Alex stared at Macklin, watched his body take the blow. And she realized maybe this wasn't about Marsha as much as it was about where Marsha's focus had been. The name Andi was the feminized version of Andy, and, with her looks, she could pull off the male persona. Not to mention any question on her name could be put down to a spelling error.

"And you loved Marsha, didn't you?" Alex said.

Andi's lower lip trembled. She nodded her head. "I've loved her since forever," she admitted. "But, for the longest time, all she had was eyes for Macklin. She would tell me about him all the time. And I would listen and smile, and she would let me love her for a while. Then she'd get bad, and she'd forget about me, and she'd focus on him again."

"But that changed, didn't it?"

"Somewhat. She got better. The doctors changed her medications, and she didn't see Macklin anymore. It seemed like maybe she would be okay," Andi said. But the tears still ran down her eyes. "And I thought maybe it would be time for us then."

Alex waited for the woman to collect her thoughts. She'd already sent a text to Lance, giving them a heads-up. They'd be here in about ten minutes. She didn't want to push Andi, but Alex really wanted to get the story.

Finally Andi said, "And then she started to go out—with other men. Other women. It's like she didn't know who she was anymore, didn't know what she wanted, didn't know what she could have. She was like a child, sampling it all. At first, I was indulgent. It was fun to see her happier. It's like she had a whole new lease on life. Then I realized it was the medications. And it wasn't really her. She'd go from crazy, wild, energetic to mad and despondent. She became almost suicidal. I talked her into seeing her doctor. But she was on one of her upswings then, and she kept telling him everything was fine, and she was only there because I was worried.

"In reality, she only wanted me to be there when she wanted me there. I did all the cleaning. Kept everything nice and neat and perfect all the time so she'd be happy with me. But it was hard. And then we had a fight. She threw me out." Andi started to bawl. "I didn't want to leave. I'd loved her for so long I couldn't imagine my life without her. But she told me that she didn't love me. That she'd never loved me. I was just convenient—said she didn't have to be alone. She didn't have to look at herself and see her lonely life. If I was around, she was happier because, in her mind, she was better than me, so her life didn't suck so bad."

Alex winced at that. She could feel Macklin's shock. But, at the same time, she sensed compassion in him.

"And then what happened?" Alex prodded gently.

"I packed up my stuff. It took a lot. I was moving it all to the door, then out to the car. And I came back to get the last load. She was sitting there, watching TV, drinking, eating, and I wanted to beg. I wanted to get down on my knees and beg her to keep me. To tell me not to go, to tell me that she loved me as much as I loved her. I stopped in front of her, and I went to open my mouth and say something, but she looked up at me and laughed and said, 'You're so pathetic.'

"I closed my mouth, walked to the bookshelf behind her, picked up the hammer she always kept there. I turned around, and I hit her. Just once but I hit her hard," Andi said, her voice low, slowly calming. "I put everything I had into it. I could feel the bones fall away beneath the blow. And I knew she was done for. But I also knew it wasn't enough. I knew she could survive. I wanted to keep hitting her. I wanted to keep pounding on her with the rage flowing through me, but I knew, I knew the cops would then think it was a crime of passion. And that I could get caught. So I laid her down, and I slit her throat."

Macklin sat back ever-so-slightly. He was keeping an eye on the door to make sure Andi couldn't run away. But it was as if he was distancing himself from the pain Marsha must have gone through. The pain Andi had gone through.

But finally they knew who had killed Marsha.

"And after that?" Alex asked. She kept her voice low, calm, quiet.

Andi sniffled several times and said, "And then I went out over the balcony. I walked around to my car and left."

"Did you ever go back inside?"

She shook her head. "No. I didn't. I wanted to, but I didn't."

"How is it you knew she was going out with all those other people?" Macklin asked. "Did you keep track of her or watch her?"

Almost shamefaced, Andi nodded. "I did, but, more than that, I went to some of the same parties where she hooked up with these other people."

"And was it you who broke into the other houses?"

Andi nodded.

"Why those people?" Macklin asked. "Why those women?"

"Because Marsha talked about them. She talked about how pretty they were, and how she would take them to bed and show them what it meant to have a real lover," she said on a sob. "She was crazy with it. We would go to a party, and she'd point out all these people. Sometimes we just walked past a house, and she'd point them out."

"But you believed her?"

"Of course she believed her. There was no other reason to go to such lengths," Alex said sadly.

"And, if that's true," Macklin added, "why the break-ins? You never assaulted the women. Even when you had a chance. The last one was out cold in front of you."

Andi opened her tear-drenched eyes to stare up at the

two of them. Her gaze was both pathetic and hopeless. And yet pleading for understanding. "They weren't attractive to me. I couldn't touch them. I wanted to hit them and hurt them. But I knew they were just people. They weren't anybody I should be angry at. But I couldn't forget Marsha's mocking words. I broke into their houses, thinking maybe I'd find proof Marsha had been there. Instead I found myself wandering through their houses, jealous, wondering what it was like to be there with Marsha. Our perfect little family that I kept hoping and dreaming would happen. I kept going back. I went back to all the houses," she admitted. "I don't even know if Marsha slept with any of those women who lived there. She said she did, but she said anything and everything to get the attention she wanted."

"But, even after she was dead, you went into more houses." Alex sat back and watched Andi's face splinter its features right in front of her. As if watching a mask disintegrate, a personality break into many pieces. "And left photos at one house?"

Andi nodded and choked out the words. "I couldn't stop. It seemed to be the only connection I had left to Marsha. If I could just keep touching those houses, touching the people, be in their spaces, be close to them, that meant I was close to Marsha because she'd been there too." She sniffled. "So I left pieces of Marsha, photos in one house, a little kitty knickknack in another—even though I took a beating at that house the one time. It made me feel closer to her… more connected."

Alex winced at that. There'd been no word on any knickknacks found that shouldn't have been there. Still, it could have been well-hidden. She'd have to talk to the owners in the morning. See if they could find it.

"You miss her, don't you?" Macklin's voice was so deep and so soft.

Alex smiled inside. He was such a good man, even when he was face-to-face with a woman who had murdered somebody he knew. He was just making the process easier for Andi.

Andi started to bawl uncontrollably. She curled into a fetal position and cried, "I loved her. I loved her. I loved her."

Alex sat back and looked up at Macklin. There was such sadness and grief in his eyes. She gently stroked Andi's hair. "Why Betty's house? Why did you go to her house?"

"After Marsha kicked me out, and I had killed her, I had no place to go," Andi admitted between choking tears. "I knew that house was empty. I'd been in there to look. It just seemed so much like a home that I stayed there. I fixed the camera feed so no one would know. I got the instructions off the internet. Sorry …" She hiccupped. "I needed to stay there. I needed a place that felt right. I didn't have any money. I had been living with Marsha for most of the last year. But it wasn't so good with us together. We were always broke, always high, always partying too much, and crying too much." She lay there, taking great big gasping breaths. "I didn't want to kill her. It hurts so much."

In the distance Alex could hear sirens.

Andi shook visibly now. "I'm going to jail, aren't I?"

"Yes. Yes, you are. And there'll be lots of questions and lots of interviews. But you'll get through it."

Andi stared at Alex through her tears. "I didn't think you'd catch me. I figured, as long as I didn't hurt anybody too bad, you wouldn't care."

"But you hurt Marsha," Alex said quietly. "And you terrorized those other people."

She started to bawl again. "I'm sorry."

"When we get you to the police station, we'll make sure to get you a lawyer, okay? And a doctor to examine you."

"I think I need help." Andi sobbed. "I just really want Marsha back."

Alex nodded. She understood. For that was the one thing Andi would never get again.

MACKLIN, NOW FULLY dressed, watched as the police came in and escorted Andi out. Alex was busy talking with the officers. When she finally separated herself from the chaos, she came to him and said, "I have to go down to the station."

He nodded. "And I'm going home and getting some sleep."

She gently stroked his arm. "Thank you," she said. "You were very good with her."

His gaze followed the police car that left with Andi in the back. "The world is a safer place with her behind bars. But I think, in her own way, she is just as sick as Marsha."

"I'm sure she was. But that's for the lawyers and the doctors to sort out. My job was to take her off the streets and to let everybody know they are okay now. I've done that."

He looked down at her and smiled, flicked a few strands of loose hair off her forehead, and said, "You're very good at your job."

She shook her head. "No. But I am learning." She kissed him on the cheek. "Lunch tomorrow?"

"Well, it's just about breakfast time, but chances are you'll sleep right through it. With any luck, I will too." He took a glance at his watch. "How long will you be at the station?"

She reached for his arm and checked his watch. "Probably at least two hours."

He nodded. "How about I meet you outside the office in two hours then?"

She turned and searched his gaze. "What about going to sleep?"

He grinned. "Sleep's overrated. I might catch a couple hours. But I might just come down to the station and wait for you."

"If I'm lucky, and I work hard, I might be done in an hour."

He held out his arm. "Then why don't you get started. As soon as we get finished, we can come back here and sleep together."

"That's all you want to do? Sleep?" she asked in a teasing voice. "Are you sure something else isn't on your mind?"

"When we get back, it will be sleep on my mind," he said in a firm voice. "When we wake up again, that's a whole different story." He stopped, pulled her into his arms, tilted her head up, and kissed her gently. "I'm very glad that's over with."

She smiled and pulled his head back down. "Hold that thought. Let's get through this next hour. And then we can enjoy life and all it has to offer."

He kissed her deeply. When he lifted his head, he said, "Now that's a date worth keeping. Promise?"

She chuckled, hooked her arm through his, and said, "Promise."

COREY

SEALs of Honor, Book 16

Dale Mayer

PROLOGUE

COREY HANDLEMAN WOKE up, surprised to find it as late as it was. Being in the navy, he rarely slept in. But it was already six-thirty. He rolled over and checked his cell phone for a text from Macklin. Corey was not at all sure what had gone on last night. But he had a suspicion his friend was taking a step that might not be in his best interests. He sent a quick text. **Where are you?**

There was no response. He frowned, got up, had a quick shower and put on some coffee. His phone rang.

It was Mason. "Did you hear the news?"

"What news?"

"They caught Marsha's killer."

Corey let out his breath with a heavy gust. "Thank God for that." He frowned. "Who was it?"

"Her girlfriend."

"But nobody said she had one."

"Marsha kept her a secret. Even though the girlfriend lived there, she wasn't allowed to let anybody know. She went in and out of the balcony door. The police only found out at the station after picking her up."

"Ouch. Makes it hard to have a relationship if you're always going out the back door. How long were they together?"

"Off and on for over a year, but they've known each

other for quite a few years. It wasn't somebody Marsha ever talked about."

"And I suppose they didn't go to parties together—do girl stuff?"

"Never."

"And how did you get all this information?"

"I contacted the station and talked to them this morning. Alex was just leaving. Anyway, she gave me the heads-up on some of the details. She and Macklin were heading to bed."

"So that's why Macklin didn't answer his phone." Corey chuckled. "Well, I could see that one coming."

"It's good for Macklin. He's waited a long while to find somebody."

"Yeah, he has."

"Your turn, Corey," Mason said. "Isn't it time for you now?"

"There's nobody special in my life," Corey explained. He walked to the window and stared out. "Maybe it'll happen one day."

Mason smiled, his voice laughing as he said, "Pretty darn sure it will happen sooner than later. You seem to have a lot of women in your life."

"Not really. Although I did meet one for coffee a few days ago. But that wasn't a girlfriend. She was my sister's best friend. And it was hardly a social visit."

"If it wasn't a social visit, what was it? What did she want?" Mason asked with curiosity in his voice.

Corey hesitated.

"If you don't want to tell me, that's all right," Mason said. "I'm just curious."

"The thing is, I don't know what she wanted. She called

me and asked to meet. We sat and had coffee. Then she suddenly seemed to get nervous. Changed her mind. I tried to talk her into staying, but she wouldn't. She just said she had to go."

"Is she okay?"

"I don't know. I called my sister, left several messages, but I haven't heard from her either."

"How long ago was this?"

"Two days. But with all this going on with Macklin and Marsha, I put it out of my mind."

"How do you suggest we make sure both of them are okay?"

"I should have heard from my sister, but she's been really busy. I don't know what's going on with Angela."

"Was she looking for help?"

"I don't know. She told me that she was fine, apologized for having bothered me. Then she stood and left. I walked out to the car with her. But she wouldn't have anything to do with me. Honestly, she pissed me off, so I just put it out of my mind."

"So it's not like she was being followed or anything?" Mason asked in a sharp tone.

"Not that I could see."

"So tell me. Who was she?"

Corey sighed. He turned to face the small room, walked over to the coffeepot, poured himself a cup and said, "Somebody from my past."

"This sounds interesting. You sure it isn't more than that?"

"No, it's not more than that. I haven't seen her since high school graduation."

"That doesn't mean much. Look at Merk."

Corey gave a bitter laugh. "Yeah, but he at least married his girlfriend. In my case, a whole lot of other emotions were tied up."

"Anything you want to talk about?"

Corey shook his head. "Nothing to talk about. She was my little sister's best friend. We fell in love—as strong as first loves are. I was sure she was the one for me. I thought she felt the same way."

"That happens," Mason said, his tone neutral. "Then what?"

"She found out she was pregnant." Corey winced, feeling the same old feelings of frustration and pain flow through him. "We didn't have much chance to sort out our feelings and what we would do when she had a miscarriage. Next thing I know, she didn't want a thing to do with me. When I saw her two days ago, it was the first time I'd seen her in twelve years."

"And yet she looked you up after all this time?"

"Yeah. She did." He frowned. "I sure wish I knew why though."

"But you saw her after the miscarriage?"

"Yeah. She had to finish school. I saw her, so it's not like she had the baby and that I didn't know anything about it." He shrugged it off. "It's old water under the bridge." He talked another couple minutes with Mason and then said, "I'll catch you later."

He hung up, picked up his coffee and stepped outside on his little deck. Those old memories were hard. He'd wanted that baby something awful. He'd always loved children, always planned to have children. No, he hadn't been ready for fatherhood back then, but that was what he'd been handed, so he would have made the best of it, and he was pretty damn happy with that plateful. When she'd lost the baby, he'd lost it too. He had never expected to experience grief when it wasn't even his body, when the child wasn't even fully formed yet in her belly.

She'd barely been through her first trimester. But it had been a keen loss that, even now, twelve years later, still hurt. With no children of his own, he wondered and worried what would have happened if they had been able to keep the child. He thought back to seeing Angela at the coffee shop—his shock, his surprise.

It had also been a joy, a bittersweet joy. She'd looked exactly the same, and it had taken his breath away. The same angelic blond hair, even in the same hairstyle, straight but curling against her shoulders.

His phone rang. It was his sister. "Hey, sis, there you are."

"Sorry," she said, fatigue in her voice evident. "It's been a hellish couple weeks."

"Work?"

"Work and studies."

His sister was almost done at Thomas Jefferson School of Law here in San Diego. She had a brutal class and work schedule, but she was coming through with flying colors. "Hopefully this will be done soon."

"Well, it would be. But two days ago something else happened."

"For you too, huh?"

Her voice piqued in interest. "What happened to you?"

"Angela walked into my life again."

She gasped. And then suddenly went silent.

Instincts on alert, he asked, "Why? What was that reaction for? What's wrong?"

"She told me that she might stop in and see you," Bridget said quietly. "Something was really bothering her."

"Well, she came, but she got up in the middle of coffee, even though we had lunch ordered, and said she had to go, that it was a mistake to see me. I walked out to her car, trying to talk to her, but she wouldn't have anything to do with me."

"Yeah, I was afraid of that."

"So why did she come?"

"Somebody was threatening her. She was hoping you could help."

He frowned. "Why me?"

"I've kept her up-to-date on your life." She gave a bitter laugh. "To make things worse, Angela's gone missing."

CHAPTER 1

COREY ENDED HIS call to his sister and dialed Mason. "I just heard from my sister," he said without preamble.

"And?" Mason's voice sounded unconcerned, as if having moved on to something else after their conversation from ten minutes ago.

Corey understood. He was like that himself. "She said Angela, the friend I met, has disappeared."

"What?" There was a long pause. "She has nothing to do with the military, correct?"

"Not that I know of. She did ask me to meet her at that coffee shop near the base."

"So that means the local police." Mason paused for a long moment. "Has your sister contacted anyone?"

"She went to the police and reported Angela as missing."

"Let's get a hold of them first. Find out if a missing person's file has been opened and if they know anything."

Corey snorted. "You know, even if they have anything, they aren't going to tell me."

"Exactly, but we might be able to ask Alex to dig into this too. Get back on the phone. Get every last detail you can from your sister." Again Mason hesitated. "What exactly did you and Angela talk about?"

Corey stared out the window. "Not much. It was just the 'Hi, how are you? Isn't it lovely weather?' awkward conversation that happens when you haven't seen somebody for years, someone you hadn't expected to ever see again."

"And yet she called you?"

"Yes, she did. And, yes, I should have been prepared. But I wasn't. Seeing her again hit me like a punch to the gut."

"But you did see her after the miscarriage?"

"Yes, I did. Several times."

"How long since the last time you saw her?"

"Two days ago. Before that it had been twelve years."

"Okay, get back to your sister. I'll call Alex."

Mason hung up. Corey was surprised to see he was shaking.

What he hadn't told Mason was the shock of hearing her voice. That slam to his heart and his gut. The reason they'd broken up had been the miscarriage. But he hadn't been the one who wanted to break up. He'd wanted to get married and try again. And she hadn't wanted anything to do with that. He understood at the time she had been dealing with the miscarriage and the grief process.

But somehow she'd been unable to separate him from that horrible event. And had walked away. He'd tried hard to understand. He'd tried to stay in touch, but, every time he contacted her, she hadn't responded. Finally he talked to several of her friends, and they all said the same things. "For her, it's over. Move on."

His method of moving on had been to join the navy. It had taken a lot of years to rebuild his life, and just the shock of seeing her walk back into it the way she had, had been very disorienting.

He'd been more than happy to meet up with her. In fact, he'd been excited to see her, hoping maybe, after all this time, they could at least be friends. But she hadn't acted normal. She'd been nervous, tired, as if under a great deal of stress.

When he'd asked what was wrong, she'd shaken her head, given him a sad smile and said, "Life just *is*. You head down a path you think will lead somewhere good, only it doesn't. But you're too far down to change direction."

He thought about every moment of that very short visit. He realized her gaze had never stopped searching the restaurant. He had even asked her, "Are you expecting somebody else?"

She had given him a false laugh and said, "Expecting? No. Wondering? Yes."

He'd leaned back and stared at her. "What's this all about?"

But she'd hedged. "What? Can't I call up an old friend?"

"Is that what we are?"

She'd sat in her seat, stared at him for a long moment, her gaze going behind his shoulder before she said, "I was wrong to call you. I'm so sorry. I didn't want to dredge up bad memories." She grabbed her purse, stood and walked outside.

He'd raced out behind her. "What do you mean, *bad memories*? I got over it. I was hoping you had too."

She'd turned her glance his way. "Of course I got over it. But one never really forgets, does one?"

He took a deep breath, realizing just how much he hadn't forgotten as he stared at the woman he'd loved for so long. But it had been a young love. He'd been an infatuated fool back then. He was much older, much wiser and a whole lot more experienced in relationships now. And what he realized today was that what they had was very sweet.

"No, we don't forget," he'd said quietly. "Plus I never went on to have a family."

She'd glanced at him, startled, and then nodded. "I'm sorry." In her vehicle, she'd turned on the engine and smiled. "Just forget I was ever here." And she'd backed out of the parking lot and taken off. But, as she drove away, she'd turned to look behind her. And it wasn't to catch another glimpse of him.

Now he realized all the telltale signs he had missed. If only he hadn't been so rattled to see her, then he would have realized she was in trouble. He picked up his cell phone, just now wondering how she had gotten his number. And then realized his sister must have given it to her. He called Angela. Instead of ringing, the phone went straight to voice mail.

"Angela, this is Corey. Call me."

Given that type of a message, the chances of her returning his call were pretty slim. But at least he'd opened the door. It was up to her if she walked through it or not. And then he winced. At least that was what he had thought two days ago.

Maybe not. There was a darn good chance she wasn't in any position to answer. And then what the hell would he do? He'd just come through a really rough time with Macklin, dealing with the murder of somebody he knew. And that had been somebody who had caused him nothing but trouble. How would Corey feel if somebody he had cared about deeply was in trouble and if he hadn't stepped up to help?

"But she wouldn't tell me what was wrong," he muttered to the empty kitchen. Remembering Mason's instructions, he called his sister back. She answered this time.

"Sis, Mason is checking with local police here. But I need you to give me all the details, everything you know about Angela. I saw her but only for about ten minutes. She looked pale, worn out, stressed."

"Yes. She was stressed all right. She went to you for help," his sister scolded.

"Well, we never got to that topic. And it would have been nice if you had given me some warning," he snapped. "I get that you don't care one bit about my history with Angela, but it was a hell of a shock seeing her."

Her tone softened. "I'm sorry. Do you still care that much?"

"It doesn't matter how much I care now. It was a long time ago. But, seeing her after all that time, remembering how she wouldn't talk to me back then, it was a bit of an adjustment." He shook his head. "No. I don't have any excuse for the way I acted. I should have forced her to sit down and tell me what was going on right now. Instead, I let her run away. I should have known better. It's what she'd done before. It's what I felt like she always did."

"She's changed. That miscarriage really hurt her."

"Ditto," he snapped. "That doesn't change the fact she's in trouble now."

"No. But she wouldn't tell me exactly what was going on. She was looking to hire a private investigator. She wondered if you would know a good one."

"No, it's more than that." He glared around his kitchen. It was still clean because he barely ever cooked in it. Just breakfast mostly. His life was simple. In many ways, hollow. "*You* could have asked me that. *She* could have asked me that. On the phone. So why meet me in person? Especially after twelve years?"

"I have been telling her about your life for the last decade," his sister said on a bitter laugh. "It really surprised me when she said she was going to see you. I feel bad. I've been so busy with my studies and work that I haven't had the time or energy to keep up with what's going on with her. Any time I asked how she was she always said fine and just brushed me off. She was more worried about me staying focused on my work, she never told me how bad it was. That makes me feel like shit."

Knowing his sister was tired and stressed, he hated to hear her take on more guilt. Her shoulders were broad, but they were overwhelmed at this stage. Corey tried to help. "I'll find her and see what's going on. And, if she's in trouble, I *am* someone who might be able to help her."

"Then why the hell did you let her walk away?" his sister cried. Almost immediately she calmed down. "I'm sorry. That's so not fair. You're right. I should have warned you. When she left my apartment, I should have called you and said that she was in trouble and that she was coming to you for help."

"Yes. You should have," Corey said. "Then I would have convinced her to talk to me more. I was just still so focused on what was happening with a friend of mine and then, seeing Angela like that out of the blue, … well, I was off my game. I'm sorry for that."

"What happened? I heard something about a murder on the base."

"An old stalker of Macklin's was murdered."

And suddenly his sister gasped in sympathy. "Oh, no. He's such a teddy bear. He's really had such shitty luck."

Corey remembered explaining a little bit about Macklin's problems in an earlier conversation. "Well, because it was his stalker who was murdered, the police immediately looked at him as a suspect."

"But he wouldn't hurt a fly," his sister exclaimed. "He's a sweetie."

"Maybe. But he's also very well-trained and could have snapped her neck in no time."

"Is that how she died?"

"No. And that's part of the problem. Anyway, they solved the case last night. I haven't heard all the details, but Macklin now has a relationship with the detective from his case."

She chuckled. "Good for him. I'm glad to see maybe his luck is turning."

"True enough. Back to Angela. I need contact information. I need to know where she lived, where she worked and if you have any idea what was going on."

"I don't have much." She rattled off the address. "Do you have her cell phone number?"

"I do. But my calls go to voice mail. What about where she worked?"

"She was a website designer. She had her own company and worked from home most of the time."

"Interesting. Do you have keys to her place?"

"Yes, actually I do," his sister said in surprise. "I never even thought about that. I drove past, but I didn't go in."

"You have a lot on your plate. No worries. I'll come and take a look."

"Good. Are you coming tonight? Because I won't be home for several hours."

"When are you out of school?"

"Never, as you well know. I'll be very glad when this is all over." She sounded more than just exhausted. "Come and stay overnight with me. It will be nice to spend some time together."

Corey hated that this was adding to her stress. "How about I take you out for dinner tonight?"

"That would be nice," she said with enthusiasm. "I'm really looking forward to seeing you."

"Ditto." He hung up and turned to look around his small apartment. He shouldn't need an overnight bag, but, not knowing where this trip would take him, he decided to go prepared to stay for several days, just in case something unusual popped up. Given that Angela worked from home, Corey imagined she had attracted a cyberstalker. Maybe it was just Macklin's recent stalker case filling Corey's mind with scenarios, but it was a start. Plus too many people were too transparent on the internet with all the various social media outlets. Based on that, he wondered which IT specialist in his circle to contact.

He had a bunch of them to choose from. Particularly doing the missions they did in the military. Some of the men in his unit were incredibly talented, and a lot were really good hackers. It wasn't what they did full-time, but it was what they did on their time off.

Corey pulled out eggs and sausage from the refrigerator. He quickly made himself a solid meal. Just as he sat to eat, his phone rang again. He fished it out if his pocket to see it was Mason. "What did you find out?" He took a bite of egg as he listened.

"Her file was opened but extremely sketchy in details. They want to talk to you."

Corey groaned. "I was heading out to see my sister. I wanted to check out Angela's place. Apparently she's a graphic artist, and she builds websites for a living."

"Sounds interesting. Yet it could be a wasted trip."

"Still, we need to check out where she was, what she was

doing, see if there's any sign of who she was running from or running to."

"We?"

Corey sat back. "I was hoping one of the many IT guys we have in our nice little circle might be available."

"Take Warrick. He's got several days off. Supposedly to see his girlfriend. They were going to the coast for a couple days, but they just broke up."

"What? Warrick and Sandra broke up?"

"Yeah. Happened last weekend. That's the way it works sometimes. Warrick is now single, but Macklin looks to be involved."

"Good for Macklin. Not for Warrick. Although he and Sandra had been fighting off and on since forever, so it wasn't exactly a match made in heaven."

"True. He needs to find somebody like Tesla. Hell, you need to find somebody like Tesla."

"Dude, if Tesla could be cloned, we'd all have made copies and grabbed one for ourselves. She's fantastic."

"Well, Devlin wouldn't take a copy. He's pretty darn happy with Bristol."

"You all make me sick sometimes," Corey said with a laugh before he shoved a bite of sausage in his mouth. "I'll contact Warrick. Then I'll stop by the police station, give them a statement before I head out to my sister's for the night. If I can drag Warrick along with me, I will."

"And I'll run interference here. Somebody needs to check some street cameras. The ideal scenario would be if we found out she was being followed."

"There's nothing ideal about that," Corey said, his heart sinking at the thought. Surely he'd have noticed, wouldn't he? "I did stand in the coffee shop parking lot for a few minutes, and vehicles were pulling in and out at that time, but I wasn't watching them."

"Tell the cops that. They can check the cameras at the coffee shop. Or at least cameras at the closest intersections and see if anybody was on her tail."

"Will do." He hung up, finished off his breakfast, grabbed a bag and started packing. Then realized he hadn't called Warrick. He dialed his friend's number. "Hey, I hear you have a few days with nothing to do."

"Yeah. Apparently I have the rest of my life free too." Warrick's tone was snippy.

"How about coming with me for a couple days to get your mind off things?"

"What's up?" Warrick asked, his interest piquing in spite of himself.

Corey laughed. "Any disaster in our world makes us happy, doesn't it?"

"What kind of disaster?"

"A friend of mine might be in trouble." He explained what had happened. "I'm heading to my sister's. We'll stay overnight. I'll go through Angela's apartment. It might be our only way of knowing what's going on. I want to get there before the police do."

"Are you allowed to?"

"I wasn't planning on asking for permission," Corey said cheerfully. "Are you in or out?"

"Hell, I'm in. Can't say I'm too thrilled about the first stop at the police station, but I'm up for visiting your sister and definitely interested in helping out your friend. When are we leaving?"

"Ten minutes ago."

★

ANGELA GRIPPED THE steering wheel with more force than necessary. She tried to relax, to unclench her grip around the leather, but it was as if her fingers were claws. She didn't have a clue where she was going. Somehow she had taken a wrong turn, and, instead of heading to her aunt's cabin, she had ended up on this bloody highway. A turnoff was up ahead. She took it and slowed down, realizing belatedly the speed she'd been traveling. Her nerves were shot, and she could swear to God she'd been followed for the large part of this journey.

A black pickup seemed to sit on her ass for the last several hours as she drove up the California coast.

Then suddenly there was no sign of it. That made her more worried than ever. She'd wanted to stop and check in with Bridget, let her know she was okay, but she was afraid her phone was being tracked, so she had turned it off. It was just way too easy to get people you loved in deep trouble. And that was something she couldn't handle.

She was desperate to get Joshua back, but she didn't know how to accomplish that.

For some wild reason, she'd thought Corey would be able to help her. But she hadn't even stayed long enough to explain it to him. How would she tell him, as the father of the child she'd lost, that the father of her second child was trying to take her out of the equation?

She gave a bitter laugh. "I can really choose men. I walked away from a good one and ended up with a crazy one."

She pulled into a gas station and got out. She not only needed to fill the tank in the car but she needed food and a rest stop.

She finished pumping gas, paid for it with her credit

card and then froze. She pounded the roof of her car and bowed her head. "Shit. Shit. Shit. Somebody can track my credit card use."

She stared bleakly out at the world around her as she parked her car by the nearby restaurant. "I was not cut out to do this."

Exhausted, worried, she walked inside, ordered coffee and a sandwich, and sat down in the far corner. She'd very quickly learned to sit in such a way where she could watch the traffic coming and going, keeping an eye on anybody who appeared to be watching her. When her coffee arrived, she stared at it with longing. It would still be at least two minutes before it cooled enough for her to drink it.

And she was rather desperate for the caffeine hit. When the sandwich arrived soon afterward, she swallowed that down in several bites and then sat back to enjoy the coffee. She didn't know where she was going at the moment. She needed to ask somebody for help, but she didn't want to draw any attention to herself. She had a GPS option on her phone, but the roads in the area were not well-enough marked to use it. She brought out the address from her pocket and the old map she had stuffed in the back of the car's glove box, then had transferred to her purse.

Once she had figured out where she was, she realized she'd taken a wrong turn about forty minutes back. She groaned. "I'll be a couple more hours getting there."

At least she had filled up with gas, and this coffee would hold her for a little bit. Her aunt's cabin was completely empty and hadn't been inhabited for at least a year, which meant there wouldn't be food or supplies. There was no getting away from the fact that Angela was already at the end of her rope and more tired than she thought possible. She needed this trip to just end.

When she finished her meal, she ordered a second sandwich and travel mug of coffee to go. While all that was being done, she used the ladies' room, washed her hands and face, brushed her hair and straightened her clothing so she didn't look like the vagabond she appeared to be.

When she walked back out, she paid for the food, collected her order and headed outside. She reversed out of the space and drove down the road, headed back to the turn she had missed. Forty minutes later, she saw the correct turn ahead. She turned right and took the final leg of the journey to her aunt's cabin. It had been a roundabout trip, so, when she finally turned into the driveway and drove up the gravel road, her heart warmed.

This was the place she had spent many hours when she was a young child. She had a lot of good memories here. She also felt a sense of homecoming—even if it had been twelve years. They'd had such great summers on the lake. She got out, walked around to the cabin door and used the key hidden underneath the mat. Inside the cabin was cold, wet, chilly. Her aunt had promised to turn on the power, and, as Angela flipped the switch, with a sense of joy Angela realized her aunt had been true to her word. With lights inside and wood outside, Angela knew she'd be warm in no time. She walked back out to her car and unloaded her belongings.

What she really needed next was the internet. And she had paid a special price to get that here. It was just a matter of setting it up on her phone and laptop. Or at least Angela hoped so. She had to keep working. She lit the fire in the old wood stove, bringing in more kindling and wood from outside so she had enough for the night. It was summertime, but it was cooler up here, especially at night. The lake was more of a hunting area but recently had become popular with wealthier families, and they were building summer cabins all up and down the shores. With a fire going, a kettle full of water on the stove, she checked out the supplies to see if anything was left.

She was delighted to find dry goods, like flour and bread crumbs, plus coffee, tea, canned goods. Added to that was the box of food she had brought with her. She unpacked everything but her clothing and then made herself a cup of tea. She walked onto the veranda, welcoming the darkness of evening settling across the shores.

What she still had to do was move her car. To make sure nobody would easily see it sitting out front. Not wanting to take that chance and getting too comfortable without having taken that last safety precaution, she returned to her car, drove it around the cabin and parked it in front of the basement doors. Her aunt usually rented out the basement to students during the summer. And one of them in particular had parked down here. But no renters were due to show up this summer.

With her vehicle now out of sight from the road and from the driveway, plus mostly hidden from across the lake because of the trees, she walked back inside, suddenly exhausted. She locked all the doors except the sliding glass one to the veranda, walked out with her tea and collapsed on the ratty deck chairs.

For better or for worse, she was committed to this step. She only hoped it was the right decision. If she was wrong, there could be devastating repercussions.

As she settled in, kicking her feet up on the railing, she closed her eyes and whispered, "Have a good night, Joshua. Mommy loves you."

CHAPTER 2

SHE CRAWLED INTO bed with the plan of sleeping well. But a strange bed and a chill in the air made it hard to drop off to sleep. Then again she hadn't slept well for days, if not weeks. Trying to figure out what to do when there were no answers didn't make for happy dreams.

The only good thing in all of this was the fact that she knew Joshua should be physically safe. Her son was six, very smart, and very compassionate and tender. He'd be suffering emotionally without her around. But a child custody case when you were up against a powerful presence with a ton of money was a scary thing.

She'd thought she and her husband could work it out amicably. But, once he had gotten Joshua for the first visit, things had gone to hell quickly. He'd refused to let Joshua leave at the end of the day—and she'd been kicked out alone.

She'd slowly gone to pieces as she had contacted lawyer after lawyer. Each one had given her a large bill and not much in the way of assistance. Without money, she'd gone to the police. But that was even more useless. She didn't think there was really anybody who could help her.

She didn't have a clue why she thought Corey was the one to call on. He'd been out of her life for so long that it made no sense to go to him.

And yet, as soon as she thought about who she could count on to have her back, his name popped up. She didn't deserve his assistance. Plus, with so much water under the bridge, she knew it wouldn't be an easy thing to reopen that old wound.

Finally she jumped out of bed, threw on a heavy bathrobe that had been left behind in the cabin, put socks back on and padded out to the wood stove. She tossed more wood in the fire, then fired up the teakettle again. She didn't really want anything with caffeine, but a hot lemon tea might be nice. She thought she'd seen some lemon juice in the pantry.

She walked in and took a look. Found hot chocolate and some herbal teas. The lemon juice was open, and she had no idea how old it was so decided not to try it. She reached for the herbal teas instead. One with chamomile in it was called Sleepytime. She figured that would be perfect. It would take a bit for the water to heat up on the woodstove, but she much preferred sitting here in the dark, waiting, than turning on the light.

She walked out on the deck. A nice cool breeze drifted by. She could see a couple lights on the far side of the lake. Her aunt had bought this place a long time ago. The family had made good use of it ever since, and it was a wonderful place to live. If Angela had decent internet service, she could work from here.

That was what she'd always envisioned for herself. In the back of her mind she thought one day she'd have the house, the husband, the two kids and something like this to come to for summers, like she had experienced when she was growing up. But those dreams never came to pass. She'd been married for seven years and had a wonderful son. Only recently she'd learned of another woman with a son fathered by her husband, a son a couple weeks older than Joshua. What did one even do with that information? How did one deal with such a betrayal?

Joshua had a stepbrother.

Her husband had been having an affair for years. Hell, she didn't know if her husband was still with his paramour. She didn't want to know. Her husband had lived dual lives. And why he couldn't play nice when it came to child custody, she didn't know. But the thing was, things had gone too far. Now not only was Joshua's peace of mind and his life with her at stake but she was afraid her own life was too.

She'd started getting letters from his lawyer and then from him as soon as she'd initially left the family home with Joshua. At first they were mild and referenced the divorce and child visitations, but then the tone had changed somehow. Becoming more demanding. Then downright threatening. Particularly after he kept Joshua. Now they were about her never seeing her son again. Of course that was after she'd dropped Joshua off to spend a few hours with his father and never got a chance to take him home again. She wondered if Greg had been listening to someone's legal advice, but he was pretty canny by himself when it came to making someone else's life miserable.

The letters had always been signed by Greg, but, after the tenor of them had changed, she wondered if she had ever known him. After several terrifying ones, she'd bolted. It hurt her every moment she was away from Joshua. She'd do anything to get him back. He had a cell phone, unbeknownst to his father, so she could send text messages. They were light, bright, bubbly, happy messages. They also used several apps to send silly pictures to each other. She was trying to keep him out of the nastiness currently swirling around her.

She hadn't seen Joshua in just over a week. He hadn't lived with her now for two weeks. Two weeks where she had desperately tried every legal loophole she could to get him back. The only reason she'd seen him last week was because she had caught sight of him in the mall. He'd seen her and come running.

She'd wanted to pick him up and escape, but she'd been quickly surrounded by her husband and his men who ushered her out to the parking lot. She'd glared at Greg and said, "Is it really so hard to let your son see his mother?"

But Joshua had been ripped from her arms, screaming, and taken away. It had all happened so fast. Her heart broke as his screams continuously replayed in her head. She'd been shaking so badly that a woman had led her to a little coffee shop close by, set her down and gotten her a strong cup of tea.

After that incident the threats had gotten much worse. Angela rubbed her face, feeling the tears once again collect at the corners of her eyes.

Her lack of sleep and too many tears shed had her eyes burning, her nose filling, and the headache just boomed twenty-four hours a day inside her skull. She was so damn tired of fighting her husband, who seemed to think that he was above the law and that he should get everything he wanted. The only thing that gave her hope was that she had something on Greg. And yet, at the same time, she knew just how dangerous it would be to take that step.

Yet she'd do almost anything to get her son back. Still, if she died in the process, that wouldn't benefit Joshua. But she didn't dare let him be raised by a man like Greg. She'd had no idea he was so low. He considered himself a bigwig. She considered him a lowlife, somebody who put pressure on other businesses to sell out so he could demolish their storefronts and put up new fancy commercial skyscrapers. And he didn't do it in a nice way. He kept his business just legal enough to stay out of the eyes of the law. It would be too easy to shut him down otherwise. And that was only one aspect of what he did. She had just learned of a second aspect. As for the rest, she had no clue.

When she'd found the documents on Greg's desk, she hadn't thought anything of them. She'd been there dropping off her son. Greg had been on the phone, and he had stepped outside to take the call in private. She'd been anxious to spend every moment with Joshua so had been playing with him. He'd been running around the room like any young boy. He'd stopped by the table, then came giggling back to her and said Daddy was taking pictures. And she shushed him at the time, saying it was all right. But Joshua shook his head and pointed to the pictures on the table. She saw photos of several politicians in incriminating situations. She pulled out her cell phone and quickly took pictures of everything she could find.

She tried to leave everything seemingly undisturbed. When her husband had stormed back into the room, she was safely on the other side, using a pillow to play catch with her son. She'd been ushered out of the house and the door slammed in her face, never to cross the threshold again.

That had been two weeks ago.

She still had the photos. It hadn't occurred to her to do anything with them until she'd taken a better look at several of the spreadsheets she'd also taken pictures of. They looked like blackmail payments. And she realized it might just be her ticket to getting her son back. How the hell she was supposed to do that without a lawyer on her side, she didn't know.

And how was she supposed to get a decent lawyer when she couldn't afford to pay one? But there had to be a way.

Greg's threats were increasing. He'd progressed from telling her that she'd never see Joshua if she asked for any of his money to insisting she sign off on everything if she wanted to see Joshua again. He had also threatened her with what he'd tell Joshua about her so her own son would hate her. Given what Greg was capable of, she didn't doubt he'd do it. He wouldn't be happy until he had her son and until she was gone—preferably permanently.

She was a fool for not having considered her son might have said something to his father about the photographs. She'd laughed with Joshua at the time, making a game of her taking pictures, the same as Daddy probably had. But the timing with the threats—could that be what was behind his change in tone? If that was the case, her life wasn't even worth two cents to Greg. But then why hadn't he killed her yet? Why hadn't Greg said something to her? Mentioned her actions in the letters?

Why wait this long?

Was he waiting for the right time? Did he know about the cabin? If not, it wouldn't take anyone used to ferreting out information long to get the exact location.

With all these thoughts running around her head, she didn't know what to do. She could hear the teakettle whistling on the stove. She got up, poured the boiling water over the tea bag and took it back out into the night.

Just as she started to calm down, her phone buzzed. She pulled it out of the bathrobe pocket, never very far away from the unit, even though it was off most of the time.

However, at night, knowing she and Joshua would exchange good night texts, she took the risk of turning on her phone.

It was a text. She didn't know the number or the name.

I know what you did.

She dropped the phone on the small table, wrapped her arms around herself tightly, and rocked back and forth. "What do you know?" she asked the endless night. "I haven't done anything."

But of course she had. She'd taken pictures of something she wasn't supposed to know about. And now she knew. Most likely her son had mentioned something to his father. She had always hoped maybe Joshua wouldn't, and she had told him not to, but who knew what would pop out of a child's mouth from one moment to the next?

Now she needed to get a new phone, unregistered, a throwaway one. And that meant a trip back into town. And a drain on her finances yet again. Which would cut out her connection with Joshua as well as to Greg. She couldn't get rid of her only tie to Joshua.

Tired, worn out, mentally exhausted, she sipped her tea while she figured out her next step. The trouble was, she had very few options.

Finally she got up and went back to bed and fell into a fitful sleep.

COREY GAVE HIS sister a big hug. "Are you sure you don't want to come to Angela's place with us?"

"No, this is your specialty. I won't know if anything's missing, and, if you have any questions, just call me. I'd come if I didn't have this presentation tomorrow, but I'm just so not ready for it."

He leaned over, kissed her on the temple and said, "It will be fine. We'll take a look and see if there's anything to see. We'll return here afterward."

She nodded. "The spare bed is made up, and there's always the couch." She turned to Warrick. "Thank you for coming."

He gave her a big smile. "No problem. Let's hope we can find out what's going on real fast."

"Please do. I feel terrible knowing Angela was in trouble but wouldn't let me know how bad it was ..." She gave them a small smile as the two men stepped out of her apartment.

Outside, Corey checked the address. "She only lives a couple blocks away. I suggest we walk."

"I'm game."

The two ate up the sidewalk with their long legs. Both men were well over six feet and physically fit. They approached the apartment building and saw it was an older complex, only four floors high and probably only four units to a floor.

Corey approached the front double doors, looking for security. There was a call box on the side. He pressed her number, not expecting to get a response, but he needed to know for sure.

Somebody walked toward them from inside the building. He pushed open the door and held it for them to enter. Corey thanked the person and entered. He had the keys to get into Angela's apartment. But, even if he hadn't, Angela lived on the ground floor. If he couldn't have gotten in through the front entryway, he would have gone inside via the sliding door.

People liked to think they were safe inside locked doors. But he could get into almost anything in less than a minute.

Walking to her apartment, Corey had the keys in his hands. Glancing around to make sure nobody was watching, he popped the lock and stepped inside, Warrick on his heels. As soon as they entered and locked the door behind them, they realized this was a bigger deal than anything they'd expected.

Her place had been trashed. Kitchen cupboards had been emptied and dumped out; shattered glass was all over the floor; food spoiled in the opened refrigerator.

They walked through the small galleylike kitchen to the dining room area, which was just a four-by-four space with a small bistro table in the center.

They carried on to the small living room, finding the couch upside down, the cushions with the zippers opened and the foam pulled out. Next was the bedroom. Relieved when he found no body, Corey took a good look at the destruction. The bedroom was in the same state as the main living area. The bedding had been pulled off, the mattresses taken off the frame and slit; the closet doors were wide open, and the dresser drawers were dumped. Only the bathroom was left to check. The apartment was damn small. Maybe eight or nine hundred square feet total.

He took a step back and turned to look at Warrick standing in the middle of the living room, his hands on his hips, slowly turning, cataloguing the damage in his mind.

"Do you think they found it?" Warrick asked.

Corey said, "I don't think so. But I'd sure like to know what *it* is that they were after."

Warrick nodded. "Yeah, I don't think they did either. But they went to an awful lot of effort looking for it."

"Which means Angela is in a lot more danger than she knows." His voice grim, he pulled out his phone, scrolled the contacts to his sister and hit Dial. "Bridget, Angela's place has been completely trashed." He heard her short gasp from the other side.

"We need to call the cops," Bridget instructed. "Let them know."

"We need to know if they came earlier. In which case, that gives us a timeline for when the place was trashed." He pulled out a pad of paper. "I need to know the name of the detective you spoke with about Angela so I can get in touch with him directly." With the name written down, he ended the call and dialed the police station. After introducing himself, he said, "We used my sister's keys to get into Angela's place. I don't know if you've been here yet or not but we found her apartment trashed."

"Trashed?"

"Yes. There isn't a single dresser drawer, kitchen cupboard or anything left unturned. It's a huge mess. If somebody was looking for a specific item, it doesn't look like they found it."

"I'll be there in five. Stay where you are," came the stern retort.

"What does he expect us to do? Run?" Warrick asked when Corey told him the detective's instruction. "I guess they have to say that. They're cops. They need to know who we are to see if we had anything to do with this."

"Right. Like I would walk into a stranger's house, completely destroy it, then call the cops and say, *Hey, this is how I found it.*"

Warrick grinned. "We've seen a lot of similar kinds of issues. So we'll stay here until the authorities get here. Is there anything you think we can look through that will help get us answers?"

"You know what I don't get?"

Warrick turned to look at him.

"She does website design. I presume she has her laptop with her. But would she need anything else? I don't see any other electronics here. In today's day and age, she's probably got several laptops. Maybe some peripherals, like a tablet. But not too many people have the big desktop computer anymore. They don't need them."

"The new wave of computers—portable."

"Look at us," Corey said. "We have laptops. I think only Mason has a desktop, and that's because Tesla keeps going in there and upgrading it."

"She can come and upgrade my system anytime," Warrick said. "Damn, Mason lucked out with her."

"I doubt Devlin's life is any better in that sense. Although Bristol is probably not concerned about his system as much as getting his help with her system."

"She's got a new drone to release soon too, doesn't she?" Warrick wandered over to the side bar, lifting couch cushions, looking for what might be of interest beneath.

"Yeah, she does. It's got some new infrared radar on it."

Warrick turned to look at him. "Really?"

Corey nodded. "Yeah, she's constantly developing cutting-edge stuff. I just want to play with the toys all the time."

"Devlin should do that, have a big barbecue, and let us come over and play."

The two men were still chuckling when a hard rap came at the door. They looked at each other. Warrick stepped out of view as Corey opened the door. There was the detective, shield in hand, held out for him to see.

He nodded and stepped back.

The detective walked in, stopped and let out a long slow

whistle. "Wow." He stopped in place and did a slow circle. "I need to get techs in here and go over the place."

"I don't know what they were looking for, and I highly doubt they left any fingerprints, but this is the biggest lead we have that she's actually in trouble."

"I hear you. I had wondered myself if she had just disappeared. She's under a lot of stress right now apparently."

"Why is that?"

"She's in a custody battle with her soon-to-be-ex-husband over her son."

Corey felt everything inside go still. "Custody battle?"

The detective nodded. "She's come down a couple times to the station, looking for help. She dropped her son off about two weeks ago. Her husband refused to release him to her custody at the end of the visit. He's launched a series of lawsuits against her, saying she's an unfit mother. And I have to admit, some of her stories about her husband sound pretty crazy."

"She's a good person," Corey said.

The detective didn't turn his gaze away. "Exactly what is your relationship with her?"

"She's my little sister's best friend. I used to see her a lot back then."

"But nothing since?"

Corey frowned. "Out of the blue she contacted me two days ago, said she wanted to talk to me. I met her at a coffee shop. She was really nervous, restless. Finally, after just a couple minutes, she jumped to her feet, said she was stupid to have come and basically ran. I walked her out to the car, trying to convince her to come back inside and have the meal we had already ordered, but she was too nervous. She got in her vehicle and drove away."

"Right. Your sister told me about that."

"Did you check the traffic cams to see if anybody followed her?"

"I did. And there's no sign of her after she left the city limits. And, no, it didn't appear anybody followed her."

"Did anybody find an address book?" Warrick asked, as he joined in the discussion.

Corey and the detective both turned to look at him. "Why?"

"Just wondering who she has for relatives, where she might have gone."

"We have a phone call in to her aunt. Of course there's the husband and her son. I believe she has a couple cousins. But we're still tracking down people."

Corey pondered that. "I'll talk to my sister a little more, see if we can dredge up some of her memories. They've been friends for a long time. She must know some place Angela would run to. Also, if you could check the city cameras and check if she's being followed, that could give us a lead."

The detective nodded. "Also I want contact information from both of you. And keep in touch. Let me know if you find out anything."

As soon as they exchanged cell phone numbers, the two men walked back out into the front yard.

"I want to take a walk around the building," Corey said. "Let's make sure we didn't miss anything."

They did a thorough search. But it looked like the intruder had gone in through the apartment door. As Corey stood there, he pondered, "I wonder if we should ask the neighbors if they saw anybody?"

Just then a forensic team came to the apartment. Warrick motioned toward them. "They're going to do that. Let's get to your sister before they come after her too."

Corey winced. "Yeah, the detective probably already called her." They walked back in the evening light, their footsteps clipping on the hard cement. "For whatever reason, Angela knew to get the hell out. That information is likely to be on her emails, laptops, cell phone, and any other electronic device she's using."

"Well then, let's hope to hell she has all that with her. Because you know, as soon as these assholes get hold of them, they'll have tracked down exactly where she is and could be there within minutes."

Corey nodded. "Which means we just have to get there first." He walked up to his sister's apartment, rapped on the door and stepped inside. She was working away on her laptop at the kitchen table.

She looked up with a smile, only to have it fall away. "Do you think something's happened to her?" Her fingers clenched and unclenched the pen in her hand.

"Yes, I do. And, if it hasn't happened yet, it'll happen soon. I'm hoping she's holed up somewhere safe." Corey sat down, reached across the table and clasped her hand in his. He covered it, warming it up. "Bridget, you need to tell me where she would run to. Her place has been trashed, but there's no sign she has been there since."

Bridget took a deep breath. "The only place I could even begin to think of is a cabin where she spent a lot of time during the summers. I was there once, and it was a place to remember."

Corey frowned. "Is that when you went out to the lake for a couple weeks? When was that, eleventh grade?"

She nodded. "I think it was somewhere around then. We spent two weeks with her aunt."

"Any idea how to contact the aunt?"

Bridget started clicking away on her laptop. "I set up a file for all my friends at one point."

Warrick laughed. "You set up a file on your friends?"

She shot him a look. "I forget things easily," she confessed, "so this file has their addresses, phone numbers, family contacts, things like that."

"Did the police ask you for it?"

She looked up, and her gaze widened. "No. And I didn't even think about it."

"Well, they'll probably ask you soon. Now, if you've got a printer, you want to hand that off to us or at least bring it up on the screen, and we'll take pictures. Then we'll head to the cabin."

"It's a four-hour drive from here," she said worriedly. "You shouldn't be leaving right now."

The two men looked at each other, then at their watches. "We could pull out at three in the morning and get there at dawn," Corey said. He looked over at Warrick for his agreement.

Warrick nodded. "That works. We can catch a few hours of sleep and hopefully still get there before she's up and panicking."

"You think I should let her know you're coming?" Bridget asked.

"If she's smart, she'll have ditched that phone a long time ago."

Bridget picked up her phone and sent a text. "She hasn't responded to any phone contact, but maybe she'll get it in an email. Or a text. I just told her that you are both on the way, and you will be there very early in the morning." She sat back down and looked at her brother. "Please help her out. I hate knowing she's in trouble. I know she was struggling to adapt to being a single mom, but I've been so buried in my schooling that I just didn't realize something bad was going on. She was looking for a private investigator, but I never really asked why. I should have."

Warrick's phone went off. He excused himself and stepped out into the hallway.

Corey hugged his sister but inside he was reeling. Why hadn't Bridget mentioned Angela's husband and child? "Why?" he asked in a strangled voice. "Why didn't you ever tell me?"

She winced. "I was afraid she still mattered and that her marriage and family would be a blow to you all over again."

CHAPTER 3

HER PHONE KEPT buzzing throughout the night. She ended up pulling a pillow over her head and burying underneath it. When she fell asleep, she slept the sleep of the exhausted and woke up the next morning feeling like dried bread that had been ground into bread crumbs. Splintered. Rough. She didn't know how to pull it all together.

Sleep was supposed to be refreshing. Supposed to make her feel better. Instead, it made her feel like she couldn't get her mind back on track. She got up, dressed and headed into the kitchen. Coffee would help. There was only instant, but she'd take it. Desperate times and all that.

She pulled out her phone to see several texts from Bridget. In all of them, there was a note saying, **Corey and Warrick are on their way.**

That even failed to impress her. She'd met Corey and had walked away. What did he think she would do this time? Still, she needed help; she just didn't know where to get it. They might be able to give her a name.

Bridget also said she was supposed to contact the detective to let him know she was alive. Everybody was worried about her. And the last message really made her heart jump into her throat.

I don't even know if I should tell you this, but I don't think you should come home. At least not to your place.

Come to my place. Your place has been broken into, and it's in shambles.

At that, she stuffed the cell phone back into her pocket, poured hot water over the coffee crystals, stirred it and took her cup as stepped out onto the verandah. It was really beautiful here. She should seriously talk to her aunt about maybe renting it for a year. Apparently her apartment was no longer an option. She didn't know if she was safe here or not. But she had to live someplace. And, at the end of all this, this little piece of heaven would at least help heal her soul a bit. Joshua would have a blast living here. He was into bugs and water and stones and every other outdoor thing imaginable.

Well, he was a little boy and very true to form. But he was also the kind who would pick up a spider and drop it in a safe place. She wasn't of the same ilk regarding spiders but understood that was who he was. When he had asked her if she wanted the spider to crawl on her, she had shaken her head politely and said, "No, sweetie. He likes you best."

It was all she could do to stop the cringe reaction when the spider came closer. She'd gotten a lot better about bugs, but she still had a lot of room to grow. Joshua was a good boy.

She patiently brushed away tears and anger at herself for constantly succumbing to them. There was a time to cry, and there was a time to straighten her spine and do what needed to be done. In the back of her mind was always that thought that maybe she could hire somebody to steal her son back. She could run to Mexico and hide from the authorities until he grew up. She had read numerous stories in the news about people doing just that. Sure, eventually they got caught. She didn't give a damn as long as she got time to spend with her son. To consider a future without him was just too unthinkable.

She walked down the verandah steps, her thin sandals making a light clacking sound as she took each riser. It was early; nobody was here; and, with any luck, they would get lost the same as she had. She had mixed feelings about having no one to help her. It'd be nice to not be alone. But the last thing she wanted was to involve two men she didn't know—at least she didn't know any longer.

She'd never seen this behavior in Greg before. But then she'd never crossed him. She would have left a hell of a lot earlier if she had realized how illegal his dealings were. Had he married the other woman too? For a moment she indulged in the thought of not being legally married to Greg. Wouldn't that be great? Although he was too canny to do something he could be caught in so easily.

She shook her head and tried not to spill her coffee as she walked down the thirty feet of the rough path to the lake's edge. An old dock sat off to the side, looking worse for wear and desperately in need of a hammer to get some of the nails pounded flat once more. Some pretty good storms were common in this area, so the cabin could leak. She'd love to spend some time here and do some house repairs. Bring it back to the way she remembered it. Her aunt was getting on in years now. Angela imagined her aunt would go stay with one of her kids, never returning to the cabin. Angela wanted to rent it, unless the family wanted to sell it.

She gave a broken laugh. "Who am I kidding? I'll be lucky if I have enough money to put food on the table when this is over."

The lawyers had pretty well wiped her out. Her husband had mountains of money, all from his own business ventures, but he certainly wasn't into sharing. If he refused her access to her son, he sure as hell wouldn't let her have access to his money either.

A duck swam by, looking at her out of the corner of his eye, cutting a wide circle around her to make sure she couldn't catch him.

"Go ahead, little one. Keep on floating. I have no designs on you."

She wanted to sit on the edge of the dock, though her body was too stiff and sore after the long drive and her rough night. She slipped her feet out of the sandals and stepped into the water from the shoreline. She dabbled her toes in the cool water. Even though it was summertime, it was a little on the chilly side. That probably had as much to do with her fatigue as anything.

She stood here, feeling a little better as she sipped her coffee and stared at her peaceful surroundings. This was the right decision. She needed this. Something inside her soul ached to be here. Hidden away, safe, not having to worry about real life intruding ... Greg didn't know about this place, thank heavens.

After wading for a few minutes, she put her sandals back on and walked out onto the dock. She remembered a ladder used to be here into the lake.

It was much deeper at the end of the dock, and they used to jump and dive off it. They had this big floatable raft thing they swam out to and played on. She had such great memories here of lots of family barbecues and late evenings sitting around a campfire roasting hotdogs and marshmallows.

She hugged her arms to her chest, feeling a chill now. She should have brought a sweater. The sun was up, but just barely. And the cabin was tucked into the trees, so the rays of warmth hadn't reached her yet. It would soon, but, for the next fifteen to twenty minutes, she'd be standing in the shadows.

In many ways, this was how she'd felt for most of her marriage. It had been much less than she had hoped for. Greg had been a big man; she had been bowled over by everything he'd promised. She thought at the time she loved him. She just hadn't realized she'd mistaken love for security. And she'd sure found out fast how security came with bars.

She'd never been allowed to do anything on her own. Greg controlled what she did with her time. He picked out her clothing, ordered her to take various courses so she'd look better, act better—even voice classes. Nothing was wrong with her voice, but he had this arrogance about him that thought she didn't sound as upper class as she could. Rolling her *R*s and elongating her *O*s was supposed to do that.

She thought back to how naive and stupid she'd been. And how quickly he'd formed her into what he wanted. She still didn't understand how it had happened. It wasn't who she was. But she had been desperate to get married and to start a family. After losing the baby way back when, it seemed she had spent years trying to get back to that stage of life again. But she hadn't wanted it to be with just anybody. She certainly didn't want a casual one-night stand. She'd wanted a long-term relationship. She'd wanted it all.

The house, the two kids, the holidays at the lake. Instead, she got a controlling, lying cheat of a husband, an absolutely adorable son, and a lifestyle where she'd felt caged. Freedom from Greg had been bliss. With her son, she hadn't even regretted walking away from the lifestyle. As long as she had Joshua, she didn't bother about anything else. Joshua was perfect.

He was perfect in every way. And yet she had no way to get him back. Her husband wouldn't let go of his control.

She sat on the edge of the dock, dangling her feet above the water. She tried to organize her thoughts as to what the day would bring. If and when the men arrived, what were her chances of getting rid of them? And how much had Bridget told them?

Not that she had told Bridget everything either. Angela hadn't wanted to get her into trouble. It was bad enough that Joshua's life was impacted. The last thing Angela wanted was to create any more stress for Bridget. This was too important a crunch time for her. Law school had been brutal. Angela had watched her friend crumble under the stress and workload, along with a job and everything else. Bridget had shunned all men, making room for only those things she could handle.

That had been a great idea, but there had also been re-percussions. And some of them had been that Bridget could not see exactly what was going on in Angela's world, and Angela had deliberately not brought Bridget in on all the details. Angela didn't want Bridget to worry. But Angela wished that she'd had someone to share this nightmare with. Being on the run was one thing. Being on the run and trying to get her son back, that was a whole different story.

Hearing an odd sound, she twisted, spilling the last of her coffee on the boards, to see a man walking toward her. She hopped to her feet, looking for a place to run. But she was at the end of the dock. The only other place she could go was into the water. Then she heard a shout.

"Angela, it's me. I'm here with Warrick."

To the left of where the stranger stood, she saw Corey

striding toward her. He still had that long, loose-limbed walk. But instead of the young man she'd known, it was the man she'd met in the coffee shop. Powerful and in control. He just looked so damn different.

She'd been stunned when she saw him again. She'd carried the idealistic young man he had been in her heart for so long. And now, after all this time, to see him grown up, and not just grown up but somebody to be respected and be proud of, she was sad she hadn't followed up on their relationship way back when. But she'd been too young, and it was too early and too … He hadn't been right for her back then.

Hell. *She* hadn't been right for anybody back then. She'd been such a mess. She hadn't treated him as well as she should have. For that, she was sorry. But to see this powerful male walking toward her as if he knew exactly what was in her mind and understood where she was coming from made it incredibly difficult to even break her gaze free. He was mesmerizing. He stepped up to the edge of the dock and held out his hand. "I'm coming toward you," he said. "This will be okay. We will get to the bottom of it."

She widened her gaze and then realized she was standing with one foot at the edge of the dock as if she were going to fling herself into the water. She took a deep breath and let herself relax, then turned and walked toward him casually. "Hi." Her gaze drifted past him to the man standing behind him. "You must be Warrick."

The big man smiled and nodded. There was something so damn compassionate in his gaze that she wondered what he possibly did for a living. She knew what Corey did. Bridget had told her of his accomplishments along the way. But Warrick had a gentler countenance. Whereas Corey had hardened planes on his face, Warrick was more of a big teddy bear.

She glanced at Corey. "Why did you come?"

He smiled, shoving his hands in his pockets. "It'd be nice if you said *hi* first before you try to send me away again."

"I did say hi." She frowned at him. "Answer the question." Her voice rang clearly across the lake.

He studied her for a long moment and tilted his head slightly. "I came to help."

She crossed her arms, her fingers tapping aimlessly on her coffee mug. "What do you think you can do?"

He leaned forward. "You must have thought there's something I could do, or you wouldn't have contacted me in the first place. The fact that you got scared and ran means you really need me."

"Nobody else has been able to help me." She was surprised to hear how much bitterness was in her tone. "I don't see that you can do anything different."

"Come back to the cabin, and let's talk," he said quietly. "You don't know what I can do because you don't know who I am anymore."

"And you don't know what kind of trouble you might have just gotten yourself into," she countered him. "For all you know, when we walk back to that cabin, somebody'll be there with a gun."

He gave her a smile and let her see his teeth. "Good," he said in a low tone. "I hope that asshole is waiting for us."

She stared at him for a long moment, and, for whatever reason, she believed him. She took a deep breath and slowly let it out.

Warrick said, "Take another few breaths, try to step back

from the panic, and then you'll be able to explain it that much easier."

Standing where she was, she deliberately took several more deep inhales and then walked up the last bit of distance to Corey and Warrick. She reached out, shook Warrick's hand. "Nice to meet you."

He enclosed her small hands in his huge ones. "Likewise."

She glanced at Corey, flashed a smile and said, "Let's head back to the cabin." She led the way. She could hear them talking behind her. She slowed to walk beside them.

Warrick nudged Corey. "Wow. There's history here."

"You have no idea," Corey said sadly. "But it was a long time ago."

"Some things just never end. And some things end so damn fast you have no idea what hit you."

"I heard about Sandra, dude. I'm really sorry about that."

"It hurts," Warrick said. "What do you do? Sandra made a decision, and it's one that doesn't include me in her life anymore."

Listening to him, Angela was surprised. He looked like such a sweet and loving man that she couldn't imagine anybody not wanting him. But then, just like her husband had been an asshole, there were women equally bad, and they didn't always know or recognize the good in the people around them.

She stepped into the cabin, stoked the fire again and put the teakettle back on. She had almost no food. As they walked in, she announced, "I don't have anything to feed you."

"We didn't come here to get fed," Corey returned.

She cast him a glance. "Maybe not, but I'm starved."

Warrick laughed, a deep rumble that eased up his chest in a way that made her look at him in surprise.

"That sounded like thunder."

He grinned. "We stopped and picked up a bunch of sandwiches. Do you want one?"

She narrowed her gaze at him. "Yes, please."

Warrick reached out, smacking Corey on the arm. "I'll grab our bags."

She frowned as soon as he left. "Your friend is taking a lot on himself. I didn't invite you to stay."

"If we feed you, we get to stay for a bit." He sat down at the kitchen table. "Are you making tea or coffee?"

"There's only instant coffee." She glanced at the teakettle, then back at his face and broke out laughing. "You do know what that is?"

"I know what it is," he snapped. "But it's right up there with green beans as far as I'm concerned. They're both poisons. Coffee should be brewed slow and hot and very, very strong."

"You'll deal with this or do without." In saying that, she took out an extra cup, poured in some crystals, poured water over them, stirred it and walked across the room and placed it in front of him. "If you brought coffee, then you could make real coffee, but, in the meantime, that's all I have to offer."

Within minutes, Warrick came back inside, several bags in one hand, and what looked like food and a couple thermoses in the other.

Corey took the instant coffee to the sink and dumped it.

"Hey, I could have had that," Warrick said.

Corey brought the cup back, reached for the thermoses

and proceeded to pour Angela a cup. Then he rummaged in the cupboard for a second cup. All the while, he never said a word.

She realized how completely inhospitable she'd been. She was frustrated, angry and pissed off that somehow walking away from Corey the other day had brought him back into her world. Yet at the same time it was damn good to see him. She sat down at the table as Warrick handed her a sandwich.

"Eat. It'll help put the grizzly bear back inside."

She didn't say a word but chowed down. But all food tasted like sawdust now. When she was finished, she sat for a long moment. "I'm sorry. I should be more thankful. I know you came with the best of intentions."

"You have us for a few days, so deal with it," Corey said.

She looked at him. "What do you think you can do in a couple days?"

"No idea. Maybe you should start talking to us, telling us exactly what the problem is."

Bitterly she said, "Do you want the whole sordid story?"

He stared at her for a long moment, then inclined his head. "Yes, we do. We need all the details. But the bottom line is, is somebody trying to kill you?"

She took a deep breath and shrugged. "Maybe."

Corey and Warrick exchanged hard glances and turned to look at her. "Start at the beginning."

"I don't really know where it all started." She launched into a short description of her marriage, her son, her walking away and thinking Greg was okay with her leaving because he had this other *woman* and son, to finding out he had planned to never let her see her son again.

"The last time I saw Joshua was in the mall." She took a

moment to catch her breath, realizing tears were already pouring down her cheeks. "After that incident, things got bad. The threatening notes came almost every day. Greg would text and email. And the last one read **I know where you live. Say your last goodbyes**."

"Well, that's definitely a death threat."

Warrick stepped in. "Did you tell the detectives about any of this?"

"I did. But I don't know if anybody really gave a shit. I think they had labeled me as a neurotic mother. And quite possibly not a fit one, as Greg was implying." She stared off in the distance. "I'd have given up my life so Joshua could have a good one, but not having his mother can't be the best for him."

"Every little boy should have a mother," Corey said gently. "And I know you would be a good mother."

She gave him a lopsided smile. "You always were a good cheerleader."

He gave her a crooked smile. "Maybe. I've grown up a lot since then too."

She nodded. "I almost didn't recognize you at the coffee shop."

"Well, you don't look a day different," he said. "A little more stressed. But then this is a pretty rough time for you."

Warrick's gaze went from one to the other.

She dropped her gaze, waiting to see if Corey would explain, but he didn't. She figured he would tell Warrick later in private.

She said, "So I have no idea what I'm supposed to do. Somebody apparently is after me. I place the blame for that firmly on Greg's shoulders. He's doing everything he can to make it appear I'm an unfit mother so he gets to keep

Joshua."

"Do you have the name or any other contact information of this other woman?"

She shook her head. "No. I don't. Oh ..." She reached up and touched her temple. "There could be another reason he might be trying to kill me." She shook her head. "I'm sorry. I'm just too rattled and tired. I should have mentioned it first."

"What are you talking about?"

"When I dropped Joshua off two weeks ago, the one and only time I actually took him to his father's place, where we used to live, his dad was really angry. Greg said he'd be with us in a few minutes and went outside. He was basically yelling on the phone. On a table in his home office were a ton of photos. But they were pretty ugly. They looked like photos of people in various compromising positions. There were also a couple spreadsheets. I didn't know what the hell it was all about. I quickly took pictures, and, no, I don't know why I did that." She looked up at the two men staring at her intently. "I didn't think of them again until just over a week ago after I saw Joshua at the mall. Greg was surrounded by all these bodyguards, and no one would let me talk to Joshua. I was so upset that I seriously started to look at what I could do to get my son back."

"And what do you think all those photos were?" Warrick asked.

She looked at him. "At a guess, I'd say blackmail. You have to understand that I thought my husband was a beautiful man. But really the facade was beautiful. Inside, he's as rotten as any man I've ever met. He was probably blackmailing other people. The spreadsheets appeared to be payouts, but I don't know for sure. I don't understand most of that stuff. And I didn't have time to look."

"Where are those photos?" Corey asked urgently. "Do you still have them?"

She nodded. "I downloaded them and emailed them to myself."

"Can you access them from here?"

She studied them both for a long moment. "If we have internet, I can. Otherwise …" She pulled out her phone and tossed it over to Corey, "The originals are still on there."

COREY PICKED UP her phone, quickly flipped through to the photos and brought them up. "It's really hard to see them on here."

She nodded. "They were hard to see anyway. But on the laptop we can at least blow them up."

He lifted his gaze from her phone. "The only thing I have to question here is why you would take pictures of all of this."

She winced. "Because I already had an inkling he might make life very difficult for me. It's not that I wanted any money out of the divorce, but I did want my son. I was open to sharing visitation in many ways. But I wanted sole custody. I wanted to make sure my son was looked after."

"But, as he is potentially blackmailing others, you were picking this up to blackmail him," Warrick said.

She sat back and stared at him. "I hadn't thought of that. I just wanted to protect myself," she said. "To make sure Joshua would be okay."

"Had he ever hurt your son? Is there any hint he would be anything other than a good father?" Warrick asked.

She shook her head. "Outside of being a disinterested yet

controlling father, no. But he was already starting to make threats about how I would end up with nothing, including Joshua. And that Greg had all this evidence, saying, if I ever crossed the line, he would make sure I didn't get custody."

She shook her head. "I don't know why I took those pictures. But the photos were all wrong themselves. Greg was up to something. And I just didn't know where it was going. It was instinct that had me taking photos of it all." She shrugged. "And maybe I'm a shitty person, but everything inside me said to make a copy."

Both men nodded. Corey handed the cell phone to Warrick. "Can you see anything there?"

He glanced at her. "How is the internet here?"

"I just arrived last night, so I have no idea. I brought my laptop in, but I haven't hooked it up."

"Why don't you bring it out then?"

"Are the pictures important?"

"Potentially. And, if the wrong person knows you made copies of those things, then you might be a whole lot easier to get rid of than to worry about what you might know."

Corey watched the color drain from her face. He had seen divorce battles get really ugly, and custody battles were worse. It was interesting she'd actually chosen to take pictures of everything. It would have been his instinct too, if he had seen the photographs were incriminating. Because, if her husband was up to something really ugly, then that gave her leverage over anything he might try to do to her. It was something all his friends would've done.

He just hadn't expected her to do it.

And he could see she was racked with guilt over it. He watched as she stood and walked into a small room.

"Interesting cabin." Warrick looked up from the phone.

"This is a perfect getaway for the summers."

"I could actually live here all year round," Corey said. "It's a great step out of society."

"And it's her aunt's?"

"Apparently. Bridget said it was. We haven't asked her specifically."

Just then Angela came back into the room, carrying a laptop. She opened the lid and hit the Power button.

"Your aunt doesn't live here anymore?" Corey asked.

"She never lived here. It was her summer cabin. I don't think they ever came up any later than October." She took a seat and picked up her coffee. "When I needed to get out of town, I didn't have any other place to go."

"It's a good thing you did leave town, considering the state your apartment's in."

"How bad is it?"

The two men exchanged a glance, then looked back at her. "Pretty bad. It will take hours to put everything away again, or it might be easier to get a Dumpster."

She sighed. "And that's not something I have money for."

"When did you start doing website work?" Corey asked.

"I've always been into graphic design. I worked for a large company before I got married. Greg didn't like me working. So I slowly wound down my work to spend more time with him, thinking that, you know, it might be what I was supposed to do in my new future. I was going to be a housewife. And, when I found myself suddenly separated and cut off from Greg's accounts, I had to come up with a way to pay the bills."

"Do you not have any money?"

"No. We had joint bank accounts. Next thing I knew,

they were emptied. And what little money I had saved went to the first two lawyers to fight for Joshua. The trouble was, that got very expensive very fast."

"Have you had any meetings over the custody yet?"

"Greg's speaking to somebody next week. He wants to force me to have a mental evaluation to confirm that I'm an unfit mother," she said bitterly. "I've talked to many medical doctors myself. But nobody so far was willing to take my side."

"Interesting tactic."

"Why? If I'm an unfit mother, he gets to cut me out of Joshua's life."

"Your husband doesn't like to share, I gather?"

She was busy clicking on the laptop. But at his words, she lifted her head, looked at him in surprise and said, "No, he doesn't. Why?"

"Joshua."

She nodded slowly and sat back. "It never occurred to me that he would be like this. I figured he'd be happy to let us go. Instead he went the opposite direction and is making sure I don't get anything."

"We often only really understand what's inside a person when something like this happens. Divorce doesn't bring out the best in any of us. But, if he's become violent or is doing something illegal, that's a different story. There's no reason you can't both have access to Joshua. And, if Greg's pulling any kind of stunt over that, then that's something the law should be able to sort out."

"Only if you have money," she exclaimed. "If I don't have that, then I'm up against his lawyers, and there's just no way to fight them."

"Why do you think he wants Joshua? Is it really because

he doesn't want to share, or do you think he has some other reasons?"

"I think he wants his son solely so I can't have him. I think he wants his girlfriend to be his new wife, and then he'll have two sons. His second son was born around the same time as Joshua. Only I was the idiot who didn't know." She added this last bit with enough bitterness for both Corey and Warrick to stare at her. "I wouldn't be surprised if he ditched the other mother as well."

"You have her name or contact information?"

"You asked me that already." She shook her head. "I just know her name is Julia. Julia Webber. Her son's name is Daniel."

Corey brought out a pad of paper and quickly jotted down the information. "Have you heard of any problems between Greg and Julia?"

"I just found out about the other woman two weeks ago, when I left and then Greg kicked me out. So, no, but then Greg doesn't talk to me."

"What about your son? Did he mention anything about meeting them or what it was like being around Daniel and his mother?"

"He was thrilled to have a brother. He was thrilled they got to play," she admitted. "But I don't know how much is real and how much isn't real. He's only six. And of course he's dazzled by all the good things that happen when he's there."

"Versus being with Mom who doesn't have the money to take him out and buy him stuff?"

She nodded.

Warrick pointed toward the laptop. "Can you see if you have internet access here please?" He handed the phone back to Corey. "I'll be setting up on that little coffee table over there." He nodded behind them. Pushing his chair back, Warrick stood, grabbed one of the bags he'd carried in and brought out a laptop.

Corey knew what Warrick was doing, just not exactly how he would do it. But then that was why Corey had brought an IT guy. Between the two of them fussing on the laptops, Corey felt useless. He went out on the deck to take a closer look at the surroundings, the neighborhood and security—if there was any in the place. He applauded her parking around back.

When he'd first arrived, he'd had no idea if she was here. As he went around the cabin, he'd seen her car. But, by that time, he'd already caught sight of her down on the dock. Even then, he was still trying to fit this current woman, who seemed to have nothing but trouble in her life, with the woman who had left him all those years ago. Everything had been sweet and simple for her back then. Until the miscarriage.

He wondered if that had started the difficulties for her or if this was new.

He wandered around, checking out the hiding places anybody skulking around could use, what he could see across the lake and whether anybody there could see them.

It was very much country living. A lot of trees on a hillside, a nice gradual descent to the lake. But the cabin was hidden from most of the neighbors. Although there were open areas where he could see across the lake to the other properties, those were a long way away. A high-powered rifle with a scope could definitely make things more visible.

Warrick called out, "Corey, come here for a sec."

He wandered back inside to see Warrick sitting on the

couch near the coffee table, laptop open, with a couple other gizmos on the side that Corey recognized as boosters. He sat down beside Warrick. "What did you find?"

"I downloaded the images off her phone."

Corey sat down and watched as Warrick brought up the images one by one. "Wow. These could be damaging." One was of two men in a sexual clench. Another was of a man and a woman in a similar clench. Another was of a man talking to somebody, handing a packet of something across. "I wonder where the hell Greg got these photos."

"He could have taken them himself. Or paid for them. I don't know," Angela said from the kitchen table. "He had a lot of strange people through the house. Less after I moved in and Joshua was born. When I asked him about it, he said it was out of consideration for us." She raised her head. "But then I realized he just used the home office more. So people came in and out of his office but never entered the main house. He had glass doors leading outside, which were on the side of the house closest to the driveway."

"So people could drive up, stop in to see him and leave, and you'd never know?" Warrick asked.

She nodded. "And it happened all the time, all hours of the day and night."

The two men looked at each other, then Corey said, "I'm sorry, but I have to ask. Did you share a bedroom?"

She lifted her gaze, locked onto his and in a shaky voice answered, "For the first few years, yes. He moved out about a year and a half before we split up."

"And is that when the difficulty started?"

She shrugged. "No. He had logical reasons, all kinds of them." She snorted. "Actually the end was well before that. Don't forget Daniel is only a few weeks older than Joshua, so

Greg obviously had an affair with this other woman at the same time he was married to me." She leaned back and raised both hands, palms up. "And, if he's got two, maybe he has three or four women. I don't know." She ran her hands through her hair. "I don't care about that anymore. I just want my son back."

Corey wasn't sure what to think. But of course it happened. He nodded silently, brought out his notepad again and started taking notes. "Do you remember what day you took these?"

"It's on my phone. All the images are dated. I don't know if it's got a time stamp or not, but it should have a date stamp."

Warrick pulled up the images and pointed out the time and date stamps on the bottom. "Any idea how long they had been in his office?"

"No, because I had just arrived. I was dropping Joshua off, but my son was upset I was leaving, so I was still there when Greg got off the phone."

"Why did you go to his office to drop Joshua off? Why not just at the front door?"

"Because that's where Greg lived. The office was his room. But that day he wasn't there, he was pacing in the yard."

"Why didn't you see him when you drove in?"

"I parked on the street and took the walkway up to the front door. When I rang the bell and knocked, nobody answered. I knew he was expecting us, so I opened the door and walked in." She gave a wry smile. "It was the last time I was allowed to have Joshua with me. Greg kept him that day and ever after. It was the last time I was allowed inside his house too."

"And the driveway, where is that in relationship to the front door?"

"It wraps around the side of the house. I could see him when he paced in front of the glass doors to his office, so I know he didn't see me take the pictures." She stopped for a long moment, thinking. "It sounds like you're accusing me of something."

"I'm not. I want to make sure we have your story straight, in case things blow up, and all of this has to go to the police. The minute there is any confusion, they start tearing apart your statements, and then they start looking for more conflicting statements."

She nodded, but he could see her shoulders slump.

Corey added, "It's only going to the police if there's a bigger issue. They already know about the death threats and that your place was vandalized. I'm not sure what we'll do with these photographs yet."

"I didn't recognize anybody in the pictures, but the sexual nature worried me."

"It's not the sexual nature that worries me," Warrick said quietly. "Several of these are high-profile businessmen, and some are in politics."

She gasped. "So they *are* being blackmailed?"

"They are images somebody might potentially pay money to stop from surfacing," Corey corrected. "But we don't know yet if Greg was actually blackmailing anyone. For all we know, he could have come across this packet in the street and had spread it out, figuring out what to do with it."

"Damn. So there is a chance he's still a good guy?"

Corey snorted. "There's a chance, but it's mighty slim. I'd say the chances are much better he was putting the screws to somebody who was refusing to pay. But again it's all conjecture. We need more information, a lot more."

CHAPTER 4

S FAR AS she was concerned, that was great news. She bounced off her chair and raced over. "Which people do you recognize?"

Warrick pointed out the image on the laptop. "He's in the cabinet. I don't have any idea who the woman is, but here's a picture of his wife." He tapped the screen. "Different women. Now that doesn't mean they haven't recently separated, but there's a good chance this photo was taken for blackmail purposes."

He switched images. "I can't identify either of these two men, but enough of their faces are showing that someone who knows them can easily recognize them."

"Well, there's not a whole lot else showing, given the position they're in, unless you're looking for moles and birthmarks."

"What about the spreadsheets?" Corey asked.

"I was just working on those. Everything's abbreviated. But it shouldn't take too long to decipher them."

Corey leaned over to see what was on the screen. "Send me the spreadsheets. I'll get my laptop up and running, and we'll see if we can figure out what we're looking at."

Warrick nodded. "Sending now."

Corey walked over to his bag, grabbed his laptop and came back. "If we can prove these are blackmail payments, then we need to track down bank accounts—preferably back to Greg."

"What will they do to him if we can prove he's blackmailing people?"

"Well, he's looking at jail time for sure, but it'll take a while for the process to go through. You will certainly have reasonable doubt for your son to stay with him. That's hardly the environment anybody wants a child to grow up in."

"Well, that's good news," she said with feeling. "I don't wish him any ill. I just want him to stop trying to destroy my relationship with my son."

With Warrick on the hunt for more clues from the pictures, she poured another cup of coffee, went back to the couch and sat in a position where she could watch the two of them. They were both fierce as they dug into the problems facing them. She hadn't been friendly when they had first arrived, but, right now, it was such a comfort to know they could actually recognize what they were up against and could find the people in the photos. She didn't know how much good it would do, but at least she didn't feel quite so alone anymore.

She sat for a long time, before saying in frustration, "I feel so useless. Isn't there something I can do?"

Corey said, "Write down everything. Record everything you saw, so we have something to refer back to. Let's not have faulty memories or contradicting statements later on."

"Everything?"

"Start with the day you took Joshua to his father's and found all these photographs until today."

She got up and found one of the two notebooks she'd brought with her. It had been on her list to do something like that, but, with Corey urging her, it seemed like a good time now. She refilled her coffee from the thermos, grabbed a notebook and headed out onto the deck. She'd loved being here before and hoped sitting outside would help soothe her soul as she ran through the list of everything that had gone wrong.

It had only been two weeks, but it seemed like her life had been flipped upside down and twisted inside out. She had shed so many tears over the loss of her son that she didn't think it was possible to have any left, but she found she was wrong as she started writing down exactly what had happened and when.

She'd had to refer to her phone several times for calendar dates. But when she got into the timeline of it, it took ten pages of writing to get it all down. By the time she laid her pencil to rest, she was exhausted. Pulling all that crap out of her brain had been like pulling roots out of her heart.

It was an emotional experience because she was afraid of missing anything. As she sat in the morning sun, she thought about what it was she really wanted out of this. And all she really wanted was her son back. She didn't give a damn if her husband got away with blackmail or not.

She didn't wish blackmail on anybody. But, if a man was stepping out on his wife, then it was time for him to go home and decide on one or the other. It had been devastating for her to find out her husband had been cheating on her during their whole marriage. To find out her husband had a son the same damn age as her own and that her husband was still in contact with his entire other family was … brutal.

She wasn't looking forward to the divorce process. Greg was wealthy, powerful, with friends in high places. She didn't hold out much hope of a happy ending. If he was a criminal, and they could actually prove it, that would give her a chance to get Joshua back. If nothing else, if he knew she had this information, he might buckle under and let her have Joshua part-time.

But then she remembered all the threats she had received and figured that wouldn't happen. She got up, wandered back inside, dropped the notebook on the coffee table and said, "That's as much as I can remember."

The men nodded, but neither really appeared to be too interested.

"Do you think, if I just told him that I have all this information, he would back off?"

Corey slowly raised his head, his gaze piercing and dark. "Hell no. All that would do is put a noose around your neck."

"I've already done that, haven't I?"

"It depends," Warrick said. "If Greg is trying to blackmail somebody, and the victim wants the goods, Greg could let the victim know what you've done so someone else comes after you. And," Warrick added, "in this digital age, it's hard for the victims to know if they received all the copies of the images or other documentation Greg might hold over them."

"Jesus." She sagged into her chair. "And then there's the problem that my son is likely the one who told my husband what I did. Will Greg hurt Joshua because of it?"

"I doubt it. Joshua's very young. Chances are he doesn't understand the photos or what you taking pictures of them actually means. But don't kid yourself, Greg certainly does. And, if he's the blackmailer, he's already playing the angles to figure out how to fix this, how to get himself out of trouble and how to put it squarely on your shoulders."

She stared at them. "I hope you're wrong. I didn't have

anything to do with this."

"And that's why we have to track down the bank accounts. It's the only way to prove you aren't the blackmailer—by proving the money went into his account—and his account alone."

She shook her head, dumbfounded. "How the hell did this get so screwed up?"

"A couple things. The company you hung with and the photos you took pictures of. I highly suspect it's very simple. He knows you took photos of what he had, and now he has sent somebody after you. If that's the case, we just have to make sure you're safe until we can nail his ass to the wall."

COREY STUDIED THE documents in front of him. Beside him, Warrick said, "You know that we'll have to tell the police about this."

Corey glanced up to see if Angela had heard. She appeared to be oblivious, sitting on the other side of the table, nursing the cold cup of coffee in her hands. She looked exhausted, her face drawn and pale. It wasn't hard to see how these last few weeks had played on her. Losing her son had to be the worst. He knew how she felt, as he'd felt the same way twelve years ago. At least her son was alive, and she remained in a fighting spirit to keep him close to her.

He still felt like there was something suspicious about her taking pictures of the photos, but he wasn't sure that was a fair assessment. "Yes, we'll have to tell the police. It would be nice if we had a little time to work on this ourselves first."

Warrick looked at his watch. "They're not even in the office yet."

At that Corey chuckled. "Sure enough."

"What are you talking about?" Angela asked.

"We need to contact the police. Not only to let them know you're alive and well but to let them know about these photos and the spreadsheets."

She leaned forward. "Are you sure that's wise? What if they don't mean anything? I don't want to end up in more shit."

"And yet, at the same time, if Greg is blackmailing somebody, you will have a much better chance of getting your son back legally."

She slumped in her seat.

He watched, seeing the fear whisper across her face. "You're really scared of him, aren't you?"

She frowned, played with the handle on the coffee cup. "He has never hit me," she said slowly. "He was never been abusive to Joshua. Greg's not a physically violent person. But there's just something about him. He's scary."

"Interesting observation. When do you think you started being afraid of him?"

She glanced over at Warrick as if surprised at the question, but she didn't toss it off. She thought about it for a long moment. "I might always have been a little wary of him. Nervous. I was always a little bit scared. He was all-powerful, very dashing. I couldn't really believe he was interested in me. I'm not even sure I loved him in the beginning. I was just mostly bowled over, picked up from one world and put into another so fast I didn't really understand what was going on. So I was always in awe.

"But when that became fear, I don't know. And yet it wasn't overt. It's not like he threatened me. At least not until he started to threaten me with Joshua's custody. But it was just that sense of power behind him, a little bit of meanness in him. When he did business deals, he made sure he always got exactly what he wanted. It didn't matter if it wasn't good for the other guy. That only made him happier. He wanted what he wanted and didn't care how he got it."

"If we showed you faces, do you think you could recognize any of his business associates?"

She frowned. "Probably. But what difference does it make who he did business with?"

"Do you know what type of business he ran?"

"No. I knew him as a property developer, but once I asked him and he said he dealt in information. But I don't know what that meant. I understood he was somebody who made deals happen. But I was never invited into that world."

Corey felt something inside of himself stall. "*Information*. Now that's an interesting way to put it."

"Did you ever hear any yelling or could you tell if there was any violence in his office?" Warrick asked.

Again she looked surprised by his question. "No. He's not some gangster. I don't exactly know what he did. A lot of IT work was involved. But all his business dealings were civil. The only time I actually remember him arguing was the day I was there with Joshua. And he was arguing outside, so I couldn't hear him."

"Did he normally work in his office at home?"

"Yes. He wasn't much of an outdoor person. He'd never walk on a beach with me or walk through a park. If he walked anywhere, it was to get from point A to point B. Otherwise we drove. Or he had one of his businessmen drive me around."

"Businessmen?"

"Man of business? One of his admins? I don't know what the title was. I remember he said it once, and it struck me as funny, kind of old world. It's like his *men of affairs* or something like that."

Corey tucked away that information away. "Can you tell us about any of the people or companies he dealt with?"

She shook her head. "I spent most of my time alone. He was in the office at home or away at his business office. But I never went there. I don't even know where it is." She sat for a long moment, thinking. "This is very strange because I realize this whole segment of my life is a blank. It's like I brushed up against him, but I was never really part of his life."

"Maybe that's a good thing," Warrick said. "If his world is about to come crumbling down because he deals in *information*"—he held up his phone and wiggled it to draw her attention—"then maybe you won't go down with him."

She stared at him, then at the photos. "Are you actually thinking maybe his business was blackmail?"

"Lots of times companies want information on another company so they have leverage against them in contract bidding, with planning commissions, stuff like that," Corey said. "Say he wanted to throw up a multilevel development, and somebody was blocking him. Information on that person he could use as leverage makes the block crumble, and he gets his way."

"Well, Greg certainly likes having his own way."

"So you can see that as something he would be good at?"

"Not only good at," she said quietly, "he excelled at it. He's a shark. Buying and selling."

CHAPTER 5

ANGELA HOPPED UP from the couch, wandered into the kitchen and said, "Are there any sandwiches left?" She turned back to Warrick. "I'm not sure why, but I'm still really hungry."

"Have at it." He pointed to the counter where he had dropped all the foodstuffs.

She grinned. "Did you guys expect me to be without food when you picked up so much?"

"We eat a lot too," Corey said, absentmindedly studying the laptop in front of him. "It's a habit when we're on the road to make sure there's enough."

She eyed the several different sandwiches still wrapped up individually, snagged a roast beef and some cold water and walked back out to the deck. It was still early, but there was a little heat to the sun now. She called over her shoulder, "I'm going to walk down to the lake."

Neither man answered. Good, she could have a few minutes to herself.

It was a little upsetting to think she'd spent so much time with Greg, and yet she had not really understood who he was. She would never have said she was naive, but, after seven years, she hadn't known her husband at all.

She hoped Joshua was doing okay. She missed him so. Of course one of the real reasons why she'd married so fast was because she'd been desperate for that family she'd always wanted. She'd always hoped for a big fancy wedding with all the pomp and ceremony, but Greg hadn't wanted the publicity and had instead taken her to the minister's office.

It had been a bit exciting because it had been so fast, as in being swept off her feet. But it had left an awful lot behind in terms of the romantic fairy-tale wedding she'd always dreamed of. Maybe she should have been suspicious of him then.

What she hadn't considered was how possessive he was. If the baby was his, then he wanted to own it. She wasn't sure he wanted to love Joshua as much as she did, but Greg wasn't going to let Joshua go in terms of Greg's legal rights. Joshua was too young to understand what was going on, even now, but he was certainly learning quickly.

She sat down on a big rock by the beach. There wasn't any sand. It was a very rocky shoreline with various plants fighting for survival among them. She could relate.

When she finished the sandwich, she folded the wrapper and put it in her pocket, then stood with her cup of water in her hand. She wandered out onto the dock. She didn't know where to go from here in her custody battle. Her only hope was those photos. But, if she turned those into the police, what was she to do then? Would that help her case or make her look worse in the eyes of the judge?

She'd have no leverage at all. And, if the police were bought off—because of course Greg dealt in information; and, therefore, that was a possibility—maybe the blackmail case would get closed without any justice being done. Of course she'd have the copies she had originally taken. She could always contact a newspaper or contact some of the people in the photos.

She winced at that idea. It just felt dirty and ugly to be part of that. And what good would it do her? It would only enrage Greg.

Just as she started to relax and enjoy the sparkling light of the sun across the water, she thought she heard an odd sound behind her. Maybe the crunch of a dead branch? She crouched and spun. Had the men heard anything? She peered through the trees, studying the shadows. That was a problem with the heavily treed area. It was great cover for somebody approaching, but she was standing in the open.

When she couldn't see anything, she straightened and returned to the cabin. It no longer felt so nice or quiet to be here. Too many things were going on. And being exposed outdoors, … well, that just gave her a creepy feeling.

As she wandered up the path, she thought she heard the same sound again, off to the left. Maybe more like the crunch of dead leaves on the ground? Was she being followed? She turned to look but still couldn't see anything. Rather than be afraid of every little thing, she was determined to take a look. Besides, if she screamed, the men would come to her aid. She took a deep breath and took several steps in that direction.

"What did you hear?" Corey asked.

She spun, looked up at the cabin and saw him on the deck. She rushed to stand underneath him. "Twice I heard a noise off to the side of the cabin."

He gave her a hard glance. "And you thought you could check it out yourself?"

She shrugged. "You're busy."

He snorted and came down the stairs—was at her side almost instantly.

She hadn't realized he could move like that.

"Somebody is after you. You've received death threats. You're in possession of blackmail material a lot of people would go after you for, not just Greg but every person's face in those photos. And you think, because I'm busy looking at the material, I want you wandering around on your own?"

Maybe it was something to do with his tone of voice, maybe it was his wording, she didn't know, but she got her back up. She glared at him. "I've been on my own for a long time now, thank you," she snapped. "I don't need a bodyguard to look after me."

Instead of being put off by her tone, he just stared at her quietly but didn't back down.

Almost as instantly as her temper had flared, it just as quickly dropped off. "Okay, so I haven't done all that well on my own," she said in frustration. "But that doesn't mean I can't walk around a little."

He held out an elbow. "Hook your arm through mine, and we'll walk together."

She did so, feeling strange. It was how they always used to walk together. During class, after class, the two of them, alone against the world. She shook her head, trying to shrug off the memories.

"You feel it too, don't you?"

"I don't feel anything," she said quietly. "It was a long time ago."

"It was. And we've both grown up. I'm delighted you've gone on to have a family. Never happened for me. And for that I was always very sad."

"You're still young. It's not like you can't have that family."

"True enough. But I haven't met the right woman yet."

They wandered around the property as if searching for

whatever she'd heard. But she'd long ago given up worrying about it. She could see his gaze going from tree to tree, searching, peering, looking for whatever it was that might have disturbed her. Finally she came to a stop, looked around and said, "It couldn't have been this far away, I wouldn't have heard it."

"Maybe not." He turned and led her back toward the cabin. "But I don't want you going anywhere alone anymore."

"And yet you let me go down to the dock on my own,"

"Not really. You went, but I was on the deck watching you."

"You didn't see anything?"

"No, I didn't. I did hear a couple things, but one was a rabbit moving in the underbrush, and the other was a doe at the edge of the clearing."

"As long as it's not armed two-legged animals, I don't care."

He squeezed her arm a little closer against his body and nodded. "At least the four-legged ones have a reason for doing what they're doing. The two-legged ones, sometimes they're just hard to understand."

Silence stood between them for a time.

Out of the blue he asked, "Were you at least happy for some of those years you were with him?"

"Yes. At the beginning. But apparently I didn't really understand who I was back then. I would never have thought I was naive or ignorant. It's almost like he took who and what I was and shaped me the way he wanted me to be."

"Was he unhappy with the result?"

She winced. "Ouch."

He glanced at her sideways. "It's not a criticism of you.

But if he made you the way he wanted you, and then was happy to discard you …"

"Still, it's an ouch when you put it that way. Nobody wants to think of themselves as being discarded."

"No. In this case, *set free* might be a better phrase. You're obviously not living life to the fullest, so this is a perfect opportunity to make some major changes."

She nodded. "Doesn't mean I was ready for that change though."

"See? That's the thing. Changes like that, those we don't have a choice about as to when or how, it's all about adapting."

Back at the cabin he took her into the living room. Warrick was on the phone. Too bad. They should have stayed out a little longer. She hated knowing everyone was making arrangements and gathering information but not necessarily sharing.

However, as soon as they stepped in, Warrick stopped the conversation. He smiled up at Angela and said, "Do you feel better now?" He studied her face. "You look better. A little calmer, a little more at ease."

"Not sure why I should be. I kept hearing sounds outside. Every time I did, I was thinking there was an intruder following me."

"And you should keep that thought foremost in your mind. It will help keep you safer."

"How does that work? I was down there at the end of the dock. I don't have any weapons or self-defense skills. I'm coming to realize I was more of a trophy wife than anything, I have few useful skills and even less life skills," she said with the hint of bitterness entering her voice.

"I wouldn't worry about it. You have the rest of your life

to be whoever and whatever you want to be. Having made some decisions, you're less unhappy with who you are now as you see yourself a little clearer. You'll make better decisions from now on. But you still need to go easy on yourself. This transition will take time."

"Are you always so optimistic?" she asked, sitting down beside Warrick.

"No, not always. But it's part of my nature."

"Did you find out anything else?" She pointed to the laptops. "Anything useful?"

"The spreadsheets do appear to be payouts. But it's in some kind of code. We'll need time to break it. And, yes, I phoned the cops. Yes, I've handed over a lot of the information."

She stared at him. "Already? Without talking to me?" She bounded to her feet, outrage rippling through her.

Corey stepped in front of her. "Easy. Just because we've handed over the information doesn't mean we don't have copies of it ourselves."

She looked at him, her expression a cross between anger and tearful sadness. He shook his head, reached out and tucked her into his arms. "You're not alone anymore. Let somebody else help you."

"Help me do what? There isn't even a way forward from here."

"No, there are several ways forward," he corrected. "And the good thing is, you have other people to help you follow those trails."

"But the police?" She pulled back so she could look into his face. "What if Greg owns them too? I wouldn't be surprised if he doesn't have dozens of law enforcement officers, lawyers and even judges in his pocket."

Corey looked down at her and frowned. "Do you have any reason to think he might?"

"I don't have any proof of anything. But he's *that* kind of a man."

"But not all police are *that* kind of police. We have to trust most are honest and care about doing right and upholding the law."

She groaned. "But if it comes back to Greg that I handed over this information …"

"He will try to get lawyers to say you concocted this stuff or stole it off the net and handed it over to make him look like the bad guy," Warrick said.

"How is it you already think like that?" she asked in wonder. "And, if he does do that, how do I counter his words?"

"First things first. Let the police do their job. We will follow up on our side, keep track of the information, see if we can hunt down the faces in the pictures, follow the money trail in the spreadsheets."

She shook her head. "But you're navy? How does that have anything to do with this?"

Both men winced. "Hey now, that's almost an insult. Sure, we're part of the navy. In an elite group." He gave her a crooked grin.

"But you're not police. You're not special investigators. You're not detectives or private investigators or anybody along those lines."

Warrick looked up. "You wound me. I've done plenty of this kind of work on missions."

"What kind of work?" She stepped out of Corey's arms and walked over to where Warrick sat. "Have you done any law enforcement work or investigative type of work?"

"It's called gathering intel. And, yes, I've done lots of it. But just because we've spent most of our time doing covert operations doesn't mean we don't understand how your husband operates."

"Ex-husband or will be as soon as I can process the paperwork," she corrected softly. "And maybe not even that if he married the mother of his other son." She spun toward Corey. "Any way to find out if our marriage is legal?"

He studied her for a long moment. "You think Greg might have married the other woman first?"

She nodded. "I can always hope."

"You don't want to be married to him?"

"It's an expensive process to get unmarried," she said. "I don't have the money. I'd like to have as few ties as possible to Greg."

Corey motioned to the couch. "Come and sit down beside me." He brought up the registry on his laptop and typed in her name. Up came the marriage to Greg. "His last name is Buffalo?"

"Yes. I'm now Angela Buffalo."

"Interesting."

He typed in Buffalo's name, and again her marriage came up. Then he started digging into divorces. "He could have married in another state. Were you always in California?"

"Yes, but he was originally from New York, I believe."

She watched as he clicked through database after database.

"It does say your marriage license is registered in California though, so chances are it is legal. And, so far, a search isn't showing up other marriages. But he probably used a different name if he did."

She stared across the room. "Too bad I don't have knowledge of any aliases Greg might have used. I was trying to figure out how to get a divorce without it killing me financially."

"Make him pay for it. He has plans and lots of them. He won't want to hang on to an ex-wife, not when he can take care of the financial issues very quickly."

"Maybe," she said. "But that doesn't mean he plans to spend any money on me."

Just then her phone rang. She picked it up and looked at it. She spun slowly. "It's Greg."

"Answer it, but put it on Speaker."

She nodded, clicked Talk and said, "Hello, Greg. What do you want?"

"How are you? I hear you ran away. Stress too much for you?" His tone was mocking, brutal, degrading. "After all, you're a fragile neurotic woman."

She reached up and pinched the bridge of her nose. "No, I haven't run away. If that were the case, I wouldn't be answering the phone. How is Joshua?"

"My son is fine," he said smoothly. "He no longer even asks for you. At that age you forget very quickly."

It was all she could do to not scream and stomp her foot. "I want to talk to him," she said firmly.

"That's nice, but you don't get what you want."

"So why did you call? Just to torment me?"

"You have something of mine, I believe."

Her gaze flew to Corey and Warrick. "What are you talking about? I don't have anything."

"Oh, I believe you do. I believe you stole something that matters a great deal."

"I don't have anything, and I didn't steal anything." Her

stomach started to churn. "Whoever said I did is a liar," she bit off.

"Are you saying your son's a liar?"

"So now he's my son. When he's a liar, he's my son. But when he's not, he's your son?"

It was all she could do to hold back the cynicism in her tone, but she was afraid now she knew what this call was about.

"According to him, you took something from that envelope."

"What envelope?" she asked.

"An envelope on my desk in my office. Enough of this. I want it back. And I want it back now." He hung up with a sharp *click*.

COREY TOOK THE phone from her frozen fingers. "Did you take something from that envelope?"

She looked at him and nodded. "I did. I wasn't thinking. Joshua was bored and started running around. I told him to leave Daddy's things alone but he brought me these photos. I went to put them back and realized what they were. So I took a few photos, moving Greg's photos around. While I wasn't looking Joshua had picked up this piece of paper, but Greg was coming back, so I took it out of his hand and slipped it into my pocket."

"What is it?"

She looked up at him, shamefaced. "I would have put it back if I had realized but I was trying to protect Joshua. Greg angers easily."

"Tell me what it is."

She looked at him for a long moment, then glanced at

Warrick who stared at her intently. She walked over to her purse, pulled out a folded piece of paper and handed it to him.

Without a word he opened it and stared. "These are bank account numbers."

She took a deep breath. "I don't know if they are or aren't. I was trying to take a picture of them. But, like I said, I had moved some of the photos around, and I could hear him coming, and I panicked. I just … I just stuck it in my pocket and raced over to pick up a pillow, like Joshua and I were playing. I was trying so hard not to let Greg know I'd seen anything."

"So you actually took away this piece of paper with the account numbers on it?"

"I didn't know they were account numbers. They were just numbers. And I was waiting for him to leave so I could put it back again. But he never did."

The two men looked at each other. "Not only could these be account numbers he needed but they could be the numbers where the blackmail money was deposited."

"Yes, but why would he have it with the photos? That should be something he kept separate."

Corey glanced at the numbers again—nothing but two separate sets of digits. He held it up for Warrick to look at. Warrick studied them, opened up a document on his laptop and typed them in. Corey put the slip of paper on the table, took out his phone and took a picture of it. "Did you take anything else?"

"I didn't, and, if I could have, I would have put that piece of paper back," she said painfully. "I just don't have any reason why I did that. I should have just put it back under the photos." She reached up and rubbed her temple.

"I'm in such shit."

"This happened a few weeks ago?"

"Yes, two weeks ago." She frowned. "So why would he worry about it now?" Then her face cleared. "Unless Joshua just spoke up. That's the only connection there could be."

"Greg also might not have needed those accounts all the time. Or those numbers could be somebody else's accounts he tucked in there for safekeeping. Maybe he went to look for it, couldn't find it and got angry, and your son mentioned it."

She nodded and sat straight in the chair. "What am I going to do now?"

"I need to give this to the detective." Warrick grabbed his phone and dialed. While Angela and Corey listened, he explained to the detective about the phone call from Greg and the paper Angela had. "I'm thinking they're account numbers."

He read off the numbers. A minute later he hung up and said, "The detective is looking into it. They'll be able to track the bank accounts pretty easily. I'll be checking as well, but it'll take me a little bit." He glanced at the sandwiches. "Corey, toss me one, will you?"

Corey pulled one out for Warrick and grabbed one for himself. He looked at Angela, asking silently if she wanted another one.

She shook her head. "I can't eat anything. My stomach is sick right now." She rubbed her face. "I hope he didn't punish Joshua."

"There's no reason to. He's a child. He wouldn't know what he'd seen before was important. If he only just now told his father, it's because his father only just now went looking for them."

"The worst of the threats started right afterward." She shook her head. "Maybe if I just lie low, the police can solve this, and I can get back to having a life."

"You have clients, businesses you can focus on. You'll need to make money one way or another."

She held up her hands, and they were shaking. "How am I supposed to work like this?"

Corey grabbed her hands and rubbed them together. They were like ice cubes. "Look. Nobody's saying exactly what those numbers are yet. Let's just stay calm and see what turns up."

They sat together on the couch while he ate his sandwich. When his phone rang, and he saw his sister's ID, he smiled. "Hey, sis. What's up?"

"Did you find her?"

Corey realized he hadn't contacted Bridget to say all was well. "Yes, I did. She's sitting right beside me."

"Really? Oh, that's great." Then her voice changed. "The least you could have done was texted me."

He rolled his eyes. "You're right. I'm sorry, Bridget. But she is here. She is alive and well."

"Can I talk to her?"

He handed the phone to Angela. "My sister wants to talk to you."

He listened as the two women talked. Both sounded like they were in tears. Their conversation was half broken, which he didn't even begin to understand.

When Angela handed the phone back, she was no longer crying. She still had tears in her eyes, but they were happy tears. "I really miss her. I just want my life back."

"That's the trouble with making left turns. It takes a while to straighten out and find the right path," Warrick said.

She nodded, curled her legs up under her and leaned her head back on the chair. Corey studied her face and realized, if they kept talking, chances were good she'd fall asleep in no time. He looked at Warrick who was demolishing the last of his sandwich. "Any way to tell what country the bank accounts are from?"

"Each bank has its own numbering system. There's nothing to identify transit numbers or even bank branches. They're literally just the account number itself."

"So not as helpful as we first thought?"

"They will be, once we find out who and where they are. What we should also do is check the photographs she took to see if this piece of paper can be traced back to a specific photo to prove it came from that same pile."

Corey froze. "That's a damn good thought."

With her now snoozing gently, he turned on his laptop and went through the photos. At the corner of one was the folded ripped off pieces of the little note. He turned it so Warrick could take a look. "Do you think that can be identified?"

Warrick peered across the table at the image and smiled. "Now that's good because that places the account numbers with all these images. We have to make sure we hang on to that." In a casual side note, he asked, "Did you take time off work? I already had the holidays booked, only to have them blown back in my face. But what about you?"

"I've got two days off," Corey answered. "I do have holidays coming if I need them. I was hoping to have this wrapped up before then. There's talk of another overseas trip next week."

"Yeah, I heard about that. Likely we're both going. Depends on how quickly you guys leave and if I'm back on duty yet."

Corey cleaned up the food wrappers and threw them away in the kitchen. As he stood staring out the window, he could feel the weird creepiness crawling over the back of his neck. In a low tone he said, "Watch your six."

Warrick closed the laptop, stuffed it into the couch and slipped over to the living room windows. With weapons ready, they waited. It wasn't long before there was a crunch and a crackle of branches being broken. Corey peered outside but saw no sign of anyone.

Between him and the living room windows was the front door and a side door. They were just around the corner from each other, but it wasn't a very large corner. Yet there was a blind spot where he couldn't see. With Warrick watching the other half of the house, Corey crouched below the window and then came up on the other side, trying to peer out. And saw a man's back.

He held up a hand, snapped his fingers, and then held up one finger. What he didn't know was whether this man was an intruder, a gunman or a curious neighbor. He waited and watched. The man stepped back away from the front door, looked at the house and then took several more steps back. Perfect, now Corey could see who it was, though he didn't recognize the man. He was wearing a red plaid overshirt with a different plaid undershirt, a pair of old jeans and hiking boots. Corey frowned, wondering what the hell he was doing here.

And then he decided, since the man wasn't armed, he'd go find out. He tucked his gun back in his waistband under his shirt, opened the door and stepped out. "Hello. Can I help you?"

He could hear footsteps inside the house, realized Warrick had shifted position to come over and guard his back. The man turned to look at Corey and frowned. "I was expecting to see a woman here. Bella's niece."

"If you mean Angela, she sleeping right now."

"So she is here? Her aunt asked me to check on her to make sure she was okay."

"She's fine. But, like I said, she's sleeping right now." Corey gave the man the once-over. "Do you live around here?"

He pointed to the far side of the lake. "I live on the other side. Had a cabin there as long as Bella's had one. It's kind of lonely out here. We normally stick together. I didn't recognize the vehicle when I came in. Last I heard, Angela just had a small car."

"That's my truck," Corey said.

The man seemed hesitant to leave as if wanting confirmation that Angela was actually here.

In order to put the old man's mind to rest and to stop any suspicious returns, Corey said, "You want to come in and make sure for yourself she's okay?" He watched relief cross the man's face.

"Yeah, I don't mind if you don't. I got to report back to Bella. I won't feel good saying her niece is here if I haven't actually seen her."

Corey put a hand behind him, grabbed the door and pushed it open. "Angela, you've got company." He motioned for the man to come in.

As he crossed the threshold, he said, "My name's Bill, by the way."

The two men shook hands as Corey introduced himself. As he walked in, he saw Warrick at the kitchen table. Corey introduced him to Bill, then Bill stopped at the entrance to the living room. Angela was curled up on the big chair, her breathing slow and even.

"She really is sleeping," he said in surprise.

Corey chuckled. "Yes. She's pretty tuckered out these days."

"That girl has always been hell-fire. I haven't seen her in years, but she still looks like she used to."

"Older, a little more experienced in life now," Warrick said. "Still, she wears the look well."

Bill nodded. "Thanks for letting me see her," he said to Corey. He turned and walked back to the front door. "I might come back in a day or two. At least I know she's okay. Tired and worn out but she's holding." He walked out the front door without another word.

Corey walked out behind him, wanting to see what vehicle he drove. But instead of driving, the old coot had walked. He headed to the road and then headed back around the lake. It could easily have been a twenty-minute trip, and that was something else to consider. If there were a lot of people living on the other side, they weren't very far away, and there were lots of options for hiding places.

After Bill disappeared from view, Corey took another quick look around the property and then stepped back into the kitchen. Angela was still sleeping. He sat down at the table beside Warrick. "Suggestion?"

"Lay low, stay out of sight and see if the police can solve some of this. And the minute anybody finds out where she is, we'll have to move fast."

There wasn't a whole lot to add to that. Corey agreed. But it really sucked. He'd take action over inaction any time.

The two men continued to do research as Angela slept.

But when a second knock on the door came, Corey was jolted out of his concentration. With a frown at Warrick, he got up, opened the front door to find no one there. Instantly he was on alert. He closed and locked the door and turned to find Warrick already standing guard over Angela. They watched and listened, but there was no sign of anyone. He glanced over at Warrick who shrugged.

But Corey refused to believe he had imagined it. Still, after a full search around the house, inside and out, finding nothing, he started to get angry. There had been a knock, and that meant somebody was here and playing games. If there was one thing he hated, it was games.

CHAPTER 6

ANGELA WOKE UP feeling better than she had in a long time. When she saw the two men, instead of being startled or scared, she smiled with relief. "Thank you for that," she said quietly. "I haven't slept so well in a long time."

"A neighbor and friend of your aunt's stopped by," Corey said. He told her about Bill.

She chuckled. "Yes. My aunt and he were friends for a lot of years. I'm not surprised she called him. I haven't called to let her know I got here. I was so tired last night, I never thought of it. And, when you guys arrived this morning, I have to admit I didn't think of it either." That was not good. She pulled out her phone and sent her aunt a text. "That should make her feel better."

She turned to the two men, but they weren't smiling or joking. "What's the problem?"

"There was a second knock on the door," Corey said slowly. "But when I opened it, no one was there."

She frowned. "No one?"

"No one," Corey said. "At least no one prepared to let me know he was there."

She slowly sank back down onto the chair she'd been sleeping in. "So do you think it's someone after me?"

"I can't imagine playing this game except to let you

know they are watching you." He held out his hand. "Let me see the phone."

She handed it over. "It's brand new. Never out of my reach." She watched as Warrick opened up the back and studied it carefully. Then he closed it up and handed it back. "It's fine."

"Great. So what? You said no one was out there. So they're watching me? What does that mean?"

"It means they're watching, and now they know I'm here too."

She stared at him for a long moment. "I don't get it. Is that good or bad?"

"There's a good chance he left because he didn't want to take us on alone. But it also means he knows I'm here and potentially you are too."

"So what do we do now?" Her voice was starting to crack. She stamped down the panic, but it was hard. As far as she could see, there was just no option; she was trapped yet again.

Warrick walked toward her. Somehow he'd already managed to pack up his bag with his laptop and the rest of his gear. He simply said, "Pack."

Corey grabbed her arm and gently led her back to the bedroom. "I don't know how much you've unpacked, but you need to consider repacking everything, because we'll be gone in thirty minutes."

She shook her head. "How are we going to do that? What about my car?"

He nodded. "I'll drive your car. Warrick'll drive my truck."

She stared at him.

He smiled, reached out and tucked her into his arms.

"This will be fine. But we have to go. You've been found, and now we need to make sure you get unfound."

She let out a garbled laugh. "It's not that easy. I don't have any place to go."

"That's not the problem right now. Right now the problem is to get gone." He marched her into the bedroom, saw her bags on the floor, lifted them, put them on the bed and said, "What did you bring?"

Five minutes later, she walked out of the room. "I hardly unpacked."

"Good," he said abruptly. "Very good actually."

He walked into living room with both bags and took a glance around the kitchen. "Did you bring food?"

She rushed over to the fridge. "I did but not too much." She quickly packed the apples, milk and cheese. "I was planning on doing some more shopping."

"Bring everything you brought, so we can leave the cabin without power. Leave it all as if you hadn't been here."

"Well, that's not going to happen. There's garbage and God only knows what else."

But as she stood and looked around the kitchen, she realized Warrick had already washed up and had the garbage bag ready to take out. She glanced over at him. "Are you always this efficient?"

He gave her a grim smile. "When I have to be, yes."

Four minutes later she buckled the seat belt on the passenger side of her car. She shook her head. "Why? Why can't we just stay here? If someone's watching, they'll see us leaving. They could follow us."

Corey turned to look at her. "We can come back later, but right now we have to make sure you stay safe." He turned on the engine and reversed the car all the way around the house and back up the hill, a feat she didn't think she could have done. He turned around at the top and followed Warrick out onto the main road.

Warrick's voice suddenly filled the car. "Bogey on the left."

Corey yelled out, "Get your head down."

He dropped his seat back and hit the gas. He roared onto the main road. She heard some weird ping hit the side of her car, and then suddenly they were long gone.

When he sat up, she asked, "Can I sit up now?"

He glanced around. "You can." He popped the back of his seat up, so it was in its normal position.

She followed suit. "What the hell was that?" she asked, her voice shaky.

"Somebody shot at the vehicle and probably would have got in a decent hit if I hadn't hit the gas when I did," he admitted. He pointed out Warrick ahead of them.

Warrick's voice once again filled the vehicle. "You two okay?"

Corey responded, "Yes, Angela's a little shook up, but she's good."

"Did you see a vehicle?" she asked.

"Not enough to help. And we're not going back to check either."

That's when she saw a cell phone sitting on the dash where the coffee would normally sit and knew the guys had set up the phone call earlier. She stared down at that simple thing and realized just how much she didn't think the way they did. "Where do we go from here?" she asked, trying for a calm and reasonable tone of voice.

"No idea," Corey said cheerfully. "Warrick, you got any suggestions?"

"I'm all for taking her back to the base and stashing her with someone there."

"Hell no," she said emphatically. "Just because I'm surrounded by military, doesn't mean I'll be any safer there."

"Well, it does because there are checkpoints everybody has to go through," Corey said. "The thing is, what we have to do is find a safe place for you to go to ground. At least then the detectives can do their job without having to worry about your safety."

She was horrified at the concept. "Why not just go to your sister's house?"

"Hell no. We're not putting her in danger. Somebody actually shot at you. You do realize that means they're dead serious about killing you now?"

She sat back and asked in a small voice, "So where can I go?"

Warrick, his voice tinny sounding over the phone, said, "We can talk to the police. I'm sure they'll have a safe house, if you prefer that."

"And how safe will that be?" she asked.

"No safer than anywhere else. Honestly, the safest place is with us."

"We do have a few safe houses available to us," Corey said slowly. "I can always get the locations from Mason."

"That's not a bad idea," Warrick said. "We don't use them often, but they are available. Only they are supposed to be used officially of course."

"What?" She turned to look at him. "What are you talking about?"

"Sometimes we have to have places to disappear to," Corey said quietly. "Places for people who need to be safe while plans are made and carried out. For that reason we have a couple houses available."

She stared at him. "You're talking about your job, right?"

"Yeah. At least mostly." He gave her a grin. "Warrick, I'll give him a call and get back to you."

"Sounds good. I vote for one in the sun." And, laughing, he hung up.

"He's not talking about Mexico, is he?"

"That wouldn't be ideal, given the circumstances," Corey said. "Let me talk to Mason, and we'll see what we can do." He shut off the call to Warrick and then dialed somebody else.

She settled back, wondering about an organization that actually had houses available, but then law enforcement all across the country had places like it. She'd much rather grab Joshua and take him with her too. But, if that wasn't an option yet, she'd do whatever she could to put an end to this nightmare.

HE RECOGNIZED WHEN Angela slowly succumbed to the stress and anxiety of the day and fell asleep again. Mason had given him a couple ideas, and, between them, they'd settled on a house in the San Diego suburbs. It was one he hadn't been in before, so he was looking forward to checking it out.

Someone was heading there now to turn on the fridge and make sure all was well. Angela was exhausted and needed to sleep in a real bed as soon as possible, but they'd be hours getting there.

Mason had also warned him about how quickly this could go south. They'd discussed strategies for several moments, then Mason had gone to his computer to keep digging into the soon-to-be-ex-husband's activities. There was enough for several of them to work on for hours, if not days.

Corey wasn't sure how he felt about Angela having been married for seven years. He'd tried so hard to convince her to marry him twelve years ago. It was a cold realization that he hadn't been enough, but this criminal had been. Maybe the tables had turned, giving him a second chance—if he wanted to try for it.

But it felt like taking advantage of her and this nightmare situation. If it was down the road a few months, he might take several steps in that direction. But right now, she was a mess.

And he didn't want to add to her confusion. That was what their past relationship had been. He wanted something very different this time around.

His phone rang again. Corey quickly brought Warrick up to speed. "It's a perfect three-bedroom family home. We'll need to stop at a grocery store and stock up first. When Angela wakes up, I'll ask her about a menu."

"She's sleeping?" Warrick asked in surprise. "Good. I wasn't sure she would."

"She's exhausted." He glanced over at her, hating to see the dark circles under her eyes. "She needs to have this nightmare over with."

"We're working on it. We work miracles, but even miracles need a day or two."

With a laugh, Corey rang off and settled in for the long drive.

He hadn't had such a pleasant afternoon in a long time.

CHAPTER 7

ANGELA DIDN'T KNOW how long they'd been driving, but it seemed like forever. She'd nodded off once. The second time she fell asleep, she fell deeper into a sleep filled with crazy dreams ripping through her head and panic for Joshua permeating every thought.

Only when a hand shook her awake did she bolt forward, coming against the seat belt. She shuddered and turned to look at Corey. "I fell asleep again?" she croaked.

"If that's what you call sleep, then we have to work on your definition," he said, his voice harsh.

She looked at him groggily for a moment, realizing he was upset. "What do you mean?"

"Sleep is supposed to be peaceful, restful. You twisted and jerked, even cried out several times." He eased back onto his side of the car and took a deep breath. "I took it for as long as I could and then realized it couldn't be good for you either."

She relaxed back and thought about it. "Everything is so caught up in my head. It's twisted and mixed up. I haven't been able to sleep for over two weeks—since I left. When we separated, I didn't have any money. That was a panic in itself—trying to figure out how to make a living and to support my son. I didn't care about trying to maintain the same status. I was just trying to survive. But since Greg got ugly about custody, well ...” She rubbed her eyes. “I don’t know where we are.” The fatigue was still in her voice. “I’ll need a restroom soon.”

“We’ll stop up here in another few miles for a meal and some coffee.”

She twisted in her seat, pulling her knees up under her. “Seems like we’ve been driving forever. But I really don’t know where we are.”

He smiled. “That’s because we’re heading to a safe house. All set up and waiting for us.”

“That sounds pretty ominous,” she admitted. “Was there no other option?”

He shook his head. “We need you safe and out of the way.”

She nodded. “Is there any way we can pick up Joshua? I hate to be away from him like this.”

“Has any custody order been signed yet?”

She shook her head. “No, I wanted to be reasonable so was trying to talk to Greg about when he’d like Joshua to come and visit him.” At his look she bit her lip. “I had no idea Greg would be so cruel as to not want Joshua to see me after that.”

“Then the issue is trying to separate Joshua from your husband. If Joshua’s back in your care, then your husband will have to fight that much harder to get him handed over. If no custody papers have been signed, then the judges tend to look more kindly on the parent who the child is living with.”

“Yes. Greg said something about that earlier. But I just didn’t have the means to get Joshua away without a major scene, and I didn’t want to traumatize him.”

“It’s always better to avoid ugly confrontations in front

of a child," Corey agreed. He pointed to a big sign up ahead. "We are pulling off here."

She read the sign, but it didn't register in her brain that she even saw it. "That sign said San Diego. Are we home?"

He nodded. "In a way. I took a roundabout route to throw off any possible tails. We're heading to a safe house in the city. We will pick up supplies, get to the house, and make sure we have enough to hole up for a few days."

She thought about that. "Will a few days make any difference?"

"Hopefully we won't be looking for bullets and strange people at the door while we search for answers about your husband."

"Did you hear from the detective?"

"Mason did. We've been talking about it while you were sleeping."

"Did the detective figure any of it out?"

"He's pissed actually. Pissed you didn't turn this in two weeks ago. One of the men in the photos is dead now. As in just a few days ago."

She turned to look at him in shock. "Really?"

When he nodded, she sagged back. "How did he die? Do you think, if I had turned in the photos, it would have saved him?" The thoughts were scrambling inside her brain. But guilt was the foremost feeling. "I just didn't know what to do with them all."

"You were afraid of your husband."

"Of course. But that fear is something I've lived with for quite a while. It's not full-blown terror. It's an insidious fear that is part of me now. By the last year, I had to do everything in secret. If I wanted to have lunch with my girlfriend, I had to sneak out of the house. I got caught once. He was pretty livid."

"How did you get caught?"

"The security cameras. I hadn't asked for permission to leave the house. So, when I did sneak out, the cameras picked up my arrival."

There was an odd silence in the interior of the car as he absorbed that information. Then he shook his head. "How could you live like that?"

"It starts slowly, and, before you realize it, it becomes normal. It's only when you get away from it that you realize just how abnormal that it was. Now that I look back ..." She shook her head. "It's hard to even imagine I would have been so easily duped. But Greg was very good at getting people to do what he wanted them to do. Even now I don't know exactly what his techniques were. I just know they worked. And here I am, a fool. It doesn't make me feel very good."

"You're older, wiser," he said, his voice low. "Relationships are tricky, and we learn a lot from the ups and downs. As we move forward, we take those lessons into each new relationship, hopefully making them better than the last."

She watched as he took the turn. The on-ramp was long and curvy. As soon as they were parked, she got out of the vehicle and stretched for a moment. "I want to use the restroom first," she said with a smile and headed inside.

Following the signs, she made her way to the ladies' room. After she used the facilities, she took a moment to wash her hands, brush her hair and give her face a quick wash. She stared at her features in the mirror. She still looked like hell. Although the nap had helped, it certainly hadn't fixed her haggard-looking appearance.

"You need to smarten up and fast," she said to the woman in the mirror. "No more being a doormat for you."

After giving herself a quick pep talk, she followed the hall back to the main restaurant. She surveyed the crowd, not surprised to see it as full as it was. In good weather thousands of people were on the road traveling. It was summertime and high-tourist traffic.

Seeing Corey and Warrick standing off to one side in the waiting area, she joined them. She smiled as Corey wrapped an arm around her shoulder and tucked her up close. In a low voice she said, "If nothing else, I'm glad I reconnected with you."

He squeezed her gently and dropped a kiss on her temple. "You didn't have to stay away so long, you know."

"I was all about trying to build a new life. It took me a long time to even figure out who and what I wanted."

"I think that is the same for all of us at that age. We were kids."

Just then the hostess said, "I have a table ready. Follow me please."

They followed her to a table in the corner. She wondered if that was standard for Corey. Wait until a table opened in the location he wanted. Seemed like he was constantly on the lookout for trouble.

He tucked her in the back against the wall with him. Warrick sat with his back to the main room.

In a low voice she said, "Do you always arrange seating like this?"

Warrick gave her a blank look, then winked. She took that as a yes. Menus were placed in front of them and coffee ordered. It felt so strange to be in this location with these two men. She barely knew the two men, and yet she trusted them. They had tracked her down when they knew she was in trouble. How many people would actually do that? Maybe a family member. But most of the time everybody was happy to let people live their own lives and not get involved. Whereas these two had gone out of their way to help her.

"If I haven't said it before, I want to say it now. Thank you for finding me."

Warrick reached over and gently patted the back of her hand. Then he picked up his mug of coffee and said, "Anytime."

And she believed him. He was the kind who would be there through thick or thin. The kind who would step up and be your best man at a wedding or be there for a barbecue or because you were digging up the backyard to put in a pool. He was just one of those all-around good guys. She glanced at him and asked, "How come you don't have a girlfriend?"

He raised an eyebrow in surprise. "How do you know I don't have a girlfriend?"

She frowned. "I overheard you talking. Sorry, I'm not trying to be nosy, I'm curious."

"Ah." He put his hands in his lap and said, "Not right now. We just broke up a few days ago."

She winced. Talk about asking the wrong question. "I'm so sorry."

"Don't be. Because of that, I'm not on vacation, so I can help you out."

"Her loss, my gain," she said with a chuckle.

"What makes you think she's the one who broke up with me?"

"Because I think you love long and hard and deep."

He stared at her for a long moment and then gave a quick nod. "I do indeed."

She turned her attention to Corey. "And you?"

Corey shook his head. "Haven't been in a relationship for at least six months."

She chuckled. "Now that does surprise me. You were always one of the most popular guys in high school."

He stared at her in astonishment. "Hell no, I wasn't. I wasn't a jock, and I wasn't a brain. And I definitely wasn't the most popular."

"Maybe not, but all the girls thought you were sexy as hell and were really upset with me when we were going out."

Warrick chuckled. "Now that I can see."

"She's making too much out of it. She was the most popular girl. I was just the incredibly grateful callow youth who was going out with her. I never could figure out what she saw in me." Corey had a big smile. "Those were the days."

"Yuck. I'm so grateful not to go back to those days." But she slipped her hand into his. "Besides, we're adults now. Things have changed."

He squeezed her fingers but held on tight. She sat slightly back into the seat and looked around the restaurant. "So can we assume we weren't followed?"

"We didn't see anyone, and we were watching."

"And, if we were, how do we stop them from following us directly to the house?"

"We'll be a little bit sly as we get there," he said. "After we finish here, the grocery store is only a few miles up the road. We will stop, pick up enough food for a few days, and then we'll head out again."

"Good. I'm glad I slept after all. It made the journey much faster."

"You don't look like you slept," Warrick said bluntly. "You look like death warmed over, if I may say so."

"You don't hold back your punches, do you?" she said in irritation, but it was mild. Because he was right. "You are correct. I don't look great. But that isn't the result of the nap or the trip. It's just been a very long few weeks."

Both their phones went off within seconds of each other. She sat quietly and sipped her coffee, waiting. Warrick's was a text, but Corey's was a call. He motioned with his head at Warrick and stood. Warrick got up and took his place beside her. Corey walked outside to have a conversation in private.

"Does that mean trouble?"

"It means he needs privacy to talk. And that's not necessarily from you or from me but from anybody close enough in the restaurant to listen."

She turned to look around, and, sure enough, other tables and other patrons probably could have heard the conversation. "How do you keep that edge on all the time? That awareness of what's going on around you?"

He shrugged. "A lot of it's just plain training. We've been doing this for a long time."

"So when Bridget said I should contact Corey, she meant it."

"Absolutely. It's too bad you didn't think to do so on your own."

"The past is a hard thing to revisit," she said with a sad smile. "But I'm glad I did eventually call him. Even if it took Bridget to nudge me."

"Corey's a good guy," Warrick said. "And sometimes the past has to be revisited to reopen the wound so it can finally heal from the inside out."

"How do you know there was a wound?" she asked, her voice dry.

He chuckled. "I can see it from looking at the two of

you. It's not like you threw your arms around him in joy when we arrived."

She groaned. "Body language is such a great information tool."

"That is the thing about body language. It doesn't lie. People can say all kinds of stuff. But watch the person's body language to find the real truth."

She nodded.

Just then the waitress returned, delivering plates of food.

"Oh, my God, these portions are huge."

Warrick shook his head. "Speak for yourself. I'll have no problem finishing mine." He switched plates so he had his at his new location, picked up a fry and crunched it. It made a satisfying sound.

Angela reached over and snagged one off his plate. "Don't mind if I try it too, huh?"

"You're fast. And, no, I don't mind. I share. But Corey's got a lot on his plate. Feel free to help yourself to his too."

And, in a mock gesture, he tucked his plate a little closer. She chuckled and looked down at her huge sandwich. It was a variation on the club, and it was fully loaded. She had a Caesar salad on the side too. With a happy sigh she dug in. With both of them eating, there was no need for conversation, which was good because she wasn't making any attempt to do anything other than fill her stomach. Manners be damned. There were times when she could eat like a lady, her husband had insisted. But then there were times to just sit down and enjoy a meal, and this was one of them. At the same time she kept an eye on Corey. "If he doesn't come back soon, his dinner will get cold."

Just then Corey pocketed his phone, took one final look around and stepped back into the restaurant. He eyed the new seating arrangement and took Warrick's seat. He glanced at their food and asked, "How is it?"

"It's great," she said. "Dig in before yours is too cold to eat."

She finished her sandwich in silence and waited while he plowed through his big burger. The waitress came back, refilled her coffee. But still Corey didn't say anything about his phone call. But then she realized Warrick hadn't said anything about his text either. She frowned. "Are either of you going to give me an update?"

The two men once again exchanged glances.

"It's really irritating when you do that."

Corey's gaze fixed on her. "Do what?" he asked innocently.

She rolled her eyes at him. "When you exchange that glance, it's as if each of you knows the other's answer to my question and whether you should say something or not. And then almost deciding as to who will say it."

Warrick grinned. "You're pretty good at that too."

She shot him a look. "You can learn a lot of mannerisms about people by watching their children. Joshua used to glance at me after a question to measure my response. To see how his luck was and whether he needed to add something else to sweeten the pot."

Warrick gave her satisfied nod. "Yep, kids. Got to love them."

"When we get back in the vehicle, we will talk," Corey said.

She glanced around, realized the patrons had changed, but still several were close to them. She nodded. "So twenty minutes to the grocery store?"

Warrick said, "Yeah, somewhere around that. Maybe a

little less."

"Good. Because, even though I just ate, I'll be starving again in a few hours. After all, I skipped breakfast and must have slept through lunch. So who's cooking?"

"Aren't you a cook?" Warrick asked in mock horror. "Because I can't cook worth a damn. And, if we're trusting Corey, we're really going to suffer."

"Hey, I'm magic with a barbecue," Corey said.

"You are indeed. But I doubt we'll have a grill at the house," Warrick said. "The only thing you ever served with the barbecue was a green salad. Though I can handle a salad, I'm not a rabbit. I can't live on them."

Angela chuckled. "If you guys buy the groceries, I will cook."

Both men in unison cried out, "Agreed."

WHEN THEY PULLED out of the parking lot and headed back onto the highway, Angela gave it a few more minutes and then said, "Update please."

"The detective just got the autopsy results in on Sam Spiegel. He was the man in the photograph who died. He committed suicide," Warrick said through Corey's phone. His voice filling the vehicle.

She gasped in horror and sank back into her seat.

"None of us know if you had turned those photos into the police if that would have changed anything," Corey said. "Once Sam knew he was caught, knew he was being black-mailed, he made a decision you weren't likely going to be able to change."

"But that doesn't mean something else couldn't have changed," Warrick added. "Maybe if he knew the cops were on it, he would have been able to hold out hope."

"You can't know that for sure either," Corey said. "For all you know, his boyfriend was breaking up with him."

"Was he one of the men in the two-man clench?" Angela asked.

"Yes, and he's married with three kids," Corey said.

"Oh, hell. I'm so sorry for the wife. I hope she never finds out."

"That'll be one of the issues coming up if the blackmailer decides he should try to get more money out of her," Corey responded.

"But you're assuming Greg was blackmailing him for money," Warrick said. "Depending on what kind of a job he did, maybe he was just applying pressure to have him cave in on something he proposed. Leverage is a very important tool in business."

"Exactly," Corey explained. "Sam was on a planning committee. He was against a large building complex potentially going up in one of the low-income areas. He had brought up the fact your husband bought several properties for next to nothing and was pushing to get a large building permit in the area. It's right on the edge of one of the poorer areas of town, but the business sector has spread out, and it looks like you can make a lot of money doing what your husband hopes to do. However some wanted the area rezoned for low-income housing. That's what Spiegel was working toward."

"Did my husband get those photographs and then let them know exactly what would happen if they didn't let the building complex go through?"

"It's possible. But we don't know that for sure." Corey shrugged. "And we can't make assumptions. What we do know is you found those photos. And the man has committed suicide. That's the end of that one."

"And the other photos?"

"The detective has run down several of the names," Corey said. "He's got appointments to contact a couple of them. The others he's still working on."

"And the spreadsheets?"

"He's got specialists on that. It looks like a couple letters of the first name of various people followed by potentially a code of a month. We're not sure what that month means, followed by a year."

"Potentially the month and the year he started putting pressure on them," Angela said. "Again who's to say? But some of these numbers are large payments."

Corey reached over, grabbed her hand and smiled. She was handling everything amazingly well. He just hoped that, as this developed, she could hold out a little bit longer.

He said, "Things could get ugly. Greg will know you gave this info to the police, and he'll know what your reason was for doing this is. What we don't want is for him to take Joshua out of the country or hide him somewhere where we can't find him. So let everything stand as it is. The detective also suggested we leave Joshua where he is."

She turned to look at him, sadness on her face. "Why?"

Corey explained the logic, and she gasped in horror when she realized just what options were available to her husband if he really didn't want her to get her hands on Joshua.

"Okay," she said in a low voice. "But I don't want this to keep going endlessly. Court cases are a nightmare. They can go on for years."

"I don't think that's what the detective's looking at. But,

once he brings in your husband for questioning, and potential charges are filed against him, then you should be able to get your son legally without any trouble."

She sagged back in the chair. "I sure hope so. But, until it actually happens, I won't be able to rest for worrying Greg'll pull a fast one and take Joshua away forever."

CHAPTER 8

THE TRIP TO the grocery store was both fun and exasperating. Angela picked up things that any cook would normally need without knowing if she had a functional kitchen. She was after meat, vegetables, fruit, and some basics, like eggs and bread and butter. And coffee. The men weren't giving her much time though. She had one chance to go through an aisle, and that was about it. Except when it came to the candy aisle and the cookie aisle. She watched in amazement as Warrick snagged up chocolate-covered peanuts, tossing them in, and Corey grabbed several bags of tortilla chips.

She said, "If you're getting those, we need cheese, sour cream and salsa for nachos."

Both men perked up and allowed her to head to the dairy area next. There she grabbed milk and yogurt for herself, plus the nacho toppings. She didn't have a clue how many days they would be stuck in the safe house, and the men weren't helpful in that regard. But the cart was half full, so they definitely had food for more than a few days.

In the meat section, Warrick chose a pack of steaks. Corey grabbed a pack of bacon. Seeing the men taking care of those basics, she grabbed an extra pound of butter, a head of romaine lettuce and one of red-leaf lettuce. She wasn't going down just eating protein. These guys were deadly for that.

At the cash register, they swept through and were back out to their vehicles. At that point, they changed places. She looked over at Warrick who was getting into her car. "Why?"

"To throw anyone off who may be watching us again."

Corey pulled her toward the truck. "Come on. Let's go."

She shrugged, scrambled into the seat and closed the door. "Wow, what a view from up here."

"It's not that bad," he said. "A friend of mine has a six-inch lift kit on his. Now that's high."

She shook her head. "Well, at least it's not stupid high."

"I get that you don't like them, but men are very particular about their trucks and don't like anyone knocking their aftermarket upgrades," he said with a big smile.

"Not to mention other things," she said drily.

He laughed, reversed the truck, backed out of the parking lot and followed Warrick who was leading them down the highway. "I forgot you had a sense of humor. We haven't seen too much of it lately."

"There hasn't been anything to laugh about. Besides, how do you know I meant that as funny?"

He looked at her, caught her serious look, stared for a hard moment and then caught her smile breaking. With a nod of satisfaction he said, "That's more like it."

She settled back for the drive. It was late afternoon, and the traffic was heavy. She couldn't imagine where they would end up, and she was already starving. "How could I possibly be hungry when we just ate?"

"That was an hour ago, at least."

They didn't have any of the groceries with them. They'd all been put in the back seat of her car, which was nowhere in sight. "We do trust Warrick, right? It just occurred to me that he took off with a week's worth of groceries—well, it'd last one week feeding only me—and my car."

At that Corey laughed out loud. "I am going to tell Warrick you said that."

She snorted. "You would. But I would still feel better if I could at least see him."

"You will. You will."

Just as she began to relax again, a big black truck passed them going way too fast. It swerved into their lane, cutting Corey off. He was forced to slam on the brakes, the back end of the truck fishtailing wildly. He pulled over onto the median between the two lanes of traffic and slowed the truck down. He brought it to a stop and turned to look at her. "Are you okay?"

It took her a moment to nod. "I'm okay. But what the hell was that?"

"An asshole. They're all around us. So as long as you're okay, we'll continue."

She nodded, but her nerves were rattled again. "Do you think it had anything to do with ..."

"No," he cut off her words. "That was nothing. Just some punk who's being an asshole."

She nodded but couldn't be quite so sure. Every time something weird happened, she had to consider it was connected.

They drove a little longer, until he swore.

She leaned forward. "What?" Her eyes scanned the traffic in front of them, but she couldn't see anything.

"Look behind us," he said. "Don't turn around, just look through the side mirror."

She stared at her side mirror. A gasp left her mouth. "Is that the same black truck?"

"I'm not sure."

"How could that be?"

"He would have had to pull over at the same time we did," Corey said quietly. "I'm going to shake him. Sit back and make sure your seat belt is tight. Let's see if he's really after us or not."

"Maybe we can just take our turn, get to our house, and hide away."

"Only if he doesn't follow us." At that Corey changed lanes, took the next exit without giving the people behind them much warning and was quickly on an off-ramp.

"Is this where we're supposed to go?"

"No," he snapped.

She turned slightly to see the black truck struggling to cross the same lanes. At the last minute it almost came horizontally across the exit and corrected enough to get on the ramp. "He is still behind us," she said quietly. "I wish I could see his license plate."

"I wouldn't worry about it. Either the truck is stolen, or it'll have stolen plates."

"Is that easy to do?"

"Sure. Find another truck at a mall, take off the plates and put different plates on it."

She sat back. "You could do that with a car or an SUV?"

"Exactly. It's not hard to do."

She watched his gaze, which never left the road, and yet he checked from left to right and behind them all the time. She didn't know how he did it. She had enough trouble just staying focused on the road ahead, following directions and not getting lost. She was a good driver, but she certainly didn't have the same inner sense of radar he seemed to have. And he was definitely not letting anything get by him a second time.

She casually looked behind them, and, sure enough, the truck was there. It caught up and was just two vehicles behind them. "Do we need to tell Warrick?"

He reached over, hit Talk on his phone and called out, "Warrick."

Pretty quickly Warrick's voice filled the cab. "What's up?"

"Black truck." He read off the first three letters of the license plate. Letters she couldn't see. "Followed us in a gravely dangerous move on an exit ramp. We're heading toward …" He shook his head. "I'm not exactly sure where we're heading. But we're off the main road. And the bogey is on our tail."

"Okay. I'm five minutes away from the house. Do you want me to come in your direction?"

"No. Get to the house. Make sure everything's still okay there. Hide the car. I'm not sure when we'll be coming in, but I'll stay in touch."

Tense, Angela waited for Corey to make another move. She glanced down at her seat belt to see her fingers almost white as they gripped the belt across her chest.

"It will be okay," he said quietly.

She stared at him in surprise. "How can you say that? You're assuming that whoever followed us started from my aunt's cabin?"

"That's definitely possible."

"And what other possibility is there?"

"The possibility these vehicles have a tracker on them."

She stared at him. "A tracker?" she asked hesitantly. "On this truck or on my car?"

"It could be on either or both. Once they tracked us to the restaurant, they would have seen the two together. It's pretty easy to make sure they keep an eye on both from there."

"When could they put a tracker on my car? What about Warrick? Will he know?"

"He would have already thought of it. He'll stop and check. If he finds one, he'll remove it before going to the safe house."

She shook her head. "But that would mean they had to have time and opportunity."

"How long did you sleep last night?" He turned to look at her. "Your vehicle was down below, behind the cabin. So, yes, it was hidden from the road, but it was also hidden from your view. You wouldn't have known if anybody placed a tracker underneath, would you?"

She sank back into the corner of the truck and shook her head. "No, not at all. Not to mention the weird knock you heard at the cabin. But why wouldn't they just come in and kill me?"

"Maybe they would have if you were alone, but we scared them off, and they came back. There's all kinds of scenarios that could work here."

"None of them work," she said emphatically. "All of this is bullshit." Angry and terrified, she stared out the window. "And Greg's not going to be happy until I'm dead, is he?"

"If he thinks you have this material, he'll probably make sure you're dead. And then he'll find your laptop and your phone and anything else you may have to make sure he's got all the copies. If he hasn't heard anything by now from the authorities or his marks, he'll probably assume you haven't said anything to the police. But he can't be sure. Too much time has gone by."

"I want to pick up Joshua."

"Not happening. Remember what the police said."

Stymied and cornered in all directions, she slumped against the seat and groaned. "How the hell did I get into this?"

He didn't bother answering.

She didn't really need an answer. It was pretty obvious what she had done. "I was just trying to protect my son and myself."

"You're a goldfish up against a shark. And the shark decided he shouldn't leave any goldfish alive to tell on him."

She swallowed hard. "I don't know what to do now."

"We get you stashed, safe and sound. And then we take a look at what the cops might still need."

She shook her head. "That won't be enough."

Her phone rang then. She glanced over at Corey. "It's Greg again."

"Answer and put it on Speaker. And don't tell him where we are or what you're doing."

"Greg? What's up?" She was proud of herself. Her tone sounded almost normal.

"I just thought I'd let you know that, if you try any funny business, your son will be out of your reach forever."

"What do you mean?" Inside, her heart slammed against her rib cage. Surely he didn't mean he would kill Joshua, did he?

"You know what I mean. Right now there's still a chance of you getting some visitation with him. But, if you hand over any of that stuff to the cops, than he goes bye-bye. I'll make sure Joshua disappears forever."

"What are you talking about? Are you threatening to kill him?" Her voice rose in panic. "Why would you do that? He adores you."

"I didn't say that," Greg said, his voice hard. "But you go ahead and keep thinking it. Maybe it'll make you fall in line. You stupid bitch, did you really think you could pull a con on me? I want all that shit back, and I want to know who you gave anything to and what you gave them."

"Has this got anything to do with that thing you seem to think I stole from you?"

"Don't play the fool. I know you took pictures, and I know you have a piece of paper you shouldn't have. Joshua told me all about it." His voice thickened with rage. "Don't make a mistake. You have too much to lose."

"Sounds to me like you have too much to lose," she said, fury seeping into her tone. "You have just threatened me and my son. What the hell do you expect me to think? I don't know what you're talking about, but obviously it's something very damning against you. And I don't know who else might have access, but I sure as hell hope somebody nails your ass to the wall, throws you in jail and tosses the key out the window."

"I won't be going to jail," he said, his voice final.

"Are you so sure about that?"

He laughed, but absolutely nothing was humorous in his tone. "If you want to play, go ahead. But you're just a little girl in this game. If there's even a hint that I might end up going to jail, you can bet your next breath will be your last. Joshua doesn't need a mother now. He sure as hell won't need one in ten years either. Just when you think you're safe and everything's good, you won't see it coming." He hung up.

She was trembling so badly she couldn't even hold the phone in her hand. She dropped it on the seat between them and buried her face in her hands. "Oh, my God. Now what?”

"You definitely pulled the dragon's tail. Not exactly a recommended tactic," he said quietly. "But we can work with this."

She stared at him. "What are you talking about?"

"You pushed his buttons. Threatened him with jail. He'll respond but not in a good way. Now we just have to be ready for anything."

"Or he hires a sharpshooter, my head explodes, and, right after that, my son's head explodes," she said bitterly. She stared out the window. "I didn't realize I had a temper until I married him. For the first few years it seemed like it was buried inside, but now it's firing all the time." She shook her head. "I would never have argued with him like that. And he wouldn't have let me."

"Which is why he'll try to put you in your place now. That was the threat about Joshua."

"But what if he makes good on that threat? I'm no more dangerous than a damn kitten."

At that he chuckled. "And I happen to love kittens."

THAT WASN'T EXACTLY what he meant to say. He did love kittens. He had also loved Angela a long time ago. But to see her like this, it was exasperating, enlightening and enraging. She shouldn't have done anything to poke her soon-to-be-ex-husband's anger. But she couldn't seem to help herself. And once Greg had threatened her with never seeing Joshua again, she'd lost all control. Corey could understand that. It was why her husband had done it.

But Greg may have miscalculated. Corey had never known Angela to be so quiet, so shy, so locked down, so buttoned-up. She'd always been a bit of a free spirit. He was pretty pissed at her husband for having curbed that spirit. But right now, no doubt Greg had unleashed a whole lot more than a little kitten. The thing was, this time the kitten wasn't alone. What they had to do now was make sure Joshua was safe.

"Does Joshua go to school?"

"Yes, he's in a private school. Greg was paying the tuition. Otherwise, I couldn't have kept him in it."

"And will he be there tomorrow?"

"I would think so. But it depends if Greg has taken him out of school to move him somewhere else."

"Greg might need a day or two to make those kinds of plans." He turned to look at her. "Do you have the right to take the child out of school?"

"I used to. But that was before the mall scene. I went a few days ago but was denied access. According to Greg, we're in a custody battle, and I am not allowed to have unsupervised visits. Of course he'd never have let me have a supervised visit either," she said bitterly. "He must have planned for this once I brought Joshua for the first visit and started legal proceedings to keep me from my son."

He stared at her in surprise. "He really doesn't want you to have any contact, does he?"

She shook her head. "No, he really doesn't."

"As soon as I get a chance, I'll call the detective. His threats to the child have upped the game. We'll have to see if we can intercept Joshua somewhere and grab him."

She looked at Corey with hope. "Do you mean it?"

He turned his head and quickly changed lanes. He knew a section with traffic circles was up ahead with several options where he thought he could probably shake the truck.

It stayed behind him, separated by three cars, not changing lanes, not moving over, just content to watch.

Corey took the traffic circle, quickly turned and came around. At the last second, he changed lanes, then made another quick turn, exiting the main highway. Halfway down this block was an alley. He popped down it and kept on going. A covered parking lot was up ahead. He pulled in underneath and took one of the spots, luckily between two black trucks.

He motioned for her to get down. "We'll sit here and see if they find us."

"But your truck is being tracked …"

He smiled, opened his door, pulled out the keys so there was no noise or lights and slid down to take a look underneath. Within seconds he was back up, tossing a metal device onto the seat between them.

She looked at it. "So they got your vehicle too?"

"Can't say I'm surprised. We had it parked outside the cabin." He held out his phone. "I need to talk to Warrick for a minute." He called Warrick but this time it was off Speaker. He brought him up to date. "We're hidden right now. I'm keeping an eye out to see if he finds us. But it's been ten minutes with no sign of the black truck."

"Wait another ten. I might come for you myself."

"No. Stay where you are. But make sure you're bug-free."

"I've got a device with me here. I've just checked the car and pulled one."

"I have taken one out too. I don't know if they put more than that on each vehicle. But I don't have anything to check with."

"I haven't gone to the house. I'm sitting in the small

mall parking lot about a block away. There's a video store, small grocery store, a liquor store. Pull in there, drive around to the back."

"I am at least ten minutes away, and that's once I get back on the road."

"Take your time. I'll expect you in an hour, no sooner."

Corey slipped from the truck and turned to tell her, "Stay down until I come back." He slumped around to the front of the vehicle, crossed several trucks until he could stand and take a look around the car park. He couldn't see any moving vehicles. That didn't mean the black truck wasn't somewhere behind them. Warrick had done the same thing he had.

What he wanted to do was put the tracker on another vehicle about to leave, but he had to know which one would move out. He could see the street from where he stood. He watched a delivery vehicle pull up. The driver got out.

With a quick move, Corey was back at his truck. "Wait here." He snagged the device from the front seat, closed the vehicle door quietly and disappeared within the car park and over to the delivery vehicle. He walked along the driver side and casually tossed it into the front seat through the window. It didn't need to be mounted; it only needed to be hidden from others. The delivery driver had several bags in front. Thankfully the device fell to the floor.

Corey kept walking, carried on down the block and, not wanting to leave her alone for too long, backtracked to the delivery vehicle where the driver was just getting back into it. Hidden from sight but still able to see the truck, Corey waited. Sure enough the black truck came ripping down from one of the upper levels of the car park and took a right, going after the delivery vehicle.

It wouldn't work for long, but Corey had just enough time to get the hell out of here. He raced back to his truck, reversed it and headed back the way he had come. He knew the little mall Warrick mentioned. But it was still a good ten miles away. He took as many corners and crisscrosses as he could to shake any tail trying to follow him.

He was right on the one-hour mark when he pulled into the back of the video store. Warrick waited for him and held up to him a small device before crushing on the cement. Corey double-checked the truck, then turned to Warrick. "The truck is clean."

The two men high-fived. "Now let's get these vehicles in the garage."

Four minutes later they both pulled up side by side inside the safe house garage, the big door already closing behind them.

Warrick slipped out under the garage door before it completely lowered and went down to close the gate at the end of the driveway. He'd set up a security alarm at the gate that they'd control from inside the house. Corey walked around the truck, opened up the passenger side and smiled at Angela. "All clear."

She looked out in relief, stood on his running board and threw her arms around him. She hugged him tight and whispered, "Thank you."

His arms crushed her close. Instantly his mind flooded with memories of the two of them years ago. He buried his face in the crook of her neck and just held on tight.

<h1 style="text-align:center">CHAPTER 9</h1>

S HE TRIED TO pull back from the hug but realized he wasn't letting go. So she relaxed. "I'd forgotten," she said.

He shook his head. "I never have." But his tone was light. He tilted his head back and looked down at her. "Just in case you think I've been holding a torch for you, I haven't. I moved forward and carried on. I've had several really great relationships. But one doesn't forget one's first." He reached up and gently flicked her nose.

She grinned at him. "Ditto."

"Hey, you two coming in?" Warrick's voice bordered on disgust. He stood in the doorway. "Some of us are hungry."

Inside the house everyone worked efficiently to put away groceries except for the pack of rib steaks staring at her. Angela looked for something to go with it. "How do you want to cook the steaks? Is there a grill?"

Both men shook their heads.

"Then I'll pan fry them," she said. "Can I use any food-stuffs in the kitchen?"

"You're welcome to anything here. But I doubt there's very much."

She nodded and went to the pantry. There she found rice and several canned goods. The rice would do for the moment. She brought it out, put it in a pan on the stove, prepped some veggies for a salad and got out a cast iron pan she found underneath the stove. By the time they sat down to the meal, she had started to relax again.

"Do you think there's any chance he'll find us here?" she asked.

"Slim to none," Warrick said. "We can't say one hundred percent because that's not possible."

She nodded. "I didn't see anybody on the last leg of the trip, so hopefully we got away free and clear."

They finished eating, did the dishes and then moved into the living room.

"I wish there was some way to move this process along," she complained quietly. "I know it's only been a day, but it seems like so much has happened, and yet the end result still looks to be weeks away."

Her phone rang. The number came up in front of her, and tears came to her eyes.

"Who is that?" Corey asked. He'd been trying to keep close without crowding her since they'd come into the house. It was obvious she was under an extreme amount of stress, and the last thing he wanted was for her to break.

She raised her teary eyes to him. "It's Joshua."

His breath caught in the back of his throat. He glanced at Warrick, the two in agreement. "Answer it. Talk to your son," he said gently.

Sniffling back the tears, she wiped her eyes and answered the phone. "Joshua. Hi."

"Mommy," Joshua wailed on the other end of the phone. "When can I see you?"

"Soon, sweetie. It will be soon."

"Daddy says it will be never. I keep wanting to call you and meet you, but he won't let me."

"I know, sweetie. Mommy and Daddy have a few things to work out. Don't you worry. I'm going to see you soon."

Corey listened as she spoke for a few more minutes.

Then she asked suddenly, "Does Daddy know you have your phone still?"

"No, I kept it in my backpack."

"Don't tell him that you talked to me, okay?"

"I won't. I shouldn't have told him that you took something. He got really angry."

"Don't you worry about it, sweetie. Mommy will be fine."

They exchanged goodbyes, and finally she hung up and sat quietly, her shoulders hunched, the phone hugged against her chest. Hearing the little boy cry for his mother had been heartbreaking. Just listening to the words he said made Corey angry.

What kind of a father would keep his son away from his mother? He knew there were cases where it was probably a good idea, but it wasn't like Angela was into drugs or alcohol or was abusive. In this case it was the father who was abusive, and everybody else had to dance to his tune, whether they liked it or not. Sometimes life was like that, but Corey would do what he could to help her and Joshua.

She pulled her phone down and sent a text.

"Who was that to?" Warrick asked wearily.

"I told him good night and that I love him."

She kept her head down, and he realized she was holding back the tears.

Warrick got up and went into the kitchen to put on coffee.

Corey sat down beside her and hauled her into his arms. He just held her. She cried, but it wasn't an all-out cry-fest.

It was a gentle sobbing because her heart was breaking.

He held her close, rubbing her back to let it all come out. "The situation will change. We just need a few days."

She nodded, her cheek rubbing back and forth against his chest. "It's just so hard."

"And, in a few weeks, a few months, this will all blow over, and you can start to forget about it."

She pushed herself off his chest and stared at him. "I will never forget this."

He winked. "I didn't mean it that way. I just meant you'll feel better because you'll have Joshua in your arms, and everything will be okay again."

"I don't know if anything can ever be okay again," she mumbled. "I just wanted to have a life with my son."

He stroked the tears off her cheek with his thumb. "And you'll get it, but we have to make sure your husband goes away for a long time. We don't want the case thrown out of court for any reason and then find out Greg's back on the streets within days."

Her gaze widened in horror. "That would be the worst because he'll just come right back after us."

Corey nodded. "Yes, he will. So let's make sure we nail his ass to the wall, and then you can have your life back."

She collapsed against his chest, and he cuddled her close.

When Warrick came in a few minutes later with several cups of coffee, he placed them on the coffee table in front of them. "I'll be working in the kitchen."

Corey nodded. Warrick was giving them space, and he appreciated it.

"I forgot how nice you were," she murmured against his chest.

"How does one forget how nice somebody is?"

"I don't know," she said, puzzled. "But I did. You were always the guy who brought me coffee or collected me instead of making me meet you somewhere. You brought me flowers for no reason and picked me up after work as a surprise. You were one of the nice people in the world."

"I'm not so sure I am anymore. The military has taken some of that out of me."

"No. It might have turned you into a man and given you the skills to be a fighter, but that Corey is still inside you."

"I can't say being nice helped me all these years."

"I think it did. It's hard to imagine what you'd be like if you still didn't have that marshmallow center."

He snorted, insulted. "I'm not a marshmallow."

From the kitchen Warrick called out. "You absolutely are. You are sugar sweet, gummy, gummy, completely meltable on the inside."

Angela let out a shriek of laughter. She straightened up and looked at him. "Even Warrick thinks you're like that."

Corey shook his head. "Warrick doesn't know what the hell he's talking about."

She grinned. "The two of you are exactly the same on the inside."

"Hey," Warrick yelled from the kitchen. "That's not fair. He's the marshmallow. I'm not."

"You're both marshmallows," she said with laughter.

Corey stroked her hair off her face. At least she wasn't crying anymore. "Do you want to stay here, or do you want to join Warrick in the kitchen?"

She gave Corey a big hug. "Warrick is working. I feel we should be working too."

"Speak for yourself," Corey said. "I've been working steadily. I can use some downtime."

But she wasn't having anything to do with that. She caught his hand and tried to pull him up from the couch.

He just laughed. "I outweigh you by at least one hundred pounds."

"But only one," she said. "Warrick outweighs me by two hundred."

A snicker came from the kitchen. "If you're trying to insult me, that won't work. I'm all muscle. He's the marshmallow."

Laughing, Corey grabbed their coffees and walked into the kitchen. He could see Warrick working away on the spreadsheets. "You figure that out yet?"

"No, not yet, but I figured, if we've already got one dead man, maybe we should contact some of these other people. Make sure they don't end up the same way."

"Aren't the police doing that?" Angela asked.

Warrick glanced at her. "Well, they might be, but how fast will they do it? According to the detective on the case, he's identified a couple of these men. But I think this one I know." He tapped the screen.

COREY WALKED AROUND to look at the man handing over what looked like packets of money. Something else was coming his way, but Corey wasn't sure exactly what it was. Maybe Warrick could blow that part up.

"Where do you think you know him from?"

"That's the thing. I can't remember, but that haircut makes me think he's military."

Corey leaned closer. "Holy crap, that's not Captain Jackson, is it?"

Warrick looked again and smiled. "It is. Damn, I knew

that face was familiar."

"What the hell? Send this to Mason. See what he's got to say."

Warrick clicked a few buttons on the keyboard and sent an email off to Mason. Then Warrick sent a text. Corey refilled their coffee cups, sat down, wishing they'd picked up dessert. Then remembered the chips. He helped himself, emptying the bag into a bowl, placing it on the kitchen table. Then made up the dip they bought the ingredients for. Just as he sat back down again, Warrick's phone rang. "Hey, Mason."

Listening to Warrick's half of the conversation, Corey understood Mason would approach the captain himself. They'd been buddies for a long time.

When Warrick got off the phone, he said, "Mason will contact the detective, and then he'll contact Captain Jackson. But the police already have this photo, so, if some shit is going down, the captain could get caught in the middle of it." Warrick shared a look with Corey and Angela. "The police may get pissed at us for getting involved."

The two men leaned forward to study the photo. Warrick put it into a photo imaging editor so he could enlarge it without losing too much of the clarity. They studied it some more, and Corey said, "Drugs?"

"Potentially, yeah. White packets. Heroin? Cocaine? No way to know."

"It'll be the end of the captain's career if this gets out."

"Look at that photo. He's not in uniform, and it looks like it was taken quite a few years ago," Warrick said quietly. "I don't know if he's paid Greg to keep this silent or if potentially Angela's husband is just hanging on to this type of information for when he might need it in the future."

"I'd say possibly both, depending on the circumstances," Angela said from across the table. "He used to laugh and say, that's worth keeping. And he'd tuck what he had away."

"So, if the police were to serve Greg with a search warrant on the property, do you think they'd find much?"

Her eyes went large and round. She nodded. "And, if they do that, they need to look in the safes behind the two pictures in his office. There's one behind each, but one is even more hidden because there's like a breaker box front panel, but behind that is a safe."

The two men looked at her with respect. "You know that for sure?"

She nodded. "I do. I also know he keeps stuff stashed in the upstairs hall. If you take the electrical plug out and reach your hand inside, something is taped inside the wall."

At this the men leaned forward. "How do you know that?"

"That's the problem when people think you're completely cowed, that you have absolutely no mind or life of your own. You become invisible. I remember seeing Greg, crouched in the hall, putting something in there." She held up her hands, approximating the size. "It was small, like about two inches by two inches, and it was taped on all four sides. He pressed it against the inside of the wall, put the cover plate back on with a screwdriver, got up and walked away."

"Could you hazard a guess as to what you saw him put in there?"

She shrugged. "If I had to say, it could have been one of those little flash drives, a memory stick."

"That is excellent," Warrick said warmly. "I don't know what it will take to get a warrant served on the house, but at the very least they'll have some idea what they're looking for, and they'll have a much better chance of finding it. Any evidence we can seize will help us nail him on these charges."

"More important," Corey said, "anything he thinks is worth hiding is something I really want to know about."

CHAPTER 10

ANGELA STARED AT the men. "I could probably think of other places he's hidden stuff. He's bad about that. Think of the old hermit with coffee cans full of coins. I'm pretty sure Greg keeps a lot of money at home too."

"Any idea whose name is on the deed?"

She looked at him in surprise. "His name is. And ..." Her voice trailed off. "I didn't sign any papers adding my name to anything I don't think. He was very controlling."

"All good to know." Warrick was busy writing down notes of everything she'd said so far. He looked up at her. "Any other hiding spots?"

"The attic," she said promptly. "I know he was up there a couple times in the months before I left."

"Any idea why?"

She shook her head. "No. He took boxes, shoe-box-size boxes, up there."

"Did he ever give you an explanation?"

She shook her head. "Never. I was more like the hired help. I'm supposed to look pretty and stay quiet, remember?"

The men nodded but didn't say anything.

She laughed and admitted, "It's funny to look back on it now. It's certainly not what I wanted."

"And not your planned future."

She nodded. "But it's hard when you make a mistake

like that. How do you trust your own judgment again?"

Warrick laughed this time. "Hey, I'm the one on the fallout of a broken relationship. I thought what we had was solid. The trouble was, a few days after she'd left, it was almost like I didn't care anymore. So then how much did I care in the first place?"

Angela smiled. "I think if, within a week or two, you're not bothered, not torn up about it, then it was time to break up in the first place."

Warrick stared at her for a long moment. "Sandra said something along the same line. That the fire and magic had long since disappeared, and we're just friends now."

"She might have been right." Angela reached across the table and gripped his fingers. "The good thing is, you know your heart, although damaged, won't be shredded because of this."

He gave a big shudder, shooting her a lopsided grin. "So true. But we were together for three years."

"So it's three years you could look back on with gratitude and a big smile. But now you get to look forward to something so much better." Her hand still held his, and she squeezed it before letting go.

Then in a gentle voice, he said, "And exactly the same advice goes for you."

She widened her gaze as she understood what he'd said. "That's not fair. You just turned the tables on me."

He chuckled. "It seemed to be the right thing to do at the time." Warrick's phone rang again.

She leaned back and laughed. "You guys are on the phone more than any woman I've ever known."

Both men gave her an offended look. Warrick answered the call. "Mason, what's up?" He listened and nodded his head.

Angela waited, hoping to catch some nuance that would tell her what the heck was going on. It was a long call.

At one point Warrick got off the chair and walked into the living room to talk.

She looked to Corey. "I gather we weren't supposed to hear any of that?"

He gave her a lopsided look and said, "You weren't supposed to hear the rest of that."

She grabbed a chip from the center of the table and chomped on it hard. She hated being kept out of the loop, particularly when this was her life, her son. But they weren't going to let her in just because she said so. She waited impatiently for another few minutes.

When Warrick returned, his face was serious. "Mason contacted the detective. The navy doesn't want him approaching anybody. But, when Mason contacted the captain's supervisor, *he* then contacted the detective. They're all meeting tonight at a coffee shop."

Silence.

"Really? With the detective?"

Warrick shook his head. "No, just Mason, Jackson, and his supervisor."

"Without the detective knowing? Is that good?"

"It's also a military police issue now, since it involves Captain Jackson," Corey said beside her. "And that'll trump anybody else's investigation."

"But it wasn't supposed to, was it?"

"Which is why Mason wanted to talk to Jackson alone."

She chewed on her fingernails. "I feel like I've opened a can of worms," she admitted. "I don't like it. I feel dirty, like I'm ruining people's lives."

"Maybe you were the final impetus in these photos coming to light. But you weren't the one in this photograph, doing what Jackson's doing to begin with."

She nodded. "The trouble is, because of me, this *has* come to light. And now Jackson's career, even his life, could very well be ruined."

"It's still not your fault." Corey grasped her hand in his. "You were part of a chain reaction that first involved Jackson, then your husband, now you. Remember that."

"Anything else come out of that phone call?" she asked Warrick.

He nodded. "We're to stay here out of sight until Mason contacts us."

She frowned. "How is that fair?"

"It's fair," Corey said. "You forget this is the stuff we do. There'll be a chain of command. We'll follow orders."

She slumped back in her chair and glared at him. "What if the orders are wrong?"

"Then we will change the orders or ignore them and do what we have to do," Corey snapped. "My ethics and morals are not on the line here. Jackson did whatever he did. And, right now, he'll have to face the music. He'll either have a reasonable explanation for this or we might get more information from him if he's being blackmailed. If he's been under this cloud for a long time, it might be a huge relief to him to open up about it."

She studied Corey's face for a long moment. "That would be nice, but how come it never seems to feel like it's a good thing?"

He shoved the bowl of chips toward her. "Have another chip. It'll make you feel better."

She shook her head. "It's hard to believe anything short

of getting Joshua back will make me feel better." She glanced at the other photos. "Do we know any of the other men?"

"This one's a politician. Ex-politician actually," Warrick said. "He was in congress for a few years. He isn't anymore." He picked up the photo. "I'd love to know why."

"Call him," Corey said. "Or at least get the detective to call him."

Warrick frowned. "Not sure he wants to take any more phone calls from me."

Corey bounced to his feet and grabbed the photos. "I'll phone the detective. It could be, because of these photos, that he's no longer in congress. Somebody has to talk. We need to break this open, so we can put it to rest." He dialed the detective and walked out of the kitchen.

Angela watched him go, then turned to Warrick. "How do you do this all the time? Dig into the dirt in other people's lives? Deal in all this murder and mayhem and war stuff?"

"It does take a special temperament," Warrick said. "It's not for everyone."

"I can't stand even being close to it. Just seeing all this stuff makes my skin crawl, and I want to take a shower."

He nodded. "Sometimes I feel that way too. Sometimes we hear some of the most debased things about people. You go home, and you have that shower, and you start all over again the next day. But while this is a relatively small issue, most of the time I'm dealing with big issues—guerrillas, terrorists, mercenaries. There are wars all over the world. That's normally where my focus is, but behind a lot of them are people like these who hire guns to go out and do the jobs they don't want to do themselves. Or drug dealers working large scale, and, instead of taking cash, they take weapons in payment."

She stared at him. "I just don't get how you could do that every day."

He leaned forward. "Because, if I don't, who will? If there aren't individuals like Corey and me protecting people in this world, who is there to protect you?"

"There shouldn't be any need to protect anybody," she said fiercely.

"And you're not that naive. The fact of the matter is, we don't live in a perfect world. And, as long as we don't, we have to have protectors and guardians of the innocent."

"Life sucks," she exclaimed as she continued to glare at him. "It's not the life I want to see."

"Nobody wants that," Warrick said. And then he offered her one more of those lovely gentle smiles and said, "So remember that's why Corey and I do what we do. So you can live a life where you are untouched by most of this, and hopefully the people being persecuted and ravaged by war right now will see an end before they're killed and slaughtered like beef."

She snapped. "It still sucks."

He chuckled. "Like Corey said, have a chip. It will be good for your jaw."

She glared at him even more, picked up a big tortilla chip and chomped on it fiercely.

"I CAN CALL him myself," Corey said quietly to the detective. "But you know it'll go down better if it comes from you."

"All I hear is you keep getting into my investigation," the detective snapped. "How many times do I have to remind you and your buddy to stay out of it?"

"We're not staying out of it as long as we have a woman and her son in danger," Corey said, his tone implacable. "Just be damn happy we're coming to you with all the information we turn up."

An odd silence followed on the other end of the call, and then the detective gave a snort. "Is everyone in your unit as hard-headed as you two?"

"Worse," he said coolly. "So contact the congressman, ex-congressman, and get back to us." He hung up and stood in the living room for a long moment, waiting for his temper to cool. He understood the detective's point. But this was going to blow. The more information they had before that happened, the better. If Angela's husband had any idea what was going on behind his back, he'd already be making plans to skip the country. And he'd likely take Joshua with him. And that meant Angela would never see her son again.

"Is everything okay?" Warrick called out.

Corey strode to the open doorway. "You could say that. The detective is getting a little fed up."

Angela looked at him. "So? He should be trying to solve this."

"The thing is, he's busy. This isn't his only case. We're not even sure this is a case."

"So then let's do it ourselves. You know any of these other men? Any of them we can call up out of the blue?" Angela asked.

"Do you really think that if we called one of these men and said, 'Hey, we have some incriminating photos of you having sex with another guy,' that they'll talk to us willing-ly?" Corey asked her.

She stared at him for a long moment. And then her lips

twitched. "Okay, so maybe not if we put it that way."

He shook his head. "Not if we put it any way."

Warrick interrupted. "On that same note," he tapped the photo on his monitor, "isn't that Elizabeth? From Royal Investment Funds? She used to be among the brass until she decided she was more suited to the private sector."

"Elizabeth Wheaton?" Corey walked closer and studied the enlarged photo. "That is her. Why is that photo important though?" He studied the lone woman standing at the edge of a cliff. She wore a business suit, but her feet were bare.

As he looked, Angela came around to see the photo as well. "Oh, interesting."

The two men looked at her. "What's so interesting? She's just standing there."

"Sure, but that's a popular suicide spot in the area. Although why that's of interest, I'm not sure," Angela muttered.

"She's the CEO of a large investment company. If anybody thought she was suicidal, it would have devastating effects on their stocks." Corey leaned closer. "But still, this photo doesn't scream that she is suicidal, just that she's standing there."

"But with her shoes off." Warrick nodded. "It's not that it's horrifically damaging, but it would likely push her buttons, let her know she's being watched. And, because her shoes are off—which is a typical sign of somebody who's suicidal and looking to jump—she might react exactly the way they want her to."

"But it's thin."

Warrick nodded. "It doesn't take much though, does it? To ruin a reputation? To create shareholder panic?"

At that, Corey had to agree. If the photos held any trigger for the people in them, it was likely to create havoc in their lives. He scrolled through his contacts and said, "I do have her number." He hit Dial. And then put it on Speaker.

"Corey?" A woman's warm voice filled the room. "What's up? I haven't heard from you in at least a year."

"And I'm sorry this isn't exactly a social call," he said. "I have a problem—a case. A woman and her son are being victimized by her husband, the boy's father. One of the things she did before she left was take photographs of some stuff lying around his office."

"What's that got to do with me?" Elizabeth asked.

"What's your email? I want to forward you one of these photos."

She gave it to him. He relayed it to Warrick. "Warrick is here with me. He's sending it to you now."

"I'm still at work, but I have my personal laptop so I should be able to open it up here."

He waited.

He heard her swallow hard, then her voice turned harsh. "Where did you get that photo?"

"In the house of a man named Greg Buffalo."

Silence.

"Elizabeth? Are you being blackmailed?"

Her voice was ragged. "Yes, I am." And she burst into tears.

Corey pinched the bridge of his nose. "Can you tell me about it? I know this has to be hard, but you know one should never pay a blackmailer because it will never end."

"And yet how does one *not* pay a blackmailer?" she whispered brokenly.

"Does he have other stuff on you, or is this the only photo?"

"He has a couple more like this. One where I actually tried to jump."

"I'm so sorry." Corey's voice was low and compassionate. "How long ago was this?"

"A year. One very long year. If I thought it was bad before, it's been just hell since."

Corey looked over to see tears in Angela's eyes. "I'm sorry to hear this bastard has his claws in you. You need to know that we're trying to bring him down. I'll do what I can to keep these photos quiet, but the police already have them."

"The thing is, it's been over a year now. I've been wondering about just stopping payments. But, if he did publish those photos, then what? Obviously I was going through a bad patch, and life wasn't worth living for a while."

"Is it something you can share with others before it goes public? The board of directors, your family?"

"That's one of the reasons why I got so depressed. My husband was diagnosed with stage four cancer and died very quickly, as you know. That was followed by a car accident that took our eighteen-year-old son."

Everybody could hear the pain in her voice. Corey hated himself for having to bring all that back up. "Anybody would understand you going through a bad period because of those circumstances."

"Yes, but, at the time, we were involved in a merger. A merger that was and has been very good for us. If anybody had any idea I was 'mentally unstable,' the merger would never have gone through."

"How are you feeling now?"

"Like I said, it's been a hell of a year. But I don't feel like jumping off cliffs anymore—if for no other reason than I never know who is taking pictures," she said, her tone bitter.

"What I need from you now is information on how you were approached, how you communicate with him and how you pay him."

"That I'll be happy to give you. Of course I'm really hoping you take down this asshole, and you can stop this. I'm not proud of what I did and how close I came to walking away from all this. Yet, when I look back, I can understand it. But I'm not now where I was then."

"All of us can understand. Never doubt that," Corey said in a gentle voice. "You'll be that much stronger for this experience too. But let's make sure we put an end to it. You aren't the only one caught in this asshole's net."

Elizabeth sighed at those words. "No. Of course I'm not, am I?" There was a hard *clang*. "Don't worry about me. That was just my scotch glass hitting the desk a little too hard. I never considered he might be doing this to other people."

"We've got seventeen different photographs. And a spreadsheet. We're still trying to decode the spreadsheet, but it entails several pages."

"Bastard. I have an email he used to contact me. I presume it doesn't lead anywhere. Otherwise he wouldn't have left it in use. And I have a bank account number. I do a transfer into the account every month."

"Because I have the spreadsheet and we're trying to decode it, and yet I know it's not something you want to share, but could you tell us how much you were paying?"

"Five thousand. Five thousand a month every month for the last year."

He thought about that. "And yet ..."

"I know. It's not very much. He could have asked for one hundred thousand. At the time I would have paid it. But

I probably wouldn't have continued to pay it."

"No, but this way it becomes something you're willing to pay just to have it all go away."

"Exactly. But I have been thinking it was time for this to stop. I just didn't know what to do about it. So your call is actually very timely," she said. "However, it would be much nicer if you called to go for coffee or dinner, maybe drinks out or barbecue in your backyard, something that was *so* not this."

He chuckled. "If I wasn't in hiding with Warrick and the woman who's involved, I would definitely have you over for a barbecue. So how about I take a rain check, and, when it's safe for us to pop to the surface, and hopefully safe for you to stand on a cliff without having people take photographs, we'll have that barbecue."

"That sounds great. I don't have too much other information. I never get confirmation. I just send a quick email, and then I send the payment." She sighed. "I'm forwarding the emails to you and sending you a separate email with the accounts and payment dates."

"No names?"

"None."

"We'll get back to you if we need more. And thanks, Elizabeth. I'm so sorry for everything that happened. Life's a bitch sometimes. But she doesn't have to turn the screw at the same time."

"Isn't that the truth? I'll talk to you later."

He could hear her swallow, presumably a good strong drink of scotch going down as she hung up the phone. He sat there for a long moment. "That's really shitty," he said with a heavy sigh. He'd always liked Elizabeth. She came across as real. "She's had a tough go of it. A part of me says it's her business if she wants to end it. But I can see how it would have thrown her company merger off-kilter if those photos had been made public at the time."

"So what does this guy do? Just sit on these suicide hills and take pictures of people trying to kill themselves?" Warrick asked incredulously.

"She said she did try to jump. How was it she didn't kill herself in that attempt?" Corey frowned at Warrick. "I should have followed up on that, shouldn't I?"

"I'll send her an email right now." Warrick started to type. Within a couple minutes, he hit Send and looked at Corey. "I've asked her to respond as soon as possible. She might even call you back."

Almost immediately Corey's phone rang. "Elizabeth?"

"Yes. A man caught me. I hadn't even seen him come up behind me. He grabbed me by the jacket just as I went over. I almost did fall, but he dragged me back up."

Corey leaned forward. "Do you know who that was?"

"No. He said his name was Reginald, I think. I just wanted to get away from him. I was so confused, terrified, scared. I don't even know how to express what I felt. But I never heard from him again."

"Unless he's the one blackmailing you?"

She gasped. "He was a big man. Six foot, dressed in a business suit. I didn't even ask him what he was doing there."

"He could have been doing the same thing you were. And maybe, by saving you, you saved him too."

"I hope so. He was nice."

They hung up, and Corey turned to face the other two. "Well, what are we thinking about that?"

Warrick tilted his head toward Angela. Her face was

pale, her eyes huge.

Corey leaned forward, picked up her icy-cold hand and held it in his. "Angela? What is it?"

"My husband's man of business. He is six foot tall and wears a suit. His name is Reginald."

CHAPTER 11

A NGELA STARED AT Corey. "It couldn't have been him, could it?"

"What's his life like? What's he like?"

"It's hard to know. He's always buttoned-down, obeys orders, does everything as he's told. He always had a smile for me though. Never spoke out of turn. He was always very respectful."

"But then your husband wouldn't have allowed anything less, would he?"

She shook her head. "No. You're right. He demanded obedience from both of us."

The two men nodded.

She sat back. "Reginald had a son. ... Something happened ... about a year ago." She cast her mind back. "It's so hard to remember even that far back." She ran through the scenarios in her head. "It was the first year Joshua started school. We had lots of meetings over that. Often Reginald drove us back and forth. He spent a fair bit of time talking to Joshua. They were quite good buddies."

She stopped and frowned. "For a while Reginald got very, very, very quiet." Her gaze widened. "I think something might have happened to his son." She tried hard to pull up the memories. "Can we do a search of his name, check to see if he has a child?"

"Sure. Any idea what his last name is?"

She thought about it for a moment and then said triumphantly, "Warring. W-A-R-R-I-N-G. Warring."

She hadn't even finished talking before both men were clicking away.

"What did we ever do before the internet?"

"A lot more running around on foot, that's for sure."

"Reginald Warring. Married in 2004, had a son in 2010. Son deceased in 2016."

"What happened?"

"He was hit by a drunk driver while walking on the sidewalk."

Everyone winced. "Ouch. That's got to be rough," Corey said.

"I remember that now. I didn't see much of him after that, so I don't know if he took longer off than I thought, or whether he was just working part-time, or whether my husband was keeping him away, off on business."

"But he's very loyal to your husband?"

She nodded. "Very loyal. I think he is also extremely well-paid for that loyalty."

"That would be very typical of the business world," Warrick said.

"So, in other words, you don't think he would talk to us?" Corey asked Angela.

"I doubt it. That would be breaking his word. And I'm pretty sure that's something he cares about. Don't get me wrong. I don't think my husband cares one damn bit about Reginald. But I think, for Reginald, its part and parcel of his makeup."

"Anybody else in the household who's not quite so well-paid?" Warrick smiled at her.

She shook her head. "When I split with my husband, he was in the process of getting rid of the staff. I felt bad because I figured he was doing it solely for that reason—to make sure nobody knew anything about what went on previously."

"He's a real piece of work, isn't he?" Corey asked. But he wasn't looking at her. He studied the laptop in front of him.

So she figured he wasn't really expecting an answer. "Yeah, apparently I suck at picking men."

At that Warrick snickered.

Corey gave her a horrified look. "Let's just say your judgment went downhill over time."

She realized what she'd said and chuckled. "Okay, so you weren't a mistake."

Warrick said, "Aha, I knew I was right."

She blushed. "And I figured he'd told you."

Corey shot her a look. "Men don't kiss and tell."

She rolled her eyes. "Which puts me in a bad spot. Apparently I'm the one who let it out of the bag."

"Doesn't matter," Warrick crowed. "I already figured that's the way of it."

She shook her head. "It was a long time ago."

"That's what they all say." His smile was cheeky, his eyes full of laughter.

"As long as you don't make too big a deal out of it, I'll let you get away with that."

He just grinned. "It's really not a big deal. I know it was a long time ago because I've been working with Corey for a long time, and you weren't part of that world."

She smiled. "No, I was too busy finding a controlling husband to make my life miserable."

"That's okay. You have Joshua," Corey reminded her.

"And, as we well know, that's worth a lot."

"What you don't know, Warrick, is I lost Corey's baby a long time ago. An event that caused the breakup, mass depression, and a lot of self-evaluation." She saw the surprise in Warrick's eyes.

He glanced over at Corey and nodded. "I'm also a big believer in things happening for a reason," he said gently. "So maybe it just wasn't the right time."

She nodded. "I went through quite a period of figuring all that out back then. I know miscarriages are common, way too common, but nobody really talks about them. It was certainly an early pregnancy that I lost, and, in the ensuing years, I've met lots of women who have miscarried. We all have one thing in common, at least the women I met. It is hard to deal with."

"But you managed to have Joshua, so that's a blessing in many ways."

She chuckled. "You should see him. He's such an angel. He's one of those kids who can take your words, twist them around backward and make you question what you might have said in the first place."

Warrick chuckled. "Kids are great. I will enjoy getting to know him when this nightmare is over."

She studied his face. "You really mean that, don't you?"

He glanced up. "I rarely say something I don't mean."

She chuckled. "And that's a really nice thing about you too. You speak from the heart. And that's worth a lot."

"We are good people." Warrick nodded at Corey. "You should give him another chance."

A stunned silence filled the room, and she sputtered, "What are you talking about? There's nothing between us."

Warrick looked at her, his gaze deep and dark and mysterious. "Isn't there?"

COREY RAISED HIS head at Warrick's words. But it was Angela's face that caught his attention. There was shock, confusion and a whisper of something else. It was that *something else* he wanted to lock on to. Did she see they still had something between them? Or rather the reasons they were together back then were even better reasons now?

She stared at Warrick, her jaw open.

It wasn't exactly the heartwarming response Corey had hoped for, but, as the color rose up her neck and cheeks, he realized maybe it was after all. He patted her hand. "He's just trying to bug you."

She switched her gaze to him, and he could see her shocked awareness.

He smiled. "Don't let him scare you off."

"Scare me off what?"

He gave her a slow drawling smile. "Me."

She shook her head. "Wow. You two are deadly." She was slowly regaining her equilibrium.

"And you two are easy to read. Both of you are doing this dance. Interested but scared. Lots of things to come between you but no real reason to keep you apart." Warrick gave a nod of satisfaction. "I'd be quite happy to end this mess with the two of you together again."

She shook her head. "It's not happening. Not that fast, that's for sure."

"It is happening," Warrick teased. "You just haven't come to accept it."

She glared at him. "Can we get back to business now? This is a little too embarrassing." And deliberately she dropped her gaze to the images in front of them. Almost instantly she gasped.

They both leaned forward to see what she was looking at.

"Is that a gun?"

Corey leaned closer and studied the photo. "It is a gun." He turned to Warrick. "Can you bring that up in the photo program? Let's see what that is behind the car he's standing by."

With Corey and Angela crowded around Warrick, he made a few adjustments and focused in on the back of the vehicle. Corey stepped away slightly, his face grim as he stared at the image. "That's a foot."

Warrick did a few more manipulations. "It looks like a man is lying there. It's a little hard to see."

"It's not that hard," Angela said in a shocked voice. "It looks like the man with the gun shot the man on the ground. There's something almost familiar about him, but I …" She shook her head and then tilted it. "It's hard to see clearly."

"But why didn't we see that at the beginning?" Warrick murmured. He leaned closer. "A lot of people are in that photo. Were they all part of it?"

"Or did nobody know about it? Looks like they're all having this animated conversation." Corey stared at the faces.

And, indeed, everybody appeared to be either laughing or talking, drinks in many hands. Also a vehicle appeared to move away from where the shooting occurred.

"That gun has a silencer. The shooter could have just walked up, popped him, helped him collapse out of the way and rejoined the group, and nobody would have known the difference." Warrick reached over and tapped the top of the truck. "Someone set down his drink glass. Either that's the killer's or the victim's."

"So what do we do with this photo?"

"The detective already has it," Warrick said slowly. "I don't know any of these men. Do you guys?" Slowly he moved the photo around on the screen, highlighting each of the faces. When he got to the shooter's face again, Angela leaned forward. "I feel like I know that profile, but I can't place it."

"Meaning, it could have been somebody you've seen?"

"Sure. It could be one of the people who came to the house or one of Greg's many associates. Or ..." she said slowly, scrunching up her face, "It could be Reginald, but it's not a good picture of him, if it is."

"It's grainy but we can look into that possibility. It gives us something to go on. We can't identify the body from here though."

"Or it's a much younger photo of Reginald," she added suddenly. "That's possible."

"We need a satellite hookup," Corey said.

Warrick turned to look at him. Together they said, "Tesla."

Angela stared at them. "The car?"

They chuckled. "No, Mason's partner." Corey frowned and looked at Warrick. "Or maybe Levi."

"The trouble is, we don't have a time or date stamp, do we?" He searched the bottom of the photograph, but nothing was there.

"Let me call Mason," Corey said. "He might want us to get Ice involved in this. If Tesla hasn't got authorization for the satellite system, we don't want to get her in trouble."

"Just call Levi anyway."

"Then I need to go through Mason," Corey responded. "I don't really know Levi."

Warrick held out his hand. "I know him."

"Then you call him." Corey picked up Warrick's phone and handed it to him. Together he and Angela listened in as Warrick called Levi. With a quick explanation he said, "I found a photo here that appears to show a man having just shot somebody. But we can't get any details on the victim. Or ID any of the men in the photo." Warrick nodded. "I just sent it to you. You should get it in a few minutes."

He hung up the phone. "They will take a look to see if they can do anything with it. He did ask if the police were involved, and of course I had to say yes."

"Why is it the police appear to be a problem?" Angela asked.

"When we're on a military mission, we can and do have access to everything we need. But we're not officially on a military mission, so we don't have access. And, by rights, it's law enforcement's case. They don't like it when we step into their cases. And we don't like it when they step into ours. So it's a matter of respecting boundaries."

"Isn't it supposed to be a matter of making sure Greg gets stopped, and I get my son safely back?"

"Those are the end results we're both gunning for—both the navy and the SDPD. Obviously we need to work together to make that happen." Corey could feel her frustration. He felt the same.

Angela got up and walked to the kitchen. "I'm hungry."

"You mean, for more than chips?"

She pointed at the bowl. "It's empty."

"Are you sure you want to eat? Will it stop you from sleeping tonight?"

She glanced at her watch. "It's eleven o'clock?"

He nodded. "Considering the late hour, I would say bed, not food." He caught sight of Warrick's face. "What?"

"I just realized I didn't even consider the time when I called Levi. It's got to be one o'clock where they are."

"Did it sound like you disturbed him?"

"No. But he's Levi. If anybody needs the least amount of sleep, it's him. And he's on top of everything, so this is up his alley."

"I don't know any of these people. But the circle of those involved just keeps getting bigger and bigger." She flung out her hands. "And yet nothing's getting resolved."

"How about a cup of tea or maybe a hot bath and then bed?"

She stared at him.

He could see the fatigue pulling at her eyes. Even though she'd napped in the vehicle, it hadn't been enough. She hadn't had enough sleep in a long time. "Come on. Let's get you set up in a bedroom. You can crash whenever you want to then." He turned, grabbed her bags and headed up the stairs without giving her any option but to follow him. He stopped at the top and looked at the bedroom layout. He put her in the bedroom at the far end of the hall.

Behind him she asked, "Why that one?"

"Because it's not at the top of the stairs," he said succinctly. He turned to see her reaction, only to catch the whisper of fear and understanding as she got what he meant.

She stepped inside the bedroom and smiled. "This is very nice. Thank you."

"There are two bathrooms up here. This one has a Hollywood bathroom. It's here." He walked through and showed her that it opened up to the other bedroom as well.

"I'll be on this side. Do not lock the door. I don't care what the reason, don't lock it. I'll be sure to knock if I'm coming into the bathroom, okay?"

She frowned at him. "Okay. I'm just tired. I want to go to bed."

He nodded. He walked back into her bedroom, checked outside the window and said, "There's nobody and nothing that can see in here, so, if you want, you can have your curtain open."

"No, I'd like it closed."

He closed it, walked to the bed and flipped back the bedding. "Do you have everything you need?"

"Towels?"

He walked into the bathroom, checked the linen closet, but none were there. He headed back to the hall, opened a closet, grabbed several towels and washcloths, and brought them in for her. "This should get you started. If you need more, they're in the hall closet." He opened his arms and gave her a hug. "Now get some rest." He kissed her gently on her temple, turned and walked out. If he didn't leave right away, he would drag it out for as long as he could. He just found something so addictive about being back in her space, having her once more in his life. He hadn't wanted to let her go in the first place.

And now to find she was even more attractive to him over a decade later, well, that was an incredible turn-on.

As he stepped through the door, she called out, "Good night."

He refused to turn and look back because he knew what he'd see. He tossed back, "Good night," in a carefree voice and quickly raced down the stairs.

As he walked into the kitchen, Warrick said, "I didn't

expect you to come back down."

"She's not ready for that."

"But I figured you couldn't leave her alone for the night."

"She needs sleep, not to mention being married."

"She's been separated for months so that's hardly relevant at this point. Do you think she'll actually sleep with all this going on?"

"No idea. But she didn't ask me to stay so …"

Warrick nodded and half smirked.

Corey walked to the fridge and pulled out a beer that Warrick had bought at the liquor store. "Do you want one?"

Warrick held out a hand behind him, and Corey placed one in his palm. He walked around, sat down at the table and took a deep drink. He loved the cold chill as it chased down his throat. "It's a nice beer."

"Any beer is a nice beer when you need one."

At that Corey chuckled. "Isn't that the truth?" He studied his friend. "What the hell are we supposed to look for now? None of this makes any sense yet."

"Focus on the spreadsheets. The answers have got to be there." Warrick reached around to a stack of papers. "I've printed off several copies. Here. Go ahead and mark them up. See if you can figure out what the hell's going on."

Corey closed the laptop and spread the sheets out in front of him. "I'll start with Elizabeth and her five grand payments."

He looked at the list of names, found four that had regular five thousand dollar payments and quickly realized Elizabeth's last name was the first three letters in one of the codes. He marked that, then grabbed a scratch pad. He wrote down the other names they knew. The sums were all about the same: five or seven or four thousand dollars. Several were much more. He circled them on the first column, wondering what somebody would have to do to be charged that kind of money.

"We need more names, so we have a better understanding of his code. I still think this is a list of his payments received." He glanced at his vibrating phone. A text from Mason. Corey spread the sheets out so they were top to bottom. Then he picked up his phone and called Mason. "What did you find out?"

"Jackson was being blackmailed. He stopped making payments a few weeks ago at the same time he put in for early retirement. He doesn't know what the blackmailer will do now but no longer cares, as he's getting out."

"Any idea what his payments were every month?"

"Three grand."

In the background Corey could hear someone calling out to Mason, "Thanks for meeting him. Let's hope the captain sees a happy end to all this."

Corey hung up the phone and told Warrick the details. Corey motioned to the spreadsheets on the table. "All these payments add up to more than a hundred and fifty grand. Several here are ten thousand, and some are fifteen."

Warrick whistled. "Murder being the fifteen?"

"I think so. But God only knows how Greg determined that figure. I'm surprised it wasn't a big payout first. Fifteen thousand is not very much."

"No, but, like you said earlier, it's enough to keep his marks paying. It's as if the blackmailer knew what the victim could afford. I bet he's taking just enough that they can make the monthly payment without leaving them dry. I don't think this is a short-term process. And I doubt he went after money with everyone. It was all about using the opportunity for gain—one way or another."

"That also explains why some of these payments start at different months. Depends when he managed to get the information, presumably to target these men."

"And we can't assume it's just men either," Warrick said. "Don't forget Elizabeth."

"No, that's true. Most of the photos though appear to be of men."

Just as he sorted out some of the other names, Angela raced down the stairs in her pajamas. He looked up as she burst through, holding out her phone on Speaker. "Joshua, talk to me."

"Mommy" came a tearful voice from her phone. "Can you come get me?"

"Where are you, sweetie?" she asked, standing at the men's sides. She placed the phone on the table and danced backward.

"I'm in the trunk of the car. Daddy put me in the trunk."

Both of the men bolted to their feet.

"Is he driving the car right now?" Angela asked Joshua.

"Yes. He's driving."

Warrick sat back down and opened a different program.

Corey walked around behind him and said in a low tone to Angela, "Keep him talking. Warrick's trying to track the phone."

"Honey, keep talking to me, okay? I'm so sorry Daddy did that. Was he really angry at you?"

"He was really scary. He didn't say much. He just picked me up. I was wrapped up in blankets, and he grabbed all of it and tossed me into the trunk. I asked him not to." The boy's voice was terrified, exhausted from crying.

"Does he know you have your phone?"

"No. I had it tucked into the blankets with me. I wanted to call you later."

"Well, you hang on to that phone. We're tracking where you are by your cell phone. So you leave it on, okay?"

"Does that mean you're coming to get me?" Joshua's voice perked up with hope.

"You bet, kiddo. Mommy's on her way." She glared at Corey as if daring him to argue.

"Good, I'm really sleepy now."

"Honey, how come you're so sleepy?"

"Daddy gave me a needle," he said, his voice going faint.

"Leave the phone tucked in the bedding against you. And you leave your phone on. Do you hear me? Don't shut this call off."

No answer.

"Oh, God. Oh, God. Can we find him?"

Corey already had his phone out and called the detective.

"Now what?" he said in irritation.

"We have an emergency." He told the detective what was happening with Joshua in the trunk.

"We need the number so we can track it."

Corey pulled the number off the phone. "Warrick is also trying to track it right now. According to Joshua, he was given a shot to make him sleepy. Now he's asleep."

The detective swore under his breath. "Does he know if it's his father driving?"

"No. He said it was his father who put him in the trunk, but that doesn't mean it's his father driving. We have to track down that vehicle."

Corey wrapped an arm around Angela and helped her sit in the kitchen chair. He raced into the living room, grabbed a blanket, came back and wrapped it around her. He placed a hand on her shoulder as the detective continued to bark orders.

Warrick yelped, "I got it."

"Warrick just found the vehicle."

Warrick relayed the street it was on and where it was heading.

Corey asked, "Do you have officers nearby? Because otherwise, we're heading out, and I'll pull as many men as I need from our units to get this child picked up safely."

"I have men on it. We're tracking it now too."

"It's only about ten minutes away from here."

"I'm getting satellite on it."

"I can get that too." Warrick phoned Levi again. "The little boy has been shoved in the trunk of a car and is on the move. Do you have satellite access?"

Corey half listened to both phone conversations as he watched Angela. She looked completely grief stricken. He shook his head. "Stay positive. This isn't over."

CHAPTER 12

A NGELA SHOOK HER head at the chaos. And yet it was organized chaos. Both men were talking to different people, and everybody was tracking Joshua. She pulled her feet onto the chair and wrapped her arms around her knees. Laying her head against the blanket, she tried to stay silent. Inside her chest, her heart seized to the point it was hard to get a breath out.

Her beautiful boy. Joshua. Drugged and in the trunk of a car. Why? Where were they taking him? What the hell had Greg done? Was Joshua of so little importance that he was literally a pawn to further control Angela? Or was Greg trying to fulfill his threat—that she'd never get a chance to see him again?

Just the thought had her body shaking. She rocked back and forth on the chair. She wouldn't let her gaze leave the two men. They were barking out orders and answering questions in the same static-type tone.

And she understood she was privy to something special. What was a panic mode for her was a work mode for them. They were in control. They were determined. And they were so focused. On her son. On saving her little boy who they didn't even know.

She clenched her arms tighter around her, her knees pulled up as close as she could into the tightest ball she could make.

And she waited. And waited.

Finally Corey got off the phone. "The police have the car tracked. They're trying to surround it. I had to get off the phone so the detective could deal with it. Let's hope they bring the car to a stop fast."

He turned to look at Warrick who responded. "Levi's on the phone. He has live satellite. They're tracking the vehicle as well. They'll see when the police come up on him."

And then suddenly it went quiet. Corey put down his phone, kneeled in front of her and wrapped his arms around her. "Let's just stay positive."

She stared at him, but she didn't know what to say. Everything in her world was frozen, waiting for word. Had they gotten Joshua, and was he alive? That Greg could have poisoned Joshua was never far from her mind. Just the thought of Greg trying to kill Joshua was too much to contemplate.

Warrick gave a shout.

Corey bounced back up.

She couldn't breathe.

Warrick said, "They have the vehicle surrounded."

Corey's phone rang. "It's the detective," he said. "What's up? Did you find him?"

"We have the vehicle. We're trying to open the trunk right now."

"Who was driving?"

"Not the husband. But I might have seen the driver in some of the photos."

"Take a picture and send it to me," Corey snapped. "Chances are it's somebody Angela will recognize." He turned to look at her. Seeing the gray tinge to her face, he gave her shoulder a squeeze.

She took a deep gasping breath.

"We're waiting. They're trying to open the trunk."

She shook her head and cried, "How can it be hard to open?"

"They've got it open." The detective's voice came through the speakerphone loud and clear. "There is a bundle of blankets in the trunk."

In the background they heard a shout.

"They've got the boy."

Angela stared at the phone and screamed, "Is he alive? Is Joshua alive?"

In the background she could hear many voices and chaos.

"We're checking." Then the detective spoke, his voice low, "We have a pulse, and an ambulance is on the way. He's alive. We don't know what condition he's in. But, I repeat, he's alive."

Angela burst into tears, her body shattering as the shock ran through her.

Corey wrapped her up tight again.

She was barely cognizant of the phone conversation still going on. She heard him ask what hospital.

And he said he'd have her there in no time.

When he put down the phone, he tilted her head back. "You need to pull it together. He'll be at the hospital in about fifteen minutes. I want you with him. We will have you to the hospital in twenty minutes. Go get dressed. Make sure you have your purse and anything you might need in case you're staying overnight."

She looked at him, swallowed, wiped away the tears and ran upstairs. Her hands shook so badly she didn't think she could get dressed by herself. She quickly donned the same clothes she had worn earlier. She hadn't unpacked, and that was a good thing. She quickly threw her nightclothes into the bag and went back downstairs. She stepped into the kitchen. "I'm ready.

Corey turned to look at her and smiled. "I have a photo I want you to look at." He motioned her to the laptop. Warrick turned it so she could see. "This is the driver. Do you know who that is?"

She stared at the photo, the color leaving her face. "That's Reginald. That's the man who lost his little boy. And the one who saved Elizabeth."

"Well, Reginald's being held by the police under the suspicion of kidnapping."

She raised her gaze to the others. "Oh, my God. Is Greg making it look like Reginald is the one who did this? Then Greg'll get off scot-free."

"Except for the fact your boy said it was his daddy who threw him into the trunk, correct?"

She nodded. "Yes." She took the phone from her purse and held it out to Warrick. "Any way to get a copy of that phone call?"

He frowned. "I'm not sure." Then he stopped; an odd look came into his eyes. "I'll consider it. We need to tell the police about it too. They can get the cell phone company to give them a lot of that information. But I don't believe they record the calls."

"What we need is for Joshua to wake up and to tell us himself," Corey said. "That will put a wrench in Greg's plan."

She shook her head. "No, he'll just toss it off as being the delusions of a child."

"We will see. Right now, I'm taking you to the hospital. Then I'll head to the police station. I want to have a talk with Reginald."

She turned to look at him. "The police won't let you talk to him."

He smiled. "That's okay. If we play this right, Reginald will turn on his boss, and we won't have to worry about it anymore. And, if not, Reginald will pay for his part in all this."

Her gaze flipped to Warrick. "Are you both coming now?"

Both men nodded. Warrick lifted his computer bag and stuffed his papers and laptop inside. "We stay together."

"And what about at the hospital?"

Corey turned to look at her. "Are you thinking Greg might try something there?"

"I don't know what I'm thinking. I just want to make sure Joshua is safe. Not just for now but forever."

Corey drove Angela's car with her in the passenger seat. Warrick took Corey's truck, following behind, watching for tails.

The trip to the hospital took way too long. She struggled with fear and panic. She kept reminding herself over and over again, *He'll be fine. He'll be fine. They got to him in time.*

Corey grasped her hand. "It'll be okay."

She nodded. "I know. I just can't believe you found him so fast."

"Cell phones are a really great technology. Particularly if they're on. If Joshua had shut off that phone, it wouldn't be anywhere near so easy."

She nodded. "He's a smart little boy." Inside, she was absolutely twisted over the concept of him calling out for help, tied up inside blankets, crying out for her, knowing he had been thrown into the trunk of a car. What he must have thought? "What an absolutely horrible thing to have done to my little boy," she cried. "Why would Greg be such an asshole?"

"And that'll be one of the things Greg tells the judge— that Reginald wouldn't have done something like that normally. And that, being distraught after losing his own boy, he was stealing Joshua for his own purposes. And it's the prosecutor's job to convince the judge that Reginald did this under Greg's urging."

"Greg can say whatever the hell he wants, but it's not the truth. Joshua knows what the truth is."

"Sure. It gives you wonderful leverage for the judge to give you full custody of your son."

"But nobody'll believe me. Greg's already tried to make it look like I'm unstable."

"Except for one thing …"

She turned to look at him. "What are you talking about?"

"You put that call on Speakerphone, and now you have two very good witnesses."

She stared at him in shock and then in understanding. "That's right. You and Warrick heard Joshua too."

Corey nodded. "And our witness testimony will carry a decent impact. Don't you worry. We won't let Greg get to Joshua without a fight."

She sat back and relaxed a bit. "Thank God you were there."

"Yes, thank God we were there. And thank God your little boy called you."

She couldn't stop shaking. When he finally pulled into

the hospital parking lot, she was out of her car in a split second.

Corey rounded the car to get to her side. "Leave your bags here and just grab your purse. Let's see what the deal is first."

She nodded. When he reached out for her hand, instinctively she grabbed his.

He smiled and tucked her close. "This is a good visit. Put a smile on your face."

She shook her head. "No, this isn't a good visit. This is a *great* visit."

As they got to the front reception area, Corey identified who they were and asked where Joshua was.

The woman took down their names, pointed to the emergency area and said, "He's down there, but he is surrounded by police."

Corey nodded, but Angela was already racing toward the uniformed officers. "Have you got Joshua? Is he here?"

Several policemen stepped forward, but she could see her son in a tiny cubiclelike room behind them. Instead of a door it had a curtain, which was drawn open. "Joshua!" She squeezed past the officers to the bed.

A doctor stood beside him. He looked at her and barked, "Don't touch him."

She came to a skittering stop and stared. "What's wrong with him?"

"He's been drugged, and he's having a reaction to the drug they used. We're flushing his system and running a drug panel on his blood, but I think he was given a sedative, maybe an adult formulation instead of something for a child of his weight. But he'll have to stay right here, so we can keep an eye on him. I don't want you in the way."

"I won't get in the way. But he's my son. I need to know he's okay."

"He's okay. As long as he stays where he is. This won't be a fast process."

She glanced around the small area, but there was no chair. She scrunched herself against the far corner, as much out of the way as she could possibly make herself, so they wouldn't make her leave.

She waited and watched. As she glanced around, she saw Corey talking to the police standing in front of the open doorway. Finally he turned his attention to her and the doctor. He then slipped over, wrapped his arms around her and pulled her up close. Against her ear he said, "Reginald is being held at the station. Warrick's gone to talk to the arresting officers."

She pulled her head back and looked up at him. "I thought you were going too."

He shook his head. "No, I'm staying here with you."

Tears came to her eyes, and it was beyond her to stop the flow. She dropped her head against his shoulder and just cuddled in close. "You're a good man, Corey."

He wrapped his arms tightly around her and said, "I am. But you're also a good mom."

She smiled and finally let herself relax.

JOSHUA LAY ON the small bed, sleeping soundly, an IV in his arm. Nurses kept a close eye on him. A steady stream of traffic was had in this emergency cubical. The whole time Corey stood in the corner with Angela in his arms.

What he had said had been correct. It was the truth for anyone who wanted to see it. Angela was a good mom. She'd do anything to give little Joshua what he needed, and he was a valiant little soldier. That he had called his mom before succumbing to the drug and had left the phone on … It had probably been an accident that he'd left the call open, but it had been what they needed to get to him fast.

Corey wanted to pound Reginald into the ground for his part in this but knew he'd never get close enough.

Maybe Reginald was happy to spend a few years in jail. When he came out, there'd probably be a nice little thank-you package from Greg waiting for him. If he got out. Jail wasn't kind to anyone.

Warrick had sent Reginald's mug shot to Corey in confirmation. Reginald looked a bit on the older side compared to the single photo they had seen him in earlier—the partying crowd with the man shooting another dead. The last few years had probably aged him. Nothing like losing a child to make one realize just how short life really was. So only the threat of a murder rap could probably convince Reginald to kidnap Corey. But why would Greg do this to Joshua, to his own son? Still the police would potentially solve that mystery as well.

Finally the doctor checked Joshua again, looked at the two of them, still in an embrace, and said, "He's stable for the moment. You're welcome to stay." The doctor turned to his nurse and said, "I want to be informed as soon as there's any change." He tilted his head at Corey and Angela and rushed away.

The nurse smiled and said, "I can get you some chairs."

Angela nodded and whispered, "Thank you." Before the nurse left, she asked, "May I touch him?"

"Gently, and just on his hands only. You may kiss his cheek, but please do not move him or pick him up. I'll be back in a minute." The nurse disappeared through the curtains.

Corey dropped his arms from around Angela and approached the bedside. The little boy had a shock of brown curls—slightly long so the curls crossed his forehead. But he had such a baby face, big cheeks, big forehead and long lashes. He slept peacefully and didn't look to be in pain. He watched as Angela picked up Joshua's hand.

She didn't lift it very high, just enough that she could slip her hand underneath. Corey watched the tears once again come into her eyes. She leaned down and placed her cheek against Joshua's for a long moment. It was such a precious moment that Corey felt his heart break. She'd been through a lot.

Finally she kissed his cheek and whispered, "Mommy's here. Mommy's here, and you'll be just fine."

The nurse came back in with a pair of chairs. She gave one to Corey, who moved it to where Angela stood. "Sit down."

She sat but didn't let go of Joshua's hand. Corey grabbed the second chair and sat on the other side of the bed. At least this way he could watch everything going on around him.

"Do you need to talk to the police?" Angela asked.

"The detective's not here. He's at the scene where they picked up Joshua—or maybe in his office by now. I spoke to the officer on duty here when I arrived, but I haven't talked to anyone else."

She nodded. "I feel like we should check in with Warrick, see if he's found out anything."

Corey pulled out his phone and sent Warrick a text. "He'll get back to us when he can," he said quietly. He looked at the little boy. "There doesn't appear to be other injuries. The doctor did check him over, and there were no breaks he could find."

She sniffled and beamed. "Thank heavens. I'll feel better when he wakes up."

That might not happen as fast as she wanted it to. But, now that the little boy was safe in the hospital, his father would have a fit. For whatever reason, he'd wanted Joshua taken away. Corey sent texts to Mason and Levi. Even though it was the middle of the night, people were waiting to find out something. He told them Joshua had reacted badly to the drugs his father had given him, but he was getting treatment in the hospital. He hadn't woken up yet but had stabilized. The responses were almost instant. Like him, everybody was concerned.

He studied Joshua's face for any resemblances to Angela. But it was hard. She was a blonde; the little boy had brown curls. Maybe he had her nose. But what Corey really needed was to see the boy awake, see his eyes and see that smile. Angela's smile was unique. A little off center, a little to the left. It was very endearing. At least he'd always thought so.

He stayed and waited with her. He figured they'd be here most of the night. After shifting her chair a little closer, Angela curled up into a ball and closed her eyes and lay her head on the hospital bed. He didn't feel he could do that. He was tired, but no way he would leave either of them unpro-tected. He wasn't sure if Joshua was meant to die tonight, but Corey wouldn't give anybody a second chance. Angela and Joshua had both become very special to Corey in a very short time. He stared down at the little boy he hadn't even met.

How would Joshua react to his father's actions? And was he ready for his mom to have a friend?

He wasn't even sure Angela was ready for that yet.

He just knew inside that he was.

CHAPTER 13

"**M**OMMY?"

Angela woke from her short nap. She'd been so afraid to nod off and to miss her son crying out in the night that she had pulled her head off the bed and forced herself to sit up in the chair, still only half alert. She moved closer to the bedside, and, in the dim light, she smiled down at her son.

He stared up at her, his eyes still not quite focused.

"Hi, sweetheart," she whispered. "Am I ever glad to see you."

His face lit up. "You came for me."

She picked up his hand, brought it gently to her mouth and kissed his fingers. Every single little finger got its own kiss. When she figured she could speak without choking up, and when her tears were firmly held back, she said, "Of course I did. I told you that I would, didn't I?"

He smiled as he nodded, but then he abruptly frowned. "Is Daddy here too?" he asked, fear sliding into his voice.

She squeezed his hand. "No, sweetie. Daddy's not here. You're in the hospital right now."

"Am I hurt?"

"Not really. It's just to check you over and make sure you're all good. If you can go back to sleep, then do so. That's what your body needs right now."

He gave her a beautiful smile, rolled over and curled up. "You're going to stay with me, Mommy?"

"Always, sweetheart. Mommy will always be here now."

"Good. I don't like being with Daddy all alone." Then he yawned a great big yawn. And by the time he was done, he was back asleep again.

She sat there, tears coursing down her face.

"I need to tell the nurse he woke up," Corey said from the other side of the bed.

She turned to look at him and nodded. "Thank you."

He laid a gentle hand on her shoulder before he left.

She owed him and Warrick. They'd done so much—not just saving her son but her soul also. She didn't want to think about life without her boy. All she'd ever wanted was to have a family. She'd been so delighted when Joshua was born. He'd been the light of her life.

Maybe it was her fault that her marriage had faltered. Once Joshua arrived, she'd been devoted to him, as he had filled a void in her life. A void she hadn't even recognized before. When she fell in love with this little angel, she'd been his slave from the moment he took his first breath.

Her husband used to mock her for it, but she had ignored him. It didn't cross her mind she was giving Greg the weapon that could hurt her the most. She wouldn't focus on that now. She wasn't alone anymore.

Although Greg might still have a lot of weapons at his disposal, she was no longer as terrified of her husband as she had been. That he would do something like this to a little boy, to their little boy, made him a monster. If he walked into this room right now, she'd likely kill him herself. She didn't know if he'd ever killed anyone or had ever ordered anyone to be killed. She assumed he was somebody who didn't get his hands dirty. But, for what he'd done to Joshua, she'd have no problem putting her hands around Greg's throat and squeezing until the last breath ran out of his body.

Since it was best that she didn't cross Greg's path right now, she hoped he went to jail for a long, long time for what he did to those people in the photos.

Corey walked back into the room. She turned to look up at him. The nurse was with him. She walked over to Joshua and motioned for Angela to step back a little bit. She returned to her chair, watching as the nurse ran Joshua through several tests.

When she was done, she gave Angela a big smile and whispered, "He's doing fine. I'll let the doctor know he woke up for a few minutes, and he spoke. He appears to be in a deep sleep now. It's the best thing for him."

Angela cut back a sob in her throat. She wanted nothing more than to have her son wake up in the morning asking for cereal and milk. He'd always had a healthy appetite and had woken up hungry every morning. She wiped away her tears and wrapped her arms around Corey. She loved it when he drew her close.

She murmured, "I can never thank you enough."

He squeezed her gently. "No thanks are required. I'm just glad we found him in time."

She nodded. "I can't even imagine what Greg was planning. And it's that *what* that'll bring me nightmares for the next twenty years."

"Joshua's doing fine. He'll survive this. He's a beautiful, bright, resilient little boy. He'll have no trouble getting past this."

"Only if he's not forced to be with his father again. You heard him. He's terrified of his father now."

"Smart boy," Corey said. "I hope you don't mind, but I recorded that, so the judge can hear a six-year-old boy talk about his father in that tone."

That Corey had had the presence of mind to do that made her even more aware of his training. She had been in a hundred percent mother mode. "Then maybe you should be here the next time he wakes up too," she commented.

He dropped a kiss on her forehead. "I have no plans to go anywhere."

It was all she could do to hold back the tears. "You're being really wonderful."

He chuckled, a warm sound that rippled up his chest and erupted out of him like gentle thunder. "I'm always really nice."

She knew that. The problem in their relationship was never because of his personality. It was just that they'd been so young, and dealing with such a loss so fast had been difficult to recover from.

"Do you want to stay here all night?"

"I'm not going anywhere," she said firmly. "I can't be sure Greg won't send somebody else after my son again."

"We do have a guard standing outside," he said gently. He tilted her chin up and her head back slightly. "You also have to consider whether you'll be of any use to Joshua tomorrow if you're exhausted."

She frowned. "But what if he wakes up again?"

The nurse stepped in, bringing Joshua's chart with her. "He'll sleeping solidly now. The best thing for you is to head off and get a few hours sleep yourself."

She frowned, not wanting to leave her son. She shook her head and finally said, "No. I can't."

The nurse looked at her, then at Corey and said, "I can

bring one cot in, but I can't bring in two."

Angela brightened. "I'd love a cot. I just want to sleep beside my son." She hated the anxious feeling twisting her gut at the thought of leaving him.

Corey brushed the hair off her face and said, "That's a good solution."

She sighed with relief. "I was afraid you'd get angry."

"Why would I get angry that you want to stay with your son?" His eyebrows rose. "I'm not Greg, remember?"

She smiled brilliantly up at him. "No, you aren't. And for that I'm so darn grateful." She lifted her arms around his neck and hugged him close. Then she let him go and cried out in a soft voice, "I can't believe I have Joshua back again."

"Now what we have to do is make sure he stays safe."

Another lady walked in after a few minutes, pushing a cot. There wasn't much room, so they moved out one of the chairs so it could lay flat.

As soon as the lady was done, Corey motioned at it and said, "Lie down. A spare blanket is at the end of Joshua's bed. Let me cover you up, and you try to sleep."

She lay down. "I feel bad if I sleep, and you can't get any rest."

"I wouldn't sleep anyway. Somebody has to be here to watch over him."

"You said a guard was outside."

"Yes, and I'm the guard inside." His tone was firm, direct and unbending.

With a happy sigh, she closed her eyes and let her mind drift. She thought she'd fall asleep immediately, but it was hard. So many thoughts and questions and fears intertwined there and went nuts inside her brain. If she could just catch a little sleep, surely that would be helpful. Even if she power-napped for twenty minutes, it would make her feel better.

But every time Joshua gave a breath that was slightly heavier than the previous one, she sat up to look at him. Finally Corey sat down on the little cot beside her. "Sleep," he said firmly. "I promise I'll sit here between the two of you and make sure you're both safe."

She stared at him in wonder. "You are a gift."

Thunderstruck, he didn't know what to say.

She gave him a loving smile. "I mean it." She let her hand drift down his to wrap her fingers around his fist, and then she closed her eyes with a heavy sigh and drifted to sleep.

COREY STARED DOWN at her. She was correct in one way; a gift was here, but it was her, not him. She'd always had a big heart, capable of forgiving so much, capable of letting others off the hook for bad behavior. When most other people would have had something negative to say, that wasn't part of who she was. She'd always been happy and bubbly. She was the classy girl who stood out. Like a moth to a flame, everybody else would come running to her.

There was just something about her personality that brought others to her. He'd been no different. He'd been attracted to her right from the beginning. Even as a young man, he'd understood solid gold when he saw it. And that was definitely what she was.

With a happy sigh—and, God, wasn't he sappy—he settled in for a long wait.

CHAPTER 14

ANGELA WOKE UP slowly. She lay on the cot, sorting out her surroundings. And then she remembered Joshua. She bolted upright only to gasp as Corey gently stroked her shoulder, pressing her back into the bed.

"Easy. Joshua is still asleep. You're in the hospital. Just take a few minutes to get your bearings."

She blinked up at him in a wide-eyed-owl movement.

He smiled, leaned down and kissed her. That was as much of a surprise as anything. But it was a welcomed one. She glanced around the room. "Did he wake up at all?"

Corey shook his head. "No, he slept beautifully.

She sat up slowly and turned to look at her son. Tears came to her eyes. "It's so good to see him," she whispered. She stood, leaned over her boy and kissed him on the temple. It was just so wonderful to see him and to realize he really was okay. She gave a happy sigh, smiled at Corey and said, "I just need to use the washroom."

She walked around him a little awkwardly because of the cot and made her way to the bathroom out in the main hall. The hospital was quiet. Nurses moved here and there. It appeared to be the start of early morning wake-up rounds.

When she returned, she sat down on the side of the cot. "I slept better than I thought I would," she noted. "I was really tired." She glanced at Corey and smiled. "Thank you so much for watching over us."

"Don't thank me. It was the least I could do." He motioned at her phone. "It went off several times. You may want to check it."

"Oh," she said as she snatched it up. She smiled. "Your sister. She's worried about me." She caught Corey's wince and grinned. "You did bring her up to date, didn't you?"

He pulled out his phone and wiggled it in front of her. "We've been talking for the last half an hour."

She read through Bridget's many messages, realizing they were basically expressing concern for her and Joshua. And then Bridget's tone changed, as she must have connected to Corey. **As long as I know you're okay, sleep on.**

Angela chuckled. "Bridget's a good woman."

"She is that."

Angela turned her attention back to the phone and sent a text, letting Bridget know she was awake, she'd had a good night and that Joshua had slept well. She didn't know what the future held, but, at the moment, she was content.

A response came in almost immediately. **And Corey?**

Frowning she replied, **He's doing fine too. He stayed up and watched over us all night.**

And you and Corey?

Realizing where this line of questioning was going, Angela wasn't sure what to say. But before she had a chance to say anything, another text came in. She checked it. Her voice hardened. "I just got a text from Greg."

"What does it say?" Corey asked.

"He said the police have been there, and what the hell did I think I was doing?" She frowned.

"Don't answer him. Don't have anything to do with him."

She looked up. "But we have an opportunity to get some information from him."

"Do you really think he'll say something incriminating? Besides, the police raided his secret hiding spots and probably found plenty to nail him with."

Still her shoulders slumped. She studied her son's face. "Did anyone ever find Joshua's phone?"

"The detectives are analyzing it right now."

She nodded. "Joshua is one of those kids who is very tech-savvy, understands it all very quickly. I know he's little, but he can do things on tablets and cell phones I never understood. He's definitely got talent for that kind of thing."

"Great. Seems like the kids are so much more aware and skilled than we were at his age."

She nodded. "The age of the internet. Technology is moving forward so fast that it's crazy."

Just then Joshua shifted in the bed, pulling his legs up, then stretching them back out again.

She nodded toward him as she got up and walked closer. "Good morning, Joshua."

He opened his eyes, looked up at her and cried out, "Mommy." He threw his arms open and sat up.

She sat down on the bed beside him and pulled her little boy into her arms and just hung on. She sat like that for minutes. He was still half asleep and quite happy to cuddle. Like any young boy, she had to pick the moments when he was still long enough to actually hold him.

Finally he pulled back, looked up at her and said, "I'm hungry."

Chuckling, Angela turned to look around, but Corey had slipped out of the room. She frowned and realized the nurses probably needed to know Joshua was awake. Sure enough he returned with one of the emergency room nurses a few minutes later.

She smiled when she saw Joshua awake and cuddling in his mom's arms. "Hey there, buddy. Let's do a quick check over."

He rubbed his eyes, but he didn't move otherwise. "Can I have some breakfast?"

"Sure you can. I've already ordered trays for the three of you. But let's get some tests done to make sure you're doing better."

He was persuaded to lie back down while the nurse ran through a few simple checks. Angela watched carefully. It wasn't that she didn't trust people, but she knew her husband. He had an extended network that was scary.

When the nurse was done, she left and came back with two cups of coffee. "I just had a fresh pot made in the nurses' station," she confessed. "I figured you might need some."

Angela smiled. "Thank you so much." She took the cup. As it was really hot, she set it down on the little table beside Joshua.

The nurse disappeared again.

Joshua was lying on the bed, staring up at her. "Are you coming home now, Mommy?"

The fear in his voice made her heart ache. "No, we can't go back to the same house," she said. "That's your daddy's house now."

He nodded. "That's what he said."

"But we'll make it so you come to my house."

He brightened at that. "Is Daddy going to come too then?" He frowned, and a shadow passed through his gaze.

"No. He won't be coming to my house," she said gently. She glanced at Corey, wondering if he realized she had no place to go. Her apartment was in shambles. It had been broken into and destroyed. That was not a memory she wanted to see every morning when she woke up.

Corey placed a hand on the child's shoulder. "Hi, Joshua. My name's Corey."

Joshua fell silent as he stared up at Corey. Angela wondered what her son thought.

"Did you help save me?"

Corey nodded. "Yes, I did." He held out a hand and said, "It's nice to meet you."

Joshua giggled and put his little hand in Corey's. They shook formally, but Joshua didn't take his eyes off Corey. In a small voice Joshua asked, "Is that a gun?"

Angela turned on Corey in surprise. He quickly shifted his shirt over his weapon.

In a quiet tone Corey explained, "Yes, it is. Yes, I'm allowed to carry it. And, remember, I stood watch over you all night."

Joshua's face lit with excitement. "Can I touch it?"

"Joshua, no," Angela said. "He has to have it. It's part of his job."

Joshua slid a sideways look her way. "Doesn't mean I can't touch it."

But Corey had already moved toward the door. "No. It's not a toy. It stays in its holster until I need it." At the door he said, "Looks like breakfast is coming."

"Great," Angela said with a comical look. "Hospital food."

"I'm starving," Joshua announced. "I'll eat yours too, if you don't want it," he added generously.

"You finish yours, and we'll see how much of mine you want," she promised. She would have given him the moon. If he wanted her breakfast, he could have it. Besides, she was pretty darn sure nothing on the tray would be palatable. But she did appreciate the nurse thinking of them. A lot of hospitals had policies against extra trays.

An orderly arrived outside the doorway, pushing a loaded cart. Two trays were delivered to their hospital room. Her son happily sat up with the table swung over and the tray placed on it. He laughed at the plastic covering and oohed at the color of the Jell-O.

Angela smiled and sat back, helping him as needed, but generally just watched. She hadn't even lifted the lid on hers.

Joshua looked at her and said, "Eat, Mom. You need to eat too."

Behind her, she heard Corey chuckle. "He's right. You should eat too."

With caution she opened the lid to watery oatmeal and cold toast. There was, however, a bowl of fruit. But it wasn't exactly the most appetizing-looking selection. She smiled at her son and asked, "What would you like?"

He'd already eaten the toast and wasn't paying attention to the oatmeal, so she refilled his toast plate and took her tray out to the cart outside. She noticed Corey didn't have one. "Didn't they bring you breakfast?"

He shot her a look. "I'll wait. I might go down to the cafeteria and get a refill on the coffee."

She brightened. "You want to grab me a couple muffins while you're there?"

He nodded. "Do you want more coffee?"

"Yes, please."

She watched as he left, then turned to sit down beside her son. He studied her with an odd look. She'd always found it weird he had such a mature sense in his gaze sometimes, as if he understood things far too advanced for him.

"He's nice," Joshua announced. "Do you like him?"

Angela chuckled. "I like him just fine. And I really appreciate the fact he helped us."

Joshua's face became sober. He turned back to his meal. He looked up as Corey walked in ten minutes later, his hands full of muffins and coffee, and said in a very formal tone, "Thank you."

Corey nodded and, as if talking man to man, said, "You're very welcome." Then he smiled a much brighter smile. "Do you know your mom and I used to know each other? Back when we were in school."

Joshua's eyes went from one to the other, and then he started to giggle. "Really?"

Corey nodded. "Doesn't seem possible, does it?"

Joshua shook his head. "You were school friends?"

Angela smiled. "We were very special school friends." She was still trying to answer Joshua's questions when the doctor arrived.

"There you are, young man. How are you feeling?"

The doctor was young, probably not more than thirty, but he had a good bedside manner, and Joshua responded well to him. While the two chatted pleasantly, the doctor made short work of checking him over. Finally he straightened and said, "How do you feel about going home?"

Joshua's face scrunched up, and he slid down under the blankets. The doctor turned to look at Angela and frowned.

She rushed to Joshua's side. "He didn't mean to Daddy's house, honey. He meant with me."

Instantly the cloud cleared, and Joshua smiled. He reached up his arms, and she plucked him from the bed, careful of his IV, and held him close. She turned to see the doctor speaking with Corey privately. She looked around and said, "Let's get your clothes and get you dressed."

She sat back down on top of the bed and rummaged through the single cupboard, pulling out his clothes. That was all she had for him. He didn't seem to care. And once he was up and getting his socks and shoes on, she turned to the doctor and said, "Does he need any aftercare?"

The doctor smiled. "No. Just watch the tummy. It might be a little sensitive. If he gets nauseated, have him lie down. Try not to put too much in there that will upset his system further."

"Does he need a special diet?"

"No. Just stick with healthy foods for a few days."

She smiled at the disgusted sound coming out of her son's mouth. "Thanks, Doctor."

Joshua hopped off the bed, reached up and grabbed her hand. Angela held him securely. She walked into the main waiting room where Corey was.

In a low tone he asked, "Do you have medical insurance?"

She frowned. "I don't, but as of two weeks ago he was under his father's."

Corey nodded. "We have to take care of the paperwork."

They walked to the reception desk and explained the situation. It took a few minutes to get some of the issues resolved, and then the paperwork was signed.

She took a deep breath and walked outside. Clouds covered most of the blue sky. Little bits and pieces poked through, along with a small ray of sunshine. In a low voice, she asked, "What about Warrick?"

"He's using my truck, so we have two sets of wheels."

Corey ushered the mother and son toward her car. Instead of letting her drive, he got into the driver's seat with Joshua sitting between them. They pulled out of the hospital parking lot and onto the main road.

Joshua piped up. "Mom, where are we going?"

Instead of answering, she looked to Corey.

Corey responded, "We're going to a house where your mom is staying with me and Warrick, a friend of mine."

Joshua went quiet for a moment. "*War-rick?*" He sounded the name out slowly.

"Yes. He's a good man."

"Oh."

She wasn't sure if his hesitation was because of the fact it was another stranger or if he was afraid his father would be somewhere around. "We're safe at the house, honey."

Joshua didn't say anything. He just stared out the window. "When's lunch?" he asked.

"You can't be hungry already. You just had breakfast."

"It wasn't much for breakfast, and that was hours ago," he explained. "I also have homework, Mom."

"Oh, that could be a problem. We can't get your homework, unless the police found your backpack, but I'm not sure."

She remembered the harried drive toward the hospital. This was so much calmer and relaxed heading back to the house. She was unsure what to do about his schoolwork. She didn't want to call the school and alert them—or Greg—to Joshua's current status.

"Looks like you might be taking a few days' vacation from school," she said.

"What about my friends?" Joshua asked, his tone plaintive, almost whiny. Then he still wasn't feeling well, and his whole life had shifted.

"Maybe we could get together and have playdates with them or something?"

"I need to at least phone them and let them know I'm okay."

"We will, but the police have your phone," she explained.

"When will they give it back to me?"

She didn't know what to say.

Corey answered, "As soon as they take everything they need off it, I'm sure they will give it back to you. And, if you're lucky, we can get it back to you soon too."

Joshua stared at Corey. "Are you a policeman?"

Corey shook his head. "No, but I work with them."

Joshua seemed to be satisfied with that and collapsed back in his seat for the rest of the journey.

Once they pulled into the garage, Angela waited until the automatic garage door closed before she hopped out. Then she unbuckled Joshua and helped him out. They walked into the house.

Corey called out, "Wait."

She froze. She'd been around Corey enough to realize he wanted to go first to make sure it was safe. But Joshua didn't understand anything about this, yet he stopped and stood with his mother.

Corey went inside and finally called back, "All clear."

She entered. "Is Warrick here?"

"I'm here. Just got in a couple minutes ago," Warrick stated.

Smiling, she headed toward the kitchen. Joshua reached up, slipped his hand into hers. She looked down at him, squeezed his fingers gently and said, "Come. You'll like

Warrick."

But he didn't look like he believed her.

In the kitchen, Warrick sat with a laptop open and papers all across the table. He looked up, saw Angela, and then his gaze dropped to Joshua.

Angela walked her son over and introduced them. "This is Warrick. He's another one of the men who helped save you."

In a smooth move, reminiscent of a much older man, Joshua held out his hand and shook Warrick's. "Thank you," he said.

Warrick gave him a gentle smile. "You're welcome. Glad to see you've been released from the hospital already. Can't say hospitals are my favorite place."

Joshua shook his head. "They didn't give me much food."

Angela sighed. "You really can't be that hungry."

He gave her a sideways look. "Depends on what there is to eat," he said promptly.

Warrick chuckled. "If you sit here, there might still be some sandwiches and muffins. I stopped and picked up some on my way home today." Warrick pulled up a chair beside him.

Joshua scrambled up and looked at all the paperwork and the laptop. "What are you doing with all this stuff?" His voice was filled with youthful curiosity that only the little one could manage.

Warrick explained in a quiet tone some of the work he was doing, but, at the same time, he gave no details. Angela appreciated that. Joshua was very impressionable and had already been through quite an upset. It was better not to give him more information than necessary. As soon as his snack was consumed, which was quickly, Joshua wanted to explore the house.

She followed behind him, laughing as he raced from room to room. When he saw the backyard with a fence around it, and he had permission to go outside and play, he whooped with laughter, grabbed a ball he found beside the door and went out. "Mom, let's play catch."

She went out with him. The yard desperately needed a bit of mowing, but it was perfect for Joshua to run around in. She'd always wanted to have a house with a fenced-in yard. A place where he was safe to get out and to just be a young boy. His father hadn't thought that was appropriate.

But that was typical. He didn't understand children. They laughed, rolled, played, and, when they were finally tired, they collapsed on the ground and stared up at the sky.

"This is a good house," Joshua said. "I'm glad we came here."

"I am too. But we can't stay very long."

"Right. So where are we going next?"

She let her head roll to the side so she could look him in the eye. "I'm not sure yet. I'm waiting for Corey to give me the answer to that."

Joshua studied her for a long moment and then closed his eyes. "I'm kind of tired."

She jumped to her feet, tugged him to his and said, "Oh, no, you can't sleep out here. It could rain any moment. Let's get you upstairs to one of the bedrooms."

"Are you staying with me?" he asked, his voice threadbare.

"Yes, sweetie." She scooped him into her arms and carried him into the kitchen.

Corey met them at the door and took Joshua from her.

"Do you want to go upstairs to a bed, or do you want to sleep on the couch? Your mom can stay with you either way."

"Couch," Joshua said.

Corey walked into the living room, laid Joshua down and told Angela, "Maybe check the closet down here, see if there's a blanket we can put over him."

She did as he suggested and found several. By the time she came back, Joshua was listening to Corey tell him a story. But his eyes were getting heavy, and he was asleep within minutes. She unfolded the blanket, stretched it out over her son and pulled a chair close to him.

"I'll just sit right here," she said with a smile.

"That's fine. I'll put on some coffee. I'll bring you a cup when it's done." Corey stood and looked at her. "Are you okay?"

She nodded. "Now that I have Joshua with me, everything is perfect."

With her chair tucked up close to her son, she put her feet on the coffee table and pulled a second blanket over her. "Forget the coffee. I'll just have a nap too." And, with that, she closed her eyes and fell asleep as quickly and as easily as her son had.

THE DAY WORE on with a series of naps, playtimes, more naps and a whole lot of waiting. They didn't get updates from the detective, even though they attempted several times to connect with him. Corey requested the release of Joshua's backpack and phone.

When they were finally given permission to retrieve those items, it was after dinner. Warrick nodded toward the trio and said, "I'll get out for a bit and swing by the station and pick up everything. Before I go though I wanted to share that when shown the shooting photo, Reginald caved in and admitted his role. So that's going to blow the case apart." He stood up and looked at Corey. "You okay?"

Corey gave him a warm smile. "Better than okay."

Warrick said, "Be back in a couple hours."

He disappeared into the garage, and a few minutes later Corey heard the garage door open, then the vehicle heading down the driveway. He locked the door to the garage, just to make sure all remained safe.

Returning, he found Joshua nodding off once again.

Angela followed the direction of Corey's gaze. "I gather that's the drugs still leaving his system."

"That would make sense," Corey admitted. "He's been through a traumatic experience." He crouched down in front of the sleepy boy. "What do you say, Joshua? Time to go upstairs to bed?"

Instead of arguing, Joshua lifted his arms, hooked them around Corey's neck and whispered, "Okay."

Together the trio walked up the stairs into the bedroom they'd designated for Joshua. There was a single bed; the windows were open but had locking window stops on them, and, if they left the bedroom door open, he could come and go as needed. Once he was tucked into bed, he fell asleep almost immediately. Corey waited at the door, wondering if Angela would be able to leave him alone for the night.

She bent down, gave her son a kiss and whispered, "Any time you need me, just call out."

Joshua mumbled something, then murmured, "Good night, Mommy."

With a smile she stepped from the bedroom into the

hall.

Corey knew it was hard for her to leave Joshua. She stood in the doorway for a long moment and watched her son sleep.

Corey gently stroked up and down her back, and then, giving into the impulse, tucked her against him. Hugging each other, they stared into the bedroom.

"I'm so damn grateful to have him back," she said fiercely.

He squeezed her a little tighter and then released her. "Me too. You've got a great son there."

She kissed his cheek and whispered, "Thanks."

He looked down at her. "What about you? Are you ready to go to sleep?"

She shook her head. "I don't think so. But I want to stay up here. I'm afraid I won't hear him call out if I'm downstairs."

He nodded.

She turned to look down the hall. "I just realized, with Joshua in there, we don't have enough bedrooms for everybody." She frowned. "We should have put him in the big bed with me," she explained. She took a step back into the bedroom and stopped when she heard her son snoring. She smiled, a beautiful look coming over her face.

Corey had always known she would be a wonderful mom. What he'd seen today had proven it. "Not a problem. Warrick will probably stay downstairs anyway."

She frowned. "That would make me feel bad. He needs sleep as much as the rest of us."

"We will be on guard, four-hour watches at a time once he gets back. So it's not an issue."

"I hope so." She walked to the master bedroom and

stepped inside. "If there were two beds, the two of you could stay here."

He chuckled. "Don't worry about it."

She nodded but appeared to still be anxious.

He walked over to the window, checked it to make sure it was locked, turned to look at the bed and said, "There is a TV if you want to turn it on."

But she looked at him and said, "What are you going to do?"

He shrugged. "I can either come up here and work, or sit with you while you watch TV, or you can have a bath and go to bed—whatever you want. I can also stay downstairs and work."

She frowned for a long moment, thinking about her options.

He chuckled. "This isn't a heavy decision. Do something for yourself for a change. What would you like to do?"

She gave him an odd smile.

He frowned, then stroked her cheek. "What?"

"You're very dense."

He raised an eyebrow and shook his head. "I can't recall the last time somebody said that to me."

She chuckled. "We have the house to ourselves. The child's asleep, and we're in a bedroom ..."

He froze.

She laughed out loud. "Like I said, you're dense."

"I'm not dense, but I was thinking down the road maybe we'd get there."

"You didn't used to be so slow."

He opened his arms, staring at her. "I didn't?"

She reached up and placed a finger against his lips. "It doesn't matter what you did then. It matters what you do now."

He raised his eyebrows, but, as he stared into her chocolate-colored eyes, he didn't see anything that gave him a reason to refuse anymore. He wasn't even sure why he had. Except he wanted to make sure she was over her husband and wasn't doing this out of gratitude.

As if she wondered at his hesitation, she started to withdraw. "Of course if you're not interested …"

Instantly he slammed his lips over hers.

She chuckled. And then her laughter turned to moans.

He kissed her hard, all those feelings from twelve years ago leashed until now. He hadn't been holding the torch all this time, but whatever feelings he'd had back then hadn't disappeared completely. She was still the woman he'd loved. He tucked her against his long frame and let her know exactly how he felt about where they were at right now.

When he finally lifted his head, her knees sagged. It was his turn to chuckle. He picked her up, carried her to the bed and laid her gently down on top. He sat beside her and whispered, "I just don't want this to be out of some sense of gratitude."

Her gaze narrowed, and a spark of temper lit inside. "I do a lot of things for a lot of reasons, and, if there was anything I could do to save my son's life, I'd have done it in a heartbeat, but this is not gratitude, although I am forever grateful to you and Warrick and Levi and Mason and Tesla and everybody else who got us to this point. This"—she pointed between the two of them—"just might be joy. Something I haven't felt in a very long time." She tugged him down toward her. "So either stop protesting or get up and leave me."

"Leaving you right now would kill me," he whispered,

and he kissed her again.

What followed next was as predetermined as when he'd first set eyes on her. He couldn't get enough. It had been a long time for him but not so long that he didn't make sure every step of the way was as good for her as it was for him.

Mouths fused, fingers caressing, skin against skin, and then the urgency took it so much further. When she finally settled beneath him, her thighs opened, every scrap of their clothing on the floor, he rested above her, holding her gaze with his, and slowly entered her.

"Over a dozen years ago," he whispered as he slowly moved deeper and deeper, her eyes closing, her body arching beneath him, "we were both first-timers."

She giggled. "What are we now, old-timers?" she asked, her lips curving in a beautiful smile. Holding her hips, he plunged in all the way and seated himself at the heart of her. He lowered his forehead to rest against hers and whispered, "I'd love to be an old-timer with you."

She stroked his cheek gently. "I was a fool back then. I was so hurt. I just didn't know who and what I was anymore."

He kissed her lips and kissed her finger and then her lips yet again and whispered, "I know. I was pretty confused at the time. But we're not those people anymore."

She looped her arms around his neck, pulled him down and whispered, "Thank heavens for that. Now, are you planning to finish this job or just sitting around talking?"

He lowered his head and kissed her. Instantly passion flared, heat raced up and down their bodies as he picked up speed, kindled the flame and quickly led them to the edge of the mountain. Just before he flung them both over, he reached down, shifted her position, plunged deeper and whispered, "I never forgot, you know."

Her back arched, her body crying, her voice breaking as she whispered, "Neither did I."

Her words rolled over his body, searching and finding a response—his climax rippled through him. And he collapsed beside her.

CHAPTER 15

ANGELA LAY WITH her back to his chest, wrapped in his arms with such an inner sense of peace and contentment. She hadn't realized just how frayed and raw her nerves had been for so long. It had been years since Greg had shared her bed. She'd found it much easier to live with him when sex wasn't part of their relationship. But she also realized it was a distance that was hard to overcome.

Now lying here with Corey wrapped all around her, it was such a different experience. One she remembered from the past. That sense of peace, sense of contentment afterward. She recalled the young woman she'd been back then and the hell she'd been through with her miscarriage. She'd retreated into herself.

Her mother and sisters had closed rank around her at the time. But she had even pushed them away. She'd gotten through the experience by being quiet, silent. He'd joined the navy soon afterward, leaving her to make peace with her world. And it had taken years.

And then she'd met Greg. What a nightmare that had ended up being. And yet now, with Corey in her life again, she wondered if she was being given a second chance. A new lease on life. A new chance at love.

He stroked the side of her cheek and whispered, "Heavy thoughts?"

She heard the insecurity in his voice, twisted slightly and said, "Only about walking away so long ago."

Surprise was in the depths of his huge brown eyes. "I'm sure you did what you needed to do at the time."

She was surprised at that insight. She nodded. "That's exactly what I was doing. I needed to go away and heal. But, as I have now learned, I didn't need to walk away from everyone I knew at the time."

"I think we all do things when we're in shock. Afterward we're not exactly sure why it seemed like the right thing to do. But we did them, so we have to live with the consequences."

She smiled. "Well, I can tell you that, right now, for the first time in twelve years, I'm happy, content. At peace, inside and out."

He tucked her close against him and whispered, "So does that mean we can repeat this?"

She chuckled, rolled over and wrapped her arms around his neck. "Absolutely."

Just then his phone rang. He swore softly, sat up in the bed, grabbed the phone and answered, "Mason, what's up?"

She couldn't hear the rest of the conversation, but he wasn't getting upset, so she figured things were all good. She rose and went to the bathroom. When she came back, he was off the phone. "What did Mason want?"

"An update on Joshua."

She smiled. "It's amazing to think so many men did so much to help him, and Joshua doesn't even know it."

"Mason, Warrick, Levi … There are so many of us. We're all good guys," he said with a smile. "You just had bad luck to hook up with Greg."

"Yes, if that's what you call it," she said. "How did you

meet Mason? Was he one of the men in your unit?"

"No. But he's been a friend for a long time," he said with a smile. "Although Mason started a trend. Something most of us thought we could escape. Apparently that might be in jeopardy for me."

She frowned at him. "What are you talking about?"

Laughing, he explained about Mason and his band of Keepers.

When she heard the story, she gasped. "Oh, my God, that's perfect."

"No, it's not so perfect," he said with dry humor. "A lot of guys are pretty protective of their independence."

She chuckled and sat on the bed. "And are you part of Mason's Keepers?"

"No. I'm not part of his unit," he said triumphantly. "So it doesn't apply to me."

"But you wish you were," she said in a low voice. "I know you. On the inside all you really want is to be happily married with half a dozen kids in a home somewhere and a way to make a living that honors that part of you that needs to do good in the world. Protecting others is what you were always meant to do."

He looked at her for a long moment. "That always was the dream, wasn't it?"

She nodded. "The thing about dreams is, we tend to turn away from them, but we never really forget them."

He pulled her onto his lap. "How did you get to be so smart?"

She chuckled. "I'm not smart at all."

Just then they heard a vehicle come into the driveway and roll up to the garage.

She whispered, "That's Warrick." She bounced off the

bed and started dressing. When he didn't get up, she said, "What are you doing?"

He gave her a lazy grin. "I wasn't really planning on going down and seeing him."

"He has to get rest too. I thought you were to be on four-hour watches," she scolded him. "Come on. Get up. Get dressed."

Chuckling, he was up and dressed faster than she was.

She frowned and grumbled, "How did you get to be so fast at that?"

"Getting dressed and being ready at a moment's notice is something we're trained to do."

She nodded. "I can see that." She raced downstairs to see Warrick at the kitchen table with her son's backpack. "Oh, excellent. Thank you so much. I know he'll be thrilled."

She opened the backpack. Sure enough, her son's homework was there. She turned to look at Warrick and caught a speculative look in his eyes. She frowned at him. "What?"

An innocent look crossed his face as he raised his gaze to Corey who was standing in the doorway. Corey, without socks. An extremely tousled-looking Corey. She gasped and turned back to the backpack. The last thing she wanted to get into was a discussion about what they'd been doing for the last couple hours. Mumbling, she asked, "Did they give you his cell phone?"

"Yes, they did." He handed it to her. "They copied all the contacts and the history."

She nodded. "I expected that. But he'll be happy to know he got his stuff back." She grabbed the phone and the backpack and excused herself, "I'll put these in his room so he sees them as soon as he wakes up." And she escaped up the stairs.

When she was almost at the second floor, she heard, "We have a problem."

She stopped midstep, realizing she'd given them an opportunity to discuss something without her. She glanced down at the items, continued to her son's room and placed them by his bed. Then she ran back down.

As she entered the kitchen, she was greeted with silence. She stood in front of Corey and Warrick, crossed her arms and said, "What's the problem?"

Warrick looked to Corey. He stared back at Warrick and shrugged. Corey turned to Angela. "There's a chance Warrick was followed here."

She frowned, her arms gripped tighter around her chest. "What do we do?"

"We stand guard."

"When did you shake them?"

"About half an hour ago. I was followed leaving the police station. But I'm pretty sure I lost them."

She understood that. He wouldn't have come home if he thought he was leading somebody to the house.

"Then I suggest we get some sleep." She turned, headed back to the stairs. "Which one of you is on watch now?"

Warrick said, "I am. I need to do some work. I have to enter my notes from today and tonight."

She nodded. "Come on, Corey. Let's grab some sleep. Then you can come down and relieve Warrick."

Obediently Corey followed her up the stairs. At the top she called back, "Good night, Warrick."

"Good night," he replied, his tone already sounding distracted by work.

In the bedroom, Angela crawled into bed after shucking

her outer layer of clothing. "Do you think we're safe?"

"Yes. I do."

She smiled, waited until he got into bed and had his arms wrapped around her. She cuddled up and fell asleep.

SOMETHING WOKE COREY. He lay still for a moment, then gently eased himself out from under the covers.

Instinct drove him to move. He didn't know what was wrong, but definitely something was not right. He checked his watch and saw it was time for a shift change anyway. But he couldn't hear a sound downstairs. He dressed quickly, grabbed his weapon and stepped into the hall. He closed the door partway behind him and slipped over to Joshua's room.

The boy still slept, and there was no sign of any disturbance in his room. Corey listened for anything downstairs, but still there was nothing. And that bothered him. Going down the stairs meant skipping two of the risers that made noise. On the first landing, he peered around the corner and saw nothing. And yet there should have been some noise, some slight movement from Warrick. Corey made it down to the main floor. And he froze.

A vehicle was parked at the bottom of the driveway. They had company. Warrick hadn't warned him, and that meant Warrick *couldn't* warn him. That was the only possible explanation. With his gun ready, Corey did a sweep of the living room. But found nothing there.

Moving soundlessly, he shifted to the kitchen. There he found Warrick slumped over the kitchen table, blood pooling around him. All the lights were off. Corey slipped over, pressed fingers against Warrick's neck. There was a strong, steady pulse. *Good.*

So the head injury was enough to knock him out but not enough to kill him. But why hit Warrick and not then steal the boy? Corey's mind flashed through all the options, not coming up with anything that made any sense. Until he heard a vehicle start up. He raced to the front door only to see somebody running across the lawn to catch the vehicle as it left. Then a huge *whoosh*, and fire started all along the front of the house.

"Shit." He pulled out his phone and called 9-1-1. But there were too many flames, too fast. He raced upstairs, grabbed Angela and said loudly, "Fire. We have to get out of here now."

She blinked at him before understanding, and then she bolted from the bed, grabbed her clothes and screamed, "Joshua. Where's Joshua?"

Corey was already in Joshua's room, grabbing the backpack as a second thought. With the boy once again bundled up in bedding, he raced down the stairs with Angela at his heels. He headed to the garage and his big truck. He tucked them both inside. "I have to get Warrick. He's knocked out in the kitchen."

Smoke filled the house already and seeped into the garage. The fire had started to eat heavily into the front rooms. He knew it would be touch-and-go. He had to get them out of the garage fast. "Stay here. I'll be right back."

She shook her head, protesting. But he bolted back inside. Warrick appeared to have just started to stack up all of his paperwork. Corey scooped it all into the computer bag, bent down, grabbed Warrick in a fireman's carry, and brought him and the computer bag to the big truck.

There was no room in the front of the cab. Warrick was too awkward to maneuver. The best place for him was in the truck bed. Angela opened the tailgate for him to lay Warrick down in the back. Snapping the tailgate closed, they hopped into the truck, tossing the computer bag on the seat. Coughing, he turned on the engine and tried to open the garage door.

But the door wouldn't open.

"What will we do?" Angela screamed.

By now the garage was full of smoke, and he felt the heat of the flames. He shook his head and said, "Hang on." He put the truck in Reverse, hit the gas hard and blasted through the garage door, heading down the driveway. Pieces of the door floated around, but they were traveling so fast that Warrick would have missed getting hit by any debris. By now the flames had reached the second floor.

"Oh, my God, would you look at that," she cried.

But he wasn't too bothered. He was more concerned about something else. The steady ping hitting the side of the truck as he drove. He grabbed her head and pushed her down in the seat. "Stay down. We're being shot at."

She gave him a horrified look of disbelief, then covered Joshua with her body, both of them tucked down well below the back of the seat. He kept driving backward down the driveway, blasting through the gate, and around the corner. He couldn't see where the shots were coming from, but the shooter had to be here somewhere.

He watched a man run, a gun in his hand. Still driving backward, Corey pressed hard on the accelerator and chased after him. In the distance he could hear sirens as the fire engines approached. But he was after the asshole who had hurt Warrick and was hoping to kill all four of them. The big truck continued backward. He couldn't turn around; there just wasn't enough room with all the parked vehicles on the street. He needed another driveway to do that, but he wasn't letting this asshole out of his sight.

Corey saw the man cross the road and get into the passenger side of the same vehicle waiting for him as before, the driver ready with the engine running. Corey hit the gas as hard as he could, plowing into their car, spinning it around, pinning it against another one. Both men were inside. He pushed open the window between the cab and the bed, shut off the engine and crawled through.

As long as the men were pinned inside their car, that was fine. But the minute they got free, he would make sure they could not get away. Sure enough, they shot through their windshield, shattering glass everywhere. He waited in the back of the truck bed beside Warrick as the two men tried to climb out of their pinned-in car.

Warrick chose that moment to sit up and look at Corey, a groggy and pained look on his face. He reached up to touch his head and groaned, "What happened?"

"It's still happening. These assholes, I presume, were the ones who tried to burn us alive, and, when we got out, they tried to shoot us down."

Warrick swayed unsteadily. Assessing the situation, he reached for his own weapon, which thankfully was still in its place, and, as soon as the men crawled out of the car, Corey and Warrick both said, "Stop and put your hands up."

The men were at least smart enough to freeze.

In seconds the street was filled with fire engines, police cars and, thankfully, an ambulance. With Warrick standing guard on the two men, Corey pulled out his phone and called the detective. "You need to get down here. Someone just tried to burn us alive, and then two men, probably the arsonists, were shooting at us as we left the safe house. I have both of them under armed guard. The fire trucks are here, but I have a very interesting set of hostages for you."

"You know them?"

"I know the driver," he said. "I know it's dark out here, but it would be pretty hard to mistake Joshua's father. The asshole driving this getaway car is Greg, the estranged husband."

The detective crowed. "Don't you let that bastard move."

Corey said, "There's no way. Just get down here before I'm tempted to put a bullet in these assholes' heads."

"Don't do that. We've got lots to put him away. Now he's just added twenty more years to his sentence. I'm in the vehicle, driving. I'll be there in five."

Hearing a voice behind him, Corey turned his weapon to see Angela poking out through the rear window of the cab. "Can I come out?"

He shook his head. "Better not. Greg and one of his henchmen are in the car. We're holding guns on them. The detective is on the way."

She shot him a startled look and shifted to the driver's side. There she could see the two men in the vehicle.

She pounded the window until Greg looked at her. His face twisted in a snarl. Greg couldn't see her face, but when her arm shot out the window with a finger in the air, he figured Greg got the message.

He chuckled. And then he laughed. "You don't have to worry about him anymore. He's not going anywhere."

At that moment a gun appeared in Greg's hand. He pointed it at Angela. She ducked and Warrick fired. Greg shouted, and his gun went flying harmlessly onto the pavement.

"Try that again," Corey snarled. "The next bullet won't take out your gun arm."

But Greg wasn't listening. He was sobbing in the front of the car.

A cop car arrived, and the detective ran up. "Did you just shoot him?"

Warrick popped his head over the back of the cab. "I did. He was trying to shoot Angela."

The detective shot Greg a disgusted look. "Wow. You're just adding up the years, aren't you?"

But Greg wasn't listening. He was too busy bawling like a baby.

Angela got in the last word. "I hope you lock him in jail and throw away the key. Assholes like him don't deserve a nice life."

The detective chuckled. "You won't have to worry about him anymore. Take your son and go home."

She smiled. "Now that's an idea I can get behind."

CHAPTER 16

ALTHOUGH THE DETECTIVE had said they could go home, it wasn't so fast or so easy. They had to give statements; Warrick had to be checked over, and Corey wouldn't leave him behind. But Warrick sure as hell refused to stay at the hospital.

When they were finally all standing outside the hospital, a sleeping Joshua in Corey's arms, Angela said, "Where the hell is home now?"

"That's a big legal mess you will have to resolve with the lawyers from the divorce settlement."

"And what about your apartment?" Warrick asked Angela.

"Trashed, remember?" She looked at Corey. "How small is your place?"

Warrick chuckled. "It's pretty small. But he'll find room for both of you, for tonight at least."

They got back into the truck, dropped Warrick off at his place, then Corey drove Angela and Joshua to his apartment. Carefully he moved Joshua from the vehicle once again. Inside, he laid him on the couch in his living room.

Angela looked around the small apartment. "Obviously a single guy lives here."

"Never any point in getting that house I always wanted as I never had anybody to live in it with. So an apartment was good enough. And I'm not here all that often to worry about keeping it nice." He straightened, covering her son with a blanket.

She looked up at Corey and wondered at all the strange steps she'd taken in her life. She could have done so much better than Greg. But she'd been blinded by his attention and his flattery. And the lifestyle. And yet here in front of her stood so much more in the form of honor, respect, courage, determination, bravery … She could go on and on. She whispered, "What about now? Any chance of that changing?"

Startled, he looked at her. "I was just waiting for the right time in your life." He opened his arms; she stepped into them, and he closed them around her, holding her tight. Above her melting heart, he said, "And this just might be it."

She squeezed him like she would never let him go. Because she wouldn't. Not in this lifetime at least.

"Is that okay with you?"

She tilted her head back and said, "Better than okay. It's perfect."

WARRICK CANTON PICKED up another box of toys, shook his head, looked down at Joshua and said, "This is a lot of toys for one little boy."

Joshua danced in place and said, "No, it's not." He grabbed a small box beside Warrick. "Come on. I'll show you my new room."

Warrick chuckled and followed the little boy. In the ensuing weeks, with all the chaos and recovery behind them, Joshua was a whole new child. He no longer went to a private school and didn't seem to mind. He attended the local public school and was settling in. It would take him a bit, but he was young and resilient and had a lot of good times ahead of him to wipe out the bad memories.

His father was in jail and wouldn't be out any time soon. The trial was scheduled but wasn't for another year. In the meantime, Joshua hadn't asked very much about his father. Apparently he'd been awake when he saw his father try to shoot his mom. That had been too much for him.

They'd explained quietly what had happened, that his father had done something very bad and was in jail. Joshua hadn't said very much, just nodded. Once he realized he would be staying with his mom, he was fine.

When he realized Corey was moving into the new home with them, Joshua got really excited. And he'd seen plenty of

Corey and Warrick. Even Mason had stopped by. Joshua seemed pretty excited by all the men. It was a good life for Joshua. He would grow up with real men as role models around him—not assholes who used others for their own gain. And he smiled all the time. The same off center smile like his mother.

Warrick was happy for Corey, yet Warrick enjoyed being single right now. But it didn't make up for the three years he had been in a relationship with Sandra where he'd thought he had had the real thing. He should have realized the breakup was imminent, but he'd been blind, not really aware of what was going on in her world. He didn't want to make that mistake again. But he hadn't found anybody else who he liked half as much.

Joshua led Warrick into the bedroom where Corey was setting up his captain's bed. Corey took one look at the boxes and said, "Whoa, tiger. I don't think all that stuff'll fit in here."

But Joshua just giggled and stacked the boxes off to the side. "We'll unpack later. I'll show you all my stuff then." And he raced back out again.

Corey looked up at Warrick and smiled. "Thanks for helping us today."

"A bunch of other guys just arrived too."

Corey nodded. "That's great. The more hands we have to help, the more gets moved in and the faster this will go."

"Are you happy, dude?"

Corey looked up, his face beaming. "I'm so happy. Stupid with it," he admitted. "I hadn't really expected this."

"Sometimes you need to let go of your expectations and see what comes your way instead. Instead of trying to control everything in your life."

Corey nodded. "How are you doing?"

"Outside of the concussion leaving with me an odd headache …" He grinned. "I'm fine."

"Time for you to find another woman," Corey said in a joking tone.

"No rush. I'm happy to watch you guys play house for a while."

"Here, give me a hand with this will you?" Corey asked.

The two flipped the bed onto its four legs and finished off the last of the installation. They added the mattress and the drawers. And then stepped back. "He should like that."

Warrick slapped Corey on the shoulder. "That kid is in heaven."

"Yeah, I'm just a little nervous."

"Don't be. Just be you. It's going to be great." Warrick smiled at his friend in sincerity. "Don't forget his dad was an ass. It can't be too hard to beat that."

"Thanks," Corey said, laughing.

The two went back downstairs. And, sure enough, the house was full of men moving furniture and boxes. In the center of it all was Angela. Her face was flushed with excitement.

She caught sight of Corey and raced toward him, flinging her arms around hm. "Your friends arrived."

He chuckled. "Yeah, hopefully so did the groceries."

Just then Ryder stepped in and held up a box. "I brought the steaks, potatoes and salads. Devlin's here with the grill. I think Mason is bringing a second one."

Warrick leaned against the doorjamb and watched as the chaos around him continued. This was what Corey had always hoped for. And Warrick was so damn glad that Corey would finally get his chance at a home and a family and happiness. Warrick had watched his friend go through one lighthearted romance after another, never settling down. But, man, when Corey found the right person, he'd settled in a big way.

Ryder walked over, looked at Warrick and asked, "You okay?"

Warrick nodded. "I just think all the good women in the world are taken."

Ryder stared at him for a long moment. "I thought that way once too."

Warrick gave him a lopsided grin. "And yet look at you now," he teased.

Ryder nodded. "When it's time, when it's right, it'll happen. Until then, just enjoy life."

Warrick shifted from the doorjamb and thought that was a hell of a decent piece of advice. He could just enjoy life for a while. And, if he was lucky, somebody would cross his path and put a smile on his face to match the one on Corey's. And Warrick couldn't wait.

This concludes Books 14–16 of SEALs of Honor.

Read the first Chapter of Ryder: SEALs of Honor, Book 17

SEALS OF HONOR: WARRICK
BOOK 17
CHAPTER 1

H ELL, YEAH, HE could wait. He could wait for eternity until the right woman showed up if she was anything like the pugnacious terror in front of him.

It didn't matter that she was only five foot nothing, her fiery long red hair in a ponytail slightly off to the side and a face full of freckles.

She glared at him and had been for the last half an hour.

He'd filled out the paperwork incorrectly on his latest injury. And, damn, if she wasn't trying to hang him with it.

Warrick had a hard time stopping his jaw from jutting out, an imitation of her own actions. "Penny, I get that you have a problem with me," he said, trying for patience. "But honestly, I'm not trying to screw you over by messing up the paperwork."

She snorted. A completely unfeminine sound that both surprised him and intrigued him. She shook her head. "You might not be trying to be difficult," she said, "but you do it naturally. The instructions are so damn clear." She tapped the paperwork. "Why aren't you following them?"

Warrick sighed, took the papers from her, looked at them, and, sure enough, it gave exact instructions. He didn't know why he hadn't followed them. Then again, it was the third time he'd been in here with the wrong paperwork.

On one of the training missions a few weeks ago, he'd hurt his ankle. It had pissed him off, and he had refused to get treatment until the guys had forced him to get it looked at. He had a hairline fracture and had severely strained his ankle, and his foot was in a cast, to keep the ankle immobile to heal properly. The doctor had been very clear how he felt about Warrick staying on his feet when he had long passed the point he should have gotten off of them before seeing him.

Warrick would be the first to admit he had more than his fair share of stubbornness. But then all the guys did. And nobody wanted to be sidelined with an injury. That just wasn't on anybody's to-do list. Not that he had a whole lot of choice. Not now at least.

He lifted his gaze from the paperwork and said, "Okay, I did it wrong. Sorry."

She blew out a heavy breath, directing it up where tendrils of red curls lifted off her forehead. Then she relaxed. "I just don't get it, Warrick. This is the third time in as many weeks."

He shrugged. "I'm really good at stuff I like to do." He plastered an engaging grin on his face, or at least he hoped it was. "You know? A lot of people don't want to deal with stuff that's boring and uninteresting."

"This is hardly boring and uninteresting," she said. "This is what gets you your medical. This is what gets you all that good stuff you need done so you can heal and get back onto the front line as fast as possible so you can go kill yourself again," she explained.

He chuckled. "It's not that bad."

She glared at him, her bottom lip jutting out. "You do remember you've got a fracture on your shin bone, right?"

"Yeah, but that's not a real break," he said, minimizing the injury. "Besides, even if it was broken, it's not that big a deal."

"A break isn't a big deal?" she snapped. "Stress fractures, damaged tendons? Because somebody is an idiot and staying on his ankle well past the point when he shouldn't have been. Now that's a problem."

Under his breath he said, "Whatever."

Only she had heard him. And that was probably not a good thing. She turned and glared at him. "*Whatever?*"

He sighed. "How come I only ever see the prickly side of your personality?" he asked resentfully. "Everybody else says you're a sweetheart." She flushed, and he watched as the wave, almost shockingly red, rolled up her alabaster-white skin.

"*Prickly? Sweetheart?*"

He raised both hands in surrender. "What? So both of those are wrong or not allowed?"

"Not when they're complete opposites, no," she said in exasperation. "Fill out the paperwork properly, and bring it back again."

"We could do it right here and right now," he said hopefully. "Then I wouldn't have to come back."

She glanced at the clock and said triumphantly, "We can't because I have to close up the offices. It's four o'clock. You're too late."

He just glared at her. "Now you're being mean."

"Try to utilize an education level above a two-year-old and fill out the forms correctly."

Inside he fumed because, of course, his education was

much higher than a two-year-old level. He was well known for his reports, but he wasn't sure why these damn medical forms were such a pain in the ass. He snatched the forms off the table and stormed out the room.

Behind him she called out, "Have a nice day."

He slammed the door in response. In the hall he tried to control his breathing.

Tanner walked up, took one look at his face and chuckled. "I told you Penny is a sweetheart."

Warrick glared at him. "How is that"—he jabbed a finger at the door behind him—"even remotely related to being a sweetheart?"

"She's a sweetheart, except when she isn't," Tanner said. "But she's the one who keeps everything flowing. So I wouldn't suggest you piss her off."

"Too late," Warrick roared. "Why is this crap so difficult?" He stormed toward Tanner, then swore as his ankle screamed back at him. He slowed his pace, taking several slower, more careful steps.

Tanner tsk-tsked. "Sorry, bud. That ankle's given you nothing but hell."

"Stupid thing. You know we had games last week, and I missed out on them. We were against the air force too."

"You missed out on the soccer and the water sports the week before." Tanner grinned.

Book 17 is available now!

To find out more visit Dale Mayer's website.

https://geni.us/DMWarrickUniversal

Author's Note

Thank you for reading SEALs of Honor, Books 14–16! If you enjoyed the book, please take a moment and leave a short review.

Dear reader,

I love to hear from readers, and you can contact me at my website: www.dalemayer.com or at my Facebook author page. To be informed of new releases and special offers, sign up for my newsletter or follow me on BookBub. And if you are interested in joining Dale Mayer's Reader Group, here is the Facebook sign up page.
http://geni.us/DaleMayerFBGroup

Cheers,
Dale Mayer

About the Author

Dale Mayer is a *USA Today* best-selling author, best known for her SEALs military romances, her Psychic Visions series, and her Lovely Lethal Garden cozy series. Her contemporary romances are raw and full of passion and emotion (Broken But … Mending, Hathaway House series). Her thrillers will keep you guessing (Kate Morgan, By Death series), and her romantic comedies will keep you giggling (*It's a Dog's Life*, a stand-alone novella; and the Broken Protocols series, starring Charming Marvin, the cat).

Dale honors the stories that come to her—and some of them are crazy, break all the rules and cross multiple genres!

To go with her fiction, she also writes nonfiction in many different fields, with books available on résumé writing, companion gardening, and the US mortgage system. All her books are available in print and ebook format.

Connect with Dale Mayer Online

Dale's Website – www.dalemayer.com

Twitter – @DaleMayer

Facebook Page – geni.us/DaleMayerFBFanPage

Facebook Group – geni.us/DaleMayerFBGroup

BookBub – geni.us/DaleMayerBookbub

Instagram – geni.us/DaleMayerInstagram

Goodreads – geni.us/DaleMayerGoodreads

Newsletter – geni.us/DaleNews

Also by Dale Mayer

Published Adult Books:

Lovely Lethal Gardens

Arsenic in the Azaleas, Book 1

Bones in the Begonias, Book 2

Corpse in the Carnations, Book 3

Daggers in the Dahlias, Book 4

Evidence in the Echinacea, Book 5

Footprints in the Ferns, Book 6

Psychic Vision Series

Tuesday's Child

Hide 'n Go Seek

Maddy's Floor

Garden of Sorrow

Knock Knock…

Rare Find

Eyes to the Soul

Now You See Her

Shattered

Into the Abyss

Seeds of Malice

Eye of the Falcon

Itsy-Bitsy Spider

Unmasked

Deep Beneath

Psychic Visions Books 1–3

Psychic Visions Books 4–6

Psychic Visions Books 7–9

By Death Series

Touched by Death

Haunted by Death

Chilled by Death

By Death Books 1–3

Broken Protocols – Romantic Comedy Series

Cat's Meow

Cat's Pajamas

Cat's Cradle

Cat's Claus

Broken Protocols 1-4

Broken and... Mending

Skin

Scars

Scales (of Justice)

Broken but... Mending 1-3

Glory

Genesis

Tori

Celeste

Glory Trilogy

Biker Blues

Morgan: Biker Blues, Volume 1

Cash: Biker Blues, Volume 2

SEALs of Honor

Mason: SEALs of Honor, Book 1

Hawk: SEALs of Honor, Book 2

Dane: SEALs of Honor, Book 3

Swede: SEALs of Honor, Book 4

Shadow: SEALs of Honor, Book 5

Cooper: SEALs of Honor, Book 6

Markus: SEALs of Honor, Book 7

Evan: SEALs of Honor, Book 8

Mason's Wish: SEALs of Honor, Book 9

Chase: SEALs of Honor, Book 10

Brett: SEALs of Honor, Book 11

Devlin: SEALs of Honor, Book 12

Easton: SEALs of Honor, Book 13

Ryder: SEALs of Honor, Book 14

Macklin: SEALs of Honor, Book 15

Corey: SEALs of Honor, Book 16

Warrick: SEALs of Honor, Book 17

Tanner: SEALs of Honor, Book 18

Jackson: SEALs of Honor, Book 19

Kanen: SEALs of Honor, Book 20

SEALs of Honor, Books 1–3

SEALs of Honor, Books 4–6

SEALs of Honor, Books 7–10

SEALs of Honor, Books 11–13

SEALs of Honor, Books 14–16

SEALs of Honor, Books 17–19

Heroes for Hire

Levi's Legend: Heroes for Hire, Book 1

Stone's Surrender: Heroes for Hire, Book 2

Merk's Mistake: Heroes for Hire, Book 3

Rhodes's Reward: Heroes for Hire, Book 4

Flynn's Firecracker: Heroes for Hire, Book 5

Logan's Light: Heroes for Hire, Book 6

Harrison's Heart: Heroes for Hire, Book 7

Saul's Sweetheart: Heroes for Hire, Book 8

Dakota's Delight: Heroes for Hire, Book 9

Michael's Mercy (Part of Sleeper SEAL Series)

Tyson's Treasure: Heroes for Hire, Book 10

Jace's Jewel: Heroes for Hire, Book 11

Rory's Rose: Heroes for Hire, Book 12

Brandon's Bliss: Heroes for Hire, Book 13

Liam's Lily: Heroes for Hire, Book 14

North's Nikki: Heroes for Hire, Book 15

Anders's Angel: Heroes for Hire, Book 16

Reyes's Raina: Heroes for Hire, Book 17

Dezi's Diamond: Heroes for Hire, Book 18

Vince's Vixen: Heroes for Hire, Book 19

Heroes for Hire, Books 1–3

Heroes for Hire, Books 4–6

Heroes for Hire, Books 7–9

SEALs of Steel

Badger: SEALs of Steel, Book 1

Erick: SEALs of Steel, Book 2

Cade: SEALs of Steel, Book 3

Talon: SEALs of Steel, Book 4

Laszlo: SEALs of Steel, Book 5

Geir: SEALs of Steel, Book 6

Jager: SEALs of Steel, Book 7

The Last Wish: SEALs of Steel, Book 8

Collections

Dare to Be You…

Dare to Love…

Dare to be Strong…

RomanceX3

Standalone Novellas

It's a Dog's Life

Riana's Revenge

Second Chances

Published Young Adult Books:

Family Blood Ties Series

Vampire in Denial

Vampire in Distress

Vampire in Design

Vampire in Deceit

Vampire in Defiance

Vampire in Conflict

Vampire in Chaos

Vampire in Crisis

Vampire in Control

Vampire in Charge

Family Blood Ties Set 1–3

Family Blood Ties Set 1–5

Family Blood Ties Set 4–6

Family Blood Ties Set 7–9

Sian's Solution, A Family Blood Ties Series Prequel Novelette

Design series

Dangerous Designs

Deadly Designs

Darkest Designs

Design Series Trilogy

Standalone

In Cassie's Corner

Gem Stone (a Gemma Stone Mystery)

Time Thieves

Published Non-Fiction Books:

Career Essentials

Career Essentials: The Résumé

Career Essentials: The Cover Letter

Career Essentials: The Interview

Career Essentials: 3 in 1